Spare Change

CHRISTOFA KAY

ISBN: 13: 9798472231145

Cover design by: Ed Turner

Library of Congress Control Number: 2018675309

Printed in the United States of America

For my children: Elijah, Sarah, Mayah and Mikaylah

CONTENTS

CHAPTER ONE

It was cold that autumn morning, not just brisk, but cold, and Jermaine, a young, recent high-school graduate from the ghetto streets, boarded the bus to his community college. He was only half-awake, struggling to survive on little sleep. Throughout the nights, the middle bar from the pullout couch in the living room jabbed him in the ribs, and he slept for only four hours. You would think he would be used to it after a year and a half of sleeping on the pullout, but it was still a nuisance to getting a good night's sleep.

Jermaine got lost in mental judo as he prepared for his commute. "High school was tough enough, and now I am a grown man sleeping in my momma's living room with just enough room for my crate of clothes in the corner."

On the bus, there were early morning service workers on the way to their daily grind with various collars poking through the zipper of their plump winter coats.

"This is why I go to this damn college," he thought. "Because my people worked hard so I can do a little better than they did."

School was hard for him, and when he was honest with himself, he thought about dropping out every chance he got. Jermaine had run with a gang since he turned sixteen, the minimum age for the Rottweilers, who claimed a set on the Eastside. He never got into any real trouble with loitering being his heaviest violation. Tony, the leader of the Rottweilers, got locked up for petty theft that past summer, and the members turned to Jermaine for leadership since he was Tony's second in command and one of the longest remaining members.

"It's a tough job, but somebody has to do it," he thought.

Jermaine got off the bus to a campus void of students. There was security at the gate, and groundskeepers raking leaves. Early morning staff members hustled to their offices with their carafes filled with coffee, to boot up their computers and catch up on email before the influx of students arrived. He pulled his red and grey skully down over his ears and put a heavy backpack over his shoulder for the trek through campus. When he approached a building full of windows, he stopped and sat out front. Suddenly the electronic locks switched off, and he walked inside the school library to find an empty study carol, pulled out some books, pens and paper and in a matter of minutes fell asleep. When he woke up, the library was bustling with people and he had less than five minutes to get to class. He threw his books back into his bag, put his jacket back on and headed for the cold blast that met him as he opened the doors to the campus. He got to his economics class just as Professor Bruce Wright was shutting the door.

"Mr. Beasley, it looks like you just woke up five minutes ago," Professor Wright said.

"That's because I did!" Jermaine said.

"I saw him sleeping in the library as I was printing my paper this morning," a classmate said.

"Why didn't you wake me up?" Jermaine responded.

"Man, it looked like you were getting it in and I don't mess with nobody when they are sleeping!" the classmate said.

Bruce was standing at the front of the class now and nodded at Jermaine and asked him if he was able to complete the assignment. Jermaine was especially gifted in Economics and found the work pretty stimulating when he found the time to do it. Jermaine looked back sheepishly.

"You know things are crazy in my house right now, but I know the material," Jermaine said. "You can quiz me."

Bruce knew Jermaine was right, but just to put him on the spot and show that he wasn't playing favorites to his star student he thought he would run him through a few sample questions. Jermaine caught a sly smile wrinkling around his professor's lips, as he prepared to be his target for the morning. Bruce shot some basic questions his way regarding different countries' economies and Jermaine knocked it out of the park. Bruce raised the bar and asked about controversial U.S. companies and their regulations. Jermaine took the challenge and expounded beyond a simple answer, but provided a frame of reference for decisions these companies make that were based in greed and self-preservation.

"Are you sure you didn't do the reading?" Bruce asked.

"I guess I retained some of it as I was falling asleep," Jermaine stated. "Countries, such as the U.S. or any capitalist society tend to repeat themselves. They are all here to make a profit. If they produce a product that actually helps someone, well that's a secondary benefit."

Bruce faced the class.

"But I am teaching you all to think ethically, right?" Bruce said. "So, we can learn from history and not repeat the mistakes of the past?"

Jermaine was off the hot seat, but tapped his pen and thought hard about what it meant to change the course of history. He let his mind drift to a world without greed and how there would be no more war and how crazy that was to even conceptualize. The girl sitting behind him kicked his chair and ended his Utopian daydream.

"Show off!" she said.

As the class ended Jermaine thought to throw a flirtatious comment her way. "I can come over and tutor you if you like."

"No, thank you!"

Jermaine smiled and watched her walk away thinking how much he would love to have a girl like that.

Bruce caught him as he was putting his things away.

"Alright, Will Hunting!" Bruce said.

"Oh, the professor's got jokes?" Jermaine replied.

Bruce changed his tone and told Jermaine that he had a special talent in economics and explained how he took the topic to a whole new level, by finding the message hidden between the lines.

"How are you doing in school?" Bruce asked.

Jermaine was honest, if not anything else, and told him how he was struggling to keep up. How he barely got out of high school and how college work was coming at him three times as fast.

Bruce asked if he was making it to the tutorial center. Jermaine said he did when could, but most of the time he didn't have the time or energy. He talked about the four other classes he had and outside work.

"You know they will cut my financial aid if I don't take at least twelve units."

The next class started filling in the seats, so Bruce told him to come by his office later and hinted that he may have a way to help him ditch his job and earn some pay, which piqued Jermaine's interest. He looked at his phone and realized he was already five minutes late for his counseling appointment and hustled out the door.

###

Bruce was sitting at his desk intently flipping through some reference materials as he graded assignments. Jermaine tapped on the door lightly and entered with a look of exhaustion.

"What's good?" Jermaine said.

"Come in, why don't you?" Bruce said sarcastically.

"My bad. I thought you were ready for me," Jermaine said.

"Yeah, I am just sitting here twiddling my thumbs," Bruce said.

He closed the book he was in and turned towards Jermaine and just stared at him. There was an awkward silence, as if Bruce forgot that he asked him to come. After Jermaine reminded him that he told him he was there at his request, Bruce finally disconnected from his previous work.

"Yeah, that's right! Something came in that made me think of you and I thought you should take advantage of it."

He pulled up an email on his computer and printed it off. As Jermaine was reading it, Bruce sat back, but then chimed in to let him know more about it. He told Jermaine that he was teaching an honors class in the spring and always wanted to make it a hands-on experience.

"I think you will be great," Bruce said.

Jermaine kept reading. He saw something about a laundromat and asked about it. Bruce explained that it was helping a company with its placement and daily operations of their coin-operated machines in the area.

"So, I am going to be like a vending machine operator? Loading soda cans and candy bars," Jermaine said sarcastically.

Professor Wright ended the conversation and asked for the sheet back, but Jermaine told him he was just playing.

"No, I am interested, especially if it will get me out of the deli at the Stop n' Shop." Jermaine said.

"First of all, you will not be in a laundromat or loading soft drinks in a vending machine. The Econ Honors class is centered around small rising companies, and we are fortunate to have one that does business in our backyard. This company has regional reps, but in order to get a better feel for the local economy they are contracting with the community college to bring on students with a strong aptitude for economics and knowledge of the area. This is an opportunity to put some of your studies to work as an insider of a rising company. Besides they are offering thirty percent of the profits to the on-site manager and it sounds like you could use the green."

Jermaine took it all in as he looked down at the sheet still warm from the printer.

"Thirty percent of the profits? It's a start-up area," Jermaine remarked. "They probably won't see a profit for the first three years."

"Well, that's where you're wrong!" Bruce said.

Bruce then explained how this company may be different. He said that was true for the majority of companies, but this company exceled in product placement. They keep their overhead low and they tended to turn a profit within the first few months. He then explained how they needed a person like Jermaine to help them figure out where the placement in the area. Jermaine did some quick math in his head and asked his professor to let him think about it. Bruce handed Jermaine a card with the add code for the Honors class.

"If nothing else, you will learn how these companies operate," Bruce said.

"Probably unethically," Jermaine retorted. "Preying on the poor in order to line their pockets,"

"Possibly," Bruce said. "But you will learn to keep your friends close and your enemies closer. Let me know something soon."

"You got it!" Jermaine said.

Jermaine grabbed his backpack and headed off towards the bus stop.

###

Jermaine got off the bus close to where he got on. It was a desolate area near abandoned property on unkempt streets. Trash was strewn everywhere. He walked up a slight hill and the destitute poverty continued in the same vein as he made his way up a small set of stairs into a dimly lit house.

"Ma, I'm home!" he called out.

There was no response. He put down his backpack in the corner of the living room next to some of his other belongings. Nearby, a nightstand served as a makeshift desk with a small lamp on it. There were milk crates with school books and another bin with clothes, all stacked neatly in the corner. Besides a few hooks in the bathroom, this was the sum of his belongings. What he had learned to call home. Just as he sat down and untied his bootstrings to breathe out, a voice rang out with demands from the kitchen.

"Jermaine, take out that trash!" his mother yelled.

Denise was a forty-two-year-old mother of three who worked as a home attendant during the day until Jermaine's two younger sisters got out of school at three o'clock when she had to take them to their after-school program. Jermaine huffed in frustration, not only because he had to take out the trash, but taking out the trash meant that the family had already finished dinner and there was likely none left for him. He grabbed the trash from the receptacle and took the large, white bag down the small set of stairs and into an alley next to a group of shared trash cans. He walked back into the house, and before he sat down, he grabbed his backpack to pull out some books where to his delight he found a half-eaten sandwich.

"Oh, I forgot I didn't finish this ham and cheese joint from work."

He took a bite and the crust left toasted bread crumbs all over the carpet.

"Jermaine, don't eat in that living room. You are going to make a mess and bring rats up in my house," Denise said.

Jermaine put his boots on and went outside to sit on the stairs and finish his sandwich in the cold winds of autumn. As he ate, a few of the members from the gang walked by in their heavy coats and hoods.

"What good, Jay?" Dookie said.

Dookie was a sixteen-year-old with his pants sagging down below his waist. Jermaine told him he just got off of work and was getting his grub on, between bites of his sandwich. Dookie let him know that the gang was meeting down in front of the corner store in about an hour. Jermaine let him know he just got home and had to put some work in, but he would try to get down there.

The guys kept walking. Jermaine finished his sandwich and then went straight to the bathroom to wash his hands. As he walked past his sisters' room, he saw one of them drawing and the other one reading in their matching My Little Pony pajamas. He thought this was good, because it meant they had already taken their baths and wouldn't be in his way. Roxie and Renee, were eight and ten and attended a newly-converted charter school. They were the result of a failed marriage Denise had in her thirties as a single mom raising a son by herself.

Greg, her ex-husband, had been very strict with Jermaine, and that did not sit well with Denise being an over-protective mom for so many years before meeting him. "Stop babying the boy, Denise!" Greg would say. "This world ain't gonna be any nicer to him. I am trying to teach him to be a man."

Greg had been around since Jermaine was eight-years old and was all Jermaine knew as a father figure since he'd never met his biological father. Greg would take him to the movies and out to the park and the two got close over time. After Jermaine got robbed of some new sneakers as a pre-teen, Greg taught him how to protect himself. This often took the form of boxing or grappling lessons. Jermaine would get bruised and didn't complain, but Denise didn't like it. By the time Jermaine was fifteen, the arguments between Denise and Greg became too intense and ended their relationship. A year later, Jermaine joined the Rottweilers.

Jermaine was working on an assignment on a small tablet on loan from the school, when he looked across to the clock on the wall in the kitchen and noticed the time.

"I should get down there."

He transferred his work to the cloud drive, put his coat on and headed down to the corner store.

###

CHAPTER TWO

It was nearly ten p.m. as two gang members, Brian and Dookie loitered harmlessly in front of the corner store. Police often rolled by to harass the boys because they had nothing better to do at the time. As often as the police searched the Rottweilers, they had never found any knives, guns or paraphernalia. This was not to be mistaken that the boys were angels. Those brothers did love to smoke and the police would sometimes question them about their slurred speech and bloodshot eyes. Jermaine turned the corner to greet the gang.

"Where's everybody at?" he asked.

The two teens, Dookie and Brian, were brothers one year apart, sixteen and seventeen-years old respectively.

"Cheech went to go smoke and Earl, man, I don't know where Earl went, but he'll be back though," Brian answered.

Jermaine checked in with Brian and Dookie asking them what's been up. Dookie told him that the streets have been quiet and suggested that it had something to do with it getting too cold to pop off. Dookie had been shot more than once in the past year and had crapped his pants both times, so his brother dubbed him Dookie, a name the gang members quickly adopted. His mother didn't find it funny, but would find herself using the name every once in a while, when it slipped out. Brian and Dookie's mom was a heroin addict and would go missing for days at a time, but usually showed back up when the social security, disability or welfare check was soon to arrive. She was also savvy enough to stay clean long enough for when the social worker was scheduled to come by. The boys knew that when the house was clean, mom was clean.

"Nah!" Jermaine said. "Weather has nothing to do with it. When it is quiet these fools get bored and are looking for something to get into. Keep an eye out! You need to find Earl."

Jermaine was like a watchful big brother and in his four years as part of the gang he learned some things that he tried to pass on to the younger members. Although Jermaine didn't smoke, he would sip some Cognac on a Friday or Saturday night as a way to wind down from the busy week.

Brian told the gang he was calling Earl to find out where he was. As Brian was dialing, Dookie saw Cheech walking back down the block.

"Why you always walking off like that Cheech?" Dookie asked.

Cheech told him that Five wouldn't let him get high on the Ave so he just took it in between the block.

Jermaine greeted Cheech some dap and while doing so told him that Dookie was right. "You never know who's watching to try to catch you when you are not watching."

Cheech was an older member of the gang and knew all this, but he liked to get high and didn't always think. He let Jermaine know that he was a grown man and knew how to keep himself safe.

"I've been out here almost as long as you," Cheech said.

Jermaine told him that meant the guys were following his lead and that it was Cheech's job to show them the way.

"That's not my job!" Cheech said. "That's your job! Mr. Second in Command."

Cheech had always been a little salty that Jermaine was asked to step up after Tony got pinched. He asked Jermaine what he knew about setting an example since he was never around much.

"I'm the one out here with these cats when the streets are hot," Cheech said.

Cheech was right. Since Jermaine had to pick up his job at Stop n' Shop to help out around the house, he didn't get home until after nine p.m. and barely had time to be a true leader. Still Jermaine puffed up his chest to maintain his dominance. Something he rarely liked to do. He let Cheech know he knew he wasn't around enough and that was why he had to make every minute count.

"I didn't ask for this role, but I got it and I owe it to Tony and those before me to make men out of boys." Jermaine said. "Do you want this torch? Do you? Because I don't think you can carry it."

Cheech was still high and wasn't up for an argument and let it squash. But he still hinted that it may be him one day.

"For now, move on Black man, move on."

There was a commotion down the street and the gang members saw someone coming their way running top speed.

"Yo, it's Earl!" Dookie yelled.

Earl was desperately escaping a heated chase by five rival gang members who were only about a half a block behind him. Brian ducked down an alley and came back holding a .44 Magnum and as Earl made his way to the corner, Brian pointed the gun in the direction of Earl's pursuers who took off in five different directions. Earl collapsed down around the corner and Brian put his piece back down in the alley. Jermaine and Dookie went to look after Earl.

"Man, where did you go? Dookie asked.

Earl, was a twenty-year-old, undersized guy. He was breathing heavily and could hardly speak.

"To...to...to see about this girl!" Earl replied.

"And you couldn't tell nobody?" Jermaine quipped.

Earl steadied his breath and quipped back asking if Jermaine told them every time he was rolling to see about a girl. Jermaine was once again forced to be stern.

"If it is in somebody else's hood, you had better believe it," he said. "I might even ask one of you to stand outside the house."

Cheech laughed in agreement and told a story about how Jermaine made him sit on a stoop over on Davis and how Cheech swore he was going to get shot.

"Man, why you gotta bring up old stuff?" he said. "That was one time and I was right inside the living room."

Jermaine turned back to Earl and told him the point was to always let someone know where he was at all times.

"Yeah man! Understood!" Earl said.

Jermaine then turned back to Cheech and told him he wasn't about to let him get shot over some girl and the two of them laughed.

"You know me better than that," Jermaine said.

###

A well-dressed man was sitting in a conference room with Bruce. The door was closed, but Jermaine could see their lips moving in what he imagined as a very formal conversation. Bruce had set up a meeting for Jermaine to meet a representative from the coin-op company. He looked at his phone. He was on time, but it appeared the meeting had started without him and he was hesitant to knock on the door. Instead, Jermaine stood right outside the conference room glass door, visible for both Bruce and the representative to see him. Jermaine was somewhat dressed for the occasion. He had on an oversized white dress shirt that fell clumsily on his skinny frame, with a black tie and jeans. This was his normal uniform at the deli, minus the Stop n' Shop smock apron that always accompanied it. As the hour neared, Jermaine grew impatient and decided to lightly knock on the door. Bruce looked up and waved Jermaine in. Jermaine took two deep breaths and entered.

"Mr. Beasley, I would like you to meet Jonathan Stone from Quarimoc Industries in Kansas City, Missouri," Bruce said.

Jermaine walked over and shook Jonathan's hand with a firm, authoritative shake.

"Mr. Beasley, your professor tells me you are skilled in economics and in fact you are one of the top students in his class," Jonathan stated.

Jermaine displayed a little shock from the compliment, but rolled with it. "I do my best sir!"

"So, has Professor Wright told you anything about our company?"

"Not much sir. We strictly spoke about the honor's class project and what my responsibilities may be."

"Let's leave the sir stuff at the door!" Jonathan said. "If you allow me to call you Jermaine you can call me Jonathan. How does that sound?"

Jermaine relaxed his shoulders and told him that worked for him. Jonathan told Jermaine that Quarimoc was a growing coin-operated company based out of Kansas City, but spreading their wings through Missouri and even across the state line into Kansas.

"We believe we have a good operation, but never want to take the local residents for granted. Although we are a for-profit business, we hold ourselves to a very high standard to treat our customers with dignity and respect."

Jermaine's hairs raised on the back of his neck.

"How does that look for a coin-op located in another state," Jermaine asked.

"That's a great question Jermaine!" Jonathan said. "This is where someone who knows the needs of the community comes in. It's easy to make bank from pushing sugar on kids in schools. That doesn't take too much talent. What does take some thought is enriching the community."

In Jermaine's opinion, a company had to ask the right questions regarding what the customers need and want. Jonathan thought he knew the answer to that by focusing on better schools and better services in low-income areas, but Jermaine challenged him to start before that with building a sense of community.

"A place where they can chill with their neighbors and friends. Free from the chaos. Where they can get to know one another as people," Jermaine said.

Jonathan wanted to know how a coin-op could engage in building community, and Jermaine focused on starting with the senior centers and the after-school centers and altering the focus from not only snacks, but meals.

"Laundromats are two hours or more of undivided attention," Jermaine began. "That attention needs to go beyond television game shows, soap operas and judge shows broadcasted from monitors with horrible reception. Quarimoc needs to think about how to make something as mundane and necessary as doing laundry an activity, where people make friends, talk with their neighbors, maybe meet their potential spouse."

"Free movies on the hour?" Jonathan suggested.

Jermaine didn't dismiss the idea of movies, but he was thinking even deeper. Into things like community lectures, book clubs, personal development classes.

Jonathan was in wonder at the way Jermaine thought and wanted him to start right away.

"Wait until you see his aptitude for growth," Bruce said.

"Jermaine, you are a bright young man and did not disappoint." Jonathan stated excitedly. "My mind is buzzing."

Jermaine and Jonathan shook hands. Jonathan handed Jermaine his card with a personal cell number on the back and told him that he would love for him to meet the rest of the reps at Quarimoc as soon as possible, but to hit the books for now, so he could maintain the necessary GPA to get this internship.

As Jermaine walked out his brain was spinning. He walked across the campus with an air of confidence.

###

It was another early morning at the library and students were powering through in their study carols. Jermaine was at a computer station with headphones on and working on a Black Studies paper that was due the next day. He had books and articles that were suggested by the reference librarian and now he was in flow. As his paragraph came to a close, he hit the period button with extra emphasis, like he was slapping the winning bone on the table in a game of dominos. It startled the student next to him. He reached in his bag and pulled out the add code for the Econ Honors class.

"Man, I can do this!" he thought.

He looked down at his phone and realized that he had about an hour until open priority registration began for special groups. Jermaine was admitted to the college as a local, low-income student and got to register before the general population. He looked at his suggested class schedule from his advisor and after thinking about it for a few minutes, decided to add the Honors class in place of his Physical Education class. Jermaine needed the PE class and loved to hit the gym, but he also realized that the amount of time it took to bring clothes, go to the locker, change, workout, shower and change back into his school clothes, was time that he could use to work on assignments.

"This will hurt, but I gotta do it! It just means I gotta find time to get in that cardio after work."

With a sigh of relief, he put his head down and started back in on his paper.

###

At the Stop n' Shop Jermaine donned in plastic gloves and a smock apron weighing sliced meat at the deli. He served customers with a smile that he seldom wore on the block. When he was on break outside, his supervisor came up to him.

"Jermaine, J-Man!" Will said, a heavy-set man with slicked back hair in his thirties, called out to him.

"What's up, boss man?" Jermaine said with a nod of his head.

Will had switched Jermaine off the schedule for the weekend because he overbooked and had to get Carlos, another deli worker at the store, some hours. Jermaine reminded Will that he turned down hours at the tutoring lab to pick up the shift and how much he really needed the money. Will dodged the conversation by saying it would give him more time to hit the books. He pleaded with Jermaine to let it slide and with Will being the boss, Jermaine didn't feel like he really had a choice.

"Thank you for accommodating!" Will said. "Carlos has a family and I gotta look out for him."

Will started walking back inside the store. Jermaine was miffed and before Will made it back in the store, he caught him and told him about his internship starting in January. When Will asked what he would be doing, Jermaine downplayed it by saying it was overseeing some video games, vending and laundry machines. Will told him about his cousin who did vending for Coca-Cola and Jermaine felt the need to clarify that he would be doing more than loading cans and pulling out coins.

"Nah, I am going to be contracting with businesses, and deciding where they go and how and where they add to the community."

"Okay, so you are going to be managing. I didn't know you had skills like that," Will said.

"I didn't know either," Jermaine replied.

"Well, good luck with that!" Will said. "Let me know if there is any information I can help you with. I have picked up a few tricks of the trade over these last eight years."

Jermaine looked encouraged as Will walked in the store. He knew that he probably wouldn't take Will up on his offer, but it somehow felt good to know that he was moving on from the store. Almost like a weight had been lifted off his chest.

###

Denise was on the floor playing Chutes & Ladders with Renee and Roxie which was their normal evening activity before their bath. Jermaine tried to walk in unnoticed, but Roxie didn't let him get away that easily.

"Come play with us Brother!" she said.

Brother, was the girls endearing name for Jermaine. He told her that he couldn't because he had to take a shower, but when Renee chimed in to badger him, he kicked off his shoes to join in.

"Okay, just one round," he said.

He loved playing games with his sisters, especially since he didn't grow up with any siblings his age. This was another reason he found the gang so attractive. He had the opportunity to be around kids his age.

Denise divvied out another playing piece for Jermaine while asking him how school was going. Jermaine shared about the opportunity that may be coming his way while Roxie rolled the dice and moved her piece across the board. Roxie was interested to hear about his internship opportunity, so Jermaine told her he was going to be putting video games around the city. This immediately piqued Renee's interest. She thought her after-school center needed more video games, because the ones they had were boring, so kids just went outside to play.

"It's good that you girls are staying active on the playground," Denise said. "Video games make it so you don't move around as much and you get lazy."

Jermaine used the opportunity to gather some information and address Renee. He wanted to know what kind of games she thought the kids would play. Roxie felt like a dancing game would be fun and Jermaine used the opportunity to take a dig at his mom.

"So, something that keeps you moving?" Jermaine said. "Like Dance Dance Revolution? Mom loves that game."

The girls couldn't hold back their laughs because they knew it was true.

"We hear her playing it in her room after we go to bed," Roxie said.

"You girls are supposed to be sleeping." Denise scolded.

This made the girls laugh even harder. Jermaine took a turn and immediately fell down a chute straight to the bottom.

In an effort to change the topic, Denise asked how the opportunity came about. Jermaine let her know that his professor for economics asked if he was interested, since he was doing pretty well in the class. Denise remembered how much Jermaine struggled in high school so to hear that he was gravitating to a subject made her happy.

"See, as much as you complained about classes in high school, I knew you would find your niche."

During Roxie's turn on the board she climbed a ladder that took her almost to the top.

"Yay! I'm about to win," Roxie sang.

"Not yet!" Jermaine said. "You still have some chutes to get by."

"Yeah, Roxie. It's not over yet," Renee said.

Denise decided to ward off the argument by diverting back to the internship. She wanted to know when it started. Jermaine explained that it was just a class project and that it was part of an Honor's Class for the spring semester. Roxie asked if he was going to make any money and everyone became interested. Jermaine told them that it all depended on if the company made any money. Then he would be able to see a fraction of the returns. Denise, never being shy about asking, wanted to know details and Jermaine told them that it would be up to thirty percent of the profits.

Roxie rolled the dice that skipped her past a big chute and her eyes got big. Renee wanted to know what thirty percent of the profits meant, so Jermaine explained that for every dollar the company earned above cost that he would get to bring home thirty cents of it.

"And for every hundred dollars they earn your brother gets thirty dollars," Denise added.

Roxie was in the third grade and was learning her multiplication tables and did some quick math as she waited her turn on the board.

"That means for every thousand dollars they make you get three hundred dollars of it!" Roxie said.

Denise quickly remarked that three hundred dollars would be just about his paycheck at the deli and that it should give him some incentive. Jermaine never thought of it that way. Now he was the one doing the math. Meanwhile, Denise was quickly climbing to the top of the board unsuspectedly. Renee wished him luck and Jermaine told her that he was sure he would do fine. With the next roll of the dice, Roxie won the game and Renee sighed.

"It's okay!" Jermaine said. "It's a game. If big brother does turn a profit you girls will get some nice gifts for your birthdays."

"What about mom?" Denise asked.

Jermaine leaned over and gave his mom a kiss on the cheek.

"Of course, the biggest gift goes to my favorite girl."

The girls giggled.

"It better!" Denise stated. "Now off to bed with you young ladies."

As the girls scrambled off to bed Denise and Jermaine cleaned up the game.

###

"Earl!" Dookie called out. "You hear back about that job at Foot Locker yet?"

Earl twisted his face. He wasn't interested in walking around in those zebra stripes to sell overpriced shoes to teenagers all day. The truth was he only put in that application to get his mother off his back about eating up all the food and not contributing around the house. She would often tell him that he either needed to go to school or get a job, but he wasn't going to sit up in the house all day doing nothing. Even though Jermaine was busy doing it all, none of it appealed to Earl.

"Jermaine said he was about to be done with the joint at the deli though. Maybe you could apply there," Brian said.

Earl wasn't trying to take orders from anyone and wanted to be his own boss.

"Are you going to start selling knock-offs on the street corner?" Cheech laughed.

"Maybe. I just know I'm not going to that interview at Foot Locker."

Dookie put it together that Earl heard back from Foot Locker. Jermaine walked up to hear the tail end of the conversation.

"What's up y'all?" Jermaine asked. "Hear back from who? That girl on the Eastside?"

There was an awkward silence that Earl finally broke.

"Nah, we ain't talking about her," Earl said.

"So, who are we talking about? Somebody spit it out," Jermaine demanded.

Brian spilled the tea that Earl got a call back about a job, which got Jermaine excited. He had always been taught that the gang members should always be moving toward independence from their parents.

"We can't live this life forever." Jermaine said. "Besides, cops give you less crap when you got a job, have a certificate or license or are in college."

Dookie shot Earl a sideways look to get him to speak up, which Earl tried to ignore, but couldn't for long. He ended telling Jermaine that he wasn't interested in working for the man and that he wanted to start his own thing. This got Jermaine even more excited, but the members knew Jermaine and figured that there had to be a lesson in it all. Jermaine wanted to be an entrepreneur himself, but realized that working for yourself, wasn't as easy as it sounded. He knew that it would be long nights and weekends to get a business off the ground. Earl didn't see it that way. He only saw it as flipping some product for more money than the product cost and referenced the street vendors he saw doing it. Jermaine had already considered that route out of high school, but once he realized that most of them were making less than minimum wage, he decided to go to college.

"Most street vendors never consider their price index. What markets to sell in? Who is their customer and what their needs are? Sure, some of them get some money, but how long do they keep it?"

Jermaine quickly broke down a hardcore beginner's economic lesson and let them know what it would take if they really wanted to consider a business venture.

"We can talk about what it would take to buy enough of a product at three percent and sell it at five percent and how much time it would take to break even and eventually make a profit in an expanding market," Jermaine said.

The gang members hadn't heard Jermaine talk like this before and their mouths dropped. He had put just enough salt on their tongue to make them thirsty, but he also knew it wouldn't last long so he had to push. He saw Earl's mind spinning like an out-of-control helicopter and wanted to catch him before he landed.

"In the meantime, I want to see you suited and booted for that interview with Foot Locker. In order to be a good leader, you have to be a good follower."

###

CHAPTER THREE

It was just after Thanksgiving and the holidays were fast approaching. Jermaine was back at school after some much needed time off. Although he was spending more time in the library, his grades were not anywhere near where they needed to be and it was nearing finals. All this time he thought it was supposed to be getting easier.

He walked through the campus and saw Bruce in line at the coffee shop. He stopped and asked him about his Thanksgiving break. Bruce enjoyed the break, but also realized that the final push toward the end of the semester was treacherous for students and instructors.

"How are your grades looking?" Bruce asked.

Jermaine was doing a little better than at mid-terms, but was still in the grind, especially with math and history, subjects he had always struggled with.

"My mind just doesn't wrap around it," Jermaine said.

Bruce thought otherwise. He knew Jermaine could do the work, but thought he was having some kind of mental block. Maybe from a bad experience or bad teaching growing up. While he ordered his craft drink he put together his words and while his order was being prepared, he pulled Jermaine over.

"Economics is a combination of what has taken place in the past. History. Along with production, consumption, and transfer of wealth. Which is math," Bruce asserted. "Your mind does a great job of grasping those concepts."

This time it was Jermaine who was caught unsuspectedly and who quickly became the student. He still didn't understand why it all felt so foreign. Bruce was hustling off to section with not much time to talk, but Jermaine was too curious to just let him go, so he walked out of the building with him. Bruce shared his thoughts on Jermaine's mental block due to having struggled in these subjects early in life.

"You don't believe you can do well in certain subjects and it becomes a self-fulfilling prophecy," Bruce said. "If you approach these things with a different mindset, like in the view of how money is made and how wealth is attained, you will begin to see things differently."

Jermaine couldn't grasp what history had to do with money. He had always viewed it as just a whole bunch of dead people, governments, laws and ancient societies. Bruce showed him how all of those things centered around money and the accumulation of wealth. Even the Church. Jermaine had been so focused on economics in the industrial age that he never considered how long it had been impacting and shaping the world since the beginning of time.

Bruce explained how it is the same story with math and how it is in everything from finance to science to architecture, but it is the grassroots of economics.

"Well, that makes sense!" Jermaine stated. "I just have a hard time wrapping my head around all those different formulas."

Bruce stopped in front of his hall and looked Jermaine dead in the eye. He knew the trick was to make his difficult subjects more relatable to what Jermaine was truly interested in and what he was good at.

"That is the beautiful thing about college," Bruce said. "You get to make the assignments into what really and truly moves you."

Jermaine wasn't fully grasping what Bruce meant and wanted more time with him, but Professor Wright had to go. He was going to be late for section if he spent any more time explaining.

"When you complete an assignment. Any assignment. You get to choose what frame of reference you put it in," Bruce stated. "In high school, they gave you information and asked you to remember it. Just tell them back what they told you. Here we are going to ask you to take the information we teach you and make sense of it. Apply it to everyday life. How can you use math, history, economics and Black Studies to impact the world around you?"

Bruce opened the door to the building and started to walk in.

"That's all I have for you today!" he said. "I am late. We are going to finish this conversation later."

Bruce continued into his class to start section. Jermaine found a place to sit down and connected to Wi-Fi. He opened his Black Studies paper and began to look at it through the lens of the uneven distribution of wealth. He immediately made edits, pulling out bloated statements and inserted deeper concepts in their place. When he was done, he looked at his paper and was much happier with the results than before. His mind was opened to new concepts. He became curious about how he could apply this to his math. He thought long and hard before pulling out his calculator and his math assignment. He took a look around the campus at the students carrying heavy backpacks, coffee cups, and mobile devices and suddenly realized that it was all economics. He quickly pulled out his Economics 101 midterm and reviewed his answers.

He added some new math concepts into his midterm and looked to see how it all worked.

Unhappy with the results, he scrapped what he wrote and began to think about it some more. He instead looked at math as being at the center of wealth accumulation. He considered the price index that these corporations used to figure out what they needed to turn a profit without overpricing and losing customers. He reviewed a simple supply-and-demand concept and realized that math was integrated throughout. He deduced that it was all hidden in a formula. He finally pulled out his calculator and punched in price indexes, cost for products and overhead and what corporations and banks in the 1990's were charging their customers and noticed that they all fit into a formula. He pulled out his math assignment and began to apply several different formulas to his equations and realized that it all repeated itself. He completed his math assignment in half the time it normally took him. Then he looked down at his phone and realized he was going to miss his bus to work and would have to Uber. His quick math made him realize that he didn't have money for a rideshare.

###

Jonathan Stone sat with four other Quarimoc regional representatives and waited for the conference call to come in. One of them was named Pablo, a long-time rep who had been around since the early days of Quarimoc and who wondered if Jermaine was the real thing. Jonathan certainly thought he was. Especially, if they were looking for someone who knew the area. Besides it was an opportunity to get their foot into the college.

"If we get this right, we can get promising economic students for years to come," Jonathan said.

Lance was a relative newcomer to the team and on his first launch outside of the hub of the company. He questioned why the onus was on Quarimoc to get it right. Jonathan told him how it was important to treat Jermaine right and invest in his future. Pablo, who was ever so salty, brought up the fact that Jermaine was getting an opportunity to get some money in the deal.

"I had to work at unpaid internships all throughout undergrad," Pablo said. "It felt like another class that I had to pay for in order to line the pockets of companies that were already rich."

Lance chalked up all the time in the trenches to experience, and Pablo agreed that it helped him get his foot in the door, but money would have been nice as a struggling student. Jonathan assured the reps that Jermaine would be fairly compensated and that it would add to his resume. He also hoped that Jermaine would be able to drop his off-campus job, so he could have more time for his studies.

"If he turns a profit," Lance emphasized.

"When he turns a profit," Jonathan corrected. "This guy gave me our money's worth in the first meeting alone. We need to have a face that the community trusts to get our foot in the door."

The call came in and the reps turned their attention to the huge screen on the wall. Jonathan composed the group and answered with Jermaine popping up on the fifty-two-inch monitor.

"Good afternoon, Mr. Beasley!" Jonathan answered the call.

"Good afternoon, Mr. Stone!" Jermaine said.

Jermaine's voice came booming through the monitor and Jonathan adjusted the volume as Jermaine adjusted in his chair located in a study room in the library. Jonathan let the reps know that they agreed to lose the formalities and insisted that Jermaine call him by his first name and that he would be introducing the team by first name only. No one disagreed and Jermaine insisted that they address him by first name as well.

"Alright Jermaine!" Jonathan began. "To my right we have Pamela. She is a fifth-year executive who oversees several districts. Next to her, we have Lance who is fairly new to the company as of March. Across from him there is Shirley, who also comes with years of experience in the coin-op field from a competing company, and across from me there is Pablo, who has been with the company since we started almost sixteen years ago."

"I came in year three, so not since the beginning beginning," Pablo corrected.

Jonathan told Jermaine that Pablo had been there long enough ago to remember when Quarimoc was just a small outsource company and was barely able to keep the lights on. Pablo agreed and wasn't quite sure if the company still owed him a check or two from those thin years. Everyone, except for Shirley enjoyed a laugh. Shirley remained very business oriented and checked her watch to insist that they get started. She immediately wanted to know what Jermaine knew about their company. Jermaine didn't know much about them at all really. Only what Jonathan had shared. Before the interview, Jermaine had combed the website and reviewed a few articles, but there wasn't much to be found.

Pamela knew this was done on purpose. "We consider ourselves more 'mom and pop,'" Pamela said.

Jermaine got that and felt that his neighborhood and neighborhoods like his would appreciate the small feel versus a big disconnected corporation. But, he still believed there was room for some branding. As a twenty-year-old, he found when he searched for a company and little came up, he became suspicious about whether the company was even legit. He didn't have to see thousands of reviews, but it helped to have some information regarding what customers and users thought. Jonathan thought Jermaine's suggestion sounded like a delicate balancing act.

"I am not the one to tell you how to market your company," Jermaine continued. "I just know that in a digital age, if my soda doesn't drop and a machine steals my money, I want to know if they are reputable and if they will do right by me."

Pablo had felt that the company could and should do more entering into the digital age. He was next in line for questioning and wanted to know how Jermaine saw Quarimoc expanding in terms of product placement?

Jermaine had already shared a few of his ideas with Jonathan back at the campus about coin-up being an addition that enhances the community. If he was going to be out at a park for hours and lunch or dinner was still a long way off, he wanted something close by to keep him from having to leave his friends to find food. Pamela gravitated to that concept and thought of the idea as starting with the people instead of the product.

Jermaine considered the people as the product and his underlying goal was convenience. "If we are able to accommodate people while they wait for their laundry or stay around at the arcade instead of leaving to just come back, we develop community."

Pablo knew that convenience was what the founders of the company had in mind, so people could have everything they wanted or needed at their fingertips. Shirley couldn't wrap her mind around how it made the company a profit and Jermaine was ready with his thoughts and impressed her by addressing her by name.

Jermaine pulled up a spreadsheet and shared it on the screen for everyone to see. On it he broke down the cost index for how much time most people spend in a four-hour window on a busy day at the laundromat, or an arcade or in a teacher's lounge. Then he factored in physiological factors such as bathroom breaks, sleep and hunger. The need to eat superseded why most people left these places earlier than they would have, so he deduced that if one out of every three patrons staved off hunger, breakfast, lunch or dinner, that it would account for fifty customers at an average of a dollar fifty per item or load of laundry, bringing in an additional seventy-five dollars per coin-operated machine. By placing thirty machines in high traffic areas, the company would be looking at roughly twenty-two hundred dollars during busy windows of time and another seven-hundred fifty dollars during slow times averaging three-thousand dollars a day, at least five days a week.

"If we pull in an average of fifteen-thousand dollars a week you walk away with eleven-thousand five-hundred dollars." Jermaine said. "After I get my meager cut."

Lance did the math and knew he was right, but Jonathan knew it was subjective. Jermaine agreed, but also believed that he was underestimating. His bet was that they made even more when factoring in adult leagues, soccer tournaments, music festivals, bowling alleys, dorms and the such.

"The goal is to get a steady flow of customers," Jermaine said.

The team got pretty excited about the pitch and looked around the room at each other. Without much of a check in with the rest of the reps, Jonathan told Jermaine that he wanted him on with the team in the Spring. He just had to make sure all the paperwork was in order. Jermaine had already registered for the Honor's class and he was jazzed about getting started.

"Great! Your professor will let you know what papers you need to sign," Jonathan said. "Thank you for your time today! We will see you in the spring."

The group said their goodbyes and hung up the phone.

###

On Jermaine's last day at Stop n' Shop, he walked in with his backpack and hoodie on and avoided eye contact with the cashiers as he headed downstairs to his locker and changed into his work uniform. When he got to the bottom step, he saw signs and banners made up for him that read "Congratulations" and was taken aback. He had been working at the deli since his junior year of high school and didn't remember seeing this for other folks. As he thought back, he realized that people rarely left. They transferred to other stores and moved up in responsibilities, but rarely left. As he was thinking this, he heard Will approaching.

"What do you think, J-Man?" Will asked.

"Did you do this?" Jermaine replied.

"Nah, dude!" Will said. "Well, I asked the ladies if they would help me put something together, but they did it all."

Jermaine got emotional as he thought about the three years he had been at the store. He was a seventeen-year-old kid when he started. Will thought it was a good thing that he was getting out and talked about how he had been at the store for twelve years right out of high school.

"I made manager after four years and never looked back. Once you get married and have kids there isn't time for much else."

Jermaine took it all in as he walked to his locker and grabbed his smock. He pictured his life ending up with getting a job and working his way up to a decent salary. Will knew there was no decent salary to be had. After twelve years, he was still working long hours doing back-breaking work and living check to check to keep a roof over his family's head with little appreciation.

Jermaine looked at the banner on his way back up the stairs.

"Well, I feel appreciated today," he said.

As he got to the floor, he was welcomed with a round of applause from the team waiting for him at the top. This garnered stares from the customers as they wondered what the commotion was about.

"Is it his birthday?" a customer said

"No, it's his last day!" a co-worker replied. "He got a paid internship through his college."

"Oh, good for him," the customer said.

Jermaine was all smiles and tried to deflect the attention by sliding behind the deli unnoticed. Carlos was working with him and helping a customer, so Jermaine started pulling salad trays. Carlos wondered if Jermaine was going to miss the deli. Jermaine would miss the people, but not the work.

“There are worse jobs out there!” Carlos said.

Jermaine knew that first hand, but didn’t want that to be his comparison. He also didn’t want to appear condescending. He knew this was probably it for Carlos. He was thankful to work with great people, but felt like he was missing the opportunity to use some of his skills and God-given talent to help people. Skills he didn’t even realize he had. Carlos tried not to think about his God-given abilities, knowing that with a wife and kids, he didn’t have time to pursue the things he dreamt about as a kid. Jermaine was still young and living with his momma. He didn’t know about responsibility and Carlos could sense it, but didn’t tell him as much. When his shift ended, he washed his hands and took off his apron and wished Jermaine good luck.

"Maybe we will see each other again soon," Carlos said.

"I am sure we will," Jermaine replied.

The store was emptying out as it neared closing time. Jermaine cleaned up the deli and began to pack everything away. A few of the remaining cashiers and clerks walked over with a cake as Will locked the front door.

"Jermaine, you have been here a while," Will began. "It's hard to see you go my man."

"I haven't been here that long!" Jermaine replied with a laugh. "But I did grow up here. Met some cool homies. Went on a few dates. It's been my second home"

"But now it's time to move on!" Will replied.

As the room went somber, Jermaine wanted to alter the mood. He held back a tear as he grabbed some forks and plates from behind the deli handed them out along with slices of cake.

"Not until we cut into this cake! Is this strawberry? The bakery throws down!"

###

Jermaine walked through his neighborhood early on a cold Saturday morning while the streets were still empty. More than likely due to the cold weather. Christmas was fast approaching and most people had already done their shopping. There were a few lights in every third house and store window and the occasional Kwanzaa candles as that holiday was set to begin as soon as Christmas ended. Jermaine normally spent most of his Saturdays working at the deli and now with that gig ended he was just looking to get out of the cramped house.

He walked through the block and saw people in the laundromat. Although his internship hadn't started yet, he figured that it was never too early to do research. As he walked in he saw that it was not overly crowded, with only about a third of the machines being used. The owner appeared to be foreign-born and Jermaine wasn't sure if he spoke English. He stopped the person he assumed was in charge.

"Excuse me!" he said. "Are you the owner?"

"Yes!" Sethi answered.

Sethi was a middle-aged Indian man who spoke the King's English.

"How can I help you?" he said.

Sethi noticed that Jermaine did not have any clothes with him.

"I just got this internship with a coin-operated machine company and I am curious who you get your machines from," Jermaine said.

Sethi explained that they didn't use coin machines anymore and that customers had to load money onto a card. Jermaine was familiar with the process. His mother had one. He was still curious about what made the laundromat go that route.

"My brother owns a laundromat in the Heights and he convinced me that it was more convenient than coins." Sethi said. "But I don't think my customers here like the cards."

"I definitely see it being the wave of the future," Jermaine said.

Sethi pointed to a machine on a wall. What he was talking about was like a MetroCard. If you had a card already, you could add more money, either by cash, debit or credit card. Jermaine checked it out and was impressed. He noticed that there were not many people there for a Saturday. The customers had not quite taken to the card system as fast as Sethi would have liked. They instead walked six blocks to go to a competitor's laundromat, but Jermaine figured that they would get tired of that as soon as the snow and cold came around. Sethi wasn't quite as confident.

"I don't know!" Sethi remarked. "Some people don't trust cards. It's seen as another way to track your every move."

Jermaine was taken aback. He didn't think the card had any personal identifiers on them and wondered how anyone could possibly track them. Sethi had been living in the U.S. for almost fifteen years now and he knew that the government didn't need to have a name on a card to know his whereabouts. Jermaine found that interesting. There was a chip in the card that told anyone who was interested when and where the card was used. Coins were much more elusive and the U.S. found a way to screw over poor people with bad credit and low wages. Sethi's customers didn't want to load money on a card and pay ahead for what they only need at the moment.

Jermaine was impressed at how well Sethi knew his clientele and could have spoken to him all day gleaning knowledge, but he didn't want to take up his time. Sethi was happy to have someone to talk the business side of things with. He offered to show Jermaine the back end of the business and went over the nuts and bolts of ordering processes, financial books and contracts. Jermaine's brain was about to explode. He hadn't even started getting into any of this stuff yet and didn't start his internship until spring. He hoped if things went well with product placement he would see some profits. Sethi loved his optimism and wanted to do what he could to help Jermaine succeed. He invited him back once he got started with his assignment. Sethi was thinking about putting a few coin-ups washers and dryers back in the store and Jermaine wondered if he could help. They shook hands and Jermaine felt as though he had already made a sale. He went back to his mother's house and threw some loads of dirty laundry in a basket and headed back out for the door.

"Mom, can I borrow your laundry card!" he asked.

"It's in the drawer next to the refrigerator," Denise said. "Do you have detergent and fabric softener?"

"No!" Jermaine replied.

"How about dryer sheets?" Denise asked.

"I will get some," Jermaine sighed.

Denise saw laundry day as more than just clothes and a machine. She was interested in what Jermaine was going to bring to do while he was waiting for his clothes. Jermaine grabbed a textbook to study for his Econ final. He thanked his mom as he walked out of the house and scurried up the block. He ran into Cheech.

"What's up, brotha?" Cheech asked.

"Laundry day!" Jermaine replied.

Cheech was surprised to see Jermaine. He normally worked on Saturdays until the evening. Cheech forgot that he quit his job and, realizing he was free, Cheech wanted to hang. Jermaine didn't have anything better to do with his free time. If he cranked out his studies during laundry, he would be free for the rest of the day. Cheech hung out with a crew of home girls down around the game room on Saturdays and told Jermaine to meet him there around two o'clock.

It was almost noon and Jermaine knew it would be tight because he still had to get lunch. He would get over there when he was done with all that. For now, he had to keep pushing to finish his laundry.

###

At the arcade, there was a mix of Skee-ball, pool tables and video games culminating into quite a ruckus, especially on a Saturday with younger kids running around, mixed in with a sizable number of teens and twenty somethings. Cheech was already there, hanging with some girls and all of them were as high as a kite by the time Jermaine arrived.

"Jay, Jay, Jay!" Cheech called. "You know all the homies, right?"

Jermaine had seen them all from time to time, but didn't really hang with them to know them well.

"Hello ladies!" he said.

Jermaine gave Cheech a homie hug and then acknowledged how hot the spot was. Cheech had been riding him to come through for a while now, but Jermaine had never made the time. The arcade didn't have all of this when he was a kid stopping by the game room on the regular. There were only a few arcade games, but this place felt like a Dave & Busters.

Cheech told him that he was satisfied that the college boy approved. Jermaine brushed off the jab and instead turned to one of Cheech's friends to get her name. Veronika, was a teenage girl with a hat pulled just above her eyes. Jermaine had met her before and she was upset that he had to ask her name.

"Jermaine, you know me." Veronika said. "Now you have to guess!"

Cheech and the rest of the homies enjoyed the game of cat and mouse and weren't going to give anything away. Jermaine needed a hint and found out that he went to junior high and high school with her older sister Tammy.

"Vanessa!" he said.

"Close!" she replied.

Jermaine looked to Cheech and the homies for help, but there was none to be found. Charlene, was a mocha-skin girl and Patrice, a lighter-skin girl both shook their heads at Jermaine. Cheech was a little more forgiving. Jermaine was close. He got the first letter and there weren't a lot of "V" names.

"Vicky, Vivienne, Valerie?" he blurted one wrong name after the other. He was really bad at this. Veronika wanted to know if he knew who her friends were and their names rolled right off of his tongue, which didn't do him any favors, and in fact, probably did more damage than good.

"See now I am just hurt," Veronika said.

"It's not Vanessa?" he said. "Veronika! Your name is Veronika."

Jermaine wasn't confident and Veronika could tell. Cheech, Charlene and Patrice remained silent. Veronika asked if he was sure. Jermaine tried to see if she was giving anything away, but couldn't tell from her eyes being all faded from the weed. He decided he would double down on his guess.

"I will bet the five in my pocket on it," he said.

Jermaine pulled out a crumpled bill and Veronika snatched it out of his hand.

"Oh snap!" he said "I thought for sure that was it."

"It was a lucky guess," Veronika said.

She thought he didn't deserve his money back for a guess. Jermaine thought it was ruthless and let Cheech know that he had to be careful who he hung with. He offered to buy Veronika a soda with the five dollars. Veronika had already claimed the money as her own, despite Jermaine getting her name right. She figured it took him too many guesses to come up with the right answer. Eventually she did give him his crumpled bill back.

"No soda?" he asked.

"No, thank you!" she said. "I'm not thirsty."

The crew picked up on the implication and couldn't hold back their facial expressions.

Cheech sung a lyric from iNi KAMOZE song.

"Out in the street, they call it murder," Cheech said.

Jermaine punched his coat and excused himself as Cheech walked him in the arcade to show him around and spoke about the lady who bought it out and renovated it. The arcade was decked out with shooting games, driving games as well as video games.

"You have absolutely no game bro," Cheech told Jermaine.

Jermaine knew this to be true, having been shot down repeatedly lately at school, at work and now even on the block. He had lost his street edge and was becoming corny and surmised that sisters didn't want anything to do with an educated man.

"You are too much in your head, Jay!" Cheech told him. "Too uptight! It makes people uncomfortable when you approach things so...so methodically."

"Methodically?" Jermaine jested. "Now that's a five-dollar word! Who is the heady one now? I'm going to call you Method Man."

"Shoot!" Cheech said. "That's better than Cheech."

Jermaine wasn't the one that started calling him Cheech. It was Tony who came up with the nickname as soon as Tony found out Cheech smoked. Cheech had never even seen the movie and wouldn't be able to tell who he was if he stepped on his Air Ones, yet he had to walk around with his name. Jermaine offered to call him Method Man if he could be Raekwon the Chef.

Cheech recited some Wu-Tang Clan verses still high as a kite.

"The RZA, the GZA, Ol' Dirty Bastard, Inspectah Deck, Raekwon the Chef, U-God, Ghostface Killah and the Method Man. M-E-T-H-O-D Man," he sang.

Cheech saw the manager and stopped his spit to get her attention.

"Donna!" Cheech called out over the roar of the machines to get the attention of a thirty something, short Black woman. She stopped, turned and smiled.

"Hello, Julius!" Donna said.

Cheech chided her for using his government name, but she refused to call him pothead.

"It's Cheech!" he said.

Donna used to run the Boys & Girls Club before she started to do her own thing. She was pretty much doing the same thing over at the arcade except she was making her own money.

"Who is your friend?"

"Jermaine, Donna. Donna, Jermaine," Cheech said. "Jermaine is an economics major."

Jermaine was not an economics major, but he was taking Microeconomics. Donna was interested in how he liked it, so Jermaine shared about the honors class and the paid internship. Donna assessed that he had become an Econ major by default and shared that she also studied Business Econ at Kent State, which impressed Jermaine and made him want to know more.

"So, are you an economist by training?" Jermaine asked.

"Hardly," Donna laughed. "I went straight S&E. I wanted to make some money."

Donna gave Wall Street the middle finger after it got too greedy for her and went straight Occupy. She cashed out at one-point-five million and came back home to work in the community.

"Wow! So, you're from the hood?"

"Yep! I graduated from McKinley," Donna added. "A few of us make it out."

"But very few come back!" Cheech added.

Donna came back to work at the Boys & Girls Club because she believed in its mission to keep kids off the street after school. They had basketball and soccer teams, study rooms, tutors and mentors and a game room to accomplish this goal, but Donna saw possibilities in that game room and asked if she could oversee it. She learned everything she needed to know to open up her own spot within three years.

"It didn't hurt that you had some capital to invest," Cheech added.

Jermaine dug down into the weeds to find out Donna took over the lease the summer before, which put her at about eighteen months in ownership. The summers were slow when kids were out of school and wanted to be outdoors, but some nifty maneuvering led to Donna putting in some great air conditioning for them to escape the heat. Donna was excited about winter approaching and people looking for a warm place to hang out outside of their homes. Jermaine wanted to pick her brain and for Donna to take him on and mentor him. His internship for a coin-op company would likely pose competition, so it was a better move to take Donna on as a client. Donna listened, but she didn't make any promises, but in Jermaine's mind he took it as a "yes." He took a card from the counter and told her he would show up on Monday afternoon to begin. Feeling confident about the interaction, he did his best rendition of a mic drop, Jermaine headed back toward the door where the homies were at, which left both Donna and Cheech in shock at his confidence. Jermaine approached Veronika and told her about a coffee spot on the avenue that made a great latte that he wanted to take her to.

"You don't take 'no' very well do you?" Veronika said.

"You can't in this world or you'll get nothing," Jermaine said.

He dapped up Cheech and told Veronika that he would pick her up by her momma's place on Wilshire tomorrow morning around nine o'clock. Veronika was impressed, if not with his confidence, then with the fact that he knew where she lived.

"I'll see you at ten," Veronika said. "It's Sunday and I will be sleeping in."

"I will see you then," he said.

As Jermaine walked off, Veronika turned to Cheech to find out if he told him where she lived, but of course he didn't. She was sure he wasn't going to get far with buying her a five-dollar latte.

###

CHAPTER FOUR

Jermaine took Veronika to a hipster coffee shop on the main street of town which was quiet on Sunday morning with only a very few lingering customers. Some people were dressed in their Sunday best, possibly on the way to a church service. Jermaine and Veronika found a quiet spot away from the counter to carry on a conversation. He asked about her sister to find how she was doing. Tammy had gone away to college for a year, but got pregnant and decided to drop out second semester. She lived in the next town over, which was only about twenty minutes away. Jermaine remembered that she was always around the same guy during their senior year of high school, but couldn't remember his name.

Veronika told Jermaine that she and Marquis broke up when she went away to college. He wasn't the father. The timing didn't suggest it, but no one really knew. It was more than likely someone she hooked-up with at college. Jermaine saw Tammy as more of the commitment, marrying type.

"Well, we all start off with a plan," Veronika stated. "Until we get hit in the mouth!"

Jermaine held back a laugh and instead pressed Veronika about her plans. Veronika had just graduated high school, but didn't feel like she learned much. She liked to do hair and make-up. Jermaine knew that his community college had a cosmetology school and wondered if she was going to take classes there. Veronika thought about it, but knew they drug tested, because of the work on human subjects. She was honest about her drug use.

"I smoke like a chimney," Veronika said. "In case you didn't know."

She applied for a medicinal use card, but was confident marijuana was going to be legal in the state soon the way the country was moving. Jermaine didn't smoke. In fact, he was allergic to smoke. He never even tried edibles. He did sip a little cognac on the weekends, but preferred to keep a clear head. Veronika was quite the opposite and believed her thoughts became clearer when she smoked, like a lot of artists. Jermaine knew that Veronika did spoken word after speaking to some of the homies about her. Veronika saw through Jermaine and knew that he wasn't trying to get with some hood chick, that Jermaine didn't see her that way. Veronika never saw herself leaving the block. He confessed that he didn't have much game, but he thought she was cute and wanted to get to know her better, which was something she picked up on already, but couldn't, for the life of her, figure out why. Jermaine had never noticed her before. He couldn't even remember her name yesterday. When she was in high school, she was all but invisible to him.

"I don't know if I am your type," she said. "I stay high. I am not college material. I live with my momma."

Jermaine lived with his momma too, Not even in his own room, but on a pullout in the living room. He did have hopes and dreams. Cheech told Veronika about his college internship. She had been asking Jermaine about too, but didn't want to admit it. Cheech had been talking him up.

"I'm hurt." Jermaine said. "How come you never asked about me?"

"Boy stop!" Veronika said. "We don't have anything in common. "Do you think I would ever step foot in this coffee shop if you didn't bring me here? I don't even come over this way except to pay my phone bill."

Jermaine knew that this meant it was a failed attempt at a date. Veronika agreed. He wanted a do over, but was denied.

"We should just keep it on the level," Veronika said.

Jermaine didn't like her answer, but could understand. He still wanted to see her perform spoken word and she said that would be cool. Veronika left, denying him the opportunity to walk her home.

Instead, he stayed back for a little while to give her space.

###

The block was unusually hot and this was uncommon for a winter night, but tonight there was an after party at a local club after a big concert downtown. Cop cars whizzed by followed by ambulance sirens and fire trucks. Teens and young adults walked up the block past the corner store hang out of the Rottweilers.

"I heard from Quincy that the concert was fire," Earl said.

Dookie and Brian were out on the corner with a crew of about ten other guys in heavy winter jackets and hats. Brian wanted to know if Jermaine was going to walk up to see what was happening at the club, but there was nothing up there for Jermaine. All Earl could think about were all the fine women up in that after party. Jermaine had been talking about his recent dating failures and Earl was trying to help him out.

Cheech wanted to know how things played out with Veronika and Jermaine told him it was another swing and miss. Earl thought he dodged a bullet. He didn't want to see him with a hood rat and Cheech took offense.

"Yo! Slow your roll!" Cheech said. "That's my people!"

"You know exactly what I mean, Cheech!" Earl defended himself. "Jay is a college boy now. That changes you."

Jermaine knew what he meant, but it hurt and he wanted desperately to be the same person he had always been. Cheech knew that Jermaine had changed too. Jermaine was around a different crowd now. He was forced to code switch in order to talk to top level executives and professors.

"That's it!" Dookie chimed in. "I've been wondering what changed about you! That higher education has sucked the hood out of you."

Jermaine was frustrated because he knew his boys were right, but he still didn't think he had changed who he was. He professed that he never had much game and Earl had to remind him that before Tony got locked up he had a shorty he used to go and see up the hill.

"She was cute!" Brian stated. "What ever happened to her?"

"She said I was corny!" Jermaine replied. "She only dated me because she knew I ran with a clique. She was looking for a thug."

The thug life was never Jermaine. Greg had made him read and study. On weekends, he was working on science kits and was in after-school programs. It wasn't until Greg left that Jermaine would even come out on the block. That's when the gang became his family and he never looked back. That's always who he was. Tony knew he was the smart one, but Jermaine had to prove he was one of them and that he belonged. He could fake it for a while, but the truth be told

Jermaine had outgrown the street life. It happened to gang members in the past. A former member, Rico, changed when he started having kids. It happened to another member, Barry, when he moved up to become manager at Walmart. It was bound to happen.

"You have never been in any real trouble," Brian said. "When we got into it last summer and Dookie got shot you basically walked through Central Booking because you were enrolled in college."

"C'mon man! I was there in the ambulance with your brother," Jermaine said. "He would have been solo if we all got arrested."

Dookie was the baby of the bunch, but was wise enough to know facts. He wanted to know why Jermaine was still out there with the gang if he had places he could be. Jermaine would do anything for Tony. When Greg moved out, Jermaine didn't have anybody until Tony stepped up and took him under his wing. Tony taught him the streets. When he went upstate, he told Jermaine to watch over things for him. This was Jermaine's way of paying it back.

"Besides I'm a damn good leader," he said.

The Rottweilers laughed, but knew he could be around more. Brian realized that there were vending machines in the club. Earl had been in there recently. They had everything from condoms, to cigarettes, cologne and breath mints and probably had tampon dispensers in the ladies' room. Earl was proud of himself and wanted recognition and a cut of the profits. If they were able to put together a few dollars to buy their own small machine, Jermaine would definitely cut Earl in.

"We can't be on these streets forever right, and I know you don't want to work for the man." Jermaine said. "Now walk down and get in this line with me. We gotta scope out the bathroom vending machines and see what kind of business they get."

###

Customer service reps sat at the main office of Quarimoc and answered phone calls while a sales force took incoming orders. It was still early in the day and people were still getting in to their desks. Most of the regional reps were on the floor, but Shirley sat in her corner office with glass windows overlooking the city scape. She called Jonathan in to deliver some bad news. She had just learned that Quarimoc's legal department found out that Jermaine was picked up on gang-related charges the year prior. Even though Jermaine never got arrested, she didn't want to hire him for fear of the company being associated with someone with gang affiliation. She didn't bring the matter to Human Resources and didn't see the need to for a short-term intern. She thought it was best to just let him know that they couldn't hire him and settle it that way.

Jonathan didn't want to fire Jermaine. Jermaine was a good guy and Jonathan wasn't about to take an opportunity away from him for something that he wasn't even arrested for and that took place over a year ago. Shirley was so used to people falling in line with her way of thinking that she didn't know what to say.

"Don't you care about the reputation of the company?" Shirley asked.

Jonathan was working off of a different mindset. He believed in second chances, especially for those who never even got a first chance to begin with. He saw Jermaine as someone who was working to turn his life around. Not only was Jermaine in college, but he was succeeding in the subject matter and Jonathan wasn't willing to be the person to stop that momentum.

"I get it. We hire murderers and thieves at this company," Shirley said sarcastically.

Jonathan saw the conversation was at an impasse and turned to walk away.

"I say we give him a chance," he said

Shirley conceded, but still needed to know if Jermaine still had any gang affiliations. They could sweep the past under the rug, but they would be liable for anything they knew about Jermaine's involvement moving forward. Jonathan agreed and as he walked back to his desk he thought long and hard about how to tackle the issue he was faced with. He called Bruce to find out what he knew.

Bruce was in his office putting his final touches on his spring-semester classes before taking off for the winter break. He was heading down to Orlando to spend some time with the in-laws, which didn't sound like a lot of fun to Jonathan, but Bruce wanted to escape the cold for three weeks and to take the kids to Disney, which he also enjoyed himself. He could tell something was on Jonathan's mind, he wasn't calling out of the blue. Jonathan let him know about the gang-related activity from the previous summer and wanted to see what Bruce knew. Bruce had formed a relationship with Jermaine and knew he had a past like so many people do, but he also knew Jermaine was a good kid. Jonathan needed assurance that it was indeed a teenage thing and that Jermaine was done with that part of his life.

Bruce didn't know for sure, but imagined that he still maintained some affiliations. "These are the guys that brought him up from the time his father figure left the house," he said.

Jonathan really didn't want to let Jermaine go and Bruce couldn't understand why the topic was even on the table. They were halfway down the road on getting him into an internship that could set him on the right path. Jonathan was hoping Bruce would have another bright student that he could give his spot to, but it upset Bruce to think of the possibility of Jermaine losing this opportunity. He also knew that he had to be careful to maintain a professional face with the company.

"Jonathan, you are correct," he said. I have many bright students. What I do not have are many bright economists. Mr. Beasley has never been the smartest person in the room, but he has always been the best economist."

Jonathan was caught, because he knew Jermaine was the right person for this job. He was going to do what he could to make it work, but realized that if it came back to bite him everyone lost.

"I may lose the internship," Bruce stated. "But I'm tenured. I get to keep my job."

They were able to laugh off a tense conversation. Bruce was assured that it was all going to work out and for Jonathan's sake it had better.

###

Jermaine rushed into his class with his books already out and his backpack wide open. The exam he was scheduled for that morning had already begun. The students stared at him sweating profusely on a twenty-degree day.

"No extra time, Mr. Beasley!" Bruce said. He sounded very upset.

Jermaine nodded and slid into his chair trying to go unnoticed. He scurried to put his books away. It was the final exam and students were desperately trying to concentrate. Bruce walked over and placed the exam on Jermaine's desk. Jermaine's sweat fell on the crisp paper and the droplets permeated the page. He wiped his forehead and brow only to produce more moisture within seconds. He only had thirty-seven minutes remaining for a fifty-minute exam. Jermaine was still hurting from the cognac he consumed into the early hours of the morning and he could hardly clear his mind to think, but was desperately trying to focus. The student to his immediate right winced at the smell that secreted from Jermaine's pores and asked to be moved to the front row. Jermaine took a few deep breaths and started his exam. Answers that commonly came second nature to him escaped him like the wind. His head whirled as he pulled out a metal water canteen that hit his desk with a bang. He threw his head back to take several large gulps. To clear his mind, he did some meditation exercises Greg taught him during

YFL halftime. His classmates just stared at him as he appeared to fall into a trance or maybe even asleep within seconds.

He straightened his posture and looked at the exam with fresh eyes. Although he was still visibly hungover, he was able to pace himself through the first few questions which were primers and was nowhere close to what was about to come.

The other students were close to half way through the exam as Jermaine flipped the first page. He changed his gaze to watch some of his classmates and took in their construed faces as they face the more challenging concepts. Jermaine knew if he could get through the rudimentary concepts his brain space would find flow.

Two seats to the left of him, there was a guy swirling his pencil on his thumb and forefinger and it distracted Jermaine to no end. He shot the guy a look of irritation, but was totally ignored. After roughly twenty minutes, Jermaine got to the meat of the exam.

The place where the terms became concepts and concepts became real world challenges. He had about fifteen minutes to get through nearly half of the questions and this is when he flipped the switch. He was no longer working to remember names and definitions, but now he was into the real-world practice of economics. He flew through two questions and then two more. Question forty-two out of fifty gave Jermaine some pause. He knew the answer, but didn't agree with it. He was caught in an ethical dilemma. A key faux pas of economics. He debated between getting it wrong on purpose and risking a full letter grade or acquiescing to the pressure. Ultimately, he decided to put the "correct' answer down, but spent extra time writing his true feelings in the margins. This time wasted left him with three minutes until "pencils down." Luckily, the next three questions only took him a minute each. He was left with roughly thirty seconds to guess at four answers.

He looked at the questions as a group. He noticed that they were a sequence, which meant that if he could get the theme of the first question and answer it correctly he could get them all. He tapped his pencil to his head as if trying to jar the right answers loose. He figured out it was a devilish trick laid out by the test maker to cause the test takers to fall in a snare of assumption. He quickly marked down the last three responses without even reading the question.

"Pencils down!" Bruce said.

Most pencils went down, but some students filled in their guesses, while still others made last second corrections. Jermaine took a big swig of water.

"Pencils down class!" Bruce repeated.

Jermaine had stopped sweating, but he was still drenched through his shirt. He finally got a whiff of the smell he was giving off and was embarrassed. He tried his best to sneak out of the class quickly.

"Leaving so soon Mr. Beasley?" Bruce asked.

"If that's okay?" Jermaine asked.

The class all laughed as Bruce suggested that a cold shower might help.

"You would be happy to know that I was up late doing research for my internship."

A girl from the back of the room recognized Jermaine from the club.

"That's funny!" she said. "Because I could have sworn I saw you at Tito's when I left around midnight."

The class gave a big "Oh!" and was assured that Jermaine got caught in a lie.

"That's right!" Jermaine said. "I was checking out the coin-op machines and seeing what kind of business they attracted on a busy night."

The class silenced down, but Bruce wasn't satisfied. He wanted to know what he found out. Jermaine thought that the club could more than cover the cost if they owned the machines outright instead of renting them. He went on to say that the machines only carried five products, and they could fill the aspirin, condoms and tampons themselves, but didn't think they were getting their money's worth paying rental rates.

"And you realized all this three sheets to the wind?" Bruce asked.

"I may have found some trouble on my walk back from the club," Jermaine said. "But business and pleasure seldom mix."

Bruce was clear that if Jermaine ever showed up to his class again smelling like a distillery he would send him home.

"Consider yourself warned," he said.

The class nodded in agreement and Jermaine got the message and walked out. The semester was officially over with all his papers and exams completed. He made his way to the bus stop and headed home.

###

CHAPTER FIVE

At Jermaine's house, it was eerily silent with Denise at work and the girls in school for the next week before their winter break kicked in. Jermaine was assigned cleaning duties to keep him occupied. He was way too tired to get out of his bed. Winter had come in like a lion and the warm bed, along with plenty of sleep, was what he needed to recover from a draining semester of classwork, finals papers and exams. He knew there was a list of things to do before the girls got out, but figured it could wait.

After a few hours, he turned over to check his phone and realized it's time to kick into gear. He rubbed the sleep out of his eyes and made his way to the bathroom. He checked the list, which for the most part were cleaning duties, but Denise had also tasked him with stripping the linen off the beds and doing laundry. Jermaine had been looking for an opportunity to spend more time in the laundromat and this was the perfect in.

He scrubbed down the counters, swept and mopped the floors, then ended his house chores with a thorough cleaning of the kitchen and bathroom just before he took advantage of his work and got into a freshly cleaned shower coated with the scent of lilac.

Jermaine was way overdue for laundry and had to wear a suit pants and a sweater vest down the block to make it to the laundromat. He looked and felt like he had already become corporate.

The patrons during the week differed vastly from the weekend crowd and Jermaine was surrounded by senior citizens and retired government workers, as well as some non-working, younger parents with small children attached to their hip.

He reloaded Denise's card and looked into the office to see if Sethi was around. He spotted him on the phone, so he put his earbuds in and waited for him to be done. Sethi hung up the phone frustrated and

Jermaine deduced that it wasn't the best time to bother him and instead walked back over to his foaming machines as they tossed around his loads of dirty laundry. Sethi walked out and got Jermaine's attention.

"Jermaine!" he called out. "I thought that was you outside of my office. Why didn't you knock?"

"You just got off the phone and it looked like you were still percolating," Jermaine said.

"You're right!" Sethi said. "But you have come on the perfect day. You have an hour of wash and an hour of drying to do before you fold. Do you want to help me?"

Sethi was not an economist, but he began to break down some basic cost analysis. He had two machines that had gone down and was trying to figure out the cost of repair versus buying a new machine with a long-term warranty. Jermaine had just taken his final with a similar scenario, but now he was faced with a real-life situation. He followed Sethi back to his office and looked over the current contract. The machines that went down were chip machines, which were one big computer that required a lot of technical maintenance. Sethi chided that it was supposed to be the future, which gave Jermaine some pause. As Jermaine's gears turned, he realized that there were some benefits to starting a new contract.

"You get a newer machine with newer technology, as well as a longer-term warranty," Jermaine said.

The downside was that he would lose all his equity in the current machines and have to start from ground zero. Conventional wisdom would say to stick with the old and run it into the ground before upgrading, but Sethi had to think about revenue lost, as well as customers lost from machines being down.

"'Out of Order' signs are not a good look in any business," Jermaine said.

Sethi knew this first-hand, relating it to his experience with airport kiosks. He rarely had issues with his coin-operated machines.

Jermaine suggested an alternative solution that departed from conventional wisdom. He agreed that chip-card machines were the wave of the future, but unless Sethi had an IT person on-site his machines could be down for three or four days at a time. Jermaine suggested a hybrid. Sethi was familiar with what he was referring to and knew that customers could pay with either cash or card, like a parking garage. Jermaine thought this was a good option. If the computer went down a customer would have a backup and that would avoid the "Out of Order" sign.

Sethi's current vendor did not offer this as an option, but Quarimoc did. Jermaine acknowledged he had some skin in the game, but still wanted to help negotiate a trade-in that protected Sethi's current investment. Sethi thought it was a brilliant idea. Feeding two birds with one hand. Jermaine made the call to Jonathan to see what price he could get for a trade-in. Simultaneously, Sethi called his current vendor to see what it would take to get out of his current contract.

###

It was still early afternoon on Christmas Eve and Jermaine's house was decked out with a reef, lights and a tree with lots of presents underneath it. Greg and Denise had done a lot of shopping for the girls and there was no shortage of gifts. The girls' eyes were as big as saucers at the site of all the wrapping paper and the stuffed stockings. Jermaine had also saved to make sure the girls and his mom had gifts from him. This was his first year truly being able to contribute since all his money from the deli usually went as fast as it came.

Denise still had last-minute stocking stuffers to wrap and it was Jermaine's job to keep the girls occupied while she did her last-minute preparations. He knew the girls loved to bake so he pulled out the mixing bowls and ingredients and called them into the kitchen.

"Roxie! Renee!" Jermaine yelled. "Guess whose job it is to make cookies for Santa this year!"

The girls came running and screamed as they tore into the kitchen.

"Wait, wait, wait!" Jermaine said and jumped in front of them. "You still have to wash your hands."

Roxie ran towards the bathroom beating out her sister for the first turn. Renee squirmed past her older brother and started washing her hands in the kitchen sink using dish soap. Jermaine pulled out two stools, purchased just for the girls, and set them next to the counter with the bowls. As the girls reached the stools, he assigned roles.

"Who wants to crack the eggs?" Jermaine said.

Roxie's hand shot up a split second before Renee's. Jermaine knew that eggs could get pretty messy so he decided that he should do that job so he didn't ruin Denise's kitchen just before Christmas. Now Renee had cracked eggs before, so Jermaine cracked them and let Renee put them into the bowl. Roxie crossed her arms and pouted, but Jermaine insisted that there was plenty left for her to do.

Jermaine opened a big bag of flour and helped Roxie pour it into a bowl. Some of the flour escaped and Roxie wiped it right into her shirt. Jermaine got the girls two aprons and helped them tie the back. Now he had two little bakers on his hands.

"You are both going to be ready for cupcake-sales this summer."

As they stirred the batter they added chocolate chips to their recipe and prepared to stick the dough in cookie shapes into the preheated oven.

"Hey brother!" Renee said. "Are you going to help us with our lemonade stand this summer?"

Jermaine sized up the competition for lemonade and suggested that the girls needed to do something to stand out from the crowd. Roxie thought that they could also have the best cupcakes known to man and Renee added cookies to the menu.

"We have to sell more than the girl-scout sisters up the block," Renee said.

The girl scout sisters always got the spot at the corner where all the cars stopped and bought cookies from them at the light. Jermaine sank immediately into thoughts of his internship and agreed with Renee that it wasn't fair.

"We can't always get the prime location, but it helps us think outside of the box," he said.

Renee had no idea what "thinking outside the box" meant, so Jermaine told the girls that they had to think of even better locations. Of course, their mother wasn't going to allow them to sell anywhere else outside of where she could watch them. Jermaine knew this as well, but still thought it didn't hurt to ask her or even their dad to come with them.

"They wouldn't stay out there with us for hours in the sun," Renee said.

"That is why you have to get a lot of sales all at once. First, think about who your customers are."

Renee knew immediately that it was mostly little kids who bought from them. He primed the pump by helping the girls figure out where they were going to find large groups of these little kids. Roxie knew immediately that kids hung out at the playground in the summer. Now they just needed to figure out when large groups of kids would be at the playground at the same time. Renee guessed that most of the parents brought their kids out around sun down, so they wouldn't get scorched by the brutal heat of summer. The girls had deduced their target market, the kids, along with their target location, the playground, as well as their target time. Late afternoon. Now all that was left was to figure out their target product.

"What's a product?" Roxie asked.

"It's what we are going to sell," Renee said.

"Yes! What is your most popular item?" Jermaine said. "What is different or better or of more value that draws people to buy from you?"

The sisters stood there and pondered this question and it came to them. They knew that everyone loved Denise's peanut-butter/chocolate-chip cookies. They always sold out of those first. Jermaine had his own favorite growing up. Brownies with caramel in them. The girls agreed that those were both yummy and gooey. Roxie also suggested that they put strawberry syrup in their lemonade. Jermaine applauded their ingenuity and believed that they would sell three times the amount sold by the girl-scout sisters from up the street in half the time.

Denise came into the room and screamed, "My kitchen!"

"We'll clean it up. Don't worry!" Jermaine said.

Jermaine recruited his sisters to help him bust some suds. Roxie would only agree to help if she got to lick the bowl and Jermaine couldn't deny her the opportunity.

"Sounds like a deal!" Jermaine replied. "Roxie, you wash. Renee, you dry. And me, I will put them in the dishwasher, deal."

There was still plenty of batter left and Renee was not done making cookies. They mixed and baked and cleaned all at once and Denise was happy that Jermaine was spending time with his sisters.

###

The holidays wound down and with that Jermaine was starting his internship the start of the spring semester. He had allowed his mind to get rusty and was now looking for ways to get it cued up again. When he pulled out a receipt for something he wanted to return to the mall, he happened on Donna's card inside of his tattered wallet. He knew immediately that was his way to grease the chain. When he called, the phone went to voicemail and he started to leave a message.

"Hey mentor! This is Jermaine, Cheech's...I mean, Julius's friend. I hope you remember me," he began.

Donna picked up midway through the voicemail. She remembered Jermaine, because he made an impression on her. It wasn't every day that Donna got a request from a young man for mentoring. She wanted to know where he had been since he told her that she would hear from him the following Monday. Jermaine didn't want to seem too assertive because Donna had never agreed to the mentor role.

"Your first lesson," Donna said. "You will need to be too assertive to get what you want in this business."

Jermaine asked if he should write that down and Donna was quick to tell him that it wouldn't hurt.

Donna's mind was racing with problems that she could have used Jermaine's assistance on just the previous week. She needed to find a way to make the arcade a year around venture if she was going to make a profit. Jermaine was ready to take on the challenge, but wanted to be sure Donna didn't see him as a competitor, but a mentee. From her days on Wall Street, Donna, not unlike Jermaine, knew that it was important to keep your friends close, but your enemies closer.

"So, I am the enemy now?" Jermaine asked. "I thought we could grow and build together. I like what you are doing for the community."

"Don't get it twisted, Jermaine!" Donna said. "I am still trying to make a profit."

"What business isn't?" he said.

Jermaine knew there was a difference between profit and greed. Companies who made money off of their community and who spent it elsewhere depleted the net worth of the community and it just wasn't sustainable. Donna knew that many business owners didn't live or spend in the hoods they made their money in. She confessed that Jermaine had challenged her and asked when he could meet up. With classes and the internship kicking in at the start of the semester, Jermaine's time was going to be short. Donna let him know that the store was open until seven that night and that he could come by that afternoon. Jermaine was curious to know how he challenged her.

"Business values change on a dime." Donna said. "It moves from helping kids get off the streets and having something to do, to the bottom line and making more money than last week, than last month, than last quarter, than last year."

Jermaine knew at twenty years old that was the nature of the beast and imagined that times ten when a company had no investment in their customer or the community and it was only about the dollar.

"I can learn from a young, unadulterated mind," Donna said.

"We can learn from each other! Hopefully you can keep me from becoming adulterated."

Donna wasn't ready to make that promise. She knew that money had a way of making you want more and more of it. She knew Quarimoc did not hire Jermaine to lose money or break even and Jermaine wanted to help them make their money and a little for himself as well, but in the process, help the community grow. Donna was excited about their meet-up. Jermaine had to run a few items to the mall, but told her he would be by before sundown.

"Right on! See you soon!" Donna said.

###

CHAPTER SIX

It was not unusual for hyper masculine cops to harass the gang as they stood out in front of the corner store, just because the cops could do so. They patted down several of the Rottweilers and told them to move on as they pointed to the "No Loitering!" sign to the left of the store's front door. Brian argued that they were paying customers and not hurting anyone, but the cops didn't want to hear it. They knew that the boys ran with a gang and called it out by name. Earl made it clear that if they knew who they were they also knew that the Rottweilers weren't out there dealing drugs or mugging people.

"We are for the people, trying to do right by the people," Earl said. "Mohammed never complains about us being here."

These cops and other gang task forces felt commissioned by the local community members and business owners to do whatever they wanted to anything that resembled a gang. The cops felt because the boys claimed a set they brought trouble to themselves. The officers knew they had rivals, so even if they didn't cause trouble they welcomed it by their presence. Earl knew his rights and knew that they were being searched illegally. He also knew that as many times as they had been searched there had never been any reason to hold them.

"Are we under arrest?" Earl asked. "If we are then read us our rights and cuff us."

The officers knew they didn't have anything so they headed back to their cruiser.

"If we see you out here when we come back in an hour we will do just that," the officer said.

The police cruiser pulled away from the curb slowly and took off down the street and around the corner. Dookie, who had been silent during the interaction, knew it was so bull, and the officers were just looking for someone to harass. Earl agreed. It was important to him that he knew his rights and where he could and could not be. The gang decided to keep it pushing either way and went to go find Jermaine and Cheech.

"They said something about the arcade, which means Cheech is with those stuck-up girls," Dookie said.

"They ain't stuck up," Brian told his brother. "They just ain't interested in you."

Earl laughed at the put down, but knew Dookie didn't want that drama. The homies were Cheech's crew. He was interested in what Jermaine was doing over there with them, especially after Veronika sent him packing. They knew they couldn't be in front of the store when the cops came back around, so they decided they would go and check out the arcade, but as they walked up the block they spotted some unfamiliar faces and paused.

"Yo! You know those dudes?" Brian asked.

"What are you thinking?" Dookie asked.

"It's either Five-0 or those punks from the Westside," Earl said. "Either way we need to split up."

Brian threw his hood over his head and turned the corner. Dookie walked up the block and Earl crossed the street and headed the opposite direction. Just as Earl crossed the street, he thought he two rival gang members come out of the building. He picked up his pace, but was all alone now and was pretty sure he was being followed. He turned the corner and started to run and before long he was being chased. He knew the streets, being born and raised there since the cradle, so he figured he could escape his pursuers. He cut through a backyard and then into an alley and ducked behind a garbage bin. As his pursuers ran past, Earl looked down the street to get a good look at who they were. He realized it wasn't Westside.

When the coast was clear, Earl left the alley and ran back towards the arcade to find Brian already there and Dookie making his way up the block.

"Yo! Who was that?" Brian asked.

Earl didn't know who it was, but he knew it wasn't rival gang members or cops. Dookie made it to the arcade moments later.

"You okay dude?" Dookie asked. "I saw them come after you. I was just about to follow, but that dude on the corner never moved."

Brian panicked and knew they had to tell Jermaine, but only saw Cheech. It was their second option. Earl decided he would go in alone and told Brian and Dookie to stay on look out.

The arcade was sparsely filled with people scattered here and there, but it was still loud with kids running around. Cheech was surrounded by his homies when he walked up on him.

"Hey Cheech! Can I talk to you for a minute?" Earl said.

Cheech was faded and not able to focus on any topic for more than a few seconds.

"What is it little homie?" Cheech said.

Earl put his back to the homies in an attempt to shield what he was about to say.

“We may have trouble.” Earl said. “Some dudes who I haven’t seen before just chased me up the block.”

Cheech was immediately paranoid and Earl had to calm him down. He led Cheech outside which didn’t make things any better. Cheech noticed how Dookie was visibly shaken by Earl being followed.

“Yo, Cheech!” Dookie exclaimed. “We are being watched.”

“We don’t know that yet,” Brian inserted. “Have you seen Jermaine?

Cheech lost it and began to say that he knew it was bound to happen sooner or later. He went on about informants following their every move, but Earl got a good look at them. He knew they were too young to be police.

“That’s how they recruit them!” Cheech said. “Who knows how long they have been on us?”

Cheech wasn't helping the situation and Brian wanted to find Jermaine to help sort it all out. Since Jermaine was not around, he figured they were on their own. Cheech appointed himself as leader and demanded to know where it had all gone down. Dookie pointed him to the avenue and asserted that the dude he saw was probably still there. Cheech paced in place then walked back inside the arcade to let the homies know that he might need back up. Earl, Dookie and Brian were confused. The homies mounted up and left with Cheech up the block.

"Yo! I will be back in ten minutes," Cheech said. "Stay low until I get back."

###

Jermaine and Donna were at the Boys & Girl Club volunteering with elementary-school kids. This was what Donna left corporate to do, but in the midst of working at the Boys & Girls Club she found her calling.

"There are many ways to give back," she said. "We just have to stay grounded."

Jermaine had suggested that they go to the club. It was something Donna had almost forgotten about her work with non-profits. Jermaine knew the term non-profits was a loaded one. There was always someone who made money off of the kids, and Donna agreed. She knew the rich got richer by donations and write-offs and it just all fed into the system of greed. It was all a game, but yet it was important to know how the game was played in order to win it.

"Man, why do they have us back here in these classrooms?" Jermaine asked. "Show me where you worked?"

"We have to hurry," Donna said. "There will be an influx of kids in here soon."

Donna walked Jermaine through a corridor towards a door that led to the outside and into a gym. She pointed out where she worked. She was immediately spotted by a custodian, named Enrique, who asked if she came back to work for the Boys & Girls Club again. She laughed, but sometimes wished she did. Jermaine told her that she had to rediscover her passion for the community. Enrique knew what she did over on the Eastside. His kids went to the arcade all the time and thought it was a great service to the community. Donna thanked him and his kids for their patronage before she led Jermaine behind a wall to a game area with pool tables, air hockey, ping pong tables and video games.

"Man, this is just how I remember it!" Jermaine said. "My stepdad had me in these rec centers all the time. Normally getting up shots for Winter League Basketball."

He walked over to a video game and noticed that the games still used quarters. Donna remembered that the Boys & Girls Club was considering moving to arcade coins when she was there, but thought it was too big of a transition for such a small population. Jermaine was interested in what changes Donna made while she oversaw the game room and Donna had to confess that she didn't change much.

"These centers stay pretty uniform across the state," she said. "There is not a lot of autonomy. What I did do is gain a lot of knowledge about what works and what doesn't work."

Jermaine wanted to hear all about it, but it would have to wait. A bus full of kids pulled up and let out a group of students at the front doors. Donna suggested that they make it back to their posts fast and get ready to greet them. They hustled back through the gym and to their classrooms. Jermaine realized that most of the kids were impoverished Black and Brown kids that needed help with basic English and Math tutoring. They came from single-parent homes or homes where their parents had to work several jobs to make ends meet. He knew there was little time at home for review or help with homework. He also noticed that the kids were smart and resilient. Although Jermaine grew up poor he found himself in a grateful place in that he was always provided for.

After two and a half hours, the kids began to head to their respective homes and Jermaine and Donna had to see them off. Donna was invigorated and Jermaine was exhausted and ready for a nap.

"No such luck for me!" Donna said. "I have to head back to the shop and get ready to count my bank."

Jermaine knew that Donna had already done a count before she left that afternoon. Donna had to remind him that there are always two counts a day and always one at the end of the day. Jermaine knew this from his days at the Stop n' Shop. Donna took on the role as mentor again to tell Jermaine how the shop operated and Jermaine was all ears as they grabbed their coats and headed for the door.

###

Jonathan was sitting alone in the same hipster coffee shop where Jermaine and Veronika met up at. A young, African-American man sat down to join him. Jonathan immediately wanted to know what he was able to find out. Jonathan hired him to look in on

Jermaine and the gang to see if there were any nefarious dealings, but the young man wasn't able to report anything of the kind.

"You just told me to trail him and that's what I did," the private investigator said. "Where is my money?"

Jonathan needed more information, but the PI was holding out until he saw his money first. Jonathan was not short on cash and pulled out a wad of it then peeled two one-hundred-dollar bills off the top. The young man took the bills and rubbed the cold hard cash together as if trying to make them multiply. He then told Jonathan what he didn't want to hear.

"So! I think they spotted me," the private investigator said.

"What?" Jonathan said. "They saw you."

He explained that he was a good distance away when he saw the police roll up and pat down the guys that were out there.

"I knew they were clean because the cops left, but I concluded that the cops told them they couldn't be there, because they started walking," he said.

That's when they spotted him. He was just standing out there minding his business, but he could tell the gang members made him out because they took off in different directions.

"They must have thought I was a DT undercover," the private investigator said.

He told Jonathan that two guys whom he brought out with him followed Earl but lost him and there was no sighting of Jermaine. The plan was that the other members might lead them to Jermaine or that Jermaine would roll up and join them, but that never happened. In that part of town if you thought somebody was after you, it was either run, fight or hide and the young PI was happy that they chose the first option.

Jonathan pulled out the money clip a second time and peeled off another two hundred dollars. He asked the PI to dig up some more information on Jermaine. The man initially refused and told him he needed to hire a professional, not just some street wise guy, to do his work.

"Right now, you are my PI," Jonathan stated. "One more time. Find me some info and this payout doubles."

"Alright!" the private investigator said. "But I am telling you. These guys just love to hang out and smoke and drink a little. Nothing you need to concern yourself with."

Jonathan hopped up leaving the man in the booth and took off out the door and got into the backseat of a car parked across the street. The driver pulled off the curb and took off down the street.

###

Cheech stared out of a second story window in a "By Any Means Necessary" kind of pose. He had been off the grid for the past week. The homies were inside an apartment playing cards when Cheech saw activity on the street below and tried to get a better look. He headed for the door and Patrice jumped up to stand look out. She knew the signal and waited for it. Cheech trotted down the long set of stairs and paused in the building doorway before peeking around the corner and catching a glimpse of the PI. Someone he didn't know and who was definitely out of place.

Upstairs, Patrice looked out the window to see if Cheech was onto something. While downstairs, Cheech bent over to tie his bootstrings and when he got up, he threw his hood over his head and started in the direction of the PI standing on the block. This was the first signal and Patrice got into position. The young man didn't see Cheech approaching. This was his first mistake. He was caught off-guard until Cheech was right up on him. Just as Cheech was square with the young man, he turned to face him which startled him.

"Yo! Who are you dude?" Cheech said. "What are you doing checking out my clique?"

"I'm just...I'm just waiting...waiting for a friend," the private investigator said.

"Yeah! What friend?" Cheech asked. "Who sent you? You Five-0?"

"No...no man!" the private investigator said.

Cheech asked him directly who he was working for if it wasn't the police, but the young man tried to lie again. Cheech cut him off abruptly and the man begged for his life. Cheech let him know killing him was not what he was there for. He wanted to know the truth. The man shaking and trembling told him that a man in a suit paid him to trail a kid he was about to hire for his company to find out any dirt. He gave the name "Beasley" and Cheech blew a gasket.

"You mother…!" Cheech began. "You trying to hurt my boy, Jay?"

"No...no! He said he wants to be sure he's clean," the private investigator said. "He's worried about the reputation of his company."

Cheech patted him down.

"I swear to you! I'm not trying to hurt nobody," the private investigator said. "I don't even carry, man."

Cheech remembered that he had two other people with him and asked their whereabouts. The man tried to deny it, but Cheech knew he didn't work alone.

"You had two dudes follow my man, Earl, last week. Where are they?"

"I...I called them off," the man replied. "I told dude that you guys are legit. I was just coming out here for a few hours to confirm."

"You didn't want to split that money," Cheech said.

His face gave away that Cheech was right.

Cheech wanted to know how much he was getting paid for a couple hours work and the young man told him only a couple of pig faces. Cheech knew he didn't come back out for free and the man confessed he copped a couple more for the second trip.

"Well, you are going to need to hand that over," Cheech told him. "And I don't want to see you or your goons around here anymore. Because if I do, you don't leave. Understand?"

The man reached into his pants pocket real slow and pulled out a couple of hundred dollar bills and told Cheech that he spent the rest. Cheech told him to leave and watched him walk for a few seconds and then Cheech started walking in the opposite direction. He put his hands in his pants pockets and a single shot rang out causing the young man to crumple in a heap. Cheech didn't bother to turn around. He took his hands out of his pants pockets, put his hood up and made his way back into the apartment building he came out of.

###

Spring semester had just started at the college and students hustled to get their books and find their new classes. The lines for financial aid and counseling were so long they blocked walking paths. Jermaine had to fight his way through to get to billing and made his way to the front of the line. He handed the cashier his ID and the woman behind the counter punched in some keystrokes and read off Jermaine's account. After confirming his name and ID number, she told Jermaine that he a had zero balance. Jermaine was confused as to what that actually meant and the woman explained that he didn't owe the college anything that semester. He became concerned that he was dropped or didn't get into any of his classes. He was enrolled in fifteen units, but his balance had been covered. She couldn't see how or why, but told him Financial Aid would have more information. He was more perplexed than confused. He looked at the line for Financial Aid as it snaked around with its end out of view. He realized it could have been worse. Some people get to the window owing a lot more than they can pay.

Jermaine's bills were not super expensive. The community college only ran him about sixty dollars a unit, but that was nine hundred dollars, plus fees that he got to keep in his pocket. He made his way to the bookstore knowing his economics and literature books would be as expensive as they were heavy. The line pushed all the way through the store. Jermaine dug through the stacks to find his subjects. He grabbed the books he needed and made his way to the end of the line. There he saw one of his counselors helping students in his program.

"Alex, what's good?" Jermaine said.

The counselor broke her gaze and looked to see who was calling her. She waved and then walked over to the line which had grown even longer since the time Jermaine stepped in.

"Mr. Beasley, we missed you yesterday," Alex said.

"What was yesterday?" Jermaine asked.

"Our back to school BBQ. We awarded some need-based tuition grants and you were one of our lucky awardees."

It hit him that was why his bill was a zero balance. They were also giving book vouchers provided by donors, so his books would be covered too. Jermaine was winning big time.

"Now if I could only avoid this line," he said.

"I can't help you with that, but they did open an hour early yesterday for our students."

"So, I not only missed free food, but a chance to skip the line?" Jermaine said.

Alex felt the need to remind him that he scored free classes and books and told him he would be alright. He tried not to complain. Alex had other students to assist, but Jermaine stopped her before she could walk away. He was interested if the grants were need-based and Alex confirmed that they were. Now Jermaine knew he was not the only person struggling to make ends meet at the college, and he wanted to know why he was the person chosen. There were a lot of factors taken into consideration, but recommendations by a professor were heavily weighted. Jermaine assumed it was Bruce, but Alex wasn't at liberty to say. She knew his department had strong corporate connections and had a strong interest in investing in young talent. The book grants were donor based too. For years, donors had taken interest in low-income students. The state was only able to cover a portion of the expenses. Jermaine was trying to follow the money. He also wanted to know whom he needed to thank. He made his way to the counter and provided his school ID. When the bookstore cashier scanned the card it was a zero balance and the cashier offered Jermaine a bag.

"Is that free too?" he asked.

"The bag is on us!" the bookstore cashier replied.

"Then I will take two of them. I can't go throwing out my shoulder."

###

As Jermaine got back to his block he saw EMT, fire trucks and police a block from the bus stop. Although curious, Jermaine knew his stepfather had taught him to walk in the opposite direction of sirens. He cut down a street, two blocks out of the way and saw Earl who told him the streets were hot after some dude got shot.

Jermaine wanted to know who it was, but it wasn't anyone they knew. Earl then told him about the same guy being on the block a week ago and the two guys that followed him. Jermaine was upset that no one told him and was trying to figure out why someone would follow him.

"DT undercover?" Jermaine asked.

"I don't think so," Earl replied. "I made a dash for it and ducked into an alley."

Earl told him that Dookie and Brian were there too, but they met up with Cheech at the arcade trying to find Jermaine. Jermaine was beside himself.

"You didn't tell him, did you?" Jermaine asked.

"We couldn't find you," Earl said.

"You didn't tell him, did you?" Jermaine repeated his question.

"Yeah, we told him," Earl said.

Jermaine panicked and wanted to know how Cheech responded. Earl tried to calm him down, but Jermaine feared the worst.

"You really need to bring this to me," he said. "You know this already."

"You don't think..." Earl started.

"What do you think?" Jermaine said.

Earl sat down on the stoop to catch his breath. Jermaine wanted to know where Cheech was when the dude was shot and Earl told him that some neighbors saw him walking in the opposite direction away from the dude. This meant that Cheech was out on the block.

"That's what I heard." Earl said. "They say dude slipped Cheech some money and then walked up the block. Supposedly Cheech was walking in a different direction with his hood up and his hands in his pockets when it all went down."

Jermaine was immediately reminded that hands in the pocket was a signal he learned from the old-timers from when he first joined the gang. He did everything he could to not let Earl in on it. He told Earl that if Cheech was walking in the opposite direction then he couldn't have done it and Earl agreed. Jermaine asked about the homies, but Earl didn't know anything about them. He told Jermaine that they were at the arcade when he told Cheech and nobody had seen any of them since.

"Okay!" Jermaine said. "Find Cheech! Tell him to get in touch with me. As far as you and the rest of the gang, stay low until this blows over. We are going to get some heat from the cops for this. Your only response is 'I don't know anything.'"

Earl got it. Jermaine was okay, but he was determined to figure this out. He told Earl to stay off the block as they took off in different directions.

###

Bruce had just ended his lecture and class was dismissed, but as the students left he noticed Jonathan standing at the back of the lecture hall. The last few students exited and Jonathan walked past them to the lectern.

"Mr. Stone!" Bruce said. "Nice to see you! Reaching out to you is on my long list of things to do today. I have hours and site visits scheduled for the internship and the syllabus for the honors class has been approved by the Curriculum Committee."

Jonathan cut Bruce off before he could get out this next statement to let him know that there were bigger fish to fry. He told him that someone was shot and killed. Bruce's reaction was visceral.

"What? What happened? Was it Jermaine?" Bruce asked.

Jonathan quickly told him that it wasn't Jermaine, but it was somebody in his neighborhood and that it might be gang-related.

Bruce didn't understand why Jonathan would be telling him this and how he even knew about it. Jonathan invited Bruce to sit down by motioning towards the seats and Bruce knew that whatever he had to say it wasn't going to be good. Jonathan admitted that he put somebody out there to see what he could find out after their phone conversation. Bruce was livid. Jonathan explained that his managing rep wanted him to pull the plug on the internship and he wanted to convince her there was nothing to worry about.

"You told me no one at Quarimoc knew anything," Bruce replied.

"Well, news travels fast," Jonathan replied. "It's just her as far as I can tell."

Bruce still didn't put two and two together about what all of this had to do with the shooting.

Jonathan had to tell him that the guy he put out there got killed.

"You got somebody killed," Bruce asserted.

Jonathan looked around in a panic. "Don't say that!" he said.

Bruce was concerned whether anyone else knew if the guy worked for Jonathan. Jonathan swore that he didn't tell anyone and he asked the guy to keep it close to his vest as well. Bruce wasn't convinced that Jonathan wasn't connected, but he knew the only reason Jonathan was coming to him was because Jonathan felt Jermaine was connected to the incident. Jonathan told him the guy got made by a few of the gang members a week before the shooting. Bruce wasn't surprised, as most of the guys from the street could smell when something wasn't right. Knowing that the PI went out there the week before, he didn't understand why Jonathan sent him out a second time.

"I just wanted to make sure," Jonathan said. "I assume the gang didn't like that."

"So, you are saying Mr. Beasley was associated with this?" Bruce asked.

"No, but I think he may know who is." Jonathan said.

"How so?" Bruce asked.

"One of the gang members, a guy by the name of Julius Parker, was seen talking with my guy before the shooting," Jonathan said. "The police brought him in for questioning. It turns out he robbed him minutes before he got shot."

Bruce didn't understand what Jonathan meant until he explained that Cheech was found with two hundred dollars on him and the police believed it was from the victim. The whole thing was shady from the jump. Jonathan eventually admitted that he got the name of the PI from a person in Junction City and Bruce knew immediately that it led to a tangled web. Even though Jonathan didn't give his name to the person, he assumed it was going to end up at Jonathan's doorstep.

"I wouldn't be surprised if the police aren't at your office right now," Bruce said.

Bruce knew that you could never be too careful! He wanted to know what happened with Cheech.

"He said he didn't know anything," Jonathan said.

"He knows something!" Bruce said. "I would put two hundred dollars on it."

As the next class started filing in, Bruce committed to bringing it up casually with Jermaine. He wanted Jonathan far away from it and suggested that they continue on with the internship as if none of it happened. "I don't need to be tied up in any mess," Bruce added. "Neither does Jermaine."

###

At the laundromat, the conversation was all abuzz with people concerned about a sniper on the loose. They talked about who was going to be next and that the shooting appeared to be random. Others disagreed and thought it was gang-related, but as Jermaine walked in the ladies quieted down. They knew that Jermaine was gang-affiliated. They had seen him hang out on the corner late at night. One even knew that it was Jermaine who called the shots since Tony went away. Jermaine felt the eyes on him as he walked past to make his way to Sethi's office and sat down. Sethi stopped his work at the computer and looked up. Sethi asked him if he had heard about the shooting

"Yeah! I just heard about it." Jermaine confessed. "Do you know what happened?"

"Not a clue!" Sethi replied. "I only know what the news tells me."

"I am sure the streets are talking," Jermaine said.

"There is so much gossip that goes in and out of here. It's all I can do to ignore it all," Sethi said.

The new machines had arrived and were working like a dream. As soon as word got out, some of the old customers made their way back to the laundromat. The machines were paying for themselves. The internship was a different story. Jermaine wasn't able to start yet because something was held up with the paperwork. Sethi asked if it had anything to do with the recent murder. He knew people didn't like to invest in a place if they felt like there was going to be trouble. Jermaine knew that was a horrible business strategy.

"Always buy when there is blood in the streets," he said.

"Right now, people are scared to come out of their homes," Sethi said. "I heard it might be gang-related."

Jermaine's ears perked up and he wanted to know what people were saying. Sethi knew the victim wasn't from around there. According to the senior citizens nobody knew him. Jermaine remarked that it didn't sound gang-related.

"Gangs normally hit rival gangs," he said.

"Believe it or not! I ran with a gang in my youth in India," Sethi said.

"Really!" Jermaine said. "I didn't know India had gangs."

"Every poor area has gangs," Sethi informed. "It doesn't discriminate!"

Sethi chose his words and the right time to ask if Jermaine ever got caught up in a gang. His seniors had been talking about Jermaine and now Jermaine wanted to know what they were saying.

"They want to know why they see you working back here," Sethi said. "They say you are part of the boys that hang out at the corner store."

Sethi knew more than he was saying. He knew that Jermaine was the leader and called the shots. Jermaine was caught off-guard and didn't know how to reply. He didn't want to lie, but he knew that sharing everything would jeopardize their relationship. He told Sethi that when his good friend and mentor went to prison that friend asked Jermaine to look after things and keep the guys out of trouble until he got home. He told Sethi that they don't cause any trouble and were, in fact, working on some entrepreneurial ideas. Sethi shared that he left India to escape all ties to his former life and found that business was a great alternative to the streets. Jermaine agreed.

"And getting an education," he said.

"And sometimes both," Sethi said.

"Yes! And sometimes both." Jermaine said.

#

The gang members were laying low, but to avoid cabin fever Brian and Dookie made their way to the arcade to play some "run and gun" games after class. When they got there, they saw Jermaine counting bank and balancing the daily ledger.

"Yo!" Brian said. "You see Jermaine over there acting like nothing ever happened? I wonder if they even questioned him."

"He told us to lay low," Dookie replied. "We just need to stay low and don't worry about him. Besides he had an alibi."

Brian thought that they all had an alibi, but Cheech didn't. He was reported to be on the block when it happened. This made the gang a prime suspect in the murder even though the brothers were in front of the store with Earl when it happened.

"Police are going to say we arranged for somebody to hit 'ol boy after Cheech vetted him," Dookie said.

No one knew where Cheech was. They hadn't seen him in over a week before the shooting, but they weren't even to say that much. Jermaine told them not to say anything, especially about being followed.

"You right!" Brian agreed. "We don't know anything.

Jermaine saw Brian and Dookie with their backs turned towards the games and put down the ledger to check up on them.

"What's up fam?" Jermaine exclaimed. "What are y'all doing out?"

"What are you doing out?" Brian asked.

"I'm working with my mentor," Jermaine replied.

Jermaine spotted two undercover detectives playing speed hoops. He told Dookie and Brian to keep playing the game and not to turn around. He wondered if the brothers were followed. He let them know that heat was in the arcade and Dookie motioned to turn around.

"Don't turn!" Jermaine insisted. "You are already getting left behind by your brother in the game. Focus and listen. I can't talk for long."

Jermaine turned his back so only they could hear him. He told them that they were going to be called in for questioning, but that the police didn't want them, they really wanted him. They knew he was the gang leader, so they were going to try to pin something on him in order to throw the gang into chaos. Jermaine caught the men looking over and told Brian and Dookie that the detectives would walk over as soon as he left. Jermaine knew that if he were still there when they approached the brothers they would have to question him too, and they didn't want to do that.

"I have an alibi," Jermaine said. "People saw me volunteering until six p.m. the night of the shooting. They used the same approach with Tony and the only reason he got caught up is because he intervened, so they got him on obstructing justice and he took a plea."

Brian wished he knew all of this earlier, but it was too late. Jermaine figured the police would come down on them once Tony got locked up. The brothers didn't have a lot of time to prepare. The cops were going to come over as soon as he left. Jermaine told the brothers what to do.

"Just know that when they walk up I am not going to come over," he said. "I am not even going to look your way. Don't resist! They are going to ask you lots of questions. You don't know anything. Just follow them outside. You ask them two questions once you get outside. Ask them, 'Am I under arrest officer?' Once they reply, 'No, you are not under arrest,' you ask them: 'If I am, not under arrest, I must be free to go at any time? Is that correct?'"

Brian assumed because they were minors they couldn't be questioned without their parents or lawyers there.

"You don't have to worry about all that if you just do what I am telling you," Jermaine

said. "Remember they don't want you. As sad as it sounds you are nothing to them. They are trying to cut off the head."

Jermaine saw the men head outside. It was time for everything to go down. He asked if they were clean and Dookie confessed to having a dime bag in his sock. Jermaine told him to go and flush it and meet his brother outside. Jermaine went back to counting bank.

While Brian was outside, he saw the officers waiting in a car up the block in the direction of his house and waited in front of the arcade for Dookie to come out. He was nervous and thought that this was more than he could handle. He wanted to call his dad in North Carolina, but now was afraid to reach in his pocket for his phone. The officers stayed put. Dookie came out and started walking in the direction of their house until Brian grabbed his jacket and insisted that they walk the other way. As they walked, Jermaine continued his count inside the store, but saw the undercover cop car roll past the storefront. It took everything within him to not go and protect his fellow gang members. Tony had assigned him to watch over them and to keep them out of harm's way. He knew Tony was counting on him, but now there had been a murder in broad daylight and everything was going to point in the Rottweilers' direction. Besides that, he had no idea where Cheech was either.

The officers rolled up on Brian and Dookie as expected. The interaction was brief. Both teens complied. The officers were surprised, as if they were looking for an opportunity to draw their guns. To flash their badges. To read them their rights. But none of that happened. The boys agreed to go to the station unassisted. As the officers tried to make small talk, Dookie calmly asked if they were under arrest. The officers were shocked at their demeanor. Brian wanted the next question and was cued to ask it.

"So, if we are not under arrest that must mean we are free to go?" Brian said.

The cops suggested that it wouldn't take long and they would be home before dinner. The teens were out of questions and sat quietly for the short ride. In their neighborhood, it felt like there was a police station every half mile. Brian was unable to keep quiet and insisted on asking more about their rights.

"It's important for you to know that we are minors and it is against the law for us to be questioned without adult supervision," he said.

The officers pulled up at the station and asked them if they would like their parents to be present.

"No, thank you officer!" Dookie replied. "I think we can handle this ourselves"

He shot his big brother a harsh look for going off script.

###

The night wound into dusk as Jermaine waited outside of the police station for Brian and Dookie to come out. They both walked out, putting on their gloves and hats before they spotted Jermaine.

"I thought you were going to meet us back on the block," Brian stated.

"Change of plans!" Jermaine said. "We are going to the park to meet up with Cheech."

Brian didn't think that was the best idea with them just leaving the station. He thought Five would be hot on them, but that was all dependent upon what was said inside the station. They followed Jermaine's instructions until Brian got uppity about the fact they were minors and Dookie had to check him. If they were released in just under an hour it meant the investigators didn't think they could tell them anymore to help with the case. The cops just asked a lot of questions about Jermaine and the brothers felt like he was keeping something from them.

"I told you. The word is out that I am taking the lead while Tony is hemmed in," Jermaine said.

"It sounded deeper than that," Dookie said. "Like it has something to do with your college stuff."

As they walked down the street, Brian allowed the questions back at the station to play through his mind. He wanted to know if Jermaine was caught up in some mess at school. Jermaine couldn't believe what he was hearing.

"What would that have to do with anyone getting shot?" he said.

Dookie thought Cheech would know because Cheech kept eyes on the streets since the gang told him they were followed.

It was a cold and quiet walk before they reached the park fifteen minutes later and Cheech was nowhere to be found. Then he appeared out of nowhere.

"Dude, where you come from?" Dookie asked. "I know you saw us come in."

"I had to make sure you weren't followed," Cheech said. "I have homies watching all the entrances to the park."

Brian knew he didn't see anybody watching the entrances to the park. That was not Cheech's concern. He just needed to know if they were about to be compromised and wanted to be ready to mobilize quickly. Veronika had hit up Jermaine and told him to meet her for a date. He immediately knew it had something to do with Cheech.

"That's right!" Dookie laughed. "You know that girl doesn't want anything to do with you."

Jermaine let Cheech know that the crew had been laying low and that Five had decided to pick up Brian and Dookie earlier for questioning. Jermaine assumed they were followed from their house until Cheech let him know that DTs had been watching the arcade. Cheech and his homies hung out there, so it made sense to Jermaine that the police would be watching that location. Jermaine didn't have a clue about what was really going on. He had assumed that the streets were hot since word got out that he was in charge. It was the brothers who were questioned, and they knew there was more to it than that. They tried to tell Jermaine, but he wouldn't listen. Cheech pushed into the circle of men and told them that he approached the guy before he got shot and asked him what he was doing around there.

"He tried to lie to me at first, but I convinced him that it was better to tell me everything," Cheech said. "He was sent out here by a guy at a company called Quarimoc. Does that ring a bell?"

Jermaine was stunned and got light-headed. All the blood rushed from his brain and he fell backward. Cheech assumed he had heard of the company and told Jermaine that he was the one they were spying on.

"I guess they heard you weren't one of their normal recruits and wanted to do an up-close and personal background check," Cheech said.

Jermaine was reeling and made it over to a tree and started puking up his lunch. Cheech told him that he had to pull it together or he was taking over. Jermaine assured him he was good as he wiped his mouth with the back of his glove. The police mentioned Quarimoc several times during their interview of the brothers.

"Did you...did you?" Jermaine began.

Cheech denied any wrongdoing, saying he doesn't carry a piece. He wouldn't tell Jermaine even if he did do it, for Jermaine's own protection. What was important was that Jermaine was going to be under surveillance for the next few weeks until they pinned the murder on somebody. Jermaine didn't know what to say and struggled to put words together.

"Listen!" Cheech said. "You need to lay low. Stay off the streets and maintain your routine. Focus on school!"

Jermaine wasn't able to focus on school. That's how he got caught up in all this. He worked hard to stand upright. His mind was in a million different places. He wanted to know if Bruce knew anything. He couldn't bring it up to him. It would be a dead giveaway. Although he did think about it. He knew Cheech was right. He had to lay low.

"Not because you said so, but because it's the right thing to do." Jermaine said. "While I'm underground I am putting Earl in charge."

Cheech had to smirk at Earl being in charge, so Jermaine had to tell Cheech that it was because he was hot too. He thought Earl could handle it.

A signal rang out and the meeting time was over. Cheech went back in the shadows and the gang left the park. Just as fast as they had arrived.

###

CHAPTER SEVEN

At the Quarimoc Industries orientation, thirty-five interns poured into a conference room to go over ethics, sexual harassment and business etiquette. The trainer pounded through a PowerPoint that was sorely outdated with actors in clothes from the nineties. The interns were dressed to the nines and chipper, each trying to outshine the next and get the attention of management. Jermaine was confident. He sat in the back and didn't say a word. As the morning session was about to end, he recognized a face from his video chat interview and made eye contact. The trainer called for a lunch break and Jermaine bee lined over to the familiar face.

"Lance, right?" Jermaine asked. "You interviewed me a few months back over video chat."

"Sorry!" Lance stated. "I interviewed so many people. What is your name again?"

Jermaine looked around the room and only spotted two other Black men out of the thirty-five interns and thought he stood out among the interviews. Jermaine brushed off the slight and put Lance at ease by stating his name for him again and Lance immediately put the name with the face. Jermaine noticed the visceral reaction, yet played it down, presuming that Lance was familiar with his portfolio. Lance was familiar with his accomplishments and was just looking at his file.

"Too bad we don't have photos in there too." Lance said. "I apologize for not recognizing you."

"I understand!" Jermaine stated. "You probably interviewed hundreds of candidates to get down to thirty-five lucky winners. Each brighter than the next."

Jermaine was an exceptional talent and one of a few of their two-year college interns. Before that year, Quarimoc only hired juniors and seniors who had made it successfully through their Analysis, Theory and Econometrics set. Jermaine was taken aback. As much research as he had done on this company, he did not think to check if he was going to be a full class level behind in classwork than those to his left and right. He knew this meant that he had to outwork them starting that moment and his natural aptitude would not be enough.

He appreciated the compliment and asked if Lance had any lunch plans, but there was preparation to be done for the afternoon session waiting at Lance's desk. Lance offered to catch up later in the week. Quarimoc wanted the interns to eat together anyway so they could build bonds before they sent them off to their prospective locations. Jermaine was thrown at the idea of sending interns off. Lance hadn't realized that Jermaine was staying in his own neighborhood to help Quarimoc break into the local economy there. Lance blamed it on the fact that Jermaine was new and was on his first go around with training. All the interns were already hired and on board when Lance arrived the previous spring.

"Were you an intern with the company before you came on full-time?" Jermaine asked.

"Interestingly enough I was," Lance said. "They normally frown upon hiring from within the company interns. Something about getting more out of someone who learned under a different system."

Jermaine didn't think that philosophy made a lot of sense, but was not going to question management. Lance pressed him for his thoughts.

"There is a business theory that says it is more difficult to 'untrain' an employee on past practices than it is to train them on new practices," Jermaine stated.

"So, you think hiring employees coming in with previous methods of doing things is a bad idea?" Lance asked. "Well, we just hired a long-time manager from a rival company in the Southwest."

Jermaine knew he was referring to Shirley from the interview. He had done his research on her. He asked how the transition was working out and apologized if he was overstepping boundaries. Lance admitted that she was struggling with adopting the company's values.

"She didn't want to hire me?" Jermaine stated.

Lance was shaken and Jermaine realized he said something wrong and may have given away that he knew something he shouldn't know. He searched desperately for a way to end the conversation. Lance pulled in close to Jermaine and let him know that he was rooting for him and to keep his head down and let his work speak for him. He patted Jermaine on the shoulder and walked down the hall towards a bank of elevators.

"Lunch on Thursday!" Lance yelled back. "I will meet you here after the session."

Jermaine gave away way too much with his assertion and had to cover his tracks.

###

Back on the block, a youngish-looking Latina entered the corner store with a slight bop wearing a puffy coat, saggy pants and a skull cap. She headed straight for the malt liquor. Earl hadn't seen her before, but he was heading into the store to get a loose cigarette and she stood behind him in line. Outside, he noticed another female in a skull cap wearing gloves. This one he recognized, but not as someone from the block. He allowed his mind to flash back into time. He remembered seeing her as a really cute college-aged girl a couple of years back with long hair and a wide-eyed doe look. As his memories came back to him, he remembered exactly where he knew her from. She was a cop. He saw her as a rookie on a ride along with some senior officers when they brought her by the block to become familiar with the gang during an illegal "stop and frisk."

He noticed that she was wearing the same skully as the woman buying the malt liquor behind him.

"Who buys a forty ounce at ten a.m.?" Earl thought.

He turned his head to inconspicuously look at the woman making the purchase and recognized her black boots and then noticed that something bulged underneath her oversized hoodie as she reached in her pocket to pull out some cash. It wasn't a gun, but it was possibly handcuffs. Either way, knew she was a cop and he knew he was about to be pinched. He was next to the counter and was conflicted.

"Hey, what's up Mohammed? Can I get a loosie?"

Mohammed gave Earl a look. "I can't help you today my friend."

As Earl was about to walk away, Patrice, walked up to the door. The cop outside stopped her to ask her for a light. As soon as Patrice pulled out her lighter, the cop revealed a gun and pointed it right at Patrice's chest.

"Hands where I can see them," the second officer said.

Patrice panicked and ducked inside the store. The cop inside put her bottle down on the counter and reached for her weapon.

"Everyone on the floor!" the first officer said.

Earl quickly got out of her way and Patrice was trapped in the back corner of the store. As the focus was turned towards Patrice, Mohammed motioned for Earl to go out the back door that led to the alley. While the officers cuffed Patrice, Earl headed for the alley. He was drenched in a cold sweat. He headed up the block on a mission. On his way, he passed Jermaine and his family without a word. After they passed, he then recognized who they were and turned around way too late. Earl turned the corner and stopped to catch his breath. Two cop cars whizzed by and Earl turned his face away in fear that they might recognize him. He was too afraid to go home, thinking that he was next to be in the back of a cop car. He instead made his way to the park and as he walked in he heard a light whistle. Not thinking anything of it, he kept walking. He then saw Charlene coming from his left side. As he was about to approach her to tell her what just went down with her homie, he froze as he noticed that she was holding a gun on her waist.

"What's up playa?" Charlene said.

"I was just walking," Earl said. "There's some heat on the corner. Your girl Patrice got pinched."

"You sure you are not leading the cops here," Charlene said.

"Wait! What? Why would I do that?" Earl said. "Did you not hear me? Your homie just got arrested."

Charlene walked up on Earl and patted him down. She then pointed the gun at his back and told him to walk. As they walked, she gave a light whistle. Cheech came out of nowhere and asked Earl what was going on. He thought Earl might have been looking for him, but Earl told him that he was just walking.

"The block is hot and I barely made it off before your homie Patrice got cuffed," he said.

Earl couldn't understand why Charlene had a gun pointed at him.

"You didn't hear this from me, but your boy Jermaine is caught up in some crazy mess," Cheech stated.

Jermaine had already told Earl about the mess just before he told him that he needed him to take the helm while he laid low. Cheech motioned and Charlene lowered her gun. He gave Earl a hug and wanted to know how he was holding up. Earl was on pins and needles. Truth be told he never wanted to be a leader. Now he felt like all eyes were on him even as he slept. Earl wanted to know why they grabbed Patrice. Cheech was very nonchalant as if he already knew Patrice was going to get arrested.

"It could be for a number of things?" Cheech said. "We do a lot of dirt. Don't worry about her. She's gonna be alright. It's not her first rodeo. Besides, she keeps a lawyer on retainer."

"So, nothing to do with that kid?" Earl asked.

"What are you asking me for?" Cheech answered.

Earl could tell it was a touchy topic and was quick to change the subject. Since the gang had been laying low, another gang from the Westside had been walking through their hood without any fear. Earl thought one of them might be dating his ex. Cheech told him not to worry and that everything was going to blow over soon enough. He told him Jermaine would be back as soon as he worked out his off-the-block issues, but for now it was up to Earl to keep the young members out of trouble.

"Now, man up and get down there and be there for our crew," Cheech said. "If not, trouble will find them."

Earl walked past Charlene to the entrance and headed back towards the block still scratching his head at what Cheech meant by "off-the-block issues."

###

Jermaine's family pulled baskets full of clothes behind them in shopping carts in the one-lane path made in the shoveled snow. They were making the trek to the laundromat. This was partly to rid themselves of cabin fever, partly to get the girls out of the house on the weekend, but mostly because laundry was piling up. Jermaine was just off the plane from his week-long training and to avoid a second and sometimes third wear of his shirts and jeans he joined the family and they made it an outing.

It was a short jaunt, but Denise was a fan favorite in the community and stopped to greet neighbors, postal workers, and shop owners on the way.

"I see you have the whole family with you today darling," one of the senior citizens said as Denise passed by.

"Yes! Just trying to get everyone out of the house," Denise replied. "How are you?"

"God is good!" the senior replied. "One day at a time! Take care of those babies."

Earl was walking towards the family in a rush. Jermaine gave him a shout out, but Earl didn't hear him and walked past his outstretched hand seeking dap.

Earl just kept his head low and pushed past without acknowledging Jermaine at all. Denise gave Jermaine a quizzical look and wanted to know if everything was okay between him and Earl.

"It looked like he had some place he needed to be," Jermaine said.

As they reached the corner, they saw a crowd gathered and sirens in the distance. Jermaine knew something was up and suggested that they cut up the block. He grabbed Renee's hand and pulled her along. Within a couple of minutes the sirens reached the crowd. Roxie tried to turn around to see what was going on, but Denise insisted, that she keep walking. They made it to the laundromat and Sethi was pushed to the glass looking at all the action as it passed by. He saw Jermaine with his family and escorted them to an open machine.

"Let me get you a basket," Sethi said.

As he grabbed the basket, he gave Jermaine a look for him to follow him. He wanted to know what was going on, but Jermaine didn't have a clue. He just got back to the state.

As the sirens came to a stop, he saw someone being cuffed and placed into a patrol car. Jermaine walked back over and helped his family sort out laundry. Sethi walked back to the door to see what was going on. He saw a young African-American woman being detained by a plain-clothes female detective.

Denise got the wash started and Jermaine got the girls settled in with their tablets. Denise found some neighbors who were also doing laundry and who knew better than to get involved in what was going on outside. Jermaine stepped inside the office uninvited to wait for Sethi to find out more. Sethi walked back in and gave a brief description of the female.

"You know her?" Sethi asked.

"If it is who I think it is, I went on one date with one of her friends," Jermaine said. "She is the homie of one of my boys."

"Plain-clothed detective. Female. Sting op?" Sethi suggested.

"Yeah!" Jermaine agreed. "The streets are hot. I am fortunate that I got to be away for a week. Most people around here don't have that option."

Sethi wanted to know if what was going on outside had anything to do with him. What he really wanted to know was where Jermaine was when that kid got shot. Jermaine got defensive. Sethi was questioning him like Sethi was the police. He told Sethi that he was volunteering at the Eastside Boys & Girls Club. He continued to tell Sethi that he had someone teaching him the gaming side of the coin-op business and they were doing some tutoring together.

"Don't worry! I'm clean," Jermaine said. "I wouldn't get you caught up like that."

The girls were getting antsy and Jermaine went to check on them.

"You ladies want to change it up," Jermaine asked.

Roxie wanted to know what all the sirens were for and Jermaine told her that it had nothing to do with her and to mind her business.

"We don't move towards chaos, we move away from it," he said.

Renee was more interested in why Earl didn't greet him. Jermaine was used to being around women, but this was becoming too much. He told her he was busy. His answers satisfied the girls for the time being.

The girls brought their homework with them and Jermaine told Roxie that she needed to work on her multiplication table. Roxie sighed, but then reluctantly pulled out her multiplication chart.

"Don't make that face!" Jermaine kidded.

Jermaine explained what he learned from Bruce in the fall semester. That math was in everything they do. He told her that Sethi could show her how it helped him keep track of his expenses and income.

"His what?" Renee asked.

"How much he spends and how much he makes," Jermaine clarified.

Sethi walked by and Jermaine joked about them while checking to make sure he wasn't "cooking the books." Sethi told the sisters that their brother was a real whiz at economics and that it helped keep him in line.

As the wash finished, Sethi helped Denise push the basket from the washer to the dryer. Denise loaded it in and got it started. Jermaine found the opportunity for a math lesson there in the laundromat.

"So, if mommy put nine quarters into the washer, how much did she spend?" he asked.

Roxie looked down at the chart and didn't see a line for quarters. Her chart only went to the twelve-times table. Jermaine told her that she didn't need her multiplication table. That she only needed to know how many quarters were in a dollar. Roxie knew the answer was four and that quarter meant one-fourth.

"Now, if four quarters make a dollar and eight quarter make two dollars, how much do nine quarters make?" he asked.

Roxie struggled with the math and Renee jumped in.

"Two dollars and twenty-five cents!" Renee answered.

Roxie got mad. She wanted to figure it out herself. Jermaine told her that he had plenty more math problems to figure out before the laundry was done.

Sethi watched as the police cars drove away and the crowds dispersed. Jermaine lifted his eyes to see the tail end of the activities as well. Renee, who was well engulfed into long division in her fifth-grade classes, had jumped in to assist Roxie on some of her worksheets. Jermaine took the remaining twenty minutes left on the dryer to join Sethi in the office and discuss his week of training.

"So, you finally got to meet the team of folks you are going to be working for this semester?" Sethi asked.

"Most of them!" Jermaine replied. "If everything goes well, I may be able to get a spot over the summer."

Sethi sounded surprised that Jermaine was trying to get a job with Quarimoc. Jermaine had already learned from Lance that they didn't like to hire from their pool of interns, so he didn't set his mind on it.

"But, he also told me that this is their first year looking at community college interns," Jermaine continued.

"It sounds like you had some good conversation," Sethi said.

Jermaine told him that he was actually able to cop a one-on-one sit-down lunch after an awkward start. Sethi was curious about why the conversation was awkward but didn't ask. He was more interested in what Jermaine learned. Jermaine told Sethi what he already knew. That the coin-op business was phasing out and they had to start looking towards the future. Everything was moving towards credit card chips, tap to pay, pay by phone and such.

"Well, what does your gut tell you?" Sethi asked.

"You already know!" Jermaine replied. "You can't force people to go where they don't want to go. I like our hybrid method."

"Technology!" Sethi said. "It's how the government is able to track your every move. I went on my search engine the other day and it was already telling me what I may be interested in purchasing."

"Data mining!" Jermaine said. "It's how businesses and the police are able to track your every move too. Free internet, downloads, ATMs, GPS on your phone. You can't go anywhere without someone knowing where you are. We are always on the grid."

Sethi committed to keeping it simple. Even if it meant losing some business. He felt as though coin-op had been good to him so why change. Jermaine didn't think he would lose business. Instead, he would capture a market of people who weren't willing to put their whereabouts in the streets. He wanted to start a movement.

"Quarters!" Sethi exclaimed.

"Better yet...Spare Change!" Jermaine suggested.

"I like it!" Sethi said. "Sell that it's discounted and it's off-grid."

Jermaine was all-in, but he knew they would have to get other coin-ops to buy-in. Sethi suggested starting with his mentor at the arcade, but they couldn't stop there. Jermaine wanted to make it a worldwide movement.

"Infiltrate Quarimoc?" Sethi suggested.

Jermaine felt as if Quarimoc had already drunk the Kool-Aid.

"Spare Change!" Jermaine repeated. "We start our own movement and go counter-culture."

Sethi was sold. He felt it was a better move to learn from the internship and just do the opposite. Jermaine knew that they were teaching him valuable lessons there. He would be tapping into the forgotten customer. Focusing on the niche not the masses. The poor who were always forgotten.

"They recruited me to break into an untapped market. I will tell them that this is how you tap in."

"Infiltrate from the inside? That's what I said," Sethi said.

"So, you were right as always," Jermaine said. "You have been doing this a lot longer than me."

"And don't you forget it," Sethi said.

The laundry was done and Denise tapped on the glass of the office to get Jermaine's help folding.

"Duty calls!" Jermaine said. "I will try to remember who is the teacher and who is the student from this point on."

###

Jermaine sat in the academic counseling office with his assigned counselor, Ms. Sheila Langford, and tried to maneuver units to make his honors class work toward him graduating on time. He hoped the internship would put him ahead. He didn't come into college with any AP units, but if he received five honor credits for his internship that would mean no summer courses. Ms. Langford couldn't understand why Jermaine didn't want to keep the internship over the summer, but Jermaine knew it was a long-shot from what he had heard from Lance. Lance had all but discouraged him to apply to stay on.

Ms. Langford was baffled. She noticed that no one had worked for the company before, and that Jermaine didn't get the opportunity from the Career Office. Jermaine told her that he heard about the internship from Bruce. Bruce was supposed to go through the Career Office in order for Jermaine to get work-experience units. He was signed up for the class and the internship served as the lab, but without the Career Office involved it left questions to be answered. Ms. Langford called the Career Office and asked for a counselor by the name of Darius. After small talk, she asked if he had two minutes to talk about a student and hung up. Jermaine thought he might have said he didn't have the time right now and was going to call back, but he was actually on his way to her office which was right down the hall. While they waited, they went over Jermaine's math requirements. As they were reviewing the plans for math, there was a knock on the partially opened door and a tall man in his early fifties wearing a tie and sporting designer frames walked in.

"You rang!" Darius said.

"Thanks for coming so soon!" Sheila said.

"This is Jermaine Beasley, a second-year econ major."

"A pleasure to meet you Mr. Beasley," Darius said. "Econ major? Are you considering an internship?"

"Well, that's exactly why we called you here," Sheila cut in. "He has an internship this semester with a company called Quarimoc, but it doesn't look like he is getting work-experience units for it, only class units."

Darius leaned over Sheila's shoulder and peered at the company name. He confirmed he wasn't one of theirs. They normally liked to vet companies to be sure they were not selling their students a bill of goods to get free labor. Jermaine didn't want to get Bruce in any trouble and said he was okay if he wasn't able to get the units. Darius explained that no one was in any trouble and that companies tend to form relationships with professors from grants and forget that there are steps to the process. His job was to make sure everyone followed procedures. Jermaine regretted making an issue out of it. He just wanted to get out of taking classes during the summer if he could. There were some unpaid internship opportunities he could take, but Jermaine was getting paid if he turned a profit. He wasn't just trying to get a foot in the door and boost his resume. It made him sound ungrateful and he thought it was probably best not to tell them what he was making at Quarimoc. He quickly realized that his agreement was made off the books and he was about to jeopardize his opportunity, but he was also conflicted because of Quarimoc's back-alley dealings leading to a person getting killed. He had to think before he said anything more. He definitely didn't want to jeopardize his education, but he also wanted to get his money. He decided to come clean and tell Ms. Langford that the company was giving him thirty percent of the profits from the product placement. The two counselors looked shocked and had a quick sidebar before they responded to Jermaine.

"Mr. Beasley, we are going to have to confer with Professor Wright and this company and get back to you. Thank you for being so forthcoming," Ms. Langford said. "I promise you, no one is in any trouble!"

Jermaine left the advising session discombobulated and rushed to Bruce's office before the news traveled.

###

Dookie and Brian stayed inside their house, but were still cautious. They didn't know who was watching them. Movies about wiretaps and bugged rooms had their minds spinning in a thousand different directions. Brian decided to turn the television volume up way too high in a crazy attempt to shield any listening ears. The game was on and the two brothers still carried on conversation amidst the deafening noise.

"You seen Jay?" Brian asked.

"Just heading up the block and going to his crib," Dookie replied. "He's on the low-low! I think he may still be working for that chick at the arcade."

Brian hadn't seen Jermaine, and Earl was pretty much M.I.A. since Patrice's arrest that past Saturday. He never really found out what she was caught up in, but he knew the streets were hot and the homies were grimy. He was sure someone had to know why she was pinched by now. Earl was there when it happened and that made the brothers wonder if he had something to do with setting her up. He had also disappeared as soon as it all went down. Dookie thought it was shady, but Brian had Earl's back.

"Nah! Earl ain't no snitch," Brian said. "He's loyal to the game. Besides, we have so much on him he would go down faster than any of us."

"Not with immunity," Dookie said.

"Man, you tripping," Brian replied.

There was a knock on the door that was barely audible over the noise coming from the television.

"Get the door!" their mother said.

Brian and Dookie's mother was cleaning frantically and spinning from heroin.

"It's probably one of your friends," she said.

Dookie was still a little on edge as he got up to answer the door. He cracked it a little to see if he could make out who it was. As he looked through the crack, he made out a badge. The detectives who picked them up from the arcade were at the door. Dookie tried to look calm.

"Just one second," he told the officers.

He saw his mother walking down the hallway making her way into the bedroom. Dookie motioned for Brian to join him outside. As Brian got up, he whispered to him that it was the police. Brian turned off the television and peeked down the hall. He yelled to his mother that they were going out and she demanded that they lock the door behind them.

"I don't want to be disturbed today," she said.

Dookie and Brian went outside to talk to the detectives. Brian was surprised to see the cops there. He thought they answered all of their questions at the station, but the brother's name had come up in Patrice's arrest over the weekend.

"Do you know Patrice Denton?" Officer Santiago asked.

"Not directly!" Brian said. "We know her from just being around the neighborhood."

"Well, she says she knows you," Officer Brooks confirmed.

"She is sort of a friend of a friend," Dookie asserted. "Can you tell us what this is about?"

The detectives had found out that the brothers, along with Earl were being followed a few weeks back. Officer Santiago asked if Dookie and Brian told Patrice that they were being followed. Dookie flat our denied telling Patrice anything and said he didn't speak to her. Officer Santiago restated his question.

"Did you tell anyone at all that you were being followed," he said. "Perhaps in a space where Patrice may have overheard the conversation?"

Dookie knew if he answered the question honestly it would conflict with what he told the detectives previously. He desperately wanted to back out of the situation and prayed that someone come to interrupt. He knew he was caught. Caught in space and time with no place to run. He looked towards his brother, as he had in times like this before, hoping that he could save him.

"Detective, we get chased a lot around here," Brian said. "There are some people who don't like us being in certain places at certain times. I am sure we have talked about some of these instances with people around and were unaware that they were listening. It's hard to say whether Patrice overheard us when we talked about being chased."

Dookie gave his brother a look of thanks and silently let out a breath that was trapped inside of him for what felt like the duration of a lifetime.

"Fair enough!" Officer Brooks said. "But we didn't ask about being chased. We asked if someone was following you. To be clear, did you tell anyone you were being followed?"

"I honestly don't remember the conversation," Brian said. "What does this have to do with anyway?"

The detectives were trying to determine if the brothers had anything to do with their homicide case, and the boys were adamant that they had no dealings with it. There was an implication made the boys put a hit out.

"That is not what we get involved in," Dookie said.

"Well, I looked up your hospital records and it appears that you do," Officer Brooks said. "It turns out that you have been involved in cross-fire twice in the last two years."

"Crossfire?" Dookie said. "I have been shot while walking down the street or standing on the corner minding my own business. Crossfire implies that I am shooting back. Man, I am just out here trying to survive these streets. If anything, I am a victim."

Jermaine's words from the arcade quickly come to Brian's mind. He asked the officers if they were under arrest because it seemed that if they were, the detectives would have taken them in already. Officer Santiago told them they were not under arrest, but that he was asking for their cooperation on finding this killer. He thought since Dookie a victim of gun violence that he would want to help. Officer Brooks pulled out a card and told the brothers if they learned anything more to give them a call and the boys went back inside their house.

###

Bruce was on his way from his office hours when Jermaine called out for him.

"Hey Doc!" Jermaine said. "You got a second?"

Jermaine chased Bruce down on his way to the bathroom.

"This will only take a minute," Jermaine said.

"I've heard that before," Bruce said. "I will only take a minute. My office door is open. Go inside and wait for me."

Bruce scurried down the hall to the bathroom. Jermaine huffed, but made his way to Bruce's office. While he was in there, he noticed that Bruce's computer hadn't gone to screensaver yet and that his email was still up. Usually Jermaine believed in respecting one's privacy, but one particular subject line caught his attention. The one that had his name in it. He knew that if he clicked it the subject line would un-bold and that would be a dead giveaway that it was read. Instead, he deleted it unopened and forwarded it to himself unopened. Before Professor Wright got back from the bathroom, he read it on his phone. It was from Quarimoc.

Bruce, I appreciate you holding our last conversation regarding Mr. Beasley close to your vest. He more than likely has some clue that there have been some inquiries regarding our company and will likely ask you what you know. It is better that the kid be absolved from all direct knowledge in case he is called on to testify.

Also, the college has a call into my HR department about the internship and us not following the standard procedures. I was under the impression that everything ran through your class. Let me know if we missed a step. By the way, the kid is doing great. We already have orders for 8 new multi-purpose machines within the first few weeks. Let's be sure we hold on to this success.

Jermaine heard a loud flush that filled the hallway as he finished reading the email. He suddenly noticed that the screen saver was still not engaged. As he went to put Bruce's computer in sleep mode he realized that the email was no longer in his inbox. He had to think quickly. He went back into Bruce's 'trash' and removed the unread email from 'trash' which sent it back to his inbox. He then put the computer in sleep mode and ran back to his seat just as Bruce walked in. All at once, there was tension.

"Were you at my computer?" Professor Wright asked. "My chair is moved."

"No sir! I swung it around to check out your spectacular view out of your window," Jermaine said. "Jealous!"

"You don't know how long it took for me to get an office with a view," Bruce answered.

The tension was broken for the moment. He wanted to know what was so urgent for Jermaine to pop up on him unannounced. Jermaine knew that Bruce didn't have office hours on Tuesdays and Thursdays due to his tight class schedule, but he had to come up with something. He pretended he mixed up his days and apologized for disturbing him. Bruce asked about the internship with Quarimoc. Jermaine told Bruce he was enjoying interning with the company and he was learning a lot. He also told Bruce he appreciated the lab Bruce taught to accompany what the interns were learning in the field. Jermaine was curious if Bruce had heard anything different and the tension built in the room. Bruce had only spoken to Jonathan a few times since the orientation and didn't hear any complaints, but was expecting a report out in his email soon. He unlocked his computer to check his email. The email that Jermaine had just been through without him knowing.

"Well, I hope it's all good news," Jermaine paused. "About the internship. I spoke to my academic counselor and she said I may not be getting work-experience credit for it. Something about paperwork for fair labor requirements needing to be completed."

Bruce stopped to think. He didn't go through the Career Center as he was used to. This opportunity just came knocking on his door and he didn't think to contact Darius to get it on the books. Now he wondered if he could do it retroactively. Darius was the person whom Jermaine's advisor called in and now Bruce knew he would be getting a call about it soon. He thanked Jermaine for the heads up and Jermaine assured him it was nothing to be worried about, but Bruce knew otherwise. He knew that the college had to vet anyone associated with the college because they were a federally-funded institution, which meant even private companies who wanted to work with them had to abide by government regulations. Jermaine was sure that Bruce wouldn't put the college in harm's way, but that he just got ahead of himself.

"I could have done more homework on Quarimoc before chomping at the bit," Bruce said. "Let's hope their nose is clean. For your sake and for mine."

###

CHAPTER EIGHT

With spring being staved off by long winter months, youngsters were still making their way into the arcade to stay warm after school. Jermaine had managed to put two trial machines into the arcade after long negotiations with Donna about what their purpose would be, where they would be located and how they would attract more customers.

Donna couldn't see how more "shoot 'em up" games were going to add to the mission of building community. "I mean, I can't picture the family gathering around and joining in the slaughter."

Jermaine picked up on her sarcasm. "While it may not be as family-oriented as dance-off games, it is a money maker and it not only inspires friendly rivalries, but sibling rivalries as well."

Donna knew the community center would never allow it. She struggled to see what positive could be gained.

Jermaine tried to teach her about the benefits of hand-eye coordination, increased balance and focus and the ultimate benefit of stress relief. “If you go downtown, you will see a lot of these young professionals playing these games on their lunch breaks or after a long day in the office.”

“Then you need to put these in the bars,” Donna stated.

“Not a bad idea!” Jermaine quipped. “I will call some places tomorrow.”

Some pre-teens came over to the new machines and got really excited.

“Yo! When did they get these?” one kid yelled out.

Jermaine was confident the games were going to pay for themselves in no time. All Donna could think about were the complaints from parents and the need to keep them in the back away from the entrance so passersby didn't see them. It didn't matter where she put the games. The kids would find them. Donna knew it to be true. She was allowing Jermaine to use the space with the promise that the games would bring in more customers. That was the beauty of economics. The idea of having an anchor store or product that would draw people in to see the other great stuff.

"You should be thanking me," Jermaine said.

"We'll see!" Donna replied.

Donna knew that Jermaine still had a lot to learn about coin-op and especially the arcade business. The warm weather would be coming soon, and she would need to find a way to keep customers during spring sports.

They retreated into her office and began where they left off in their planning.

###

Pablo and Pamela retreated into the snack room at Quarimoc main offices to refresh their coffee carafes and found themselves discussing the latest and greatest news regarding the company, which included acquiring some off-shore companies in Australia and New Zealand. Pablo remembered that the company did something like this years ago in India, but the currency exchange threw them all off. Pamela preferred to operate domestically. She knew the industry had become proficient at exchange rates, but determining the cultural trends would take them some time. Many Third World countries were behind in recent technology and it would take years to catch them up. Pamela was fortunate enough to get a vote on decisions like these. She knew that New Zealand and Australia were more developed, but they were so far removed and that it would be more work establishing the company model and philosophy than it was worth. Pablo reminded Pamela of the Second and Third World living situations domestically and that people living in impoverished situations weren't adapting as quickly to tech either.

"That may be true, but they own the capability or access to pivot quickly," Pamela said. "It's all about getting them on-boarded."

"How do you propose we do that?" Pablo asked.

Pamela had ideas about providing incentives like the credit-card companies did with their cash back offers.

"People do love a deal," Pablo agreed. "This kid Beasley is making some in-roads in his community. Have you looked at his numbers?"

There was a chart on the wall in the breakroom of the most recent intern revenues. Jermaine's name sat at number three among the highly touted interns. Pamela was very impressed. She knew that area and that its income level was far below the national average.

"What's his strategy?" she asked.

"Well, I spoke to Jonathan, and he pitched community-building locations such as gyms, playgrounds and laundromats."

Pamela thought the approach was counter-intuitive. She assumed vending worked best in

grab-and-go places. Pablo reminded her that they were hanging out in community space right then even if it was only for a few minutes to get coffee. Jermaine was definitely onto something.

"Sometimes it's important to meet the customer where they are at," he said.

"I would be curious to see where his numbers are at past-the-midway point," Pamela said. "It could just be a hot start."

"Maybe, but he is chomping on the heels of some of our returning interns and graduating seniors," Pablo said. "It appears like more than a hot start."

###

Charlene and Veronika were inside of a dimly lit apartment searching the floor intently with flashlights. It was late and the sun was not providing any assistance.

"It's gotta be here somewhere," Veronika said. "I heard it fall not far from here."

Charlene didn't know what they ended up pinning on Patrice. Veronika assumed it was probably Suspicion to Commit Harm.

"That doesn't make sense," Charlene said. "They couldn't hold her on that."

Veronika reminded Charlene that the police could hold a person on anything as long as they posted a high bail. They knew the court-appointed lawyer wasn't going to fight for her to get an early trial date and figured that Patrice would have to sit this one out. Patrice had been in prison before and they figured she could handle herself.

"I'm thinking they got prints off the casings," Charlene said.

Charlene and Veronika searched the apartment for a shell they thought had to still be there. Veronika saw the shell fall, but Charlene wasn't sure if the investigators had already been up in the trap before they arrived and picked it up.

"We didn't sweep up when we left."

"We got sloppy! Veronika agreed. "But there is nothing we can do about that now."

As the two of them keep looking in the dark, they heard someone at the door and panicked. They kept their voices low and hid behind the counter. Heavy footsteps entered the room. Via the street light coming through the window, Veronika saw black boots covered by khaki army pants pace the floor. The intruder was alone. Charlene was shaking and Veronika put her finger to her lips to get her to quiet down. The boots were now near the window, and there was a silhouette of a tall figure cast onto the far wall. Veronika reached for her blade that was tucked in her ankle. Her plan was to attack before someone attacked them first.

The shadow moved back towards the door as if about to leave. The door opened partially, but stopped suddenly when Charlene leaned against the counter door causing it to creek ever so slightly. Veronika was on edge now and quickly and silently pulled her knife out. The person looked back into the room, but decided to exit, walked out and closed the door.

The homies stayed put for a full minute in silence waiting until the footsteps were out of earshot. They moved out slowly, trusting the coast was clear and let down their guard. Veronika put her blade down on the card table and relaxed for a moment.

All of a sudden, the door opened and a flashlight shone directly in their faces, blinding them instantly. Veronika struggled to relocate her blade on the table, but it was no use. Charlene tried to dash towards the opened door, but it was blocked by the stranger. The homies both rushed to attack the intruder, but without a weapon they didn't stand much of a chance. Seeing them rushing forward the stranger addressed them in hushed voice.

"Yo! It's me!" Cheech said.

The homies recognized the voice.

"Cheech?" Veronika asked.

"Yeah!" Cheech replied. "Keep your voices low! We may have company."

Charlene couldn't tell if it was him who just came in. Cheech closed the door and ushered the girls back away from the window.

"Yeah! I came by yesterday too," Cheech said. "I needed to make sure we didn't leave any mess. It's a good thing too. I found the shell casing."

Veronika was upset that Cheech didn't tell them that he had already found the casing the day before since that was what they were there looking for. Cheech figured Charlene and Veronika would come by after Patrice got picked up. He had skipped town and didn't tell anyone.

"They are trying to pin that murder on our girl," Cheech said.

"With what evidence?" Charlene asked.

"They are saying they found some gunpowder on her clothing they collected," Cheech said. "They don't have a murder weapon, so I don't believe anything will stick. They will just run her ragged to try to get her to confess, take a plea, or rat somebody out."

Veronika knew that was how the corrupt justice system operated. They had to leave the trap house. It was hot there. People were saying they heard a shot come from that direction and the police were questioning the neighbors.

Cheech opened the door and looked both ways before ushering the homies out. He told them to keep their heads low and their hoods on. He said, "We don't need any heat."

The three of them left in a clandestine fashion being sure they didn't leave anything behind.

"My blade!" Veronika said just as the door was closing.

She ran back in to get it from the card table knowing it would not have been a good look if she left it there to be found.

###

Shirley sat at her desk at Quarimoc as Lance walked in with Pablo.

"Has anyone seen Jonathan?" Lance asked. "I thought maybe the brass sent him out to the field."

"He took a last-minute vacation," Shirley replied.

"He couldn't tell anyone?" Pablo asked. "So, who is covering his area while he's gone?"

"The board has added it to Pamela's workload," Shirley replied.

"Work her to death, why don't we?" Pablo replied. "They only do that to her because she's a woman."

Shirley defended that she was being compensated fairly and added she didn't have any kids and loved to travel. Lance reminded Shirley that he didn't have any kids either. He thought Pamela was taking on far too much.

"Does she also have to take on his interns?" he asked.

"Of course!" Shirley replied. "The busy only get busier."

Lance was interested in helping her if it meant he got the opportunity to work with Jermaine. Which meant traveling out of state. He had family in Kansas. Now Shirley was curious why Lance wanted to work with Jermaine. Pablo felt the need to remind Lance that they had reason to believe that Jermaine was dirty. Lance knew that he ran with a gang, but he also knew he was smart.

"I'll let Pamela know," Shirley stated. "She will be excited. She hates doing business in the ghetto."

"You mean she hates Black people," Pablo asserted.

Shirley wouldn't say that Pamela hated Black people, but acknowledged that she was very privileged, and was uncomfortable with the unfamiliar.

"So, she is uncomfortable around all minorities?" Lance said.

"That doesn't make her racist!" Shirley stated.

Pablo thought it pretty much did. Shirley thought that Pamela just needed to stop believing what the media was feeding her about people who were different from her. It was killing her productivity so, in order to pick up her numbers, she had a wide area to oversee. Shirley told Lance and Pablo that she had been asked to mentor Pamela.

"So, you can let her know I want to work with this kid while Jonathan is away?" Lance said.

"If you want him, you got him," Shirley says. "I'm not fond of this kid. Not because he's Black, but because the things he's mixed up in could hurt the company's reputation. Your funeral."

Pablo heard through the grapevine that Jonathan had hired somebody to watch Jermaine. He told Shirley that the streets were talking.

"Well, don't believe everything you hear," Shirley replied.

"I try not to, but when it comes to this company I become interested," Pablo said.

He had been around since they put the studs in and didn't approve of the company operating in the dark. Shirley had been in the coin-op business longer than Pablo had been with the company and believed that sometimes a company had to operate in the dark in order to bring things to the light.

"Even if that means getting someone killed?" Pablo asked. "Yeah, I watch the news. Was that us?"

The room got super quiet. Shirley called the conversation over. Pablo was upset that as soon as things got tense she didn't want to talk anymore. Shirley was upset that she was being accused of murder.

"So, you know exactly what I am referring to," Pablo stated. "I think you have answered my question."

He walked out leaving, Lance standing in Shirley's office awkwardly. Lance decided to break the silence.

"So, you are still going to hook up that transfer of the CC intern to my caseload, right?"

###

Jermaine was one of roughly fifteen students in the honors class working on individual projects within the arena of economics. Each had individual time set aside to meet with Bruce. Bianca Reynolds, was a petite, second-year econ major in her second semester of the honors class. She was working on a yearlong project and led the discussion that day.

"So, I am realizing that buying overseas is going to cut my cost by almost one-third, allowing me to gain more of a profit without raising cost," she began. "This essentially helps my customers."

Bruce scanned the room for any rebuttals to Bianca's idea. Jermaine hesitantly raised his hand.

"Yes, you cut costs, but at whose expense?" he said. "If your product is that cheap you have to ask several questions about how it is being manufactured."

Bianca raised up, ready to defend her approach. "I did my research, and most of the stuff we are hearing -- about a lower quality of product coming from the East -- is made up. It's to get us to pay more to buy American. Meanwhile, our politicians and billionaire business owners are in bed with whom they claim produces an inferior product."

Bruce looked to Jermaine to see if he had any rebuttal. Jermaine confessed that she was right, and that ninety-nine percent of the time these were not inferior products. His comment about the products being less expensive was really pointing to the wages and conditions the factory workers were being paid. Many times, pennies to the dollar.

Bianca insisted it had to do with the cost of living being drastically cheaper in those countries.

"Their minimum wage doesn't equate to what we in the states require for a living wage," she said. "Commercials say for something like forty-eight cents a day we can feed a hungry child. My lunch alone cost me nearly ten dollars."

Jermaine was stumped and struggled to find the words he wanted to say. His mind was filled with his own problems and to him the school stuff had become secondary. His family, his friends, this internship and now the murder had taken up all his brain space. He fought through the distractions to compliment Bianca on her excellent points, but then told her that there was a huge difference between what she chose to eat and the scraps left for the slave laborer to eat.

"I don't think for a moment you would trade places with a slave laborer," he said.

Bianca confessed that was not her lifestyle. They weren't really living. Jermaine contested that the laborers worked in unsafe conditions and made just enough to make it through the night in order for Americans and other First World citizens to have clothes on their back.

Jermaine's classmates were confused and wanted to know what he meant, so he offered an example with the help of a student in the class.

"Tom, what are you wearing right now?" he said.

"Jeans, a shirt and a sweater," Tom replied.

"And what are they each made of?" Jermaine asked.

"Cotton, I guess!" Tom replied. "What does that have to do with anything?"

"Where do you believe that cotton is grown and harvested?" Jermaine asked.

Tom didn't have a clue. Jermaine was sure Tom must have known that more than a half-million African slaves were brought to the United States to grow and harvest cotton.

"I knew that!" Tom said. "But slavery ended with the Emancipation Proclamation."

"Did it now?" Jermaine continued. "So where do we get our cotton from?"

"There was the creation of the cotton gin," Bianca said.

Jermaine agreed, but told her and the class that cotton manufacturing was still very labor intensive. So much so, that without slave labor it was not even worth the labor or cost of that labor to produce it. He added, "Yet we have so much of it."

He challenged them to look around the room and told them that they would find that cotton made up over ninety percent of what they wore, but not one everyone questioned where it came from. The room got quiet.

"My guess is that some of you know the answer," Jermaine asserted. "It's produced overseas in the Third World, under slave-like conditions for pennies an hour, so we can click a button and buy it cheaply." He addressed Bianca. "So, again, I ask at whose expense are we able to make a profit and get a cheaper product for our customers?"

Bruce lifted his hand and ended the debate. He reminded the class to think about the ethical decisions they made while at the same time making a profit and repeated the mantra of buying local, fair-trade, sustainable, socially-conscious products. He reminded them that there were a lot of companies who worked hard to try to get it right, but it was next to impossible to know for sure.

"We have to take all of this into consideration and be able to sleep at night with our decision," he said

Bruce shifted the class to the lab portion where the students had time to work on developing business strategies they could present to their employers.

Jermaine was suddenly wiped out and had a hard time focusing on his work. He stood up and stretched to try to get some oxygen to his brain. Bianca came over to him while his back was still turned.

"So, you like challenging people's ideas, huh?" Bianca said.

Jermaine was caught off-guard and still wasn't all there. He apologized and told Bianca that he wasn't trying to cause any trouble.

"You know, I am just here trying to get the 'A' like everybody else," Bianca said.

"I hear that!" Jermaine said. He told her that she had a great concept, and he thought she was smart, but that wasn't going to get him off the hook so easily.

"What was that whole diatribe about?" Bianca said. "Making us feel bad about the clothes we wear."

Jermaine couldn't even remember what he said.

"Hell, I'm no better. I'm sure my hoodie is a hundred-percent cotton," Jermaine said. "I'm really sorry! My mind is just on other things. Sorry, if it felt like I was taking it out of you."

Bianca accepted his apologies. She thought he was smart and liked that. She suggested that they study together some time.

Jermaine thought he was picking up a flirtatious tone in Bianca's voice. He wasn't quite prepared for it. Bianca was very cute and very put together. Someone he had previously considered out of his league. She was also very self-assured which, if Jermaine were being totally honest with himself, intimidated him a little.

"Whoa, you are killing the game?" Jermaine stated. "Are you sure I wouldn't slow you down?"

Bianca took Jermaine's pen and wrote her number on an open page in his decomposition notebook.

"I'm sure you can keep up!" she said.

Bianca walked back to her seat, confident that Jermaine was watching.

A male student seated next to Jermaine looked at him and nodded.

"I guess I better do the reading," Jermaine said.

Both of them knew that she had more on her mind than just books.

###

The buzz that had claimed the block calmed down. Some of it was due to the onset of spring weather with jackets, hats and gloves coming off. More people were outside, and the vibe of new life was in the air. Along with the birds, bunnies and bees, the gang had added to their numbers as well by way of recruiting new members. Young cats who had come of age and who looked up to the older dudes for guidance and mentorship. Cheech had even come out of hiding and decided to hit the block. He met the newbies, who were led by Earl, in front of the corner store.

"Hey! What's up boss?" Cheech said. "I see you have been busy with some initiations. Look at all these new cats." Cheech went around introducing himself.

"It's amazing what you can do when you are given some authority," Earl replied.

Earl had struggled with the leader role when he was first handed the baton. Things came way too fast for him. Patrice had been arrested, and the gang was being investigated. Now, he felt more in control.

"It sounds like you are trying to keep it," Cheech said.

"I don't know," Earl replied.

Earl knew that Jermaine had some big fish to fry over the next couple of months and that was going to keep him busy. Cheech knew that summer was coming fast and with warm weather came trouble. He didn't think Earl was prepared for it.

"Why not?" Earl said. "Tony has worn it for all these years. You forget how young we were when he brought us in. He'll be out of prison soon."

Earl thought if they could just make it through summer without any incidents they would be alright.

"Speaking of incident, what's new with your homie, Patrice?" Earl asked.

The cops were working on pinning the whole murder on Patrice without any cause. The word was they found some gunpowder on her jacket, but Cheech wasn't convinced. He knew she had lawyered up, but wasn't confident that her lawyer would fight for her. He figured that she should have been released and out already if the family had made bail.

It sounded like a set-up to Earl. He was ready to point the finger at Quarimoc. He said, "It sounds like they set up a murder so they could pin it on the gang that Jay runs with, so they can avoid hiring him without a discrimination case."

"That's a stretch!" Cheech said. "But I'm picking up what you're putting down. I wonder if the detectives are looking into that."

According to Dookie and Brian, the detectives were saying the gang initiated a hit because they were chased. The real question became: Why did the detectives ask them about Quarimoc? There was a connection, and Earl and Cheech had to help the detectives put the pieces together. When the detectives went to interview Dookie and Brian a second time, they wanted to know if the brothers said anything to Patrice about being followed. Now Cheech was wondering if the gang could put together the narrative that Quarimoc was the one who put this guy on the street, and when he came back and told them he wasn't going to snitch, they shot him.

"Cheech, you were the last one to talk to him," Earl said.

"Yes, and they were watching us the whole time," Cheech implied. "When he paid me off to protect him, they took it as a sign that he was switching sides and was about to rat them out. So, they killed him to protect the image of the company."

Cheech and Earl knew they would be taking on a big corporation with money to burn and with lawyers that would try to get the case thrown out in a heartbeat. Cheech was playing the long game. He thought it would be too late by the time they could get the case dismissed, and the story would have gained enough momentum.

"Quarimoc will do whatever they can to avoid the attention," Cheech said. "The police will have to let Patrice out just based on lack of evidence and there being another potential killer on the loose."

"The media will have a field day!" Earl said.

"The community will too!" Cheech said. "I can see the protest signs now. I will get on it, but in the meantime, let's get Jay back out here. He's good for us."

Earl reluctantly agreed.

"If he still remembers who we are," Earl said.

###

Sethi was outside of the laundromat early on a Tuesday morning as big trucks with the Quarimoc logo on them unloaded machines. Lance was there with Pamela to oversee the delivery to their newest client.

Pamela spotted Sethi and walked over to introduce Lance and herself. Sethi was confused, as he remembered Jermaine setting up the contract through Jonathan.

"That is correct!" Lance said. "This is Jonathan's contract. I am only overseeing this delivery and any immediate concerns until our colleague gets back from his family vacation."

Sethi thought that Jonathan picked an odd time to take a vacation, as Sethi knew Jonathan ordered new equipment months ago to be delivered this week. Pamela intervened, saying that his wife insisted that they travel while their kids were on their spring break. She apologized on his behalf and assured it wouldn't happen again.

"So, two sales reps for one?" Sethi asked.

"We wanted to make sure the job was done right," Lance kidded.

Pamela had been assigned Jonathan's contracts while he was away, but Lance was very interested in working with Jermaine and flew out to meet Pamela on his own dime. Sethi remembered that Jermaine had lunch with Lance during the orientation and brought it up. Lance was shocked that Jermaine would share that information with a client. Jermaine and Sethi had formed a bond over the past few months, with Jermaine helping Sethi with the books a few times a week. Pamela was impressed, and even more impressed that it paid off with a sale. More than a few of the coin-op places in that area had taken notice of Jermaine's talent.

"He is only scraping the tip of the iceberg here," Sethi said.

Lance knew the industry was moving away from coins. Casinos had started a trend towards cards, and it was inevitable that companies like Quarimoc were going the way of the dinosaur. Sethi saw the writing on the wall, but also knew that poorer areas were resistant to the change. Pamela couldn't understand why. She has been a leader in the move from coins for many years and was excited to see it finally come about. In fact, she had been a major proponent of moving the company to credit and debit payments and had to be reeled back to a card system as a first step.

"Why would businesses not want to move toward the future?" she questioned. "They are able to get payment upfront and don't have to worry about coin collection every few hours. They can even identify customers better and provide direct services to them. There are so many advantages."

"Everything you are saying is true," Sethi agreed. "Yet, everything you are saying is the very concern of our customers. Our clients don't want to pay for something before they get it, and they sure don't want anyone tracking their whereabouts."

"I don't understand these people," Pamela said.

Lance was stunned by her choice of words and tried to explain. But it was too late, Sethi had already picked up a vibe.

"Ms. Pamela. I can tell that you were raised with an air of privilege. Am I correct?"

Pamela didn't answer for fear of saying something else wrong. This wasn't her first time being called out, and it probably wouldn't be her last.

"When you don't have very much, you want to hold onto everything you have for as long as you can," Sethi continued. "Conversely, I am sure you are very familiar with data mining. I am sure your sales division does it. When the people in power don't have a great history of treating the underprivileged well, the last thing you want to do is give them access to your whereabouts."

Lance was amazed at how eloquently Sethi's explanation was and made a mental note.

"Mr. Sethi, you and Jermaine can teach us a lot about untapped markets," Lance said.

"That was a freebie," Sethi said. "The next one will cost you."

Sethi walked towards the door to oversee the product placement. He reminded Pamela and Lance that Jermaine was an asset and that if they did right by him, he would be the one that would teach them to reach unheard voices.

Jermaine was still at the college, but Bruce sent them out for field work in the early afternoon. Sethi said that they should come back then. Pamela had more sales visits to make in the area and punted to Lance.

"I'm going to grab a latte before I head North," she said. "You want one."

Lance looked at his watch and told her that he wanted to stick around until the installment at the laundromat was complete and then wanted to go over to the CC to check out the campus.

"I will see you back at the ranch on Thursday?" he said.

"Possibly Friday for me. I drove, remember?" Pamela said.

###

CHAPTER NINE

It was late evening, and Jermaine was finishing a study session with Bianca. Very little studying got accomplished, but he had to gather his books and materials from the dining room table before her roommates came home and complained about the mess. He filled his backpack and tried to head for the door just as Bianca was coming out of her room wearing a long t-shirt that extended past her knees.

"Off so soon!" she said.

Jermaine was caught trying to make a quick exit without being noticed. "Yes! I actually have to get some real reports done before I meet with these area reps tomorrow morning."

"Sorry to keep you from your work!" she said. "I will try not to be such a distraction next time."

Jermaine heard the sarcasm dripping from her words and knew he couldn't just leave on that note. He apologized and clarified by reminding her that she was far ahead of him on her project. With the little cash he had, he offered to take her somewhere over the weekend. This brought a smile to her face, but she didn't want to go out anywhere. She wanted Jermaine all to herself. She walked over to the front door where Jermaine was standing.

"Are you sure you have to go so soon?" she whined.

Jermaine considered the time and his mother's rules and how early he had to get going the next day. He wished he could stay, but he knew his mom would trip if he got in too late. He opened the door. As he did, Bianca followed close behind him. He turned to say goodbye and found himself face-to-face with her. She leaned in and kissed him goodbye as if to say "stay a little longer," but Jermaine was familiar with this tactic and stood firm.

"I will come over and make dinner on Saturday night," he said.

Bianca watched him as he exited down a flight of stairs and onto the street. She didn't live far from the campus and realized that he could catch the late bus from the campus to his house. As he entered the bus, he saw the usual library crew already seated, along with some late-night employees on their commute to their perspective homes. Jermaine's eyes were heavy, but he still managed to pull out some reading material for the twenty-minute bus ride across town. As he exited the bus, he saw a crowd gathered down at the corner. His better mind told him to cut through the block and avoid any late-night drama, but he also knew he hadn't seen the gang in a while and thought he could just pop in for five minutes to say "hi" and keep it pushing.

As he arrived, he saw a lot of the newer members and saw that a few of them were carrying weapons and drinking out underneath the street lights.

"Rottweilers, where's your mind at?" he said as he approached the corner.

The new members knew him, but didn't truly respect his authority since Earl was standing in for him and was the one who brought them into the gang.

"Yo Bee! Chill! We ain't bothering nobody," a teenager named Matthias said.

Jermaine lunged at him and grabbed him by the jacket. Earl stepped in to intervene.

"Yo Jay! Jay!" Earl said. "Let him go!"

"Then you better check your boy," Jermaine said.

Earl stopped all his new recruits and told them that they needed to show Jermaine their utmost respect if they were going to run with the gang.

"He is our leader," Earl said. "You know this. I am just standing in for a minute, but he is the dude. Alright?"

Matthias and a few of the members were drunk and high. Jermaine told everybody to clear out.

"This is not who we are," Jermaine said. "This is the type of behavior that brings us heat. Go home! Tomorrow night at seven o'clock, we go through initiation the way it was taught to me when I came in five years ago."

The new members cleared out, dragging their tails behind them, but Earl stayed behind. He took full responsibility for the new members' behavior and said it was on him.

"You damn right that on you!" Jermaine said. "How are they going to respect you if you let them behave however they want? Is that what Tony taught you?"

Earl thought they should be able to have a little fun since it was late, and the block was quiet.

"So, you think it's okay for those guys to carry out here on the block?" Jermaine said. "You know if one of us goes down, we all go down. We are a unit."

Earl couldn't tell the guys were holding, but Jermaine could tell from a block away. He knew if he could tell, so could the police. Jermaine acknowledged that the streets had cooled down some, but let Earl know that they had to remain vigilant.

"We are trying to make men out of boys," Jermaine said.

Earl knew he was right. Jermaine suddenly noticed Earl's behavior was strange and sweat poured from his forehead. Jermaine asked him what he was on. Earl had just taken some pills that the gang was passing around. Jermaine asked to see them, but Earl had taken the last one. Jermaine could tell by looking at Earl that what he took was a hallucinogen. He called Cheech.

"Yo! I need you to come get your boy and watch him tonight," Jermaine said. "Can you get here in ten minutes?"

Jermaine sat Earl down on the curb and then went into the store and bought him a thirty-two-ounce bottle of water to drink. Cheech arrived within five minutes, and Jermaine told him what just went down. Cheech said he would take care of it.

"The homies and I will keep a watch on Earl until morning," Cheech said.

Jermaine went to go let Earl's family know what was up. He told his sister, Tanja, that Earl was with him and would be back in the morning. He wanted to be sure they weren't worried. Jermaine then made it to his front door and had to knock so his mother could take the bolt off to let him in.

###

After drifting off from a page of uncompleted reading, Jermaine woke up to four missed calls and was still in his clothes from the night before. He knew he was late and screamed a cuss just low enough for the girls to not quite make out what he said. Roxie screamed back from the bathroom with mouth foaming with toothpaste bubbles to ask if he was okay. He assured his little sister he was, but he also knew he had a product meeting with Quarimoc in less than ten minutes. He was lucky it was a video chat like his interview, and he didn't really have to worry about how he was dressed below the waist. He jumped up as soon as Roxie exited the bathroom to splash water on his face and do a quick brush of his hair. A shower would have to wait. He knew the internet was spotty in his house, and he put on his shoes to make it to the laundromat. He looked at his missed calls and saw one was from a Missouri area code that he didn't recognize. There was also a local call he didn't recognize and two missed calls from Cheech.

He suddenly remembered that he still had to check in with Earl. As he ran out the door, he called Cheech who picked up immediately.

"Yo, Jay! It's about time you called. Where you at?" Cheech said.

Cheech was rushed and out of breath. Jermaine knew something was wrong. He let Cheech know he was on his way to a product meeting.

"Is everything okay?" Jermaine asked.

"No! Hell no!" Cheech said. "Earl is in the ICU. Whatever he took was laced. He woke up in the middle of the night convulsing. He is on life support, Man!"

As Cheech was telling Jermaine all this, a second call was coming in. Jermaine looked down at the number, and it was the local number he still didn't recognize. "Hold tight Cheech! I am going to make it to the hospital as soon as I can," Jermaine said. "Does his family know?"

"I found his sister's number in his phone," Cheech said. "You need to call her." Cheech rattled off the number.

It was the same number that had been calling in. Jermaine told Cheech that she was calling him now and would call him back.

"Fifth floor of the D ward," Cheech said. "They are only allowing family members back there with him."

Jermaine switched the call over just before Earl's sister, Tanja, was about to leave another message.

"Where is Earl?" Tanja asked. "You said he would be here by morning."

Jermaine was a full five-minutes late for his video chat, but knew that this call was important. "Calm down Tanja!" Jermaine said. "I have bad news, but I need to know you are calm."

"What bad news Jermaine?" Tanja asked. "You didn't get my brother killed running around with you hoodlums?"

Jermaine was miffed, but he knew that it was not the time to get caught up in his own feelings. He told Tanja that Earl was in the hospital and that he needed his family by his side. Tanja screamed at him on the other end of the phone. Jermaine heard her call to her mother and sister telling them what he just told her.

"Why didn't you tell me this last night?" Tanja said.

"He wasn't in the hospital last night." Jermaine said.

"But you knew he was shot or stabbed or hurt when you came by last night," she said. "You were keeping him somewhere. I can tell."

He told Tanja that Earl had overdosed on some pills and that he was in the ICU now.

"Get your momma and them down there as soon as you can," Jermaine said.

Tanja hung up. Jermaine was a block away from the laundromat and looked in. He saw the new Quarimoc machines had been delivered and tried to sneak a peek. When he turned the corner, he saw Lance seated in a booth looking at his watch. He tried to stay out of sight and ducked into Sethi's office.

"What is corporate doing here?" Jermaine said. "I was supposed to video chat with Jonathan today."

Sethi saw that Jermaine was not dressed in attire for a face-to-face meeting.

"This guy, Lance, and a woman named Pamela came in yesterday to see off the delivery of the machines," Sethi said. "He said he called you to let you know that he can meet in person."

Jermaine was caught off-guard and wanted to know where Jonathan was. Sethi told him about Jonathan's extended vacation and that Lance asked to take over Jonathan's caseload while he was away.

Jermaine knew he couldn't meet him dressed the way he was. He was already fifteen minutes late for the video chat. Sethi assured Jermaine that there was no video call and told him to check his messages. Jermaine punched in his passcode and heard Lance's voice on the other end.

Mr. Beasley, this is Lance Dordenhurf from Quarimoc. We had lunch during your orientation. Listen, Jonathan is out on vacation, and I asked if I could oversee your project while he is away. I know you were scheduled for a video chat, but I am here in town and I thought we could meet up instead. I'm at the laundromat checking out how the new installation is adapting. Grab some coffee and meet me over here. Later.

Sethi disappeared and came back with some dress pants that were way too short in length and too big in the waist.

"No way!" Jermaine said.

"It's either this or what you have on," Sethi said "I am not running a retail shop."

Jermaine looked in the mirror and reconsidered. He changed into the pants and pulled the belt extra tight. Sethi asked if he took a shower and alluded to him smelling like the previous night's activities. Jermaine told Sethi that maybe he should consider rescheduling. He was already late and his friend, Earl, was in the hospital.

"I am sorry to hear that, but I have to say this guy is on your side," Sethi stated. "If you are going to present, there is no better time than the present. Just be sure your presentation outshines your appearance."

Jermaine reluctantly agreed. He took a hard look in the mirror and tried to pull his loaner pants down to reach his Air Force ones. He sniffed at his armpits and left the office. Lance had his head down and Jermaine was able to sneak into the booth without too much attention to what was below his belt.

"Sorry I am late," Jermaine said. "I just received bad news that a friend of mine I was up late with had to be taken to the hospital this morning."

"No problem!" Lance stated. "You look like hell! We can reschedule until the afternoon. Go take care of your friend."

Jermaine considered the offer and realized he just put on those ridiculous pants and it wasn't going to be for no reason. He told Lance that he wanted to show him the progress he made with the coin-op expansion in the local community.

"I will make it brief so I can check on my friend as soon as we're done," Jermaine said.

Jermaine shared about the relationship with the laundromat and the arcade and expanded to opportunities at the local bars and clubs and even conversations he'd had with his auxiliary department at his college. Lance acknowledged that Jermaine was quite the salesman with an eye for opportunity.

"The clientele here is looking for something a little different than most clients," Jermaine said.

"That's what I am hearing," Lance replied. "I had a great conversation with the owner yesterday when we did our delivery. It's one of the reasons I wanted to meet here instead of some local coffee shop or on campus. I got here an hour before our appointment just to see who our clientele is. Yesterday, I walked up the boulevard at dusk. Even with gentrification around, I still garnered some looks. Folks might have thought I was a cop."

Jermaine was interested in Lance's perspective. Lance saw that the people in the neighborhood used cash or cash cards to buy their laundry cards. He saw the occasional debit or credit card, but they were few and far between. He also noticed that most people came in with change already. Sometimes they cashed a bill, but it seemed like a lot of folks were doing laundry once they had accumulated enough coins to do so.

"Spare change?" Jermaine said.

"Yeah! It made me think. What if our machines took more than quarters?" Lance said. "What if we created a slot for dimes and nickels too?"

That sounded way too complicated to Jermaine, but Lance was ready to think outside of the box to accommodate a new brand of customers. The customer that other companies were not paying attention to.

"You have been talking to Sethi," Jermaine said.

Lance knew that Jermaine was the brainchild and told him he should take credit where it was due. Jermaine was looking at the clock on the wall. He had to go, but asked if everything was okay with Jonathan.

The question was way above Lance's paygrade. He hadn't heard from or about Jonathan for weeks. Jermaine told Lance that he was grateful that he filled in for Jonathan and didn't leave him hanging.

"You have been helpful," Jermaine said. "How long are you around for?"

"My flight leaves tonight," Lance said. "Otherwise, I would stay longer. Let's get lunch the next time I swing through. I'm scheduled to come back in a couple of weeks."

Jermaine anticipated that he should have a few more commitments by then. This time Lance looked at the time and shut his laptop.

"I need to get going too, if I am going to get my luggage and check out of my VRBO before noon. Do you need a ride anywhere?"

Jermaine considered the ride, but quickly remembered his attire and passed. Sethi saw Jermaine and Lance stand up and was gracious enough to throw Jermaine a lifeline and walk Lance to the door. Lance gave Jermaine a firm handshake as the two parted ways. As soon as Lance got to his rental car and drove off, Jermaine beelined to the office to change back into his tattered jeans. He thanked Sethi for the save before he ran out the door.

###

Cheech was in the waiting area at the hospital while Earl's family peered through a thick glass window and watched doctors and nurses work to resuscitate Earl from a drug-induced coma using paddles and pumps. Tears flooded the faces of Earl's mother who was named Phyllis as well as Earl's sisters, Tanja and Amber. They held hands and embraced. Earl's father, Thomas, a tall, strong man with an athletic build and shaved head, stopped every nurse and doctor who was not working on Earl to ask questions. In a neighborhood where many fathers were not in the house, Thomas was a dedicated dad who worked hard to provide for his family. He knew Earl ran with the local gang and figured it was a phase.

As a youth, he and his friends would make up turf wars and chase people from their part of town too. For him, the phase was short-lived. Once coaches realized he had a talent at football, they took time to mentor him.

He was a starting tight end at the university when he met Phyllis, as a college freshman. Phyllis was unassuming but gorgeous when Thomas laid eyes on her. He never considered himself a ladies' man, but his exposure as a top athlete made him quite popular with wide-eyed women who wanted to say they were with one of the football guys. That all changed when he met Phyllis. His tough exterior melted, and he found himself struggling to put together the words to ask her out. They dated off and on, until Thomas's senior year when a back injury side-lined him, ending any chances of playing or of entering the NFL draft. Although he was a smart student in high school, the coaches had not encouraged or rewarded academic-achievement at the university, and they had often put him in "cake" courses, hiring tutors to complete his assignment. This left him ill-prepared to take on any job in the real world that required a college skill set. He found himself graduating after a fifth-year and working in manual labor until his back would no longer allow him to do any heavy lifting, squatting or tugging. Being the physical specimen that he was, he was offered security roles at the same warehouses he lifted boxes and crates at.

Meanwhile, Phyllis graduated with a degree in engineering and became the breadwinner. Despite her father's objections, they got married, and a few years after graduation, had a baby girl, Amber. Although Phyllis was a skilled software engineer, she found herself getting passed over promotions along the raises that came with them. She was a woman in a male-dominated field. Their combined income and child expenses made it nearly impossible for them to save to buy anything in what was considered the "safe" part of town, and they stayed where they could live. Working security meant long evening hours and time away from the family for Thomas. Without someone there to teach about manhood, Earl sought mentorship from the streets.

Earl's EKG machine flat lined and more people rushed into the room. Jermaine arrived in the waiting area and saw Cheech asleep in the corner.

"Yo, Cheech!" Jermaine said. "You need to go home and get some rest. How long have you been here?"

Cheech was startled and at first didn't know where he was. He recognized Jermaine and sat up.

"Yo Jay! My dude!" Cheech said. "Is Earl all right?"

"I just got here!" Jermaine replied. "You need to go home? When did you get here?"

The ambulance had come and picked up Earl at four a.m. that morning. Cheech called Jermaine as Cheech rode in the back of the ambulance with Earl.

"Go home! You could use a shower," Jermaine said.

Cheech stood up to hug Jermaine as he left.

"Dang, Homie! You are the one who could use a shower," Cheech said. "You still have the smell of old girl on you. I guess you found your groove, Stella."

Jermaine was embarrassed that he was going to be around Earl's family with that smell still on him. He wanted to see Earl first, but he knew that they were only letting family members past the downstairs waiting room. Jermaine had been sneaking past security his whole life. At this hospital, they had police officers checking tags and ID's. Jermaine was up for the challenge.

"You get home," he said. "I gotta see Earl."

Cheech dapped Jermaine up once more and then left. Jermaine went into action. He saw someone come out with a tag and watched that person leave. He noticed that some of the guests were coming and going, but others were leaving for good, often with their loved one in tow. Jermaine waited for someone leaving from the hospital and then watched when they discarded their tag. He found one to see what was on it. He noticed that the picture was grainy and hard to make out which would make it easy to use someone else's. He then waited for a time when the officers were distracted with a large group and then flashed the ID with confidence.

He got to the floor with Earl's family and paused when he saw them holding hands in prayer. He thought Earl must have died and felt he was to blame.

"Why didn't I call the ambulance right away?" he thought to himself. "Why did I send him away with Cheech?"

The family closed prayer, and Tanja saw him standing distraught at the end of the hall and walked over.

"I am so sorry Tanja!" Jermaine said. "This is all my fault! I should have..."

Tanja cut him off. "You should have done a lot of things, but nothing is your fault," Tanja said. "You didn't give him those drugs."

"How are your mom and dad?" Jermaine asked.

"Mom can hardly breathe and dad wishes he was in there with those doctors and nurses," Tanja replied.

"They haven't let you in there yet?" Jermaine asked.

"They want to be sure he is stable before we are allowed in," she said.

Jermaine surmised that Earl was still alive, but comatose. Whatever he took last night was not what he thought it was. It turned out that it wasn't an overdose after all. When the doctors pumped his stomach, they only found traces of a small tablet. They sent it to the lab to deduce what was in it.

"They said there is some nasty stuff out there now," Tanja shared. "There were four other cases like Earl's this week alone."

Jermaine wanted to see Earl, but he could only look through the glass.

"Come on. Let me walk you over," Tanja said.

Jermaine greeted Phyllis, Amber and Thomas on his way to the glass and offered them his heartfelt condolences. He then walked over to the paned glass and looked at Earl. The doctors and nurses were all gone now. Earl's body lay limp with tubes down his throat and in his arm and wires attached to his chest. Jermaine was overwhelmed with emotion and almost lost his balance. Thomas watched him go limp and rushed over to stabilize him.

"He's gonna be all right, Son," Thomas said. "Everything is gonna be all right!"

Before Thomas, Jermaine was embarrassed not only about how he smelled and was dressed or even that he was brought to tears, but because Thomas knew that Jermaine was a fellow gang member.

"I'm so sorry sir!" Jermaine said. "I didn't want any of this to happen."

"No one ever does, Son!" Thomas said. "You just make sure you tell your friends to stay away from things when they don't know what is in them. You're a good young man. Earl looked up to you, going to college and interning at a big company. You have nothing to be sorry for."

"Thank you, sir!" Jermaine said. "I just can't help but think that this is my fault."

"Ain't that something?" Thomas said. "I think the same thing. What if I was around more? What if I made more money and moved out of the hood."

Jermaine was shocked that a grown man could have those same feelings of blame.

"But then I came to realize that drugs are everywhere," Thomas continued. "It doesn't matter if you are rich or poor, Black or White, educated or uneducated. This could have happened anywhere. The fact of the matter is: you as a gang leader starts with you being a leader and teaching these young boys how to be men. You're not out there causing any trouble. They will follow your example."

Jermaine was taken aback by Thomas' kind words and was impacted to the core. He realized that he had to take charge again, now that Earl was down, and he had a bunch of newbies to train up. Knowing this, he found a new purpose and mission. He straightened up and touched the glass. He looked Thomas in the eye.

"Sir! I will not let you down," he said.

Jermaine stopped at Phyllis and grabbed her hand. No words were exchanged. He then said goodbye to Earl's sisters, walked to the elevator and headed home.

###

Jonathan sat at a desk of a hotel room in an undisclosed location. He was writing and receiving emails when his phone buzzed. He looked at the number and could tell it was from a LAN line which probably meant it was from the government. He let his phone buzz a few more times before he picked up. It was Detective Brooks, and Jonathan went numb on the other end.

"Mr. Stone, I am going to need you to come into the station and answer some questions regarding an on-going investigation," Brooks said.

Jonathan panicked and tried desperately to calm himself and think logically. He said, "I don't know what this is regarding, but you will need to talk to my lawyer."

"Mr. Stone, we are hoping that it doesn't have to come to that as long as you cooperate," Brooks said. "When is the earliest you can come down the precinct?"

Jonathan knew that wasn't going to be possible. He was on an extended vacation seemingly out of the country. Brooks told Jonathan that he would need to cut his vacation short and that the police were investigating a murder and it required Jonathan's cooperation. He invited Jonathan to have his lawyer present, but assured him it wasn't necessary because he wasn't under arrest. In fact, Brooks told Jonathan that he wasn't even a suspect at that time, although the detectives weren't ruling anyone out. He told Jonathan that he thought the police had the shooter but were covering all their bases.

"Well, my lawyer will be in touch," Jonathan said. "In the meantime, I will look into changing my flight to see if I can get in by Friday."

"We truly appreciate your cooperation," Brooks said.

Jonathan hung up the phone and wrung his hands. He picked up the phone to call his lawyer, but then hung it up again. He decided instead to call his assistant to let her know he would be coming back early and to reschedule his travel. He then called his lawyer and told her the whole story from soup to nuts. She asked if there was anything he was leaving out, and Jonathan assured her that he told her everything.

"Are you sure?" his lawyer insisted. "You have the privilege of lawyer/client confidentiality. Is there anyone else who knows that you know this kid?"

Jonathan told his lawyer that Shirley brought Jermaine's gang-affiliation to his attention. This opened up a whole new line of questioning. She next wanted to know if Shirley suggested putting eyes on Jermaine and what her role was in the company.

"She is a twenty-year vet who came over from our competitor," Jonathan answered. "She mentors a few of us from time to time."

Shirley had, in fact, worked with Jonathan on occasion, and his lawyer gravitated to that mentor relationship. "So, this was more than a suggestion? This was a directive," his lawyer implied. "She pretty much told you to find out more about Mr. Beasley."

Jonathan knew that it didn't go down like that. Shirley told him to fire Jermaine, and he fought against it and landed on finding out more about his gang affiliations.

"Was that your idea or hers?" the lawyer asked.

"It was mine," Stone confirmed.

"But she didn't fight it," the lawyer asserted.

Jonathan was silent and got a sense of where the conversation was going. He concluded that it was better for him to not say anything else. Lawyer/client privilege aside.

"Listen, Jonathan!" the lawyer said. "I am going to do some homework on this case to find out who they are holding and what they have on them. This may indeed be perfunctory, but whether it is or not we have to find a way to make sure this does not land with you. You understand?"

"Yes...yes...sure!" Jonathan said.

He hung up the phone and sat wondering what he had gotten himself into. He desperately wanted to call Shirley, but now he was thinking that it was not such a good idea. She was the one who suggested that he take an extended vacation until everything calmed down. Now he wondered if it was Shirley who connected his name to the crime. He couldn't figure out how they got his name, especially after his PI died.

###

Brian and Dookie got home from school while it was still early. They got wind that Earl was in the hospital, but realized it was too late to go visit. They instead headed to hang with some of the new members gathered down near the playground.

"Rottweilers! Where's your mind at?" Brian said.

The phrase was a familiar colloquium amongst the members. They believed it got its start from Rico and Barry saying it as a call-and-response to one another back in the day. Rico had since moved to the suburbs to raise his growing family, and it was hard to catch up with him. Every once in a while, Barry used to come through to see the old gang on his days off, and share embellished tall tales about how rough the streets were in his day.

"Chilling Bee!" Matthias said.

Matthias went to high school along with most of the same members, but didn't move around the way until the age of ten. He came from a home of two hard working parents, and his reason for joining the gang was really to make more friends with people who had his back. He approached Earl right after his fourteenth birthday and told him he wanted to be down. Earl gravitated towards the attention and liked that these young kids were looking up to him. He ignored the tough-guy exterior and put him through initiation.

Brian didn't take to the attitude of Matthias. "Yo! Drop the 'tude!" Brian said. "We are all your family here."

Matthias rolled his eyes.

"What's that all about?" Dookie chimed in.

Brian knew exactly what it was all about. He could see a lot of his brother, Dookie, in Matthias. He figured that Matthias would shake it when he was ready. There were five new members at the park with more on the way.

Brian turned to a scrawny kid named Craig.

"What's happening tonight?" Brian asked. "You guys are just chilling?"

"Nah!" Craig said. "That dude Jermaine told us he wanted to go through some other initiation since he missed ours."

"I guess you guys didn't train us right," Matthias interjected.

Dookie didn't realize that they saw Jay or that he was even back around. Matthias told him that Earl handed the keys back over to Jermaine late the night before. Craig told Brian and Dookie how he rolled up on them while they were wilding out.

"What does that mean?" Dookie asked.

"Drinking, smoking, straight West Coasting!" Matthias answered. "He didn't like that."

Brian asked if anyone was carrying. Matthias claimed he didn't remember, but knew that Jermaine was on his way and would tell Brian and Dookie everything.

While they stood there, Alexander and Cyrus rolled up and joined the group. Along with Matthias and

Craig, there was Rudy, Tim and Stevie. Rudy and Tim were cousins. Both of them had parents from the Caribbean who arrived in the states within a few months of each other. Stevie was sixteen, the same age as Dookie, and more reserved than the other members. He had always been a gang affiliate, but never chose to join until then. He was a foster youth, a ward of the state, and was about to age out of the system. He thought the gang would provide a sense of family for him before his future became truly uncertain.

It was ten minutes after the hour, and Jermaine was late. The gang was becoming pessimistic about whether he would show and wondered if he forgot about them. That was when they saw him turn the corner with a bag full of items.

"Rottweilers, where's your mind at?" Jermaine said. "I am glad to see that you all made it. Are we missing anyone?"

"Yeah! Where's Earl at?" Matthias asked.

"Earl had a rough night last night and won't be joining us today," Jermaine said. "He's getting some necessary rest and hopefully will be able to be back with us soon."

Brian and Dookie gave Jermaine a look because they knew that Earl was in the hospital and was not likely to be back soon, if at all.

"I was reminded today that the mission of the Rottweilers is to make men out of boys," Jermaine said. "I was hoping Cheech and Earl would be here to help me, but Brian and Dookie will need to fill in."

When Cheech and Jermaine came in five years ago, Tony taught them principles that set them apart from everyone else their age. Jermaine pulled several binders out of his bag.

"It started with knowledge of how and why we began," he said.

He went over the gang history and how due to over-policing, drug infestation, and a lack of options, older teens would mentor younger teens on how to stay out of trouble. That philosophy began to wane when Brian and Earl came in and Rico and Barry took off, but they never lost the mission of who they truly were. A brotherhood.

Jermaine pulled small toys out of the bag and spoke about the need to build trust. Brian had heard about this. Even though he never went through it. He knew it had to do with team building.

"That's right!" Jermaine replied. "We are learning our history and building trust today. Whose down?

The gang members gave a weak cheer.

"I said. Rottweilers, who is with me?" Jermaine repeated.

Jermaine screamed it this time loud enough for people passing by to hear him. This time the Rottweilers yelled back at the top of their lungs.

"Then form a circle!" Jermaine demanded. "This is how we used to initiate folks."

Jermaine circled them up and ran the new recruits through a series of exercises while having them repeat the gang history. They were holding each other up. Catching each other as they fell. Hugging out success and sometimes failure. At the end of about two hours, Jermaine led them through a ritual where they each got a stone and discussed their greatest dream and biggest obstacle to getting there. They then tossed the stone representing the obstacle and replaced it with a stone for accomplishing their dream. They circled up again in brotherhood, having grown closer and with a sense of not only who they were, but where they came from.

"From this point on, you are no longer friends," Jermaine said. "You are brothers."

As they hugged it out, Jermaine pulled one last item from his bag. It was the "Principles of Being a Rottweiler" and was hand written on index cards.

"When I came in, we had to learn this by heart and be able to recite the principles at the drop of a dime,"

Jermaine said. He handed out the index cards and gave the guys a week to commit them to memory. "You get to determine the punishment for the man who let's down his brotherhood."

As Brian, Dookie and Jermaine cleaned up, the new members were coming up with far worse penance for not remembering the principles than Jermaine could ever dream of.

"That was fun!" Dookie said. "How come we stopped doing that for initiation?"

"Like I said, we lost our way after members left," Jermaine said. "We have to commit to staying on the path from this point on."

###

Donna was closing the arcade for the night. She saw Jermaine walk by and realized that he did not have late classes. He was scheduled to help close the books that evening, knowing she was overwhelmed with new projects. Business was on a downturn with students in school all day, warmer weather and spring sports. Jermaine had promised to drive up business with the installment of new popular machines. There was rain in the forecast and that would help, but Donna was a little miffed and waited to see if Jermaine was going to even acknowledge her. He didn't, and she ran to the door and called after him.

"No class tonight!" Donna said.

"What's that supposed to mean?" Jermaine responded.

Donna picked up on the double entendre and made the most of it.

"Whatever you think it means," Donna said.

Donna was ten years Jermaine's senior, but still young enough to be flirty with him when she wanted to be.

"Well, I am going to take it at face value and hope you meant I didn't have any courses tonight," he said.

"I guess you can take it that way too," Donna smiled. "I thought you were going to help me close tonight so I could focus on this new inventory."

Jermaine realized he totally forgot and had the feeling of egg on his face. He told her he could stop by after he dropped his things off. Donna offered for him to leave the things in the arcade.

"I am closing up soon, and I wanted to talk to you anyway," she said.

Jermaine thought about it. He had other things to put his focus on at the moment, but instead chose to honor his commitment. He walked back inside, and Donna held the door for him.

"What's up?" Jermaine asked. "I'm not in trouble, am I?

"No, not at all," Donna said. "Julius came by a few hours ago and said that your friend Earl was in the hospital. I wanted to check in on you and see how you were doing."

Jermaine appreciated the check-in. He really had not stopped to see how all this was impacting him.

"I'm sad that it had to happen, but being in the hospital, talking to Earl's dad....it gave me a new perspective."

"Yeah, how so?" Donna asked. "You're not thinking about dropping out of school, are you?

"No! Nothing like that," he said. "On the contrary, I realize that I need to step up and be more of a leader. I had some good people mentor me when I was coming up. My step-father, Greg. My homeboy, Tony. People invested in me to get me to a place where I saw value in myself."

"So, it's your time to give back?" Donna asked. "I can feel that."

Jermaine pulled out the ledger for the month and looked at the numbers compared to the quarterly average. He saw Donna's dip in take home, and Donna reminded him that they needed to plan for the reduction in customers before business started to decline.

"You said you had some ideas," she said.

She then realized that Jermaine was trying to change the subject and told him that they could review the books later. She was more interested in Jermaine's plan for becoming a better leader. Jermaine told her that it had to start right where he was by providing more spaces for kids and adults alike to pull together. Jermaine looked around the arcade and shared his idea of setting up activities outside.

"Like, like a mobile arcade," he said. "Something for the little ones to do while they watch their older siblings play sports."

Donna thought of carnival games where they sold bracelets or tickets. Jermaine thought that they could offer them for free as a way to draw people into the arcade.

"The prizes would be tickets for things they collect at the shop," he said.

"Once they come in the door we got 'em," Donna said. "Great idea! But who is going to work the stations?"

Jermaine thought of his new recruits, and Donna didn't like it. She considered them all hoodlums.

"Whoa, Ms. Priss!" Jermaine said. "First of all, my crew are not hoodlums. We are making men out of boys. Second of all, beggars can't be choosers. I am trying to teach these kids about economics and financial literacy. Tools they don't pick up in school."

Donna was caught up on the term "we" and her mind started putting pieces of the puzzle together. "Are you the leader of that gang?" she asked. "Is that why you and Cheech and Earl are so tight? You're the ones that got that boy killed?"

Jermaine was taken aback. He didn't expect that kind of response from Donna. Someone from the same hood he was from. He didn't know if he should tell her the full story. He assumed that she must have known. She saw him with Dookie and Brian. She knew that he hung out at the corner, but he had been away from direct leadership since he started working with her. Now he was going in full-on and would be investing in the gang members all the time. This was what he believed he was called to do. He risked losing not only her business, but also her mentorship if he told her he was the gang leader.

"Donna! You are jumping to conclusions," Jermaine said. "The Rottweilers had nothing to do with that guy's murder. We are part of the solution, not the problem."

He saw the distress on Donna's face. She could hardly sit or stand. He could tell immediately that she no longer felt safe around him because she fidgeted at his every motion.

"So, you *are* the leader?" Donna asked bluntly.

There was no hiding from the truth now. He was backed into a corner with nowhere to go.

"I am!" he said. "That is my clique! Ride or die. We are brotherhood."

Donna started to shake. She told Jermaine to leave.

"I can't have you in my office," she said. "Have you been casing the place? Planning for a break in?"

Jermaine didn't know where all this was coming from. They had been working together for nearly three months. Doing community service and getting to know each other on a personal level.

"Donna, you know me!" he said.

"I don't know you," she said. "I thought I knew you. The Rottweilers? My kid brother was a Rottweiler."

Donna had never talked about a younger sibling. As much as they had shared with either other; he had no clue that Donna had a brother and wanted to know more about him.

"That's until your gang got him killed over some petty shit when I went away to college," she said. "That's all I know about gangs."

Jermaine was broken and didn't know what to say. He got up to leave after almost being brought to the point of tears for the second time of the day.

"I'm sorry!" he said. "I didn't know."

"Yes, you did!" Donna said.

"I swear! I didn't know," Jermaine insisted.

Donna pointed to his right arm.

"Let me see your tattoo!" she said.

"My what?" he said.

"Your brand." Donna corrected herself.

Jermaine pulled up his sleeve and revealed a brand he received when he was sixteen years old after one year with the Rottweilers. On his arm there was a symbol of a wave and a letter "r" at its crescent.

"How did you know about this?" Jermaine asked.

"It's for my brother, Roderick," she said. "The whole gang showed up at the burial site with this on their arms less than a week after he passed. It became their symbol."

Jermaine reached for his bag and pulled out a book on the history. He was upset that he didn't know this. He had just reviewed the history of the gang with the new members for over two hours. He should have known. He turned to the page with the symbol on it and opened it for Donna to see. They read it together:

Why we choose peace over war? Why we value life over death? RIP Brother Rod.

Both of them were crying now and found themselves in need of each other for support. They hugged tightly. Neither one of them wanted to be the first to let go. They wept bitterly. Donna for the memory of her brother, who had died more than ten years ago, and Jermaine for a fallen gang member whose memory was forever inscribed on his arm and whose death would lead his mission moving forward.

They finally released their long embrace. Jermaine left without words. No words needed to be said. They both knew that everything was made right with them and that they shared a bond that would be unbroken. Words could be said another day. Right then, they needed to leave words unspoken and allow the gravity of the task before them to sink in.

###

Roxie and Renee were playing in the living room as Jermaine was coming out of the shower after a very full and heavy day. He shooed the girls into their room so he could get some peace and quiet. Renee told her mom that Brother was being mean, but Denise realized that Jermaine had a long day and could use some space.

"Come on girls! Brother is tired," she said. "He will play with you in the morning. It's past your bedtime."

The girls sighed but complied. Meanwhile, Jermaine noticed that there was still food on the stove and made himself a hot plate. Denise tucked the girls in and read them a bedtime story. Jermaine had become proficient at ear hustling and could make out their conversation from the kitchen.

"Mommy! Is Brother going to move out?" Roxie asked.

Denise was caught off guard and asked Roxie where that question came from. The girls knew he was almost finished with his associates degree, and he was working. They loved their brother, but the house was cramped with him there, and they liked playing in the living room sometimes.

"It's late girls," Denise replied. "It's way past your bedtime."

"I know Mommy, but brother's bed takes up almost the entire space, and we can't have our friends over," Roxie said.

"Your friends can play in your room," Denise replied. "Why are you girls discussing Brother not being here anymore?"

The girls got real quiet. Jermaine pretended not to be listening, but in spite of his exhaustion he was also curious about why they didn't want him there. In his mind, he treated the girls well. He wondered if people were beginning to talk about him.

"I just thought he was going to move out when he was done with school," Renee said.

"He might!" Denise suggested.

"I meant high school," Renee said. "We always have to save dinner for him."

"Yeah and we have to be super quiet in the morning so we don't wake him," Roxie added.

"Your brother is normally up and out of the house before you girls are even wake up," Denise defended. "Are people at your school talking bad about Brother?"

The kids at school were asking if he was still living there with them although it was none of their business.

"It's time for bed girls," Denise said.

She tucked the girls in, turned off the light and walked down the hall to her room. She was none-the-wiser that Jermaine was privy to the whole conversation.

Jermaine was exhausted emotionally and physically and now his mind spinning with what he'd just overheard from his sisters. He thought maybe if he took summer courses, he could finish his degree and get a job. He was finally enjoying school and didn't want to throw it all away, but he also didn't want to be a burden on his family. Now he wondered who else felt like he needed to move out. Maybe Denise thought the same thing and maybe even Greg.

He thought about calling Greg. Greg was remarried now and had a young son of his own he was probably investing in and Jermaine thought he wouldn't want to hear from him.

As he brushed his teeth, he took a good hard look at himself in the mirror. He knew he was being called to be an example to these young members and a leader of men. As he pulled out his sofa bed and rested his head on his lumpy pillow, he made the decision to start acting like the leader he claimed to be. He drifted off to sleep.

###

Cheech was out on the corner smoking a cigarette in the middle of the day as if waiting for someone to arrive. He figured the crew was probably caught up with a million other things and the homies, Charlene and Veronika, had been on the low. Cheech was always on the move. Earl was still in the hospital in the deep ocean of a coma. Cheech had recently been by to visit him, but it just made him depressed. He hadn't seen Brian, Dookie, Ted or any of the new members, since they went through their initiation with Jermaine, and he started to wonder if he missed anything.

As he started walking up the block, an unmarked car rolled up on him. Cheech thought it was the police looking for someone to harass early in the day. Unfortunately, it wasn't the police, but rival gang members still awake and cruising from the night before.

"Yo, Cheech!" a rival named Fuego called out. "It looks like we caught you out here all by yourself. You ready for this beat down?"

Cheech took off running, but was out of breath before he could even make it around the corner. He ducked down, hoping the car would pass him, but he was unlucky for a second time and was spotted right away.

"You should know you can't out run us," Fuego said.

The rivals were out for a little fun. They taunted Cheech and just wanted to humiliate him a bit before doing any damage.

"My brother tells me your man Earl is in the hospital, Cheechie," Fuego said. "I heard that he got ahold of some of that laced heroin that was put out there a week ago."

They started to hit and punch Cheech, but his mind was on Earl now.

"What, what do you know about it?" Cheech said as he was covering his head from the incoming blows.

"I know that he should have been careful about what he puts in his body," Fuego said. "My man Chachi told me that fools are dying off of that stuff sold at that spot off the Eastside."

"What spot?" Cheech demanded. "Tell me, Man."

The rivals stopped punching long enough for Fuego to talk to him.

"Listen!" Fuego said. "The only reason I am going to tell you this is because I don't want to see your boy die."

Fuego got down almost nose to nose with Cheech, who was battered and bruised. He told him about pills being sold at Market that were laced with PCP.

"But there is some crazy shit in there that doctors are calling Killer Coke," Fuego said. "Over at

Metropolitan West, they just figured out something that stops the brain damage."

Cheech tried to speak, but was too beat up to get the words out.

"Alright boys!" Fuego said. "We have had our fun here."

The rivals headed back to the car. Fuego yelled back to Cheech who was still slumped over.

"Get your boy to Metro West!" he said. "He'll live!"

As the car drove off, Cheech worked to pull himself off the curb. He headed back up the block but still didn't see anyone. He reached for his phone, but the screen was smashed from the loss he had just caught. He knew Jay wasn't home, so he had no choice, but to try to make it to Earl's family. He walked up the block and up the stairs to the door. Tanja answered.

"Cheech, oh my God, what happened to you?"

"I fell off my bike!" Cheech said. "I'm alright!"

"Come in and wash off or something!" Tanja insisted.

Cheech was out of breath and worked hard to squeeze out the words he needed to say. "There is no time for that," he said. "The streets are talking. That stuff Earl took. Jay said it had a brand on it. It's dangerous. We have to get him over to Metro West before it's too late."

"What, what? How do you know this?" Tanja asked

"It doesn't matter how I know," he said. "What's important is that Metropolitan can help him."

Tanja ran into the house and told Amber who immediately called the hospital. The family arranged an emergency transport to the new hospital within a matter of minutes. Cheech walked back down the stairs and made it halfway home before he found a curb to sit on and passed out.

He woke up to the buzzing of his smashed phone. He couldn't answer it, but he saw it was Jermaine. He hoped that he would leave a message. No sooner than

Cheech wished it, he saw a faint message between the cracked glass:

At Metro West with the family! Come through!

Cheech was in no condition to make it to the hospital or to even stand up on his own. He was comforted to know that Earl was being taken care of and hoped that Fuego wasn't lying to him about Metro West having the antidote. Cheech passed out again and this time was awakened by some of the new gang members on their way back from the basketball court.

"Yo! Yo! That's our brother!" Rudy said.

"Get him up!" Cyrus said. "Yo, Tim, bring him some water."

The gang members got him to his feet and leaned him up against a car. They called Jermaine and told him what was going on. Jermaine had learned from his previous mistake with Earl. He put in his Uber account as well as the destination, and the members immediately got Cheech to the ER which happened to be connected to the main hospital at Metro West.

Cheech woke up hours later with Jermaine by his side.

"Jay!" Cheech said. "How did you get here?"

"I was right next door," Jermaine said. "The new recruits did good by getting you here."

"How is Earl?" Cheech asked.

"He's still out, but he's going to live. Thanks to you and that beat down you took!" Jermaine said.

"You heard about that?" Cheech said. "Fuego told me about that junk they are pushing over on Market. He saved Earl's life."

Jermaine wasn't so quick to thank Fuego. He knew that the only reason he knew about the drugs was because Fuego's new gang members were mules for the dealers over there. His boys were about to get snitched out, and he figured he'd make good. Cheech figured that either way it saved Earl's life and he was thankful.

"Are you thankful for that beat down you got handed?" Jermaine asked.

"If it meant helping Earl, then 'yes,'" Cheech said. "My mother used to say that you have to break a few eggs to make an omelet."

"Well, I don't make omelets!" Jermaine said. "But, I am glad Earl is okay."

The nurse came in with a wheelchair, told Cheech he could be released and asked if he wanted a wheelchair to go down in the elevator.

Cheech propped himself up. "No!" Cheech said. "I feel great. I don't know what you put in these IV bags, but I have to know the street name for it."

"Too soon, Bro!" Jermaine exclaimed. "Too soon!"

###

The detectives that Cheech had hoped were in the car were elsewhere. They were sitting in an interview room at the precinct as Jonathan and his lawyer walked in. Jonathan sat down, and his lawyer sat down right next to him.

"Can I offer either of you a cup of water?" Detective Santiago asked.

Just as Jonathan was about to answer, his lawyer, Ms. Adebayo, lifted her hand and Jonathan paused.

"We are fine," Ms. Adebayo replied. "We got some while we were waiting."

Santiago and Brooks looked at each other.

"Counselor, just so you know, this is not a deposition," Brooks stated. "There are no lawyers here. We are just asking your client questions that we expect him to answer truthfully. The only communication that we are going to ask you to have is directly with your client."

"Well, I thought you asked us both if we wanted water?" Adebayo replied.

"I did!" Santiago replied. "And I am sure that doesn't require you to answer for both you and Mr. Stone."

"Understood!" Adebayo conceded.

"So, Mr. Stone! I just want to confirm that you are not under arrest and that you are here on your own volition and by your own will," Brooks asked.

"On my own will? I didn't choose to be here," Stone replied. "I was enjoying my vacation that I had to cut short...."

Adebayo whispered in Jonathan's ear.

"So, you are not here on your own volition?" Brooks continued.

"Yes! I agreed to come in and answer some questions," Stone abruptly reframed.

"Good!" Santiago said. "You are free to leave at any time."

"I will stay for the duration of questioning," Stone replied.

Brooks pushed a button on his small handheld recorder, then opened a tablet and began on a list of questions. He asked exactly how long Jonathan had worked at Quarimoc Industries and how long he had been supervising interns during that time. He then asked if he had ever worked with colleges in Kansas before.

Adebayo whispered in Jonathan's ear.

"I have worked with colleges throughout the Midwest," Jonathan replied.

"Does that include Kansas?" Brooks asked again.

"Yes! I have recruited interns from within the state of Kansas."

"Thank you!" Brooks replied.

"Within the state of Kansas, have you worked with any community college interns?" Brooks asked.

Jonathan knew that the detectives already knew the answers to their questions and began to get frustrated. Brooks asked the names of the community college interns he had worked with.

"I have only worked with one," Stone answered. "Mr. Jermaine Beasley".

"How did Mr. Beasley get selected out of the hundreds of qualified candidates in our state?" Brooks asked.

Jonathan told Brooks that he was recommended by his professor, Bruce Wright.

"What led you to choose the community college here?" Santiago asked.

"It was a strong program with some published authors and awards," Stone answered. "We figured we would call the economics department and see if we could get some names. Professor Wright recommended Mr. Beasley right away."

"We?" Brooks asked. "Who was part of the selection team?"

Jonathan rattled off the names of his colleagues. Santiago was curious if any corporate executives were part of the selection team. Jonathan told the detectives that reps get to select, interview and train the interns for the most part.

"Does anyone have seniority on the team?" Santiago asked.

"Pablo has been around the longest, but Shirley has the most experience," Jonathan answered.

Adebayo whispered in Jonathan's ear again, and Jonathan immediately asked what their questions had to do with. Brooks and Santiago looked at each other and decided to cut to the chase.

"Mr. Stone, there is footage of you at a coffee shop on Main Street with the murder victim," Brooks said. "We believe you were instructed by someone to put a trail on your intern, Mr. Beasley, after you got word that he had gang affiliations."

"Don't answer anything!" Adebayo said out loud.

Brooks kept talking despite the lawyer's interruptions. "We also have an anonymous tip that Quarimoc was not happy that Mr. Beasley turned up clean," Brooks continued. "So, your company put their hired man back out there to do more digging, and that's when he turned up dead."

"My client is through here," Adebayo insisted.

"Ms. Adebayo, sit down," Santiago demanded. "No one has accused your client of anything."

"No one told me to send him back out again," Stone blurted out. "I sent him back out there myself."

The room went silent. Adebayo demanded that the previous statement be removed.

Brooks reminded Jonathan that he was free to go at any time, but whatever he decided to say would be entered into evidence.

"Do you want to take a moment with your lawyer?" Brooks asked.

Adebayo tried to whisper to Jonathan, but Jonathan suddenly realized that he had said too much, and he found the need to cover his steps.

"I didn't break any laws, and I damn sure didn't have that guy killed," Stone said. "I was not even in the state during the time of the murder. Someone is trying to frame me. It could be one of you or it could be someone at my company, but my reputation is impeccable. That's all I have to say."

"Just one more question Mr. Stone," Santiago insisted. "Who else knew that you were having Mr. Beasley followed?"

Adebayo looked Jonathan dead in the eyes, and after a long pause, Jonathan answered.

"Shirley. Shirley Betancourt."

###

Bianca was working on mid-term presentations with a group of new interns in the honors class. The interns had the chance to get feedback from their company as well as from Bruce and now it was time to present. Jermaine had been working with his academic counselor to see if his units could push him towards graduating that summer, and now he needed to confirm with Bruce that his internship was going to yield him the units he needed.

"Are we any closer to getting the work-experience units?" he asked.

"I haven't heard from Jonathan in over a month," Bruce said. "He seems to have fallen off the face of the Earth."

Jermaine told Bruce that Lance had been meeting with him on his project since Jonathan left. Bruce wasn't sure Lance could sign off of the internship since he wasn't the person who set it up, but Jermaine decided to give him a call anyway.

Bianca caught Jermaine while he was on his phone and shot him a wink. His classmate, Tom, saw the interaction and gave Jermaine a smile. The phone rang in Lance's office and he picked up.

"Hello! Lance Durdenhurf speaking," Lance said.

"Hello, Lance! It's Jermaine Beasley. Do you have a minute?"

"Sure, Buddy! What can I do for you?" Lance replied.

Jermaine told him about the signatures he needed in order to get work-experience units toward graduation. He added, "Jonathan started the process, but never had the opportunity to complete it."

"Good news!" Lance said. "Jonathan is back at his desk. I guess his vacation got cut short. Do you want me to transfer you to his line?"

Jermaine was perplexed and a little thrown by the runaround. He thought it would be easier to just continue to work with Lance, even though he knew Jonathan was the one who started the process.

"Sure! Put me through," Jermaine said. "Hey wait! Does this mean we don't get to work together anymore?"

Lance assured him that he wasn't going anywhere and that he could call him anytime.

"You have my personal cell from when I called you from the laundromat," Lance said. I will patch you through to Jonathan."

Jonathan was in his office with the door shut as if he did not want to be disturbed. He was frantically deleting files from his computer when his phone rang. He tried to ignore it but saw Lance motioning from outside of his glass that it was Lance on the line. Jonathan wondered why Lance didn't' just walk over. He picked up.

"What's up Lance?" Jonathan said. "I'm kinda playing catch up over here."

"Hello, Mr. Stone. I mean, Jonathan," Jermaine said.

Jonathan was caught off-guard by the last person he expected to hear from. Now he wondered if Jermaine was in on blaming the murder of the PI on him too. Jermaine told him that Lance transferred the call from his office and that he could call back later if he was busy.

"I'm a little busy, but what's up?" Jonathan said.

Back in the classroom, Bianca had made her way over to Jermaine and started doing things to distract him. He tried to shoo her away, but she was quite persistent.

"So, I am doing my best to graduate this summer, and my counselor is hoping that my work- experience units can count towards graduation," Jermaine explained. "Were you able to complete that paperwork with the Career Office at my school?"

"I'm sorry Jermaine," Jonathan said. "I've been a little distracted over these past couple of weeks."

Jermaine was being distracted too during his phone conversation. He moved to the hallway which didn't help matters as Bianca followed behind him.

"I understand," Jermaine said. "Is there someone else at your office I should get to complete it? Maybe Lance or Pamela?"

This last suggestion threw Jonathan for a loop. "Are you working with Pamela?" Jonathan asked.

Jonathan was dumping computer files into oblivion while Jermaine was being unbuttoned in the hallway.

"Yes, while you were gone, Pamela and Lance assisted me," Jermaine said. "How was your time away?"

"Not long enough!" Jonathan replied. "Things are getting hectic around here."

"Well, I for one am glad you're back," Jermaine said "I can't wait to update you on my project."

"Yeah, yeah! That's good, Kid," Jonathan said. "I can't wait to hear about it."

Jonathan came across an email from his contact in Junction City while he was still on the phone with Jermaine. It read,

They know it was you!

As soon as he opened the file, it loaded a virus on his computer, and his computer crashed. Jermaine could hear Jonathan clicking his computer keys frantically, but Jonathan had gone silent.

"Jonathan?" Jermaine called.

While Bianca was kissing Jermaine's neck, Jonathan was silent. In a fit of desperation, Jonathan pulled a gun out of his desk drawer.

"Mr. Stone!" Jermaine called out again. He pushed Bianca away to get her to stop.

"I gotta go, Kid," Jonathan said.

As Jonathan went to hang up, the receiver missed the base. On the other end of the line, Jermaine heard a fatal gunshot ring out and then a panic in the office with people were rushing in and out. Jermaine hung up, fully aware of what had transpired. He stared at Bianca who saw his shock and decided Jermaine was best left alone. She retreated back into their classroom.

###

CHAPTER TEN

Sethi closed the laundromat for the evening and straggling customers made their way out. He heard some of them talking about a planned rally to take place in the park, and he wanted to find out more. Sethi interrupted the conversation and asked what the rally was for and two patrons pointed to the flyer posted on the board next to the door. The young man, in his mid-thirties assumed Sethi would know what material was hanging in his laundromat.

Sethi looked at the flyer and saw that it had to do with what people were calling "the wrongful conviction of Patrice Denton." The woman with the man was convinced that there was a cover-up going on, and that the police were trying to pin the murder of a Black man on one of the young sisters. Sethi knew the two patrons were a couple who had frequented the laundromat for the last six-to-eight months. He gathered from their attire that they were working professionals, but he also overheard that they attended local activist meetings.

"Do you know this woman who is being accused?" Sethi asked. "Patrice Denton?"

"The arrest happened right in front of the store down the block," the man said.

Sethi's mind was flooded with images of the day of the arrest and Jermaine telling him about Patrice and that he went on a date with one of her friends.

"Did she do it?" Sethi asked.

The couple knew he was being naïve, but his mere question garnered angst.

"Just because they pick up a sister doesn't make her guilty," the woman said. "They don't have any evidence. Nothing that would stand up in a court of law."

"I didn't mean to say that I believe that she is guilty or innocent," Sethi said. "Not that you would know. I am just trying to figure out why they arrested her and why people are demanding her release."

"We are just tired of the criminal justice system unfairly policing our youth," the man said.

"Innocent until proven guilty in a court of law."

"They target the poor because they know most of them have limited resources, can't post bail, and don't have legitimate legal representation," the woman said.

"Well, instead of a rally, I say we do a fundraiser," Sethi said. "Let's figure out a way to raise her bail and get her out of there. I know several of the business owners around here. I can call them together."

"The people who own businesses around here don't care about the community members," the man said. "They just want our dollar, to take it out and to spend it in their suburbs."

Sethi knew it to be true, but he wanted to change that narrative.

"It's time to demand that business owners contribute to where they do business," Sethi said. "So, whether you like it or not I am starting a movement. Are you with me?"

The couple was shocked at Sethi's passion for the issue and didn't know how to respond.

"I guess we are with you," the man said. "We still believe a rally is important though. To bring light to the unfair arrest. I heard that there might be a major corporation behind the murder."

Sethi was interested in how that narrative got out there, but it turned out to be just word on the street. There was more and more evidence coming out that was pointing the finger toward Quarimoc.

"A few people are saying that a company from outside of the area hired the victim to follow one of their new interns to find out dirt on him," the guy said.

Sethi immediately knew the company was Quarimoc, and the intern they were referring to was Jermaine.

"Have the police confirmed this?" Sethi asked.

"They have not denied it -- which is all we need to know," the woman said.

"The rumor is one of their representatives who was a part of it nixed himself late yesterday afternoon," the man said.

Sethi only knew Lance and immediately figured that it must have been him. "That can't be true," Sethi said. "That must be made up." Sethi was in total denial until the woman pulled up the article on her smartphone.

"Here! The company is based in Missouri and is publicly owned," the woman said. "Its name is Quarimoc."

Sethi looked at her phone and scrolled to see if he could find a name. He didn't see Lance or Pamela's name mentioned. Only Jonathan Stone who set up the contract for the machines and was Jermaine's initial rep. Sethi was convinced that the suicide must have been connected to the crime. His shock left him speechless. He handed the woman her cellphone back.

"I will be at the rally as well," Sethi said.

He was tempted to call Jermaine on his cellphone, but it was late. Instead, he saw the couple to the door, said his goodbyes and locked up after them. When he got home, his mind was spinning. He couldn't sleep, so he decided to do his own research. He knew that Jonathan was the original rep for his area and found an article with a picture from the training luncheon showing Jermaine on his original team. He looked up information on the murder victim and found out that he was a low-level street PI for hire. Sethi was fully aware of Jermaine's gang affiliations by now, and it was not a far jump to see how the puzzle fit together.

Sethi still couldn't figure out why the police would pin the murder on Patrice. He was dedicated to finding out more about her. He looked up the arrest and the arresting officers. He found out that Patrice was arrested as a minor on a felony charge for assaulting an officer. It turned out the officer rolled her ankle during the arrest of minor drug possession, but the article said the injury happened as a result of Patrice resisting arrest. The judge threw the case out, saying that there just wasn't enough evidence. It just so happened that the detective assigned to the murder investigation was also associated with the case that was thrown out.

"They finally got their girl," Sethi said. "Smells like a set-up to me."

###

"Can you grab my bag, Sis?" Earl said.

Earl was out of his coma, but his muscles were so atrophied that he was wheelchair-bound for the following couple of weeks. The doctors had already scheduled physical therapy to begin right away, but at that moment he just was excited about sleeping in his own bed.

Earl's family was there to gather him and his belongings to take him home. Thomas pushed him to the elevator, and his mother pushed the button while his sister, Tanja, carried his belongings.

As the elevator opened and the family entered, Earl looked down at his phone and saw that he was getting an incoming call from his older sister, Amber, who was not able to get the day off from work.

“Hey, Sis!” he answered. “What are you up to?

Amber was just getting home and was glad to hear Earl’s voice.

“Hey, Old Man!” Amber said. Old Man was her enduring term for Earl since he was a kid. “Are you on your way home?” she asked.

“We are getting out of the hospital now,” Earl said. “I can’t wait to see how Pops is going to get me into the back seat of his car.”

“Boy, you can walk!” Amber said. “Stop messing around.”

Earl wasn’t playing. He had lost a lot of muscle memory when he was under.

"You don't even want to know what it's like," he said.

"Oh, I know," Amber said. "I work with patients who can't hold their fluids."

Earl wished it was just his fluids he couldn't hold. "I coughed the other day, and all the pudding came out."

"Well, don't expect me to clean up after you," Amber laughed.

"Gee! Thanks, Sis!" he said.

"I will see you when you get home," she said and hung up.

Thomas assisted a feeble Earl into the car while holding on tightly to support him from the possibility of a fall.

"Great job, Old Man!" he said.

Thomas opened the door for Phyllis and then made his way to the driver's seat and took off. As they approached the house, Earl saw signs, streamers and balloons. He lit up.

"Look at this!" Earl said. "My family does love me."

Thomas, Phyllis and Tanja looked at each other confused.

"Uh, we didn't do none of this," Tanja confessed. "Maybe Amber knows something."

There was a makeshift ramp made of plywood boards on the side of the staircase that led up to the front door. Thomas pulled the wheelchair out of the trunk and loaded Earl into it to get him to the door. After an initial push, he was able to get enough momentum to get Earl on to the porch. Phyllis opened the door to a pitch-black house. She hit the light switch, and as soon as Earl got in the house Amber and the Rottweilers jumped out with a shout: "Welcome home!"

"I got home, and I found your friends decorating the outside of house," Amber said. "I told them that you were on your way, so we should surprise you."

Earl was surprised to see the old and new members of his gang all together in his home. Once Thomas got him seated, they walked over to him one by one to show him love. Again, he was overwhelmed. Jermaine and Cheech walked over to check in on him as the younger members congregated out on the porch.

"How you feeling, boy?" Cheech said.

Earl saw Cheech's wounds. "Better than you look," Earl replied. "What truck hit you?

"You know!" Cheech said, "Sometimes when you live by the sword, you die by the sword."

Jermaine told Earl how Cheech caught a beat down out on the boulevard in broad daylight. He added, "But it was all for the best if you ask him."

"What's that supposed to mean?" Earl asked.

"It was that fool Fuego who told me what was in your system and that Metro West had the antidote," Cheech said.

"I told him that he just felt bad because his dope boys were the ones that were peddling it over on Market," Jermaine said.

Earl told them that he wasn't anywhere near Market. Cheech and Jermaine looked at each other quizzically. Now they wanted to know where Earl got his product from. Earl had to think, the coma had messed with his memory as well. He remembered that it was from somebody out on the corner that night.

"One of the new members?" Jermaine asked.

"It had to be," Earl said. "We were all doing Molly."

"But none of them got sick?" Jermaine said.

They lowered their voice out of the earshot of Earl's family. Cheech told Earl that he thought somebody was trying to put the drop on him. Jermaine again wanted to know if it was one of the new guys.

"I think we have a mole in the hole," Cheech said.

Jermaine was determined to find out who it was. He knew that Earl almost died, and he wanted the mole smoked out. They looked out on the porch and tried to make some deductions.

"Matthias was the one acting out when I first got there," Jermaine said.

"Yeah, that's because he was high," Earl said.

Cheech didn't think it could have been Matthias. He thought it had to be somebody who was on the low.

"Who was handing out the pills?" Jermaine asked.

"There were people passing them around," Earl said "But I was the last one."

"So, there was only one left when it got to you?" Cheech asked.

Cheech looked over the group again. He realized that the math didn't add up. How could they have been perfectly counted?

"What are you saying, Cheech?" Jermaine asked.

"I'm saying that whoever took just before Earl emptied out the whole bottle and slipped the poison pill in there before passing it to Earl," Cheech said.

Now Jermaine wanted to know who passed him the bottle. Earl was mad now. He knew exactly who it was and was upset that he didn't see it coming.

"It was...it was...Cyrus," Earl said.

Cheech left to go confront Cyrus, and Jermaine followed him outside. He told Cheech now was not the time. Cheech was still sore from his beat down, but, for a second, he forgot about the pain.

Jermaine walked Cheech past the group and down the stairs.

"All right, Rottweilers!" Jermaine said. "It's time to mobilize."

The gang members said their goodbyes to Earl and began to head out. As Cyrus started to head home, Jermaine got his attention and told him to hold tight for a minute.

Cyrus was a little hesitant, but followed orders. Earl's family was making sure Earl was comfortable, but Earl told them he wanted to sit outside for a while, due to being inside for the past few months.

"I can use some fresh air," he said

Thomas got him up and onto a chair on the porch and then went back inside. Jermaine and Cheech walked Cyrus up the stairs and joined Earl.

"Cyrus, how do you like being a part of the Rottweilers so far?" Jermaine asked.

"It's cool!" Cyrus replied. "I really liked the team building. That was dope."

"I'm glad you liked it," Jermaine said. "Listen, Cyrus, is there something you want to tell us?"

"Like what?" Cyrus asked.

"Like why you roofied me?" Earl blurted out.

Cyrus was stunned and felt cornered. He couldn't figure out how they knew it was him. He was looking for a way out, but there wasn't one. His only options were to either lie or come clean.

"Man, don't hurt me, Man!" Cyrus begged. "Your family is right inside."

"You almost killed Earl, and you expect to just walk away," Cheech said.

"I'll tell you what you want to know," Cyrus said. "Just don't hurt me."

Cyrus spilled the beans that someone he didn't know paid him two-hundred dollars to slip a brown pill to the leader of the Rottweilers, and they told him exactly how to do it. The man told him to make sure the leader was the last person and that Cyrus was to empty the container and leave the gang leader the pill he gave him.

"He promised that there would be no way it would ever come back to me," Cyrus said.

"You messed up, Son!" Cheech said. "You would have never been found out if you put more than one pill back in the bottle, but now your time is up."

"Wait!" Jermaine said. "That pill wasn't meant for Earl. It was meant for me."

"Two-hundred dollars, you said?" Cheech asked.

"Yeah, two-hundred dollars," Cyrus said.

"Why do fools have to be so predictable?" Cheech said.

"You know who did this?" Jermaine asked.

"Yes, and so do you."

###

"Mom! I'm bored!" Roxie screamed from her room.

It was dumping rain outside, and Denise was not in the mood to get the girls dressed to go splash in puddles. She suggested that they build something on their Minecraft game, hoping that would divert their attention. She was still in her pajamas and cozied up on the couch reading a novel that she had been planning on getting to for some time now.

"That's what we have been doing all morning," Roxie screamed back.

The Renee, Roxie and Denise never made eye-contact as they called out from the bedroom to the living room. This prevented Denise from noticing all the eye rolling and the attitude dripping from behind the walls.

"We want to go somewhere," Renee said.

Denise knew this typically meant the library on a day like today. The girls had gained an infatuation with reading, and the books they had in their rooms had been read twice over.

"It's raining girls," Denise said. "You'll catch pneumonia." Denise regretted her statement as soon as it came off her lips.

The girls loved putting on their rain gear. They had fancy jackets, boots and umbrellas that they didn't have the opportunity to use much, but with the spring showers they got to play dress up and show off their stylish looks.

The house went quiet, and Denise assumed that she had won the battle, but it was a little too quiet. She should have got up to see what the girls were up to, but she was so cozy underneath her blanket with her fuzzy slippers poking through the bottom.

Renee and Roxie finally emerged from their room dressed to kill, head-to-toe in rain gear with their umbrellas opened. They both stepped onto the living room carpet and turned it into a makeshift runway.

Denise was speechless. She knew she should have headed this off before it went too far, but her novel was just getting good, and she was in her happy place. Just then, she heard footsteps coming up the stairs and thought that the mailman must be working late. As the door opened, she saw it was Jermaine getting ready to strip off his wet clothes and get into something warm and dry.

"Hi, Sweetie!" Denise said. "How much do you love your mother?"

Jermaine looked and saw the girls in their rain gear and Denise underneath her blanket and heard the question for what it really was. Although he was cold and wet after his walk from the bus stop, he knew it was not that much more work to take the girls back out again given he was already drenched.

"All right!" he said. "But I'm not standing out in the rain with them while they run around. I will walk them over to the arcade."

The girls gave a cheer. "Thank you, Brother!" they screamed.

Jermaine zipped his jacket back up and grabbed his mother's big golf umbrella from behind the door. The girls ran outside and immediately started splashing on the sidewalk in every puddle they could find.

Jermaine turned to Denise, as he closed the door behind him. "You owe me a steak dinner tonight," he said.

He quickly herded his sisters away from the curb, and they began to walk towards the arcade. The walk was plenty long enough for the girls to get lots of splashing in before they arrived, yet short enough for Jermaine to get out of the rain before he got sick.

They arrived at the arcade, and it was packed. It was school break and apparently everybody had the same idea. There was a huge trash can for umbrellas at the front door, and Jermaine and the girls placed their umbrellas in it. It was kind of an honor system and more than once someone who was caught without rain gear had swiped an umbrella, leaving an unsuspecting patron to make it home in the elements.

Donna was happy because she was raking it in. There were lines for almost every machine. Jermaine had brought the girls to the arcade before, but he had never introduced them to Donna. He sought her out and found her reloading tickets on a machine. Jermaine surprised her as she turned around.

"You need some help with that?" he said.

“Jermaine, what are you doing here? I thought you had school,” Donna said. “And who are these precious angels hanging onto you?”

The girls were playing shy and holding tightly to Jermaine's rain soaked hands.

“These are my bodyguards,” Jermaine kidded. “These streets are real, and I hired some protection to watch my back.”

The girls laughed.

“The only catch is they only take payment in arcade tokens,” he said. “Ain’t that a trip?”

Donna pulled out a handful of tokens and offered them to the girls.

“Well, because I need you around I will make sure they get their money,” Donna said.

They were taught not to take anything from strangers, so Jermaine let them know that Donna was a friend and she would be sure to make him work it off. His comment earned him a swat on the arm.

"What do you girls say?" Jermaine prodded

"Thank you, Ms. Donna!" Renee said.

"Thank you, Ms. Donna!" Roxie repeated, as she held out her hand to collect the offering.

"Well, that's not fair," Donna said. "You girls know my name, but I don't know yours."

The girls looked at Jermaine again, wondering if it was okay to tell Donna their names. Jermaine told them that Donna was a friend and was safe. Renee introduced herself and her sister, but Roxie was still playing shy and held on to her brother's hand tightly. Jermaine let the girls know that Donna owned the arcade and that she used to work in the community center and still returned from time to time.

"Yes, Ladies! I have been fingerprinted and my background check is in order," Donna joked.

She made the girls laugh which caused them to relax and loosen their grip on their brother. He told the girls to go find a game to play. He promised to keep a close watch from where he stood. Roxie finally let go of Jermaine's hand and followed her sister to the Mario Brothers games where they watched some of the other kids, as they waited their turn. Jermaine stood over in the corner a safe distance away, but close enough to make sure the girls didn't escape his vision.

There was an awkward silence between Donna and Jermaine in the midst of the noisy arcade. It was finally broken after it became deafening to them both.

"I'm sorry I didn't tell you that I was gang affiliated," Jermaine said. "It was important for you to know, especially since we are working together, and you are mentoring me."

"It's okay!" Donna said. "I can understand why you would keep something like that close to your vest. I'm sorry that I didn't tell you about my brother. That might have been useful information for you to know."

"That's your business," Jermaine said. "I can understand why you didn't. It must be difficult to share with people."

There was more awkward silence as they watched the girls who had finally made it onto an arcade game and were popping in tokens two at a time.

"Were you and your brother close?" Jermaine asked.

"The closest!" Donna replied. "He was not only my brother but also my best friend. It was hard for me to go away to college and leave him, but my parents insisted that I didn't let my scholarship go to waste by attending CC. After he was killed, my grades plummeted. I went on academic probation and then on dismissal. I had to petition to get back in. The dean was sympathetic to my situation and put me on an ed plan that included meeting with a therapist once a week for grief counseling."

Jermaine had no clue about Donna's background. He imagined how hard it had to be to lose a sibling while trying to stay in school. He was ten-years older than Renee and was still convinced that he would lose it if anything happened to her. They both looked over at the girls who were in their own world at this point.

"Did the counseling help?" Jermaine asked.

"Yes, for a while, but they gave me prescription medication too," Donna shared. "That didn't turn out good for me."

"What do you mean?" Jermaine asked. "Bad reaction?"

"No!" Donna said. "They worked a little too well. It made me forget all my troubles. I was in La- La Land all the time. I became dependent. I went from depressed and anxious to drug addicted. Talk about a roller coaster!"

"Well, look at you now," Jermaine said, trying to add some levity to the conversation.

Donna knew it had been a long road to get to where she was. One that she didn't wish on her worst enemy. She lost twenty pounds and destroyed all of her relationships with friends and family members. She started dating a dealer of prescription meds who kept her high all the time. Her parents tried to get her away from him, but she wasn't having it. She started doing great in school because of the Adderall, but in order to fall asleep at night she would cocktail the Adderall with Xanax. Wall Street didn't help. It was the land of the walking dead over there.

"If you think there are drugs in the hood, Wall Street is ten times worse." she said.

Jermaine was trying to keep a straight face, but he could feel his judgment creeping through. He realized that she accepted his gang lifestyle, even though she blamed it for killing her brother. Now that she felt comfortable enough to open up to him about her past, he found himself judging her for it. He wanted to walk away. Maybe to go check on the girls. Maybe to even slip out the door into the rain and disappear, but he fought the inclination. He stayed and listened. He knew this wasn't easy for Donna so he stayed and listened.

"So, how did you get clean?" he asked.

"I hit rock bottom," Donna said. "I know I told you that leaving Wall Street was my choice, and it was, but I found myself at the end of my rope. Waking up in places and not knowing how I got there. Compromising deals for the sake of making a profit. If I didn't get out when I did, I would be dead or out of my mind by now. So, I cashed out."

"Just like that?" Jermaine asked.

"Yep! I took my stock options and walked away from millions," Donna said. "I was too embarrassed to come home, so I checked myself into a rehab in the country and spent the next nine months getting clean."

"What made you decide to come back here?" Jermaine asked.

"I missed my mom and dad," Donna said. "They didn't know where I was after college, and they took the death of my brother harder than me. I knew if I showed up at their door they would take me in, so I just showed up. No phone call. No letter. No nothing. I got a job at the community center, and I never looked back."

Jermaine thanked her for sharing her journey and said how proud he was of her of overcoming her demons. He reached out to give her a hug. This was their second hug, and it felt natural at this point. Only this time they were not alone. They were surrounded by a hundred teens and pre-teens all caught up in their own worlds.

There was a break in the weather just as Renee and Roxie ran out of coins. They both ran up to Jermaine and pulled on his jacket.

"Brother, Brother! The sun is coming out. Let's see if we can see a rainbow and make a wish," Roxie asked.

"Are you ladies ready to go home already?" Jermaine asked.

"Yes! I am ready to splash you with a puddle," Renee said.

Donna walked them to the front door and pulled out their umbrellas from the huge can of umbrellas and walked the three of them out to the sidewalk.

"You get him once good for me," Donna said.

Renee smiled, and Roxie grabbed Jermaine's hand.

"Thanks, Friend!" Jermaine said

Donna was planning on catching up with Jermaine the next day. He was out early and told her that he would get to the arcade as soon as he got back.

"You have to work off those tokens I paid your bodyguards," she said

Renee giggled and then splashed Jermaine with a puddle when he least expected it.

###

Lance walked through the campus in search of Bruce's office. He was already running late because his parking pass was not at the gate, and he had to circle around the lot a few times. Now he was all turned around on the map and finally stopped a groundskeeper to try to point him to the Business and Entrepreneurship Building.

Mark, the groundskeeper, told Lance that the building he was in search of was clear on the other side of campus. "Past the gazebo, then the garage and then a fountain," Mark said. "You would be better off driving over there."

Just then Lance realized he was parked in the wrong lot and that was why his pass wasn't there.

"Drive over there and park in the green lot!" Mark reiterated.

Lance saw that Mark had a cart and tested the temptation to ask him for a ride.

"I heard that you guys are pretty nice at this campus," Lance said. "Any chance I can bum a ride?

Mark was a little hesitant. He would have to load everything back into his cart and drive all the way over there and then drive back. Lance noticed the hesitation and realized that it was not quite the lunch hour. He pulled out a crisp ten-dollar bill.

"It will take you five minutes, and lunch is on me," Lance said.

Mark threw his equipment into the back of the cart and cleared out the front seat. "Hop in!" he said.

Lance hopped into the cart without hesitation, and the cart took off. The campus was beautifully landscaped with stunning architecture. They passed the lot where Lance was supposed to park, and he realized that he would have a long walk back. That was if he would be able to find his car at all.

Mark dropped him off in front of the building without a minute to spare. Lance thanked him and handed him the ten dollars. He ran up the stairs to the third floor and searched out Bruce's office in the midst of a bank of faculty offices. Bruce was inside with soft music playing, as he went through items on his desk.

"Professor Wright?" Lance asked.

"Yes!" Bruce said. "You must be Mr. Durdenhurf."

"Please! Call me Lance"

"Lance, you must be exhausted having just flown in this morning," Bruce said. "We could have met later in the day."

"No, this worked out better," Lance assured. "I have to work my way upstate to meet a few clients for dinner, and I wanted to make sure I met you."

"So sorry about what happened to Jonathan!" Bruce said.

Bruce acknowledged how shaken the office must have been.

"It's really tragic," Lance said. "It was hard for many people to even come back into work for a few weeks after the incident. Many of the staff worked remotely from home or just stayed on assignment. This is really a horrible way for the two of us to meet."

"Any idea about why he did it?" Bruce asked.

"No clue!" Lance said. "The detectives went to find anything on his computer or at his desk that might give way to a motive, but everything was wiped clean."

Bruce thought that wiping his computer clean was a clue within itself. Lance questioned if someone else might have wiped his files.

"You don't think..." Bruce began.

"There were a lot of people in that office before the police arrived," Lance continued.

"Interesting!" Bruce said.

They sat quietly before Lance broke the silence by commenting on how nice Bruce's office was.

"I am happy with the view," Bruce said. "My last office overlooked the parking lot you are in."

"Uh, yeah, about that!" Lance began.

"You didn't get lost did you?" Bruce asked. "I gave you precise directions in my email."

Lance confessed that he was parked clear on the other side of campus, but luckily copped a ride from one of the groundskeepers.

"Anyway, I am here now," Lance said. "I know Jermaine needs some documents signed, and I thought I would meet with you before I met with him."

Bruce pulled out the paperwork. All the documents had Jonathan's name all over them. Bruce thought that they might have to start all over, but Lance assured him that it was nothing a little correction tape wouldn't fix.

"Are you sure?" Bruce asked.

"Do you have another form?" Lance asked.

"No!" Bruce replied.

"So, it is what it is," Lance said.

Bruce didn't have any correction tape either, but Lance kept some in his bag for situations like this.

"I make a lot of mistakes and sign way too many contracts to run back to the office for duplicates,"

Lance said. He did a quick read of the forms, then placed Wite Out tape on Jonathan's name and put his own name on top of the Wite Out.

"So, who needs to get this in order for Jermaine to get his work experience units?" Lance asked.

"The Career Center and then they will get it to his advisor," Bruce said.

"Where's that at?" Lance asked. "Can we walk it over now?"

"Sure! You can," Bruce said. "It's back over by where you parked."

Lance implored Bruce to take the walk with him. He wanted to hear about the projects his other students were working on in his class. He offered to buy Bruce some lunch for his troubles.

"I can use the walk. It's nice outside!" Bruce said.

"And you have a beautiful campus. It makes me want to go back to school," Lance said. "I heard that you are one hell of a professor."

They left the office and started walking to the other side of campus. Bruce taunted that Lance wouldn't survive a day in his class. Lance welcomed the challenge.

"There is a little bit of myself I see in Jermaine," Lance said.

"What does a rich kid like you from the suburbs see in Jermaine that's anything like yourself?" Bruce asked.

Lance knew that Jermaine had done his share of dirt, but he believed the same thing that made Jermaine gravitate towards the grime was the same thing that made him great. Bruce felt uneasy and didn't like where the conversation was going, but Lance asked him to hear him out.

"I have some natural talent, but I struggled in high school," Lance began. "When I got to Uni, I knew I wanted to make money, so I learned to hustle. I got into sales, and I did whatever it took to claw to the top."

"Jermaine might be in the streets, but he has integrity," Bruce said.

"I'm not doubting his ethics," Lance said. "I'm sure after Enron and Tyco, professors spend enough time talking about integrity and ethics. I'm talking about the willingness to do what it takes to get the sale. That's special."

"He has that, but he also has the book smarts," Bruce said.

"So, he should be able to go twice as far as me," Lance said. "I am sure I will work for him one day."

They made their way to the Career Center and turned in the form at the front desk. They then continued on to the cafeteria. Lance saw Mark and pointed him out as the person who gave him a lift.

"Mark, you never gave me a ride anywhere!" Bruce said.

Mark looked back and saw it was Bruce and that he had Lance with him. "You never asked and you never offered to buy me lunch!" Mark said. He flashed the ten dollars Lance gave him.

Bruce was getting a better picture of Lance and said, "I see your hustle."

"Hey, I am just trying to stay ahead," Lance said. "How do you think I was able to land a spot at Quarimoc right out of college?"

"Don't tell me!" Bruce begged.

Lance told a story about dating the boss's dog-ugly daughter as an intern. He knew that they frowned upon hiring interns. He didn't have two nickels to rub together, but he offered to buy the execs lunch every day. He even found out what they liked in their coffee and had it waiting for them when they got in. Lance told Bruce that he marked down everyone's birthday and sent them expensive gifts.

"I left that internship that summer eight-thousand dollars in debt," Lance said.

He paid for lunch, and they found a seat to continue their conversation. Bruce informed Lance that his approach to winning was contrary to everything he taught in his class.

"How do you justify that kind of spending?" Brue asked.

"I know it doesn't meet today's standards of ethics, but I not only got the job, but my signing bonus more than made up for the lunches and gifts."

"Well, I hope that's not what you think Jermaine is like," Bruce said. "He is going to do everything by the book."

"And he's still going to win," Lance said. "I admire that. He's a winner. He's overcome some hardships. Poverty, loss, even subpar education, and he is coming out on top."

"He still has to finish his degree," Bruce said.

"Why?" Lance asked. "The greats never do. They find their passion and go. He is ready. He's figured out his market and his approach. Now he just needs encouragement. He needs you and me in his corner. What do you think?"

"I looked at his latest mock-up. It can definitely catch steam," Bruce said.

"That's what I'm talking about! That's what I wanted to hear!"

###

The word of protest was hot on the street. Residents and community members were up in arms. "No justice, no peace," was the rallying cry. People carried their picket signs to the gathering area. Those without signs were provided materials and the space to create what they wanted to say. A rather large woman with a bullhorn was gathering people to a grassy area in the park where the march was set to begin. The streets were cordoned off, and police were prepared to stop traffic. The people were silent but out in force. They believed that Patrice was innocent and got framed. Popular Black leaders, authors, poets and politicians made the trips to support the cause. The cause...the cause...the cause had gone national.

Earl, Cheech, Brian and Dookie had been busy spreading the word that Quarimoc was the group behind the shooting and that Patrice was the fall guy. A storyline that caught wind in the news was that one of their sales reps for the area was being questioned by police about the murder and had killed himself.

Sethi had also been an advocate since finding out that the police had it out for Patrice. He had rallied local business owners and raised money for bail by letting them know that the police were holding Patrice without any real evidence except what was purely manufactured. That gave the movement legitimacy. The money and tax dollars in those areas made politicians take notice. They could no longer dismiss the claim as a "conspiracy theory." The police were also not as resistant as the courts might have hoped. Detectives on the case wouldn't rule out the possibility of Quarimoc's involvement and demanded access to Jonathan's phone, tablet and computer.

The rally began and the woman with the bullhorn was getting everyone pumped up. She screamed into the bullhorn in order to get a call-and-response from the gathered crowd of nearly three- hundred-and-fifty people and counting.

"What do we want?" she said.

"Justice!" the crowd replied.

"When do we want it?" she said. She knew the crowd didn't have to be primed at this point.

They screamed back, "Now!"

"Let's take it to the streets!" she said.

As the marchers left the park, the police cleared the streets and stopped all cross traffic that threatened to cause harm.

The woman continued her rallying cry and received the appropriate response.

She said, "No justice!"

"No peace!" the crowd replied.

There was some pushing that got the police officers' attention. The organizers quickly intervened to let the rabble-rousers know that was not what they were there for.

New mothers were pushing strollers. The elderly joined hands. Some raised their fists in an air of Black Pride/Black Power. Others sang and hummed, as they marched on. Still others chanted, going back and forth between monikers on their way down the street.

"The people united will never be divided," they said. "The people united will never be divided."

A smart aleck threw a bottle. This time Rottweilers intervened. They identified the culprit and shook him down. No punches needed to be thrown. The kid knew who they were and who they rolled with. He didn't want any trouble. Stevie, the older of the new members, made the message clear.

"Cut that out or go home!" he said.

The kid was scared out of his mind. He thought he was being cool and his behavior was quickly checked.

Sethi and some other business owners handed out material about the crime. It read: *Find the real murderers*!

Some didn't believe that the police were doing all they could to solve the case. It had been going on for six months, and the community felt the investigators might have given up.

Ultimately, the rallying cry was heard. Bail was accepted. Patrice was released, but the war was not over. The people were not satisfied and wanted answers for what many saw as another young Black body laid waste in the street. Maybe not at the hands of the police, but something far worse. Corporate money. Capitalism gone rogue. Above the law. Able to operate in the shadows and have the poor get blamed.

As the marchers dispersed and the people went their separate ways Cheech and Earl recognized they needed to find some way to keep the momentum going.

"What do we do now?" Earl asked.

"We need to organize," Cheech said.

"We ain't never organized anything in our lives," Earl replied.

"That's alright!" Cheech replied. "That's why we have Jay around. He will know what to do."

Brian and Dookie came and joined the conversation. "Yo! Where is Jermaine?" Dookie asked.

They needed Jermaine to stay low after finding out that somebody tried to drug him and take him out. Brian and Dookie didn't know that the pill that got slipped to Earl was meant for Jermaine.

"Dang!" Dookie said. "So, you took the hit for Jay?"

"I guess I did," Earl said. "And if it wasn't for Cheech getting his ass whupped I probably would have died."

"That's for real though!" Brian said. "So, what are we going to do about Cyrus?"

"Jay says we have to take it to a vote," Cheech said. "That's how Tony dealt with internal strife."

"I got my vote right here," Dookie says putting his fists up.

Earl had to remind Dookie that Cyrus was a brother now. He had forgiven him.

"He came on for the wrong reasons, but he's learned some things," Earl said.

"How can we know we can trust him?" Brian said.

"He is going to have to earn our trust back," Earl replied.

Cyrus had to tell the whole gang what he did. It wasn't going to be easy, but he had to decide for himself if it was worth having people question his intentions and calling him out on every mistake. He would be excluded from some activities. It was going to take some time for things to become normal for him.

"He'll come out a better person if he lasts," Cheech said.

Brian and Dookie headed home as Cheech pushed Earl's wheelchair down the street back toward the avenue.

###

Sethi decided to put up more flyers on his way back from the rally. Jermaine stayed behind at the laundromat and was acting as Sethi's proxy in his absence. He kept the area clean, assisted customers, and answered the questions he could. Meanwhile Sethi stopped by local grocers and struck up a conversation with the owners. Most of the business owners in this section of town rented their space and worked to cover their overhead through sales. This meant that customers, like in most places, were taking the hit on any rent, utilities or fee increases. Sethi realized that the grocers' products were different in these stores compared to the wealthier parts of the city. Many products had expired dates, the produce was browning, there were few organic choices, and the overall quality of food was just unhealthier -- high in sugar, soybean and high fructose corn syrup. This was much different from his grocers in the suburbs, where he drove from at five in the morning to open the laundromat. He didn't hesitate to approach owners and managers.

“Why do you not offer more healthy options for our community members?” he said. “You are killing your customers.”

“These folks don’t know the difference,” the shop owner said. “They are looking for the best deal.”

“These outdated canned goods and the rotting produce,” Sethi said. “How can you sleep at night?”

“It’s what the truck gives us,” the shop owner said. “You think I picked out the bad stuff to get a cut rate?”

“That’s exactly what I think,” Sethi said.

The fact was that a box of string beans in Jermaine’s neighborhood cost the same as a box of string beans downtown, and the distributors knew that the customers in poor areas didn't have the advocacy to complain. Sethi wanted to change all that and buck the system.

"Why do you care so much?" the shop owner asked.

"Why don't you?" Sethi said. "This isn't just where we make a buck. It's where we spend our time and invest in futures. If you see an injustice you have to call it out."

This was a part of the reason Sethi was putting up his flyers, but the other part was that he believed that if the powers-that-be could do it to the people who lived in Jermaine's neighborhood, then they could do it to the shop owners too.

"They already do by giving me outdated products," the shop owner said. "What do you want us to do?"

"We need to ban together as business owners and be the voice for those who don't have a voice," Sethi said. "We can't just stand by and be silent and take our slice of the pie and then go home to our wives and kids in the suburbs. This is where we spend ten, twelve, sixteen hours a day. This is our home too."

The shop owner took a flyer and posted it in his window. He then walked Sethi out and shook his hand. As Sethi made his way up the block, he walked past some of the younger Rottweilers heading in the opposite direction. He was immediately intimidated by the on-coming group. The hairs rose on the back of his neck as the group of young, Black and Latin teenagers walked his direction. As they got closer, he recognized them as the kids Jermaine led.

The Rottweilers saw the flyers Sethi was handing out.

"I see you are down for the cause," Alexander said.

"I am!" Sethi said.

"That's all right!" Alexander continued.

"In fact, Jermaine is keeping shop right now over at my laundromat," Sethi said. "You should come over and learn how to become business owners yourself. Jermaine is well on his way."

"That sounds dope," Craig said. "We may take you up on that."

"May?" Sethi repeated. "Do you want to keep giving your money to people who don't live in your own neighborhood or own the shops that serve you? This isn't how most other communities work you know. Most shop owners live in the communities they work in. They don't take that money somewhere else."

The Rottweilers were listening. They were already motivated from the march earlier in the day. Ownership seemed so far off for them. Most of them came from welfare dependency, broken homes or low-income families. They didn't have mentors or examples of what ownership looked like.

"I am going to ask Jermaine to bring you guys by the laundromat after closing so we can talk," Sethi said. "He is on his way, and I know he doesn't want to leave any of you guys behind."

Stevie told Sethi that his grades were not strong in school, but Sethi let him know that being a business owner had nothing to do with grades. That it was about understanding key practices and having someone show him the rest.

"Nobody cares about us man!" Stevie said. "I'm about to age out of the foster system in a year and a half and then I am on my own."

"Even better!" Sethi said. "You have nothing to lose. You start tomorrow."

"What?" Stevie said.

"Ownership!" Sethi said.

Sethi wanted the Rottweilers to learn the ropes through paper trades in public companies. The teens agreed, and Sethi told them to bring their friends and he would have Jermaine set it up.

###

Back at the laundromat, Jermaine was hustling. Pushing baskets, sweeping, getting change and detergent, all while trying to manage the office. A customer came in fresh from the march and saw Jermaine managing the shop.

"Why did you skip out on the rally, brother?" the man quipped. "We could have used as many bodies down there as possible."

"Man, you know I wanted to be there," Jermaine answered. "Conflict of interest."

The man looked down and saw Jermaine's polo read, "Quarimoc Industries."

"I see!" the man said. "It looks like more than that, looks like a part of the problem. Why are you working for the enemy? Those folks got that young man killed?"

Jermaine tried to explain that it was more complicated than that, and he shouldn't be so quick to doubt his loyalty to the movement. Jermaine was for the people, but there were times to work from the inside. To keep your friends close and your enemies' closer.

"I hear you, but don't get dragged down in all that mess," the man said. "They are always looking for a fall guy, so the corporation stands and keeps its corruption intact."

The man walked out of the laundromat. He didn't have any business to conduct in there but just came in to rib Jermaine about not being at the rally. Now Jermaine wondered who he was. There were almost thirty people in the shop, and for some reason, the man had decided to pick on him.

Jermaine thought: "I'm over here busting my butt trying to serve folks, so they can do their laundry, and he stopped to give me a hard time."

Jermaine's mind was playing with him now, and he wondered if someone told him he was there. Or was the man ever part of the rally at all? If he was, did he attend the rally just to see who was and wasn't there? Or was it possible that he was another Quarimoc informant?

After Cyrus was paid off to try to have Jermaine OD, lots of thoughts had been flying through Jermaine's head about who was out to get him. He now realized he had to keep his inner circle tight. He saw Sethi walk through the door and was excited to finally get a break. Jermaine had to skip lunch and couldn't wait to get to the Chinese restaurant for some wings and rice with hot sauce.

"About time?" Jermaine said. "The rally ended over two hours ago."

"I had to make some stops," Sethi told him. "To talk to some business owners I rarely get to see. I also saw some of your friends."

Jermaine really didn't have many friends. At least none that Sethi would know.

"Cheech?" Jermaine asked. "I saw him pushing my friend Earl up the block about an hour ago."

"No, no!" Sethi said. "Some younger teenagers."

Jermaine thought to himself that maybe it was Dookie or Ted. Sethi told him that there were about five or six of them walking back towards the avenue. Jermaine immediately realized he meant the new recruits.

"Yes! The new guys," Jermaine said. "How did you know they were with me?"

"I don't know," Sethi said. "I just knew. The way they carry themselves."

Jermaine made sure that none of the gang members wore identifying colors, beads or bandanas. They didn't throw up gang signs or have a specific walk or call. That circumstance had been passed on to him by Tony when Jermaine first got into the gang.

"People should recognize us by the way we conduct ourselves," Tony would say. "We should stand out as not being like everyone else."

Sethi let him know that Stevie saw him with the flyers in his hands and stopped him to asked if he was down for the cause.

"And what did you tell him?" Jermaine asked.

"I said somebody has to be," Sethi said, as a way to throw a slight jab at Jermaine.

"You sound like a guy who just walked in here," Jermaine said. "He was asking me why I wasn't at the rally."

Sethi was immediately curious and wondered why someone would walk all the way over to the laundromat to ask him that. The guy was not there long, he just scolded Jermaine and disappeared. Jermaine described him, and Sethi knew exactly whom he was referring to.

"Middle-aged Black guy wearing a knit kufi? Yeah, I saw him at the rally," Sethi said. "He was by himself. He looked suspicious. As if he was looking for something or someone."

"Police?" Jermaine asked.

"Maybe!" Sethi answered. "I wonder why he came over here. It makes me think he knew you were here."

Jermaine was thinking the exact same thing and thought he was going crazy. Sethi wanted to call the police, but knew that was not how Jermaine handled things.

"So, what are you going to do?" Sethi asked.

"I will see if he decides to show his face again," Jermaine replied. "If he does, I will put somebody on him."

"Be careful! That's what they are saying you did when your friend was chased down."

Jermaine became curious how Sethi knew what people were saying. He immediately looked at Sethi sideways and wondered who he had been talking to. Sethi told him that he did his homework.

"I may not be the smartest in my family, but I am the most informed," Sethi said. "Working in the laundromat and searching Google has given me all the education I need to know about almost everyone."

Now Jermaine wanted to know what other news was spreading. The narrative was slowly changing in the media. It started with Patrice being a trigger man for the gang, to her being a trigger man for police, to her being a trigger man for Quarimoc, to her not having anything to do with it at all. Jermaine wanted to know what Sethi believed.

"I don't think she pulled the trigger," Sethi said, "But she may know who did."

As customers got a bit too close to the conversation, Jermaine pulled Sethi into his office and shut the door.

"I don't know who pulled the trigger," Jermaine said. "I don't even know if the gang set it up. That's Cheech's crew. They do what he says. I just know I didn't make the call."

Sethi pointed at Jermaine's polo and alluded to Quarimoc's involvement. Jermaine knew that Jonathan had something to do with that kid being out there and maybe even following Earl. He couldn't waste his time on theories and guesses though. He had bigger fish to fry. He had just found out that Cyrus was paid the same amount to slip him a poison pill as the PI who got shot.

"What?" Sethi asked. "How did you find this out? Never mind. Can Cyrus identify him?"

"Slow down!" Jermaine said. "This will all play itself out. Let's be patient."

"Be patient!" Sethi screamed. "One kid is dead. A young girl is in prison. The sales rep blew his brains out, and your friend OD'd on a pill that was meant for you. This is no time to procrastinate."

"Whoever is behind this may already know we are onto them," Jermaine said. "It's the cornered dog that will bite you."

"Well, they are certainly biting," Sethi said. "And it looks like they are spreading rabies."

###

Donna saw the flyer posted on her front door and pulled it down. Business was slow due to the rally, and she asked an associate to watch the arcade for ten minutes as she marched down to the laundromat less than a half mile away. She knew about the shooting and had promised herself that she wouldn't get involved. Her family history made it far too difficult to get too close to a conversation about murder, especially with the victim being so close in age to her brother. She had never been inside the laundromat in her two years of being in business and found her way to Sethi's office. She opened the door without knocking.

"Did you put this flyer on my store window?" she said.

Sethi was stunned to have Donna walk into his office, although customers had done it before. He had seen Donna before and knew that she owned the arcade. Sethi looked up from his books.

"Well, welcome!" he said "Why don't you come right in?

"I thought we were beyond asking permission for things once I saw this flyer on my arcade window," Donna said. "Mi casa es su casa, right?"

Sethi laughed and closed his ledger.

"I'm sorry I didn't ask your permission before I put the flyer up," Sethi said. "I did go in and speak to most shop owners beforehand. You were tied up, and I assumed you would be okay with it."

"And what do you assume now?" Donna said.

"That I was wrong," Sethi said. "And in order for you to walk all the way to my place to tell me about it, you must be pretty upset."

"Why did you assume I would be okay with it?" Donna asked.

Sethi knew that they shared a common interest in working with Jermaine, and Jermaine had helped him put his self-interest aside and become more interested in the community needs.

"I heard you were working with him," Donna said. "I am surprised that he is not here now."

"He was just a minute ago," Sethi said. "He helped watch the shop while I was at the rally. He went to get some food."

Sethi was curious what issue Donna had with the flyer. It seemed like more than just a case of not asking her permission for her to confront him. It was a personal matter and none of Sethi's business and Donna did not hesitate to tell him.

"Just because we share some time with Jermaine doesn't make us friends," she said. "He has helped me gain a wider perspective on the community as well, but you don't see me telling other shop owners that they should volunteer their time."

"Well, maybe you should!" Sethi said. "I would be down for that. I don't mean to invade your privacy, but we are in a crisis here. Sometimes it is easier to ask for forgiveness rather than permission."

Sethi read Donna's facial expression which had moved from one of anger to sadness. He decided to take a risk and find out more.

"Let's start over!" Sethi insisted. "Sit down! Maybe we can become friends."

"I have to get back to the arcade," Donna said.

"It looks like you have a lot on your mind," Sethi said. "I may not look like it, but I am a good listener. I obviously upset you. Something about the flyer caused it."

Jermaine walked into the laundromat and saw Donna in the office talking with Sethi. He didn't know what to make of it. He knew better than to interrupt grown folks when they were talking, so he ate his lunch at a table outside the door.

"Jermaine is back from getting food. I can ask him to watch the laundromat for a while longer." Sethi said. "Let me walk you back to your shop."

Donna looked down at her phone and saw her ten minutes were up. Sethi opened the office door for her and asked Jermaine to watch the shop for another ten minutes while he walked Donna back to the arcade. Jermaine nodded and gave a "thumbs up" with a mouth full of food. He tried to say goodbye to Donna, but she was already on her way out the door. Sethi had to catch up.

Donna was hesitant to open up to a stranger about the true feelings that the flyer brought up in her, yet Sethi was easy to talk to. He was very soft spoken with searching eyes. She felt comforted that her story would not spread like wildfire, but she had already spent almost a year in drug rehab hashing out her feelings to addiction counselors. She didn't see the need to bring up things that had been pushed down for so long. Her conversation with Jermaine kept her up that night with thoughts of self-medicating. She called her sponsor early the next morning to have her talk Donna back off the ledge and now this flyer had her spinning into oblivion again.

Sethi and Donna walked almost three blocks without any words being spoken. "It's okay!" Sethi said. "We can talk when you are ready. I see that whatever it is it isn't easy."

Donna began to tear up. "The young man who was killed," Donna began. "He reminds me of my brother. He was killed by a rival gang here in town."

Sethi paused. He wanted to give Donna space to say everything she needed to say.

"I know the flyer is about the young girl and her wrongful arrest, but I can't help but think: What if she did it and now we are all rallying in support of a murderer?"

"I can see how that would stir emotions," Sethi empathized. "Did they ever catch your brother's killer?"

"They arrested some people," Donna said. "Minors on lesser charges, but no one was talking then, just like no one is talking now."

Sethi knew that was the code of the streets. It was the same way where he grew up in Bangalore.

"We never think about how much hurt it causes to family members to not have closure," he said.

"You were in a gang in Bangalore?" Donna asked.

"Sadly, I was!" Sethi confessed. "And I hurt many people. We were not peacemakers, like Jermaine's friends. We were ruthless, doing whatever we could to survive."

Sethi didn't choose to come to the United States. His parents gathered all the resources they could to ship him out of the country, as they feared that either he would kill himself or the rival gangs would kill him. Those were the possibilities, or the legal system would sentence him to death.

"They have the death sentence there?" Donna asked.

"They used to when I grew up," Sethi said. "We didn't care. We weren't afraid of death. What could be worse than the lives we were living?"

"My brother, Roderick, was a gang member with the Rottweilers," Donna said. "He was my best friend. It really hit hard when he died."

"I imagine," Sethi said. "I hope you have people you can talk to when those feelings come up. Even if it is not a flyer left by some idiot, something is bound to pull at those emotions and cause you to spiral."

Donna wondered who Sethi turned to when he thought about all the people he hurt.

"Well to be honest," Sethi said. "I used to smoke a lot of ganja. That would suppress a lot of my emotions. Now I get proper sleep, eat right and exercise to make myself feel better."

"No counseling?" Donna asked.

"Not yet!" Sethi said. "It's not that I don't believe in it. It's just not my method of healing. We all have our things."

They made it back to the arcade, and Donna was much lighter. Donna was grateful that Sethi shared his story, and Sethi caught on that Donna made him do all the talking.

"Very sneaky of you!" he said

"Well, it helped me," she said. "Thank you!"

"Anytime!" Sethi said. "Take down the number to the shop and call me if you ever want to talk."

Donna wrote down the number before walking into her shop. Business had picked up since she left.

###

CHAPTER ELEVEN

Patrice got released from prison after scathing accusations of a cover-up, along with there being no charges or court case pending. It helped to have media, politicians and known activists support and even come to town for the rally.

She was back around the way, but did everything she could to avoid the circus. Veronika, Charlene, and she were at an undisclosed location, one they all knew to meet up at in case anything went down. The apartment was furnished and well-lit with nice pictures on the wall. It almost looked lived in, but also as though no one had lived there for a while. It was very clean, almost immaculate, as if there was a cleaning service that came through regularly. Unreal, like a model apartment.

Patrice hadn't touched her phone since getting it back. She imagined there were four hundred messages on it, and it would be next to impossible to get through them all, so she didn't bother to try. She moved in with her sister. Her parents were older, and her lifestyle had become too much on them. Her sister had a good job with the city, and they always got along, yet also stayed out of each other's way, so she asked if she could move in with her. Her sister and her long-term boyfriend were practically married without the rings. She kept most of her belongings over at his place but was maintaining her own apartment until the actual ring came. This gave Patrice amazing freedom to come and go as she pleased. Something she never had living under her parent's roof. But her sister did have rules:

Don't be bringing a whole bunch of people up in my place! No smoking! Let me know if you are having guests, especially if you have somebody sleeping over. Clean up after yourself, and if you break it, you replace it. Other than that, we will get along fine.

Obviously, that left out the option of committing high crimes, such as murder, kidnapping and extortion. People don't think of such things when they are putting together house rules. The parents tell the babysitter, "*Don't let them stay up past 9:00 p.m. or give them sweets or let them watch scary movies,*" but they never say, "*by the way, don't kill or kidnap my children.*" Maybe it's considered too much to ask.

As the homies hung out in this immaculate apartment, they rolled up a joint being sure to disengage the smoke detector before they lit up. Veronika passed the joint to Patrice.

"It must feel good to be out," she said.

Patrice was unusually silent. Almost eerily silent as she took a pull off the smoke

"You alright, homie?" Charlene asked.

"Yeah, I'm alright!" Patrice said. "I guess it's gonna take me some time to readjust to being out."

"They didn't do anything to you in there, did they?" Veronika asked.

Patrice shot a look at Veronika as if that question was off limits. In prison, there was always somebody who tried to test you. Patrice was fortunate enough to have people in there who had her back. She passed the blunt to Charlene.

"That's cool!" Charlene said. "So, everything's alright?'

"You can say that!" Patrice said.

"There's something you're not telling us!" Veronika said. "I know you P! Spill it!"

"I guess you can say that I met somebody," Patrice said.

The room went quiet as if all the air got sucked out of it. Charlene passed the weed back around to Veronika.

"I'm not tripping!" Charlene said. "It gets mad lonely in a spot like that. We all need somebody."

Veronika looked over at Charlene and then back to Patrice. She took a hit and blew out the smoke before asking Patrice how long she knew she was gay.

"For a while!" Patrice said. "Pre-teen at least. It just took the right timing and circumstance for me to act on it."

"So, they didn't turn you out in there?" Veronika kidded.

"No! Nobody turned me out," Patrice said. "We were cellies and just mad cool with each other until we finally made a move."

"Who made the first move?" Charlene asked.

Patrice took the smoke from Veronika.

"Dang! Y'all are nosey," she said. "I guess you can say it was me. We kinda were just talking and we both leaned in. It was just a matter of time."

"You miss her?" Veronika asked.

"Like crazy!" Patrice said. "Like, so bad that I want to get locked up again."

Veronika had known Patrice since junior high school and had never seen her like this before. She was happy for her and at the same time worried that she could do something stupid. Charlene took the blunt from Patrice and tried to find out where the relationship was headed.

"When does she get out?" Charlene said.

"Who knows? The court system plays games with your life as if you are not real. Changing your court date, moving you from place to place, putting you before a parole board that has no intentions of helping you. You hear about people in there that thought they were going to be in less than a year and have spent half their lives in prison."

"She doesn't have a release date?" Veronika asked.

"July next year. With good behavior and a good lawyer, possibly December."

"You're all lawyered up!" Charlene said. "I'm sure you could hook it up."

Charlene passed the trees to Veronika. Patrice's lawyer was her family's lawyer, and she didn't do a lot to get Patrice out. Charlene and Veronika encouraged her to not give up on love, but also implored her to not do anything to get herself arrested.

"That doesn't help anybody," Veronika said.

"I know!" Patrice said. "We will come up with something. For now, don't tell anyone about this, especially Cheech. You know he gets weird about things like this."

"We got you!" Charlene said. "Mums the word!"

The three finished the weed and aired the place out.

###

Denise was in the kitchen when Jermaine walked in. He had something on his mind, and she could tell, but she waited for him to start talking while she kept on cooking. He was able to get his work experience approved for credit which would finish up his units for the summer and make him eligible to graduate.

"You thinking about where you want to transfer?" Denise asked.

"No, I haven't thought about it," Jermaine said. "I think I am going to work for a while."

"Really!" Denise said.

Denise faked her surprise. She assumed Jermaine was considering employment, but she didn't know what had spurred it on.

"Yeah!" Jermaine replied. "It's time for me to get a real job and stop being a burden on you and the girls."

"What makes you say that?" Denise asked.

Jermaine summarized all that he overheard when the girls told Denise about his taking up space in the living room, eating up the groceries and using up her toilet paper. He felt it was time to grow up and move out on his own. Get a room or small apartment he could afford.

"You're not thinking about moving too far away from your mother, are you?" Denise asked.

"That depends on who hires me," Jermaine said. "I want to stay close. I want to see the girls grow up. Be around to beat up any boys who come trying to holla at them."

Denise laughed, but she knew the girls would love to have him close by.

"So, what brought on this change of heart?" she asked

Jermaine hesitated and then changed his words after taking a breath.

"It's time!" Jermaine said. "I'm going to be twenty-one soon and this internship is setting up my future prospects pretty well. When you know, you know."

"I guess you're right." Denise said. "Just promise me that you will go back to school one day and finish."

"I will, Momma!" Jermaine promised. "I will."

#

Roxie and Renee got home from school, and the house was buzzing again. They saw Jermaine on the pull-out couch wearing headphones, hard at work on his computer, and they tried not to disturb him, but it was inevitable with him being in the living room and their running back and forth. He put down his headphones, closed the computer and decided to take a break.

"How was school today?" Jermaine asked. "Did you pick up any financial wisdom?"

"Brother!" Roxie exclaimed. "They are not teaching us that yet."

"Well then, you have to learn it on your own," Jermaine said. He scooped up Roxie and sat her down next to him. "Do you want to see what I am working on?" he continued.

The girls got excited. They always saw him hard at work, but never got to see what he was actually doing. He opened his computer and showed them an earning sheet. He went from showing them small businesses to large corporations and governments and even various countries' economies.

"I'm doing word problems like this," Renee said. "They ask us what we would need to do to make our goals."

"So, you are learning financial literacy?" Jermaine said.

"Literacy?" Roxie asked.

"Yes!" Jermaine continued. "You are learning how to make and grow money. It's a rare thing that schools don't typically teach."

"We aren't talking about our own money," Renee said. "They are made-up stories".

"Well then, you have to pretend as if it is your own money," Jermaine said. "Show me one of your math problems."

Renee ran into her room and got her math book out of her book bag and hurried back. She turned to the page where they left off in school. She showed her brother a word problems involving Girl Scout cookie sales and ice parlor inventory. She then showed him a problem that hit close to home regarding candy machines.

"Ooh! This is exactly what Brother is doing now," Jermaine said.

"Buying candy?" Roxie asked.

"You're silly." Jermaine said. "I am trying to count how many quarters, dimes and nickels it would take for me to buy a candy bar."

"That's not what you are doing in college!" Renee exclaimed.

"Pretty much!" Jermaine said.

He related the math problem to corporations and how companies need to have stuff to sell and told the girls that they needed to buy or make that stuff before they could sell it.

"If Brother buys a candy bar for twenty-five cents, I need to find out how much I can sell it for to make fifty cents. That minus all of my expenses of buying and maintaining my machines, renting space and paying for electricity. That is what I am learning in college."

"Well, that's not what I am learning in fifth grade," Renee said.

"All that confuses me," Roxie said.

Jermaine tried to convince the girls that it wasn't as hard as it sounded, but if it were easy, anyone could do it. He wanted them to look at things differently than the other students in their class and put themselves in each of the word problems seeing themselves as the ice-cream-parlor owner or the girl scout.

"Then you will start to envision yourself as owners," he said.

The girls' eyes started to glaze over. He knew that was all they could handle for the day. He was boring them and that was not the goal.

"It is fun! But it also makes my brain hurt to think so hard," Roxie said.

"That's what coffee is for," Jermaine said.

Denise shot him a look from the other room.

"Just kidding!" Jermaine laughed. "Milk or juice for you girls."

###

With all the house a-buzz, Jermaine grabbed his books and headed to the coffee shop downtown. It was about a fifteen-minute walk, and the weather was nice. As he walked, he made a call to Bianca. When she saw his name up on her phone, she answered right away.

"Hey, Boy! It's been a while since I heard from you," she said.

"Yeah, sorry about that!" Jermaine said. "I was going through some things."

"Well, I'm not trying to disturb your flow. I know you are on your grind, as am I."

"How is your project going?" Jermaine asked.

"I just received a shipment of metal from overseas this week that cut my overhead to less than half," Bianca said. "My company is super excited about the savings that are being passed on."

"Wow!" Jermaine exclaimed. "It sounds like you are putting in work."

"Not so much that a Brother can't stop by and say 'hi' to a Sister," Bianca said.

Jermaine told her that he was running to the coffee shop to get some work done, but he wanted to see what she was up to later.

Bianca told Jermaine that she was trying to get out of her roommate situation and was looking at a place downtown, so she could be on her own.

"You should come with me," she said.

He couldn't. He had to put some work in before pleasure.

"I didn't know you were looking for a spot," he said. "Aren't you transferring?"

"Yes, but my company wants me to stay on full-time, and they are paying for me to go to the university here."

"That's dope!" Jermaine said. "So, you found a place?"

Bianca hadn't actually secured a place yet. She was still looking. The place she was stopping by that day was nice. It came fully furnished and looked like an executive suite at the Marriott.

"I can't wait to roll around with you in there," she said.

Jermaine smiled and tried to find out what she was doing later. "I was thinking about catching a movie around seven-thirty p.m."

"I can do a movie," Bianca said.

"So that's a 'yes'?" Jermaine asked.

"Let me get back to you in an hour to confirm," Bianca said. "I still have to get up early."

"No, that's cool. We could just grab some food and stay in and stream a movie," Jermaine suggested.

"Now, that I can do!" Bianca said.

Jermaine spoke of some ideas about food and he wanted to pick the food up on the way. But was shot down. Bianca wanted to order once he arrived.

"Make sure you stop by the drug store though," she said.

"No doubt!" Jermaine said. "I can get there around seven-thirty p.m. How does that sound?

"Perfect! See you then," Bianca said.

Jermaine hung up but was still about a block away from the coffee shop. That was when he realized that he needed to be with his boys at the laundromat that evening as they went over business ownership and trading stocks. He also hadn't seen Bianca in a while, and it was about that time. He called up Sethi to let him know he would be skipping the session that night and made sure it was okay.

###

The spotty internet at the local coffee shop was frustrating the hell out of Jermaine. After about an hour and a half of connecting and reconnecting, he called it quits. He had got through about ninety percent of his project. He looked at his watch, and it was six-thirty p.m. The "Rottweilers Investment Club," as one of the members coined it, was just getting underway, so Jermaine decided to pack up and see if he could catch the first half hour.

As he walked in, the laundromat was still buzzing with midweek patrons who came in after work to get laundry done. Commonly, the group met on the weekends, after the laundromat closed, but many of the Rottweilers now saw the club as a great way to meet up during the weekday and avoid hanging on the corner.

Jermaine's appearance surprised many of the gang members. He still had his books in hand, and they were suddenly curious about his Honors project. He had given them bits and pieces of what he was working on, but now was a perfect time to find out more.

Matthias spoke loud enough to get the attention of the rest of the gang. "Jay! What's up with your business?" he said. "We are all curious. I hear you are ready to drop something good on the hood."

"I don't know about all that, but I know I still got work to do," Jermaine said.

"He is being humble!" Sethi said. "What he is putting together is not only counter culture, but is also community focused."

"You are gassing my head up, Sethi!" Jermaine said. "There is a lot still on the drawing board. Besides, I just stopped by for a hot second to see what you guys are learning tonight."

Craig was upset that Jermaine wasn't staying. Sethi didn't have time to tell them that he had to ditch. Craig threw out a penance for ditching.

"In that case, you gotta tell us about what you're working on," Craig said

Jermaine agreed, but needed to think of a way that made his work relevant to all of them. It was simple to break down economics to the girls and explain how Renee's word problems related to his business ideas. Now he had to take a step back and make it simple, yet also complex enough to explain to high school students.

"Okay! So, you guys are learning about investing, right?" Jermaine asked. "When you invest in a business you become part owner of that business right?"

"Yes!" Matthias said. "You own stock in that company."

"You care about if it is doing well or if it is not doing well," Jermaine said. "Well, think about the community as a company. We all invest in this community daily. We shop here, do laundry here, our parents pay rent or mortgage here. This is essentially our company."

"I think I am following you," Alexander said. "So, it's important that we invest in where we live?"

"More than that!" Jermaine continued. "It's a two-way street! Money in and money out!"

Jermaine explained how important it was for the people who lived in their communities to own their apartment buildings, stores and shops, and what he was trying to do through coin-op was create a company that was "community ready." To think about who they were serving and their likes and dislikes.

"The only way to really do that is to get people from the community, who live in it and breathe it in every day, to be invested in the creation and ownership of the company," he said.

"Jermaine is putting not only customers first, but the community first," Sethi said. "If he is successful, it could revolutionize how business is done in neighborhoods like yours all over the country."

"What does all that translate to?" Stevie asked.

Jermaine used the laundromat as an example. How patrons shouldn't have to be limited to putting money on a card so that they had to pay in advance and have their information tracked.

"Many people like to spend as they go, so we put in an option of coin-operated machines and hybrid machines," Jermaine said.

Jermaine knew that as the community went through more and more gentrification it was going to become increasingly important to ask the question of what served the current customer, rather than what would attract future customers.

"It sounds like you are feeding a dying dog," Cyrus said. "It's a survival-of-the-fittest world, man. Machines will eventually take over manpower."

"I'm not arguing with that," Jermaine said. "All I am saying is that we still need manpower to turn on the machine and to provide it maintenance when it goes down. I'm not against progress, I am just advocating for room for those who don't fit nicely into that box.

The box is designed for the 'haves' and like it or not there are still plenty of 'have nots.'"

Sethi told the boys about how Jermaine was looking at creative uses for spare change in everyday life.

"Think about the spare change you have accumulated just today among the six of you," Sethi said. "Now think, instead of putting the change into your top drawer or old piece of pottery that's collecting dust, you actually put it to good use for services in the community."

"Yeah, but nobody likes spare change," Alexander said.

"It's not that they don't like it," Jermaine said. "It's money. Cents make dollars."

Jermaine found that there was never a practical use for spare change. It seemed as though there was never enough, and when there was enough, people didn't have time to count it out at the registers. It was just easier to just pull out another bill, so more change collected, and by the time you got home, you would have over a dollar of spare change in your pocket.

"Now imagine that six to eight different coin-ops accept every piece of change in your pocket, or better yet, you let it gather and get something like a vending-machine meal two or three times a week. You are winning!" he said.

"I follow you!" Craig said. "I just don't know how it's going to work."

"Me either, Brother," Jermaine admitted. "Me either."

###

Bianca sat home with her housemates surrounded by a bunch of material and information from the apartment she had just seen. She brought home floor plans and layouts for the entire complex, even though she knew exactly what apartment she wanted. There was some competition for the place, and she knew the rental agency would prefer someone with a stable career over a twenty-one-year-old college student, but she was in sales and knew how to pitch herself better than any product she had ever sold.

Her housemates were either never home or always in their rooms, so to have them in the kitchen when she came in was a bit of a shock. She told them that Jermaine was on his way over, and they were going to be ordering food and watching a movie in the living room. They promised to disappear as soon as he arrived.

Bianca had on her fancy clothes and shoes from viewing the apartment, but now it was time to lose the bra and relax. She had grown pretty comfortable around Jermaine and knew that sweatpants or pajamas would be fine, but she opted for the yoga pants which were comfy with a flair of style to them. She had a few "go to" restaurants for ordering in. Although she was a tiny thing, she ate out at least three times a week just due to being busy with school work and her internship. She decided to wait for Jermaine to arrive before she made any decisions. He was already ten minutes late, and he hadn't called. She knew it was no big deal because he was often running into class late or just as class was beginning. Just as she sat down to put on the TV, he knocked on the door. She couldn't contain her excitement as she jumped up. Her housemates were still wrapping up some cooking in the kitchen, so they got to witness the glow from over the counter. She opened the door and welcomed him in with a big hug.

"Took you long enough!" she said. "I thought you may have gotten caught up and forgot about me."

"Never that!" Jermaine replied. "I actually ditched my project and decided to hang with the fellas for a few. They had a million questions about what I am trying to do."

"Yeah! What did they think?" Bianca asked.

"You know! That I am feeding a dead dog," Jermaine said.

Jermaine saw Bianca's housemates trying to finish their meals and stay out of sight.

"Enough about me," he said. "Who are these young ladies you have been hiding from me?"

"Sheri and Dawn!" Bianca said. "I sometimes forget they are even here."

Sheri was a third-year graduate student at the university and was a little older and a lot more mature. Besides spending all her time in the library and lab, she also was an introvert and a recluse. Typical professor behavior. She had tried to meet people, but typically just found herself off in the corner of a bar sipping on a coke by herself and hoping some people would invite her into their conversation.

Dawn was an undergraduate student at the university. She worked and went to class and was hardly ever around. She maintained a strict schedule which meant: no television, music or social media. She only used the apartment to sleep and shower, and on a night like tonight, have an occasional meal.

Tonight, found them both in the kitchen at the same time, which was odd, but a great time to introduce them to Jermaine.

"Come over and meet Jermaine!" Bianca said. "You may see him sneaking out of the apartment some early mornings, so I don't want you to be afraid."

"I heard him leave once before," Dawn said. "At least, I think it was him."

"You can never be too sure," Jermaine said. "I'm Jermaine!"

"Hi, I'm Dawn," she said.

Jermaine pointed to where Sheri was in the kitchen

"And this must be Sheri," he said.

Sheri waved but did not introduce herself. She grabbed her plate and snuck off to her room.

"Not very social?" Jermaine said. "I won't take it personally."

"I am sure she has a wild side," Bianca said. "We just haven't seen it yet."

"I better be sneaking off too," Dawn said. "My food is getting cold."

Dawn grabbed her plate and headed down the hall to her room, leaving Bianca and Jermaine by themselves. They made their way over to the couch and got comfortable.

"So, what do you want to order?" Jermaine asked. "Or, would you like to go out somewhere?"

"It's too late for all that," Bianca said. "I have my fav spots for ordering in. They know my order before I call."

"Oh yeah! So, what are we having?" Jermaine asked. "Since I don't have a choice in this order."

"I'm just letting you know what's good," Bianca said. "We should go Chinese or Mexican."

"What if I was in the mood for Thai?" Jermaine said.

"Lucky for you, I have just the place for that as well," Bianca quickly replied.

"Where do you put away the food?" Jermaine asked.

"I'll show you later," Bianca answered.

"Oh, you're good!" Jermaine said.

"I know!" Bianca replied. "Are you trying to say that I am too skinny?"

Jermaine knew to be careful with his words. Especially in dealing with women and weight. You could never be too careful. He found the same was true for men, although men aren't fat-shamed nearly as much as women. In fact, men like Earl were shamed for being too small. "Get your weight up!" tended to be a common moniker around his neighborhood. Jermaine sensed Bianca was secure and was just trying to get a rise out of him, so he had to show her that he was able to give it back.

"I didn't say all that, but I can't have your ribs and hip bone stabbing me is all," Jermaine said.

"You can leave now," Bianca said, half kidding.

"I'm sorry! Don't be that way," Jermaine said. "I was just kidding. You know I can work with it."

"Let me catch you looking at one of these big-booty girls on the campus," Bianca warned.

"Well, if she got that ass, I got to look. Sorry!" Jermaine said, quoting a Kanye West song lyric.

That earned him a quick jab in the chest. He grabbed Bianca and pulled her in close before the second one could land. Bianca didn't struggle long. This was exactly where she wanted to be, and the circumstance warranted her the perfect excuse to get there. As they embraced, their conversation circled back to food.

"Let's order some Chinese," Jermaine suggested. "I can pick the movie while you call it in."

Bianca agreed and ordered some of her favorite dishes.

"Do you mind spicy?" Bianca asked.

"The hotter the better," Jermaine replied. He flipped through the suggested movies and then landed on some of the classics. "Have you ever seen 'The Wood'?" Jermaine asked. "It's a classic. Taye Diggs, Omar Epps, Sanaa Lathan..."

"I haven't seen it, but it sounds good," Bianca said.

Bianca called in the order and sat back down on the couch with Jermaine, as he cued up the movie. As the open credits rolled, they snuggled in and got cozy. It was not cold, but Bianca pulled out a blanket for them to wrap themselves in. The movie started, but they hardly watched any of the scenes, as they were more enthralled with one another. Ten minutes later, the doorbell rang, and the food arrived. Bianca answered and got the food. Jermaine was off the couch and right behind her as she turned around. He took the food in one hand and grabbed Bianca with the other. In one move, he placed the food on the kitchen counter where Sheri and Dawn had been and swept Bianca down the hall and into her room. The movie continued to play in the living room, as the food grew cold on the counter. An hour later, the two of them reemerged, Bianca with ruffled hair and Jermaine with his shirt off. The movie was almost over, but they grabbed the food, sat back on the couch and watched the ending all the way through the closing credits.

"Maybe next time, we will actually watch the movie?" Bianca said.

"Maybe!" Jermaine replied. "Who knows?"

###

CHAPTER TWELVE

Lance was in the corporate offices snack area when Pamela walked by him and asked him if he was travelling that weekend. Lance was suspicious of the question. Pamela had guessed that he was going to visit Jermaine, someone Pamela previously didn't want anything to do with, but now Jermaine had climbed up to number two on the intern leaderboard and was the talk of the office.

"I have to find out what kind of niche market he discovered, so I can replicate his success in my areas," Pamela said.

Lance could have guessed that her interest was self-motivated. Pamela figured Lance was no better and told him that he snatched up Jermaine before Jonathan's body went cold.

"Wow!" Lance said. "So, we're not pulling any punches today."

Shirley walked by as soon as the conversation started to escalate.

"Everything good here?" Shirley asked. "I have some gloves and headgear in my car if you need it."

As Lance started to make his way down the hall, Pamela followed close behind.

"Lance! Lance!" she called out. "I'm coming with you to Kansas. It's a done deal. I'm working on getting us seats next to each other on the flight."

Lance was forever the smart aleck and remarked snidely, "What? Are we going to share a room too?"

Pamela gave Shirley a look that said it all. Lance wasn't thrilled about Pamela invading his territory for selfish purposes, and Shirley picked up on it. Shirley had originally assigned Jermaine to Pamela, so she felt entitled to infringe.

"I just hate hanging out in the ghetto," Pamela said.

"Racist much?" Shirley said.

Pamela immediately realized that she was not among her friends or family, and the word "ghetto" was frowned upon in the workplace. "I didn't mean anything by it," Pamela said. "My college roommate was African American."

Pamela was making things worse. Shirley knew that this was why she had so many varied assignments. The executives had to find markets where she wouldn't offend anyone. Pamela was working under the assumption that her circumstance with markets was solely because she was a single woman with no children. But she didn't do herself any favors with her closed-minded attitude.

"You really want to know why Beasley is doing so well? Do you?" Shirley asked. "It's because he knows that the market is pricing people out. The writing is on the wall. It used to be rich White folk like us stayed on our side of the tracks and kept the Black and Latino poor in the 'ghettos,' but not anymore. We are moving into the 'ghettos' and taking them too."

"That's not my fault!" Pamela said. "They should have bought property when they had the chance. Just because the middle-to-upper-class folks can pay the higher rents and they can't, is not something I created."

"Yeah! You kinda did," Shirley said

"How?" Pamela asked.

"Do you see your attitude towards those who aren't as well off as you?" Shirley asked. "That's called systemic racism. Because of that attitude, certain people were not allowed to buy homes in certain areas, get bank loans, or more less buy land at all. All the wealth that you and your family accumulated came from access that many Blacks didn't have."

"Well, I can't help that now," Pamela said. "What do you want me to do?"

"You can start by reading a book?" Shirley said. "Then by changing your attitude."

Shirley walked back to her office, leaving Pamela there thinking.

"I'm still going!" Pamela said. "I already have my ticket, so I'm going."

She walked by Lance's door on her way back to her desk. The door was slightly cracked open, so Pamela took the opportunity to poke her head in a take a last jab at Lance, "So, Roomie, what side of the bed do you want?"

###

After fighting through a crowded ticket line, Lance arrived at the airport to find Pamela waiting for him. She was much more serious that morning, as she was anticipating her group number to be called.

"Where were you? They are getting ready to board," Pamela said.

Lance knew he didn't want to spend any additional time in the airport with Pamela if he didn't have to. She had become much more outspoken since the passing of Jonathan, and it didn't sit well in the office. He ignored the comment, as he made his way to a seat.

"I'm here now. Let's get this over with," Lance said.

Pamela picked up on the attitude and was prepared to give it right back. "Well, good morning to you too," she said. "I know this isn't what you pictured, but you are in your second year with the company, and I thought we could use this time to get to know each other."

"Not interested!" Lance said curtly. "It's better if we just focus on the task at hand. You can take a look at some of the coin-ops on the eastside of the city, and I will look at what's working on the westside. Deal?"

"No, Partner!" Pamela said. "We do this whole dog-and-pony show together. I want to see every venue we have a machine in. Even the night clubs. I bought an outfit for the occasion."

"That's all you!" Lance said.

"You wouldn't let me go out alone," Pamela said. "Your parents raised you better than that."

Lance got really upset by the comment regarding his parents and walked towards the gate as their group number was called.

It was a short flight, and given the time it would take to check in, fly, and deplane, it made more sense to Lance to drive instead. On this trip, however, Lance chose to fly for convenience. And Pamela chose to fly to bug Lance. Lance liked to get work done on the plane that he couldn't do driving. The area they were heading to was his focus area. While Pamela travelled to several places she had to maintain her portfolio, Lance catered to a niche clientele.

"My parents told me that you make the bed you lie in!" Lance snapped back while they boarded. Boom! Right cross to the jaw.

Pamela followed Lance onto the plane. She said, "Fine! Let me get roofied and raped!"

Pamela was not very attractive. Some would even say dog ugly, but that would have been offensive to most dog owners. Lance thought there was a chance that she could get raped, although someone would have had to have exhausted all other choices and even then, would have had to be pretty desperate.

Lance got to his seat in business class and put on his headset before the flight attendant had a chance to offer him his first drink and before Pamela could say anything else that bugged him.

As soon as the pre-flight announcements were about to end, Pamela pounded down two Old Fashioned cocktails made with Knob Creek and caught Lance before he got his headset back on.

"So, what're your thoughts on Shirley?" she said.

"What do you mean?" Lance said. "She's your mentor."

"Yeah! I think I may end that relationship," Pamela said. "She's been giving me fits about my views."

"What does that mean?" Lance said.

"She had the nerve to call me 'racist' because I don't agree with her point of view," Pamela said.

"First of all, I doubt if she called you 'racist,'" Lance retorted. "She probably said you have a racist attitude."

"All I heard was 'racist,'" Pamela said. "I think I am just being smart. Not everywhere is safe."

"Meaning poor neighborhoods?" Lance asked. "So, why are you coming on this trip?"

"I told you!" Pamela answered. "Poor people spend a grip on coin-op. I have to figure out how to sink my teeth into this market."

"Wow! Could you be more…?" Lance began.

"Don't say it!" Pamela cut him off. "Don't you dare! You sound like Shirley. Well, at least I'm not a murderer. That's the pot calling the kettle black."

The alcohol had kicked in, and as the altitude of the plane got higher, it appeared to be having a greater effect. Pamela knew something, and this was an excellent time for Lance to find out what she knew. He knew what Pablo's thoughts were regarding Shirley's involvement in the kid's murder. Lance also knew that Pamela and Pablo had been talking.

"See, I hang out with Pablo, so I can't be racist," she said.

The flight attendant came by, and Pamela ordered yet another drink.

"You might want to slow down. It's a short flight," Lance said.

"I'm not driving," she defended. "We can rideshare when we land. Have a drink!"

Pamela got the flight attendant's attention and ordered a second drink for Lance. When it arrived, she slid it next to his tablet on his tray table. Lance, like Jermaine, liked to sip only and was more likely to sip on the weekends than during the work week, but he didn't refuse the offer of a complimentary drink.

"I was there when Pablo accused Shirley of knowing something," Lance said. "We will probably never know the whole story, now that Jonathan is dead."

Pamela was full on slurring after twenty minutes in the air, and Lance found out that she was not only an open vault, but an emotional drunk, as she began to apologize for her comments in the office regarding Jonathan. She knew that Lance and Jonathan were close. Lance knew that the comments weren't personal. She was just rattling his chain because she regretted giving up Jermaine. Pamela figured somebody knew the truth about what was going on. She'd caught wind that Shirley was being subpoenaed and let that information slip. The alcohol did all the talking for her, and then it was too late to retract her words.

"So, Pablo was onto something?" Lance said. "I wonder how he knew. Maybe he is in on it too."

"Shirley is not as clean as you think," Pamela said. "She had the nerve to call me 'racist' when she told

Jonathan that she didn't want Beasley to be an intern because of his gang-affiliation."

Lance pretended to be shocked at the news to keep his advantage. He was already tipped off a while ago about Shirley's bias on hiring Jermaine, but he didn't want to let on that he knew.

"Uh huh! He's the gang-leader," Pamela said. "I read it in a file on Shirley's computer. She keeps files on all the interns."

"Holy…!" Lance exclaimed.

"I know, right?" Pamela said. "They don't do any major crimes, but they still get harassed by the po-po!" The third Old Fashioned had unlocked any story box that may have been hidden in the attic. Pamela said, "The former leader is doing a bid now, so he put Jermaine in charge until he gets out."

"You know what this means, right?" Lance asked.

"Um-hmm!" Pamela said. "That Shirley was having him followed."

"Yes!" Lance said. "But, also that you have the proof!"

The plane began its descent, and Lance put his tablet away, his tray table up and his seat back up. Pamela had to get a second reminder from the flight attendant to follow suit. She made Lance promise that he wouldn't say anything to Shirley.

"No, I won't say anything," Lance said. "Only because you will. We are talking about murder."

Pamela went silent. She knew sharing what she saw on Shirley computer was the right thing to do, but she was too drunk to think about it. She was more concerned with getting her carry-on down from the overhead when they landed. She thought the conversation need to happen at some point, but not right then. Instead, it was time to think about getting checked into the hotel, getting a good night sleep and going about business in the morning.

###

The streets were quiet and empty, as Donna unlocked and rolled up the gate for the arcade. She knew the kids wouldn't come in for a few hours, but it was a great opportunity to get some work done while it was quiet. She tended to get the occasional early riser trying to get a game fix in the morning hours, but usually someone who stopped in was asking for change for the bus or to buy a soft drink from the vending machine. That morning, she was greeted by Pamela and Lance who came in about a half hour after she had opened her doors for business.

"Wow! An old-school Space Invaders game!" Pamela said. "I haven't seen one of these since I was in high school."

As Pamela walked around the arcade like a kid in a candy store, Lance used the opportunity to take a quick inventory of what other companies the shop did business with. He looked at the service tags located on the sides of the machine. Both of them were on a strict schedule, and Lance wanted to meet with Bruce to find out any new developments in their marketing strategy.

Donna lifted her head from her work and came out of the office. She asked, "Is there anything I can help you with?"

"We are just casing the joint out for a break-in later," Lance said.

Donna didn't find the joke particularly funny.

"Where do I get coins for the machines?" Pamela asked.

Donna pointed to a machine on the wall. The machine spat out the coins for Pamela, and she went into her own world of playing video games for the next thirty minutes. Lance saw this as an excellent time to discuss Jermaine and his connection with the shop. He told Donna that he worked for Quarimoc, and that they had a few machines in her shop.

Donna had worked with Jonathan on the installations, but barely remembered him since Jermaine took the lead on the installment. Donna said, "Jermaine interns at your company, I believe."

"Yes, Ma'am, he does," Lance replied. "He is one of our top-seller interns. We are lucky to have him on board."

"Well, he won't be here for a few hours," Donna said. "How can I help you?"

"I can't help but notice that you are pretty thin on customers during your morning hours," Lance said.

"Yeah. It gives me some time to catch up before the rush in the afternoon," Donna said.

"Business does drop a little in the months of spring to summer, but Jermaine and I are strategizing a way to attract customers."

Donna mentioned that Jermaine asked her to take him on as a mentee, because she was a former economist. She added, "Honestly, he has taught me just as much as I have taught him."

"He is doing pretty well," Lance said. "What do you attribute his success to?"

Pamela heard the question over the electronic noise of the machine and immediately became interested. In under a minute, she had left her game and completed the circle of the conversation.

"This is my colleague, Pamela," Lance said. "She came on this trip to find out more about Mr. Beasley's success strategies, so she can use them in her area."

"Well, this was my area for a few weeks when our former colleague went on an extended vacation," Pamela said.

"Whatever happened to Mr. Stone?" Donna asked.

"He is no longer with the company!" Pamela replied.

"Oh, because I heard he got caught up in some shady dealings and offed himself," Donna said.

"The case is still open, so we are not allowed to comment," Lance intervened. "Jonathan was a dear friend and will be missed."

Donna got Lance to admit there was a case, and she also acknowledged that she had known Jonathan was no longer with the company. Lance explained that Jonathan's caseload was reassigned to Pamela, but because Lance truly admired the work Jonathan had been doing with Jermaine, he'd asked if he could supervise Jermaine.

Satisfied with this answer, Donna decided not to continue her line of questioning. "Jermaine is a special talent," Donna said. "He has the pulse of the community and figures out what they need before they know they need it."

"What a knack," Pamela said. "Steve Jobs had that same mind. It's rare."

"Wow! Can you give an example?" Lance asked.

"Sure!" Donna replied. "The other day I was discussing with him how the kids know when someone is done with a game. We know most kids just linger nearby or stand behind the person and wait for them to be done. Jermaine is thinking of how we can send an alert to their phones or even put up a "Now Serving" electronic board. The kids wouldn't have to worry about somebody beating them out for a game. The machine would freeze out anyone who wasn't next for two minutes until the next person was able to scan in their phone and play."

"That's crazy!" Lance said. "I love it!"

"Just when I thought we were staying in the dark ages, this kid is launching us into the future," Pamela said.

Some patrons slowly came in, but not enough entered for the three talking to move into the office. Pamela latched on to the comment Donna had made about being an econ major. Donna explained that she worked on Wall Street for a few years before deciding to come back home.

"So, you're from around here?" Pamela asked.

"Born and raised," Donna answered.

"And you decided to come back?" Pamela continued.

"I sure did," Donna answered.

Donna could see the puzzled look on Pamela's face. She then looked over at Lance who looked as if he wanted nothing to do with the conversation. He suggested to Pamela that it was time for them to leave.

"How about we see if your colleague Pamela is going to ask her real question first," Donna said. To Pamela, she said, "You want to know why a wealthy successful person would choose to move back to the hood."

Pamela's facial expression gave it all away. Busted. That was the crux of her question. She knew that Donna could live anywhere she wanted, so why would she choose to live here?

"I'm sorry!" Pamela said. "I am still learning."

"It's okay!" Donna said. "Many of us are."

Donna explained that when a poor person breaks the poverty cycle and leaves their community, the community stays impoverished. The people who break the poverty cycle take their tax dollar, their business, their influence and their wisdom into a community that doesn't need or sometimes even want them. Given that, Donna came back to the neighborhood for her parents. But now she had a greater purpose. Jermaine taught her about the influence of owning and investing in their own communities, something that was revolutionary and could change the way people viewed the world.

Lance and Pamela left the shop thoroughly grateful for Donna's time and insight. Now it was on to the next spot, as they put together a very tight schedule for the day that ended with a trip to the nightclub that night.

###

Earl was back on his feet and walking, fully recovered from his overdose that had put him into a coma. He had even made an effort to join the rest of the gang to learn about business ownership. His near-death experience had him a little shaken up and seeing life through new eyes. He also had been talking to Jermaine who had been preaching the idea to him for some time.

"It's definitely not for everybody," Jermaine would say. "But you never know unless you give it a chance."

When he was incapacitated, Earl had taken the time to contemplate life and what he would actually be interested in doing. He knew he didn't want to just peddle t-shirts and hats, but his capital wasn't really allowing him to do much more. A year before Earl had joined the gang, he was a petty drug-dealer, pushing dime bags a few blocks from where he lived. He had regular customers and a few more random buyers, but his take home was barely enough for a few runs to McDonalds and a new pair of shoes. Besides, he knew word would get back to his mom and dad and already they were suspicious which made things hard around the house. He always had a knack for finding low-cost items, and often thought if he could buy a box of products that people wanted wholesale, he could break down the box and take orders door to door. He thought, "Before you know it, I will have my own website and grow it into a store."

Cheech came by Earl's house, driving in a car that Earl hadn't seen before. He laid on the horn, and Earl came down to meet him. He had the homies in the car with Patrice in the front seat. Cheech asked her to squeeze in the back seat with Charlene and Veronika which wasn't really a squeeze since the back seat was spacious. Earl slid into the passenger seat, and Patrice sat directly behind him.

"Whose car is this?" Earl asked.

"It's mine, Brother!" Cheech said. "What do you think?"

"You for real?" Earl said. "I didn't know you had a little side hustle."

"My uncle was trying to unload it after the IRS came after him for some back taxes," Cheech answered. "So, he sold it to me for peanuts. He's hoping that I sell it back to him in a year when he's in the clear."

"What are you thinking?" Earl asked.

"I think I'm going to put the tags in my name, and we are going to ride," Cheech said.

"Alright! That's what's up!" Earl replied. Earl turned to the back and showed the homies some love. "What's new with y'all?" he said "It's good to see you, Patrice! I hope they treated you well on the inside."

"No doubt, no doubt!" Patrice answered. "You know I can hold my own."

"Oh! I never questioned that," Earl said.

"I saw you in the store when I got pinched," Patrice said. "Word on the street is you flew like a bird."

"Fly, little bird, fly!" Veronika mocked.

Earl got defensive, but he knew she was right. He tried his best to keep his composure and to give his rationale for running. He honestly thought the police were coming after him. All those in the car were quiet for almost a minute.

"So, what I heard was that you were snitching to the police," Charlene said. "That's what I'm hearing."

"I heard people were saying some junk like that," Earl defended. "That don't make no sense! What would that benefit me?"

"To keep them off of your behind," Veronika chimed in.

Cheech pulled onto the highway. "Yo, chill out!" he said. "Earl is just getting back on his feet y'all. Let's talk about this later."

"There ain't nothing to talk about," Earl said. "I ain't no snitch."

"I heard you OD'd and were in a coma," Patrice said. "Serves you right!"

"Chill, Patrice!" Cheech said. "Why are we bugging right now?"

"You know what, Cheech? You're right," Earl said, "I'm not even going to justify that with a response."

"Because you're a punk-ass snitch!" Charlene said.

Patrice pulled a lace from her boots, and, as soon as the car was in between exits, she wrapped the string around Earl's throat, cutting off his oxygen. Earl struggled to breathe and to get the string off. Patrice leveraged her weight with her foot in the back of the chair. She had the advantage. Cheech looked for a place to pull over safely. Not finding one, he used his right hand to try to salvage whatever air Earl had left. It was no use.

Veronika pleaded with Patrice, "That's enough!"

Charlene tried to pull her off, but Patrice wrapped the lace around her hands twice to get a better grip. Earl was still not fully recovered since his coma and didn't have any more energy to keep up the struggle and eventually succumbed. Cheech finally found a place to pull over and get the lace from around Earl's neck.

"What's wrong with you girl?" Cheech said.

Veronika and Charlene were in shock. Cheech worked hard to revive Earl's limp body, but it was of no use. He thought about calling the paramedics, but realized that it would take just as long to drive him over to the ER. When they pulled up to ER, Cheech jumped out of the car to try to get an orderly's attention. All three girls jumped out of the car and scattered. By the time Earl was on the gurney, his lips were turning blue. The first responders worked tirelessly in an attempt to revive him, but it was of no use. Earl's life slipped away from him as quickly as it had been restored to him just a few weeks ago. He could not cheat death twice.

###

Cheech was the one left to contact Earl's family now, knowing this was the second time they would receive a horrific call in as many months. Jermaine sat unaware in a meeting with Bruce, Lance and Pamela. He turned his phone off after the first missed call in order to not be interrupted. He had no clue that the worst awaited him on the other end of the line and that the life of his friend Earl's had been snuffed before his twenty-first birthday.

The four of them sat in the same cafeteria as before over a late lunch in a semi-filled room. Pamela led a conversation filled with questions but no answers that satisfied what she wanted to hear. She had visited four vendors with Quarimoc products in their locations already and still sat unfulfilled. She hoped the man behind the sales could help calm the hurricane of thoughts mixed with a tirade of emotions that stormed within her.

"Mr. Beasley, how do you do it?" Pamela said. "Your product placement is stellar. I have been with the company for almost six years and have visited hundreds of our stores and have yet to see anything near your success in such a short amount of time."

"Thank you!" Jermaine said. "And please call me Jermaine. I thought we said we were going to lose the formality."

Pamela brimmed with flattery in order to reach her ultimate goals. "Well, I thought I might have to bring it back, since I might be reporting to you one day," she said. "I can't disrespect the boss."

Jermaine revealed his age by blushing in embarrassment. Bruce knew that Jermaine still had much to learn. Nothing was more telling of this than the holes in his final project. Jermaine was quickly brought back down to earth. He knew he had a lot of work to do in order to get to his project to where it needed to be. There were so many questions left to answer and holes he had yet to fill. His mind had been in a thousand places. He had been thinking about graduation, moving, gang leadership, who was trying to kill him, the murder, the suicide and, not to mention, Bianca. Six months before this point, it seemed to Jermaine like dating was a faraway prospect, and now he was in the throes of a budding relationship with a soon-to-be university student.

"So, Bruce tells me that you are considering full-time employment after summer classes," Lance said.

"Yeah! Either that or starting my own company," Jermaine replied.

"How about both?" Lance said.

"Are you sure you don't want to finish up college?" Pamela courted. "If you get a bachelor's degree, we can possibly get you right into a position at Quarimoc like we did for Boy Wonder."

Pamela nodded toward Lance. Lance knew he was no Boy Wonder, but that he was a slick-talking salesman. He sensed that everyone around him knew it too, but he had lasted this long so why stop now? If he rode Jermaine's coattails to some automatic success, he wouldn't need to worry about Jermaine getting a job with the company. He would take all the credit for Jermaine's sales when he left and reap the rewards over the long haul. Bruce saw Lance's game as it played out.

"A bachelor's is something to consider," Bruce said. "That way you don't close the door on future opportunities."

"I am definitely going back to school," Jermaine said. "I am looking for a company that would provide college tuition as a benefit of employment."

"Hmm! That sounds strangely familiar," Bruce said.

Jermaine knew he was busted. Bruce had seen him spending time with Bianca, and he was the one who helped her get the part-time job at the company that was paying for her college tuition.

"So, Jermaine," Pamela said. "What is your five-year plan?"

Jermaine was annoyed by the question. Maybe it was because he didn't know the answer. He knew he wanted to help his community the way Donna did. He knew he wanted to own a business and promote business ownership. He knew that he eventually wanted to finish college. But a five-year plan? Who knows when happenings might happen? It came off as such a corporate question.

"Whose five-year plan actually plays out the way they draw it up?" Jermaine thought.

He knew it was good to have a plan, but why couldn't he just see where the road might lead? Whether that was to business ownership, or working for a company, success or failure, college or dropping out. Either way, he didn't want to have a plan, but Pamela wanted to hear something, so he thought he would tell her what she wanted to hear.

"I am thinking of working for a few years to learn the business side of things and then finishing college once I save some money," he said. "After college, I want to come back to the community and start something here."

"We spent some time this morning viewing some of your placements," Pamela said. "Donna, who runs the arcade, sounds like she really admires your insight."

"I really appreciate her," Jermaine said. "I consider her a mentor for what I hope to do."

"Wall Street, huh?" Lance said.

"No way!" Jermaine replied. "I meant coming back to where she grew up and starting a business here. That's powerful. We don't get to see a lot of that. Most of the shop owners don't know much about the area except for their interactions at the store. I guarantee you, if I saw them on Market Street they would walk right by me."

"It never used to be that way," Bruce said. "We knew the shop owners, the laundry owners, the barbershop owners, even the liquor store owners. All that changed after Vietnam. Some people say integration, but the economist in me says that integration paved the way for the gentrification we are seeing today."

"Professor Wright," Pamela said. "Don't tell me you blame the middle and upper class for coming in and buying cheap property in low-income areas".

"I didn't say that I blame them," Bruce said. "It's disheartening to know that the poor are being priced out due to gentrification. In the 60's, when Blacks were moving into the inner cities from the south to escape Jim Crow, my parents witnessed 'white flight' into the suburbs. As a kid growing up, I remember we had the poor side of town and the well-to-do side of town. You wouldn't see a White face past Martin Luther King Blvd. Now MLK looks like Elvis Presley Way."

"Doesn't it also bring with it better schools, roads and services?" Pamela defended.

"If folks could afford to live there long enough to enjoy them," Bruce said. "You can't live there on a teacher or bus driver's salary any more. The Westside has become like Silicon Valley without the start-ups or Fortune 500 companies."

"I have to side with Bruce on this one Pam," Lance said. "Gentrification is forcing people to relocate to a point where they can't afford to raise their kids where they grew up. I don't like it."

"Well, like it or not, it's progress!" Pamela said.

"Professor Wright teaches us about the cost of progress and to what end," Jermaine said. "The slaughter of millions of indigenous people was considered progress, so the pilgrims could move West. We need to move with ethics and integrity if we are going to move forward at all. That's really what is at the base of my project. The effort to conduct business in a way that respects those we are serving."

"I believe that is what is going to make us the greatest nation in the world," Bruce said.

"And it's what we need more of at Quarimoc," Lance said.

###

On the bus ride home, Jermaine remembered that he had turned his phone off during the meeting, and as he powered it on, a flood of messages and voicemails came in. He decided to listen to the voicemails and the first one was from Cheech.

Yo Jay! Something has happened. You have to call me as soon as you get this.

Jermaine knew that he couldn't make a personal call on the bus, so he decided to keep listening to his voicemails to see if he could find out more information. The next voicemail was from Tanja and she was screaming and crying, almost unintelligibly, but Jermaine could make out that something tragic happened to Earl. The next voicemail was from Veronika. She was calm, but apologetic:

Jermaine, this is V," she said. "Patrice flipped, yo! I didn't have anything to do with it. You have to believe me. I know that Earl is your boy, I would never have signed on for that.

Veronika went on, but it all became white noise at some point. Jermaine pieced together that Earl was dead. He didn't have to hear it. He knew. He put down his phone and went catatonic. He saw that he had missed his stop and would have to walk nearly five blocks to get to his house. He didn't want to go home now. He didn't know where he wanted to go, but as the gang leader, he knew he couldn't go into a shell. He had to do something. The pressure was overwhelming. He crumbled to his knees in between two parked cars and cried harder than he ever had before in his life. He lost track of all time and space, until finally his phone rang and he knew he had to answer it. The number popped up as Tanja's. Jermaine's voice went somber as he picked up.

"Hello!" he said.

It was not Tanja on the line, but rather Thomas, Earl's father.

"Jermaine, it's Thomas!" he said. "We need you, Son! We all need you!"

"Text me the address. I am on my way!" Jermaine said.

Thomas handed Tanja back the phone, and she texted the name of the hospital Earl was at. Jermaine, in the meantime, pulled himself off the blacktop and propped himself up on a car. He pulled up his rideshare app, and a car arrived within five minutes. Jermaine called Cheech.

"How are you holding up?" Jermaine asked. "Where are you now? I'm on my way."

"Are you coming to the ER?" Cheech asked. "They are about to move Earl's body to the morgue."

The bluntness of the statement caused another well of emotions in Jermaine. That was his confirmation. He knew he had to be strong. There would be time later on to take care of himself. At that moment, he had to be strong.

"Cheech! How are you holding up?" Jermaine repeated.

"I'm not, Man! We need you," Cheech said. "We are all falling apart. Patrice man! I want to put a bullet in her."

"Calm down and tell me what happened!" Jermaine said.

"Where are you?" Cheech asked.

"I'm about eight-minutes away," Jermaine said.

"I will tell you when you get here," Cheech hung up.

Jermaine was left to imagine the worst. Two gunshots to the head. Twenty-six stab wounds. A slit throat. The worst. The driver tried to engage him, but Jermaine was not having any of it. He tried to shut his eyes for the next eight minutes. He knew he would be up all night.

###

Donna had heard the news and was triggered. She knew Earl as a baby and was even friends with his older sister, Amber, before she left for college. Earl used to come around the community center as a younger teen and get up shots. She didn't know what to do, but it didn't seem like the right time to be at the arcade. She told her assistant Ayiesha she needed to go for a walk.

The arcade was unusually busy with kids just out of school. Some older teens who went to school with Earl were there trying to take their mind off of things, but the conversation kept coming back to the murder.

"When will you be back?" Ayiesha asked.

"I don't know," Donna said. "I really don't know.

She walked out before Ayiesha had a chance to respond.

Donna walked and walked. Not really knowing where she was going, she ended up across the street from the laundromat. She saw that some people had gathered there. A lot of young teens and some older adults.

The Rottweilers had all come to seek comfort and advice from Sethi. This had become their new gathering place. Donna hesitated, but crossed the street to seek the same comfort. The boys, though most of them non-religious, were kneeling in a circle and being led in prayer by a middle-aged man who witnessed them from across the room and asked if he could pray. The boys did not refuse. Donna closed her eyes for the end of the prayer herself.

The man consciously and considerately hugged each of the young men and put a hand on Donna's shoulder to display his empathy for her as well. The kind act triggered a range of emotions in her, and the man was unsure why. Sethi intervened and the man stepped back.

"Is it okay if I give you a hug?" Sethi asked.

Donna reached out her arms, and they embraced. That was the comfort she was seeking. The comfort that she was longing for in her half-mile walk to clear her mind. She extended the same warmth to the young men that the stranger extended, offering each of them an embrace. As she hugged the two cousins, Tim and

Rudy, she saw their brand. Her brother's brand on each of their forearms.

"When...when did you get these?" Donna asked.

"Right after the march," Tim said. "We each got them."

The rest of the boys revealed their brand.

Sethi intervened. "If I may?" Sethi turned to Donna to ask her blessing for him so he could talk about the connection. "Rottweilers, this is Donna. You may know her from the arcade. The brand you wear on your arm is not only a fallen Rottweiler, but Donna's brother, Roderick, who was killed senselessly on these streets just like Earl. It is more than just a symbol, Men. It's a commitment that you have all made for non-violence, and in doing so, we keep the memory of Brother Rod alive."

Donna didn't know why or how Sethi knew this, but she welcomed his sharing her connection with the gang. Sethi pulled up his shirt sleeve to reveal his own brand. Still fresh. Still healing.

"Why we choose peace over war? Why we value life over death? RIP Brother Rod," Sethi said solemnly.

Although Sethi may not have meant his comments to rouse his listeners, he knew many of the members stored up wrath in their heart for Earl's killer, Patrice. They wanted her maimed and murdered. Some still did, in spite of their oath. They wouldn't. They couldn't. They were to operate as a whole. If one of them caused harm, it would be as if they all had.

Sethi put his arm around Donna. Donna put her head on his shoulder. Sethi pulled the boys all into a circle around them.

"Rottweilers! Where's your mind at?" Sethi exclaimed. With this question, they knew that everything was going to be all right.

###

The sun had gone down on a long day.

Brian and Dookie did not make it to the laundromat, they had other plans. Plans that included revenge. They didn't come into the gang under the oath. The lowercase "r" had always meant Rottweilers to them. They had no excuse. They knew the values of the gang. They had heard them a thousand times from Rico, Barry, Jermaine, and even Tony. With Earl going down, all bets were off the table. They wanted blood.

"Yo! I heard that Patrice is staying with her sister up in those condos they just put up last year." Dookie said.

"She ain't there," Brian retorted.

Brian had already put eyes on the condos. He knew the homies had a hideout. One that Cheech didn't even know about and had only seen in pictures. An upscale place. Dookie was putting the pieces together as Brian spoke.

"You talking like barely lived in?" Dookie asked. "Like showrooms?"

"What? You know something like that," Brian asked. "What are you not telling me?"

"It's not around here," Dookie said.

"Well, I knew that!" Brian said.

"Those are company suites one block off of Market Street in the downtown area," Dookie said.

"Charlene used to be a housekeeper or something like that down there. I bet you a hundred dollars that she still has access to those suites."

While Brian and Dookie were making plans to try to catch Patrice off-guard, the homies were busy with in-fighting.

###

The homies were, in fact, at the corporate suites where Charlene still worked some evenings. She kept a schedule of when they had executives in town, and there was no one scheduled until mid-week which gave her plenty of time to clean up beforehand.

"I'm not going down for this," Veronika said. "I'm not saying I'm going to snitch, but you need to make the right choice here."

Patrice was panicked now. She smoked a bowl on her own. Her friends knew that it was more than likely something stronger than weed.

"I got this," Patrice said. "I'm going to hop a bus tonight to my cousins' house in the country. That will keep the cops and the streets off of me until things cool down."

"Cool down?" Charlene retorted. "You killed somebody. Nothing is cooling down."

"You forget that I just got off for putting someone down," Patrice answered "This is not my first rodeo. I live by these rules and have for some time now. I'm not about to stop now."

"It's gonna catch up with you!" Veronika said. "I'm not getting caught up in your mess."

"This is all me!" Patrice said. "I have everything I need in this one bag. I paid for my ticket in cash, and I'm going straight to the bus with no waiting in the terminal. It's bullet-proof. You girls don't have to worry. This is all on me."

Charlene wanted to know what happened back in the car. Patrice sat still and inhaled. She couldn't answer. She honestly didn't know. It was something inside of her that took her from talking smack right back to the prison yard. She saw an opportunity to get Earl's attention and took it. Her plan wasn't to kill him. Just to get his attention.

"So, you knew he didn't snitch?" Veronika asked.

"Those DTs had been trailing me way before the store. They had an image of me on a traffic cam, and they had my prints from a prior. It's a miracle I got out. I know they have everything they need to pin Earl's crime on me too."

"What do you mean?" Charlene asked.

"They don't just let convicts go these days," Patrice explained. "They strap an ankle bracelet on you."

Patrice pulled up her pant leg to reveal her monitor.

"They know where I am at all times," Patrice said.

Veronika and Charlene panicked.

"So, they knew we were in the car that pulled up with Earl to the ER?" Veronika asked.

Patrice knew that it would only take them a few hours to figure out where she was, so she had to roll out that night. Charlene knew that they could just track her down again, but Patrice had other plans, which included putting that monitor in the bottom of the river.

"People on the inside have put me in touch with folks who can break this thing off," Patrice said. "Trust me! If you thought of it, I thought of it twice."

The girls were satisfied with that answer, and they packed up to leave the suite. Patrice took her bowl and left to go downstairs to finish it, as Charlene and Veronika did some last-minute tidying up. She took the stairs to avoid running into anyone. When she reached the bottom, she was met by two men in masks. She tried to run back up the stairwell, but the potion had everything moving in slow-motion. She was stabbed once and then again and was left bleeding in the staircase. The men exited the same way they came in unnoticed. Charlene and Veronika took the same staircase and found a wounded Patrice trying to make her way upstairs.

"What happened?" Charlene screamed.

"Don't worry about it!" Patrice said. "I'm okay! What's important is that I make that bus."

Charlene found an emergency kit, and while Veronika bandaged up Patrice's cuts, Charlene tried to clear away any evidence that could point to them being in the building. Patrice was badly hurt but was determined to make it to the bus station.

"Just put me in a cab," she said. "I'm okay! These bandages should hold until morning."

The cab pulled up, and they got her in and slid her bag in next to her. The time it took to clean and bandage Patrice up had put her down to the wire. When she arrived at the station, the bus was already boarding. She struggled out of the car after paying the driver and made her way to an evaporating line of passengers. As soon as she boarded the bus and found a seat, the Sheriff's Department made their way on and arrested her.

###

Earl's body was identified and carted away to the morgue right past Jermaine as he arrived. Earl's family was still in shock while Cheech was curled up away from it all in the corner of the waiting room. The bond that Earl and Cheech had formed over the years had left him feeling like his right arm had just been cut off. Jermaine attempted to move him. To get him to talk. To comfort him. But he remained inconsolable. Although Earl's family was all together as a unit, Jermaine felt it was only appropriate to go over and join them while Cheech battled his own demons.

Cheech still hadn't talked to the police. They came over to ask him about the cord marks around Earl's neck and how he was asphyxiated. He just waved them off. Part of this was because he was unable to intelligibly talk about what led to Earl's death. How was he to explain that he picked him up just minutes before to show off his car? That he had just pulled onto the highway? That his homie, Patrice and her friends were razzing Earl, as weak as he was from his recent coma, about being a snitch? He couldn't form the words to say that Patrice took a lace from her boots, wrapped it around Earl's neck, pulled as hard as she could and wouldn't let go. Or the more Veronika and Charlene tried to fight her off, the harder Patrice pulled. Or that even when he was able to pull over on the shoulder of the highway he could not revive Earl's lifeless body. That's just a part of the reason he waved the detectives off.

The second part of everything was that there was a strict code against talking to the police. Many people thought that it had to do with protecting a friend or loved one, but in reality, most people knew that the police were rarely on the side of the poor, especially poor Black and Brown folks. That they would use whatever you say against you. So, the mantra had become, "I don't know nothing!" In this situation, Cheech couldn't even put those words together which probably meant he would be looked at as a suspect, or at the very least, an accomplice. He figured that Earl's family thought the same thing. Thomas and Phyllis had barely said two words to him. No questions. No accusations! Not even a "thank you" for getting him to the ER. Nothing. Tanja stopped and put her hand on his shoulder and then on his head and then on his moist cheek. She knew the bond Earl and Cheech shared. She knew that he wouldn't hurt her brother, who had become his brother, as well. She also knew that he likely knew who murdered Earl and that he couldn't say. Veronika had already spilled the beans on a voicemail to Jermaine. Although it may be considered in some circles as a "dry snitch," Jermaine let Tanja listen to the voicemail, which pointed to Patrice as the killer. This was enough to satisfy Tanja that Cheech was innocent.

Phyllis held onto Thomas as if he was the only thing keeping her upright, as the gurney with Earl's body rolled by. She was desperate to see him once more, but Thomas restrained her, figuring that now was not the time. Being the rock of the family, Thomas had to be strong. There was family to contact and arrangements to be made. The viewing, funeral and repast all needed to be scheduled. It was not the time. His daughters needed him too. Thomas was a strong man but also a proud man. His tears would come, but not at that moment. It was not the time. He and Phyllis both knew that there had been a chance they would be burying one of their children. Something no parent should ever have to do. But with a war on Black men, lead poisoning, low birth rates, gang-violence, drugs, and the unhealthy foods available in the hood, the odds were high. There was a funeral once a month in these underserved areas with the young dying at the same rate as the elderly.

No. No parent should ever have to bury their child, but sometimes, in some places, it almost seemed as if it was no surprise. Even inevitable. Though that didn't make it any easier. It was never easy. No matter how old or young the person who died. It somehow seemed unnatural. Although we all have to do it. Die, that is. We all must die. Somber, but true. We just hope that it is not a tragic death. Not one that comes too soon or too sudden. We wish for a pain-free, quiet passing from this world into the next. Or into nothingness. Whatever you determine in your mind to believe.

Earl's sister's eyes followed the gurney all the way to the door and out of sight. It was time to go. Earl was gone. They had to go too. Cheech was lifted to his feet by Jermaine. He was better now. Not whole but better. Thomas took his family to their car parked in the hospital garage. Jermaine considered calling a rideshare. He knew that Earl had sat in the passenger seat of Cheech's car and thought of what that must have felt like for Cheech. He thought about how much Cheech would have had to pay if he parked the car overnight. He offered to drive and let Cheech sleep in the backseat the whole ride home.

###

Roxie awakened tired and emotionally drained Jermaine who had barely slept with the reality of his good friend's death circling his mind all night. Denise, of course, knew, but she had not told the girls. She could not quite gauge how much they could digest at such early stages in their life. How do you explain something like death to a child?

Roxie was chipper and energetic from a full night's sleep, and she asked her mom if Brother could take her to school that morning. Denise, always protective of Jermaine, let her know that Brother needed his sleep. Jermaine couldn't sleep. He had been in and out of sporadic catnaps all night. Beforehand, he had dropped Cheech off and finally got a few words out of him before walking home at around one thirty in the morning. Now, he would much rather be up and moving, but his body was physically exhausted. He overheard the conversation and answered for Denise.

"I'll take her!" Jermaine said.

He dragged himself into a lukewarm shower and got dressed with just enough time to get Roxie to school on time. Renee was sick and stayed in bed. Denise was doing her best to care for Renee, but she also knew that she had to get work. She called her client and asked if she could bring Renee with her as she did home care. Fortunately, she got a positive response. That was not the first time. The girls had fallen ill before, yet the work of a home attendant must go on. Without wanting to, Denise had taken on her fourth and sometimes her fifth child to attend to.

Jermaine put on his fresh kicks while Roxie tossed her backpack over her shoulders. Denise threw a lunch in the bag before Roxie could escape.

"I'll be right back," Jermaine said.

He gave Denise a kiss on the cheek. Denise took the opportunity to comfort Jermaine. She knew it was probably too soon to call Earl's house, but she could hold on to her boy. Jermaine tried to make it short, but Denise held on a little longer. Jermaine finally relented and hugged her back. He didn't want to cry. He was about to go outside. There would be lots of kids making their way to school and adults making their way to work and he had just washed the morning crud out of his eyes. He held his tears back. Then let out a heave that said it all. The exhale of a long-awaited breath yet to be released.

"Mom! I have to go," Roxie said, demanding that her mother let go of Brother.

Denise got the hint. She knew her job as a mom to her adult son had been accomplished. She knew Jermaine and knew he didn't want to talk about Earl's death. He hadn't wanted to talk about things when Dookie had been shot or when Earl had OD'd. He compartmentalized his emotions. The street was the street. Home was safe, where he was a son, a big brother, and yes...a kid.

Roxie and Jermaine left the house just as many other teens, pre-teens and not yet pre-teens made their way to school as well. The streets and crosswalks were congested. Jermaine didn't want to make conversation with anyone, so he worked hard not to make any eye contact. Of course, Roxie wanted to talk his ear off, like many kids do. He obliged. He loved his little sister and would not deny her anything. He was the one that would give her candy before dinner and then again before bedtime. Although he knew it could have kept her up all night with the jitters and an overactive brain. Denise would sometimes find the candy wrappers stuck on the bed sheets or underneath the bed and knew that it was all Jermaine's doing. She figured this was the way he was there for the girls. She knew that he would not be there for much longer. Graduation was only a blink of an eye away.

They crossed the street and Jermaine dropped Roxie off at the playground just before the bell rang. He said, "Hi," to the crossing guard and saw the charter school principal greeting students as they made their way to the yard. Roxie reached up for a hug goodbye, and Jermaine stooped down to hug her.

"Bye, Brother!" Roxie said affectionately and loud enough for her friends to hear.

She was proud of her brother. Because he was so much older, he was like a superhero to her. He could do things that she could only hope to do one day. Their relationship was special. She had no clue how much he was hurting inside that day. She would have comforted him if she had.

Jermaine walked back toward their home, and on the way, he saw a few of the gang members at the bus stop on their way to school. He didn't want to engage. Not like this. He wanted to be a leader. Someone who was in charge. Who had the right words to say. He didn't have time to prepare, but they saw him and he saw them. He knew he had to cross the street and talk about what happened. They knew. They knew he knew. It wasn't easy for anyone, but they had to talk about it.

"Rottweilers! Where's your mind at?" Jermaine said, stating the moniker in a somber tone.

Cyrus, Matthias and Tim were all somber too. They didn't look like they got much sleep either. Jermaine knew where their mind was at. It was not on school. That was for certain. He knew there were no words to be said. Especially with a group of teens at the bus stop with them.

"We are sticking by each other, Bro!" Matthias said. "It's hard!"

"I know!" Jermaine said. "Earl was like a brother to me. Hell! He was my brother. Neither one of us had brothers, so we were each other's brother."

"Hey Jay!" Tim said. "Come through tonight! We can all use it."

Jermaine looked over to Cyrus. He was frozen. As if already dead inside. He knew he was the one who poisoned Earl. He was the one who gave Earl the Killer Coke and almost killed him the first time. Earl's death meant something different to Cyrus. It was as if he had killed Earl. Jermaine was still torn. He hated Cyrus, but he forgave him for what he did. The pill that was meant for him may have weakened Earl so much that he couldn't fight off his attacker. The what-if's were tormenting him. At that moment, especially in front of Matthias and Tim, he had to push aside his anger and hate. He walked over to Cyrus and put his arm around his shoulder and told him:

It's all right!

Cyrus broke down crying in front of all the teens and the pretty, young girls at the bus stop. He pushed into Jermaine's shoulder to hide his face. He was embarrassed but couldn't stop the water works. Jermaine saw the bus coming. A middle-aged woman reached in her bag and pulled out some tissue and handed it to Jermaine. Jermaine took it with a nod and handed it to Cyrus. The moment bonded them. Cyrus, the tough kid at school, was willing to show his vulnerability and laid down his reputation. Jermaine handed him to Matthias and Tim who got him on the crowded bus headed to the high school. Jermaine knew he was in good hands.

###

Bianca walked through the campus on her way to class. She was oblivious of the whole matter with Earl. In fact, she was happy and care-free because she was making great progress on her project. She dashed into the lab and looked around for Jermaine, but his seat was empty. She thought nothing of it. Jermaine was often late for class. She walked up to Bruce to show off her progress.

###

Across town, Pamela and Lance were leaving the hotel a little late that morning after a full night of clubbing. What was meant to be a visit to check out progress placement turned into a drink, and then dancing, and then another drink. Before they both knew it, they were the worse for the wear. Lance, being aware of the time, tried to let Pamela know that they should leave, but Pamela was having too good of a time. She had another and another. Lance called a rideshare, and Pamela refused to leave for a fourth and fifth time. He made his way back to the hotel, and left Pamela to find her own way back.

###

Bruce, knowing that Bianca might have some idea of Jermaine's whereabouts, asked subtly if she had seen him. Bianca answered that she hadn't, and her mood suddenly switched from excitement about her project to worry about Jermaine. She went back to her seat and pulled out her phone which was a strict violation of class policy, according to the syllabus. She put it on her lap and began to type a short message:

Hey boy! Where are you?

After not hearing back immediately, she became a little agitated. She knew how important this project was to him for finishing his coursework and graduating and that he was already struggling to come up with his findings. She asked to be excused and walked out into the hallway to call him. Still no answer. She found her way back into class, but her mind was somewhere else. Somewhere far away now.

###

Pamela finally made it into the hotel and through the buffet area where patrons were enjoying their morning cup of coffee, toast and eggs. She tried to sneak in undetected, but her room adjoined Lance's room. Lance heard her door shut, her shoes come off and the shower turn on. He looked at his clock on the nightstand and saw that it was six-thirty a.m. The club closed at three a.m. which meant Pamela had found some trouble to get into.

Lance scraped himself out of bed and made his way to the shower. He knew that there were at least three more stops they needed to make that day before getting on the road to the next town. He fought his clothes on and commandeered a corner seat at the buffet. No more than fifteen minutes later, Pamela joined him with a fresh do of make-up, lipstick and hair done.

"How was your night, Young Lady?" Lance asked slyly.

"Oh, I left right after you did," Pamela replied.

"Liar! I heard your door shut this morning," he said.

"I came down early for a cup of coffee to bring to the room," Pamela said. "I needed it to wake up after all that dancing."

"And alcohol!" Lance said.

A small child in the booth next to them waved at Pamela. Pamela, with a friendly gesture, waved back.

"I saw you down here earlier," the little boy said.

"Yes! I came down for coffee," Pamela said.

"You changed. You weren't wearing a black dress before," the boy said. "My mother said you looked like something the cat drug in."

The mother, super embarrassed, shushed the boy and pulled him back into the booth.

"Coffee, huh!" Lance said.

"Okay! I just got in," Pamela confessed.

"The club closed at three," Lance pointed out. "What were you up to?"

"Minding my own business," Pamela said with a smile. "Well, no one can accuse me of being a racist anymore."

"Ooh!" Lance said. "I'm not telling."

###

Class was about to let out, and Bruce figured that Jermaine must have overslept or had something to take care of on campus. As he opened his phone to check the time, he saw something flash across his newsfeed regarding the murder of a local gang member. He typically abided by the same rules he enforced in his class regarding cell phone use, but he immediately thought about Jermaine being out of class on a major report day and considered whether the worst had happened. He let the class out five minutes early so he could check his computer. As the class filed out, there were students with questions. Ninety-nine percent of the time he gave his students his full attention, but today he instructed them to make an appointment or to visit him during his office hours.

Bianca could see the worry on his face. She felt the same worry in the pit of her stomach. She rushed to Bruce.

"What's wrong?" she asked. "Is Jermaine alright?"

Bruce hardly heard her over the buzzing in his head. He frantically searched for local news stories and pulled up a page related to the murder. It read:

Long-time Member of the Rottweiler Gang Strangled to Death.

The blood left Bruce's face. Bianca saw his anguish and walked behind his desk to see what he was looking at. She read the same headline. It was a gut punch. She took over the mouse and scrolled down looking for Jermaine's name. She didn't see it. The name in the article was "Earl Waiters." Earl. She remembered that Earl was Jermaine's friend.

"It wasn't Jermaine," Bianca said. "It was his friend Earl. I have to go see him."

"Go!" Bruce said. "Do you have his address?"

"Yes! I called him a rideshare once. I have it," Bianca said. She rushed out the door.

###

That day took Pamela and Lance to a familiar place. The laundromat where they were both on-site for the installation, not so many months ago. At that time, Jonathan was still alive and somewhere in hiding. What they assumed was an extended vacation. Pamela had just handed the reins to Lance, and he had been excited to meet Sethi. This time, they were at the mat under different circumstances. Sethi knew more than he wanted to know about Quarimoc and had been instrumental in leading the charge to bring the company to accountability for the death of the man killed in their community. What Sethi didn't know was that Patrice had been arrested again, this time under suspicion for the murder of Earl.

Pamela and Lance felt the heaviness as soon as they arrived at the laundromat. It was like a funeral procession. The televisions were muted. The patrons were silent. The only sound was the whirling of the machines. Lance cautiously knocked on the door of the office. Sethi was not expecting them. He reluctantly waved them in.

"We were in the area and hoped you didn't mind if we stopped through to see how the machines were holding up," Lance said.

Sethi didn't bother to look at them. "They are just fine," Sethi remarked. "Is that all you wanted to know? You could have called to ask that."

Pamela noticed the shortness of tone in Sethi's response. She looked over at his desk and saw some leftover flyers that Sethi was posting up regarding Quarimoc. She walked over and picked one up.

"I don't know what you think we know," Pamela said. "But we had no knowledge of whatever Jonathan was doing. For God sake, he took his own life."

"Someone above him was calling the shots," Sethi said abruptly.

"Yeah! Who?" Lance asked.

"If I knew that for sure, they would be in jail right now," Sethi answered.

"For what? Putting a tail on someone," Lance replied. "There is no evidence that anyone from Quarimoc initiated a hit."

"So, you admit that you were having Jermaine followed?" Sethi asked.

"There is evidence to support that Jonathan had him followed," Pamela said. "And I believe someone put him up to it."

"So, is it so far-fetched to imagine that that same person wanted the P.I. silenced?" Sethi asserted.

"I personally believe it is...without proof," Lance responded. "Besides, it turns out the person they brought in initially was picked-up for the murder of a gang member last night."

Pamela looked at Lance. Sethi whipped his head around in disbelief.

"How long have you known this?" Pamela asked.

"Why are both of you so shocked?" Lance said. "Don't tell me you really thought Quarimoc was in the killing business, Pamela."

Sethi scrambled to search for the local news on his computer.

"How long have you known this, Lance?" Pamela demanded. "Answer the question!"

"Get your underwear out of a twist," Lance said. "I get local news alerts on my phone based on the area I am in. I saw it in the cab ride over."

Sethi found a feed that mentioned Earl's death. As he scrolled down, he read that a suspect had been detained. He saw that it was Patrice. He felt embarrassed. He had fought for her release just so she could come out and kill again. No less a member of the gang that he now belonged to. He felt flush, as if he was about to vomit. His eyes watered, and he put his head between his knees.

"Are you going to be all right?" Pamela asked.

She was still upset at Lance for dropping this on them both so casually. Pamela believed that Shirley might have been involved. She saw information on Shirley's computer. She thought Lance should have told her as soon as he found out. She wondered if he was holding it as a trump card to show off.

Now Sethi was visibly ill. He ran to the sink to wash his face. After a minute of continual dousing, he dried himself off and took a deep breath.

"The young man who died -- he was a good friend of Jermaine's," Sethi explained.

"You mean one of his gang members," Lance said. "If I understand correctly."

Sethi didn't like the tone and lunged to put a finger in Lance's face. He said, "I warn you not to speak on things you know so little about."

Lance saw the fresh brand on Sethi's arm. He had seen the same brand on Jermaine and took it for a scar or a beauty mark, but now he saw that it had a duplicate. He quickly put two and two together and realized that it was a gang brand and that Sethi was a part of the gang.

###

Bianca arrived at Jermaine's door. She had never been to his house before. She didn't know what to expect. His mother might answer. His sisters could be inside. He may have even had a side-piece who rushed over to comfort him before she could arrive. Despite all her worries and fears, she knocked on the door and waited. After about thirty seconds, she knocked again. Before she turned to leave, the curtain pulled back, and she caught a motion out of the corner of her eye. Jermaine was wrapped in a towel. He thought the knock must be for some certified mail or package that his mother was expecting. He saw Bianca and looked for some pants to throw on before he unlocked the door. He cracked it a little and yelled to her.

"Come in! I will be right out," he said.

He ran to the bathroom, and Bianca walked inside. She saw his pullout couch that was still not made and his crate of clothes and books shoved in the corner. She knew he wasn't rich, but this gave her a real picture of how he had been living for the past few years or at least since the girls had become old enough to need their own room. She didn't quite know where to sit. She made her way to the kitchen and sat at the table. Jermaine came out in a hurry, so as not to keep her waiting. He sat down opposite her at the kitchen table.

"Hey! You surprised me!" he said. "I didn't even know you knew where I lived."

"I was worried about you," Bianca replied. "I heard a gang member was killed, and I thought it might have been you. And then..."

"My friend," Jermaine said.

"I know," Bianca replied. "I'm so sorry! I rushed over as fast as I could. I was worried when you didn't come to projects class. I knew you wouldn't just skip."

"I couldn't today," Jermaine said. "My mind was racing after I went to bed past two a.m. I was in the ER until Earl's parents left. Then I had to drive my boy Cheech home and then walk from his place. I finally got some sleep after my mother and sister left."

"Is she going to freak out that I am here?" Bianca asked.

"Probably," Jermaine said.

Jermaine was a little embarrassed, but also glad that Bianca finally got to see his house. He rushed to put the bed away, so she could sit on the couch. Bianca couldn't hold in what was racing through her mind.

"We should move in together," she said.

"What?" Jermaine said. "We barely know each other."

"Just for a little while," she explained. "I just got approved for my place. I wanted it to be a surprise."

Jermaine tried to pull her back into the station. "How about I just sleep over as often as I can?"

Bianca didn't think he should have to sleep on a pullout at twenty-one years old. She knew he was thinking about moving out anyway and thought it could be a temporary move, just until he had enough saved for a down payment and some furniture.

"Can we talk about it after graduation?" Jermaine asked.

"You don't want to move in with me?" Bianca said.

"I just lost my good friend," Jermaine said. "It's too much to think about right now."

Bianca felt horrible. She thought she was being sensitive, but now she felt judgmental and pushy. She had come over to be a shoulder to lean on, but instead, she took the conversation in a different direction after seeing his meager living arrangement. Bianca did not grow up rich and had shared a bedroom with her sister until she went out of state for college. Her parents worked well-paying jobs, but they struggled to pay bills like most American families do. Even now, she shared an apartment to make ends meet by splitting the rent, utilities and the cable bill three ways. She was hanging her hat on this job that was going to pay her tuition. That would give her breathing room and reduce her school loans. It would also give her a little extra cheddar to get her own place.

"I'm sorry! I was being insensitive," Bianca said. "Can I give you a hug?"

They stood up simultaneously and embraced. This was real. Their relationship may have been thrust from their loins initially, but this hug meant more than that. It was from her concern about his missing class which had prompted to her to come over to check on him in his time of need and from her worry about his sleeping arrangements. Their relationship was quickly becoming more than a twirl in the sheets. Bianca cared for him. The real question was how long would it take for Jermaine to figure out Bianca cared or for him to realize he cared for her too.

###

Pamela got in between Lance and Sethi and reminded them that they were there on business.

"You're right!" Lance said. "I was out of line. Please forgive me. You are the customer. I work for you. Please let's start over."

Sethi backed off and sat back down in his chair.

Pamela decidedly took over the conversation. "I am sorry that you had to learn about Patrice this way," Pamela said. "I am just as caught off-guard as you. Did you know her?"

"No!" Sethi said. "I just didn't like the idea of another young Black girl getting blamed for something with little to no evidence to prove it".

"Well, something has got your rattled. What is it?" Pamela continued.

"I fought so hard to get her off," Sethi began. "I believed in her innocence. Maybe she still is innocent. Who knows? But now she comes out and does this. Strangles Earl. Over what? That's what has me shaken."

"You knew Earl?" Pamela asked.

Sethi explained that he knew Earl, but not as well as the rest of the members. That the younger guys would come in and go over business and investment strategies. How he was trying to get them to think like owners and not workers.

Lance perked up. "That's it!" Lance said. "That's the model"

"What are you talking about?" Pamela said.

Lance held his hands high. "Spare change!" he said. "Jermaine has been talking about how we disregard spare change, and how the coin-op business can make use of it. Well, what Sethi is doing right here is taking those folks who were disregarded and retooling them and putting their minds to good use."

“Spare change,” Sethi said. “I like it. I can’t take the credit though. It was Jermaine’s idea.”

“Either way. I believe we can start a group with gang members in other areas based off of what you are doing here and teach them how to build their own businesses,” Lance exclaimed.

“I want to run it by Jermaine,” Sethi said. “I can’t have some white man co-opting his idea.”

###

CHAPTER THIRTEEN

The Rottweilers were once again in front of the corner store. Their old stomping grounds. Cheech, Brian and Dookie were meeting up for the first time since Earl was killed. Jermaine rounded the corner.

"What's up fellas?" Jermaine said.

The space felt empty without Earl there. It was almost surreal. Like he was going to walk up the block at any moment. It wasn't going to happen, though they couldn't help but think it might.

Brian and Dookie felt somewhat justified, knowing they had some part in Earl's revenge. Despite the code. They believed what they'd done was the right thing to do. That Earl would have wanted it that way.

Cheech was still distraught over having witnessed the whole thing and having not being able to stop it.

Jermaine, hoping to change the vibe in the atmosphere and get a rise out of his friends, called out Cheech.

"Cheech, where's your mind at?" he said.

Cheech was still speechless. He didn't look as though he had showered or eaten in the last few days. He was using marijuana to try to numb his pain. He believed that if he came down he would have to relive the anguish.

"You have to talk about it, Brother," Jermaine said. "What happened in the car that day?"

Cheech avoided eye contact, but still tried to speak and tried to recant what he could have done differently. How could he have kept Earl alive?

"Man, I..." Cheech began. "I just went to pick him up to show off the new whip I copped. I had the homies in the car and maybe there wasn't enough room for them and him. I should have dropped them off first, right?" Cheech paused halfway through his rant, looking for an answer, but the question was rhetorical. There really was no right or wrong.

"I asked the homie P to get in the backseat, so Earl could sit up front with me," Cheech continued. "I wanted to show him the wood and the system, you know. Either way, the homies get into it with him about being a snitch. That he was in the store with the DT's and that he dipped out as soon as everything went down. So, I'm like chill. Earl ain't no snitch."

Cheech was high as a kite now and was caught up in the story. He continued, "So, before I know it, this chick has unlaced her bootstraps and has Earl in a strangle hold from behind the seat. Straight mob movie with the plastic-bag type stuff, and I am tripping. I'd just gotten on the highway, and traffic was moving like seventy miles per hour."

Cheech paused for a minute. He took a hit off the weed to calm his nerves, as a flood of emotions came pouring through. He took a deep breath and finished the story. "I was trying to reach over and get this damn lace off his neck while not crashing the car," he said. "By the time I found the shoulder to pull over on, he was gone. I was going to call 911, but it was faster to just get him to the ER myself."

Brian and Dookie were stunned. They knew the sheriffs had already picked her up. They figured she was going to get hard time for Earl's murder. That too many people saw what went down, but Cheech knew better. He told them that she knew the court system inside and out and could get out of this one if she wanted to. Also, Cheech believed that she wanted to go back inside. The time inside had changed her, and she had adapted to it. Her mind began to think like a convict's mind, and prison had become her world. It was going to be too difficult for her to become a civilian again. She had her network inside, and it was easier to live in there than out here.

Jermaine wasn't thinking about Patrice. He was more concerned with the young Rottweilers who were hurting. Earl had brought them all into the gang, and they looked up to him. He needed to figure out how to get them through this.

"They want to meet up," Jermaine said. "Let's roll over to the laundromat as soon as Sethi closes up in an hour."

###

Donna was getting ready to close up the arcade when Charlene and Veronika walked in. She really only knew them from hanging out with Cheech, but remembered Veronika growing up. As she counted change, she saw them kind of hanging around, not really playing any games and not really talking. They looked as if they just needed someplace to be. She stopped what she was doing.

"Can I help you ladies?" Donna asked.

Charlene and Veronika looked at each other to see who would go first.

"We kind of need somebody to talk to," Charlene said.

Donna hadn't heard that their friend, Patrice, was arrested for Earl's murder. "You girls alright?" Donna asked. She saw Veronika starting to shake.

"You haven't heard, have you?" Charlene replied.

"Heard what?" Donna asked.

Charlene and Veronika watched as the last few patrons left. They asked to sit down. Donna locked the front door behind them and pulled up a chair in her office for Charlene to sit on. She offered Veronika her chair, and Donna remained standing.

Charlene began to tell her all about what happened. Donna was visibly shaken. She had known Earl. Maybe not as well as Jermaine or Cheech, but she had known him. Charlene told her that Patrice was his executioner. Donna tried to keep it together, but a tear rolled down her face. She knew how much Sethi believed in her innocence of the murder of the young PI. Charlene and Veronika didn't know Donna's family history, much less that her brother was a member of the Rottweilers, or that he was killed in gang violence.

Donna knew that the girls needed her help, and they had no place else to turn. They told her as much. They told her that the night Patrice was arrested, she had been stabbed and left for dead in a stairwell, and that they feared they could be next.

Donna was confused about why they came to her with all this information. She didn't know them that well, and they didn't really know her. Then it hit her. As a Black woman who owned a business in the neighborhood, she had become a pseudo role-model for them. They didn't know it. She didn't know it herself. But it was true. They didn't go up to the other business owners who didn't look like them and share their story. Most of the other business owners wouldn't have understood. Charlene and Veronika didn't even approach their parents or aunties. They chose a stranger who wasn't really a stranger after all. She had always been more than the person who ran the arcade. She was also a role model of Black success.

Donna listened to how Patrice was arrested and how Charlene and Veronika feared the police would come to them and ask them questions. They didn't want to go home, so they went on the lam. Donna offered them something to drink and provided whatever comfort she could. She assured them that their story was safe with her. She asked if she could find out from Jermaine and Cheech if the gang was after them. They gave the okay, and Donna called Jermaine right there in front of them. The homies heard the intimacy that Jermaine and Donna shared, and it provided them with an even stronger trust for her. Donna asked Jermaine how he was doing, offered her condolences and then asked what she could do to help. After about five minutes of conversation, when the time was right, she asked if the Rottweilers were mad at Charlene and Veronika for fleeing the scene.

Jermaine was with his boys. He checked in with them while he was on the phone and confirmed that they did not hold anything against the homies. Cheech knew that what Patrice did was outside of their control. Charlene and Veronika could hear Jermaine's voice on the other end of the line. They felt safe and were glad they had come to Donna for help. Donna ended the call by asking Jermaine again about how she could help. Without being prompted or even knowing that the homies were there with her, he told her to be there for Charlene and Veronika because they must be terrified.

Donna had just received her marching orders from a twenty-one-year-old kid. She already knew from the moment Charlene and Veronika sought her out that she was going to be called on. They would be her spare change. The discarded and forgotten-about ones that she would put to good use and that she would invest in.

The girls were still very worried about the police. They knew that they would be questioned, but, they wondered, would it be as suspects or as witnesses? Either way was terrifying. They would never snitch, but they were not necessarily clean either. The cops could have pulled up their records and blackmailed them by threatening lengthy sentences. Cops lied during interrogation. A strategy they used was to separate those under interrogation and to tell each one alone that the other person had already indicted them. The cops would tell them Patrice blamed the whole thing on them. The girls knew that Cheech was not arrested. That gave them some solace. They didn't know if he was questioned, but they wanted to know.

"Can you call Cheech?" Veronika asked.

"Julius?" Donna asked. Donna was almost the only person who called him by his government name. Once in a while they would hear an uncle or cousin say it when they were around his family though that was next to never.

"I think he would rather hear from you," Donna said.

The girls had dumped their phones, so they could not be traced. Donna dialed the number and offered up her phone. Cheech picked up on the second ring. He had been concerned about Charlene and Veronika. Thinking they may have been caught in the same web with Patrice. Guilt by association. Veronika, the thug, became Veronika the scared little girl.

"Hey Cheech!" she said "It's V!"

"V! Are you with Donna?" Cheech said. "Stay there! We will come by and see you."

"No! I am on my way out now," Veronika said. "I wanted to know what you told the cops."

"They caught me too, soon after Earl passed away in the hospital, and I couldn't put any words together," Cheech said. "They tossed me a card and told me to get in touch, or they would. Where have you been?"

"Oh, here and there," Veronika said. "C and I just stopped running and stumbled into the arcade."

"Are you sure I can't come by and check in on you two?" Cheech asked.

"No! You be there for your boys," Veronika said. "I have C. We are pretty good together."

"Listen!" Cheech said. "Donna is good people too. Lean on her. She knows what we have been through."

With this Veronika looked over at Donna. Donna didn't hear what Cheech said, but she could imagine. He probably said what she was beginning to understand. That though she had left the hood, the hood never really left her. She was tethered to her community and always would be.

Veronika hung up the phone and handed it back to Donna. The girls were okay. Not perfect, but better than when they had come in. There would be questions to answer, but the girls knew the standard response, "I don't know nothing." And that would suffice.

###

People gathered in a packed church on a gloomy overcast day. Funerals tended to carry gloom with them. There was an open casket and family members, friends and community members lined up for the viewing to see Earl lying peacefully in an oak box one last time before he was seen no more. He was dressed in a nice suit. One that he would never wear if it was up to him, so it seemed like it was someone else lying there in that oak box and not him at all. He still had the same face, and that was what his friends and family focused on. Thomas and Phyllis paused a long time to watch their child lying there, stolen from them at the tender age of twenty, hardly able to experience life. Earl's older sister, Amber, had to hold Tanja up, as she could barely stand at the site of her brother's lifeless body. The hood had many funerals, but no one was ever prepared, especially when it was someone they loved lying in that box.

The Rottweilers were there. Very well-dressed. Even Cheech was in a nice suit and tie. He wore dark shades to not only compliment his ensemble but also to cover his water-soaked eyes. The gang members consoled each other, but Jermaine had an extra duty. He was there for the gang, but he was also there for Earl's family as well. He rushed to help settle Tanja. He checked in on Thomas and Phyllis. He even handed out tissues to people he didn't know. When the service was over, he rallied the Rottweilers to serve as the pallbearers. He didn't rest until Earl's body was in the ground.

At the repast, he saw Donna and Sethi talking to each other. He couldn't recall seeing them leaving the laundromat office after the rally, so seeing them together seemed out of place. They both helped with contributions for the costs of the funeral, and even though neither one of them were especially tight with Earl, they felt as if it was important for them to be there. Jermaine left his seat with the Rottweilers and walked over to join them.

"I didn't know you knew each other," Jermaine said.

"It's a small world," Sethi said. "We met after the rally. You remember, I walked Donna back to the arcade and asked you to cover for me. We were just talking about your class project."

"It's like my worlds are colliding," Jermaine said. "In a good way. So, what are you thinking?"

"Well, right now might not be the best time for that discussion," Donna said. "We can talk about it later. Right now, I want to check in with some of the people here."

"Cheech could use an encouraging word from you," Jermaine said. "He can't stop blaming himself for everything that went down."

"Charlene told me that he was sitting next to Earl in the driver's seat when everything went down," Donna said. "I will go talk to him now."

Donna left Sethi and Jermaine and pulled Cheech aside from Brian, Dookie and the rest of the Rottweilers. Sethi used the opportunity to catch Jermaine up on a few things.

"How is the gang today?" he said.

"Same, same," Jermaine said. "Cyrus is taking it bad because he feels responsible for causing Earl to be comatose. Cheech is feeling bad because he was helpless. Brian and Dookie are on edge for reasons I can't figure out. It's all surreal. I am just appreciative that you were able to pull the newbies aside and provide them some comfort in the midst of all the chaos."

"Donna is being a real support to the girls who were in the car when it went down as well," Sethi said. "But they say out of tragedy comes something good."

"What's that supposed to mean?" Jermaine asked.

"I know Donna wanted to wait to tell you, but we feel this has really opened the eyes of a lot of people to how broken our system is and how much we need to come together for everyone," Sethi said.

"I get that, but what does that have to do with coin-op," Jermaine said.

"I don't want to steal your thunder, because you have been saying this the whole time, but it really is about paying attention to the disregarded. Isn't that what you wanted to do with the coin-op business?"

Jermaine's mind had to catch up with the concept. The disregarded. Coins. People. It was right in front of him the whole time. He couldn't figure out why he didn't see it. He always talked about helping the community members become owners. The same concept applied. It was always about reinvesting in what's already there, instead of coming up with something new or pulling in resources from the outside. About retooling existing resources and figuring out how to put them to good use. At the repast in the wake of Earl's death, a new concept had been birthed. A seed fell to the ground and produced a tree that would bear fruit to feed the many.

###

While Cheech was talking with Donna, two unfamiliar faces appeared and sat at the Rottweiler table. Matthias immediately suspected that they may be undercover DT's, and he tried to get Cheech's attention. He knew that he was talking to Donna about what went down, and Earl and Matthias wanted to protect him in case something nefarious slipped out. Cheech caught on, and from the back of the strangers, he made out a familiar face. He pardoned himself from Donna for a second and came around to the front of the two men.

"Rico and Barry!" Cheech said aloud. He hadn't been this exuberant since Earl died.

Rico stood up to give Cheech a hug. "Where's your mind at?" Rico said.

The Rottweilers immediately recognized the phrase that was only used between the gang members with each other. They wondered if these two strangers were the infamous Rico and Barry that they heard so much about. A funeral could bring people out of the woodworks.

Donna overheard the celebration. Rico and Barry were kids when her brother was in the gang. Fifteen-years-old and-sixteen-years-old when her brother died. She remembered them from her brother's funeral. Now she saw them again as adults at another funeral. A flood of emotions came back. She felt as if it were her brother that just went into the ground. The young Rottweilers knew her story from the night Earl was killed. She came around and supported them then. Now she needed their support. Alexander and Rudy saw the tears and immediately came by her side. Cheech saw this happening and was trying to put the pieces together. Barry recognized Donna from over ten years ago. She had put on a little weight since college, but her face remained the same. The moment went from exciting back to somber in a matter of seconds. Barry was a chaplain for convicts now. He had left the gang and the area, put down the booze and the drugs and had gotten into the church. This was the first time he had been back in almost five years. He left as Earl was just joining the gang.

"Ms. Donna!" Barry said. "Where's your mind at?" He asked in a somber tone. Not as in addressing a fellow gang member, but as if he really, really wanted to know what she was thinking about. Cheech was amazed that he knew her.

"You remember me?" Donna asked. "You were a kid when we last saw each other."

"I keep a picture of Brother Rod on my bookcase," Barry said. "You are in it too. Why wouldn't you be? You two were inseparable. I pray for your family almost every night."

"That's a trip that you know each other," Cheech said. "She knew you as a kid, went away, came back and knew me as a kid." Cheech looked at Donna. "You truly have become a matriarch of our community."

Alexander and Tim were itching to meet the two legends, but also realized that it was a special moment and didn't want to interrupt. As Barry took over the role of comforter, Alexander and Tim tried to ease back to their seats. Cheech saw this and instructed Stevie to go bring Jermaine over but not to tell him why. Barry turned to Donna.

"How have you been?" he said.

"I've been okay!" Donna replied.

"No! How have you really been?" Barry repeated.

Donna knew that she couldn't just skirt the question as she did with most people. Barry was an adult now. Not as old as she, but close enough to have a real conversation with. He was married and had a daughter. He had real-life experiences unlike the other members of the gang.

"I'm hurting, Barry!" Donna said. "I fell into a dark place when Roderick died. I got strung out on prescription meds and ended up in a detox. When I got clean, I knew I had to come back home."

"Your parents took it hard," Barry said. "Rico, Tony and I would go by and check on them. We became their adopted kids after Rod died."

"They never blamed you?" Donna asked.

"Not once!" Barry said. "They loved us and taught us to love one another. It was because of them we put our wicked ways aside. They showed us what true forgiveness looked like. We did our best to pass that along to Jermaine, Earl, Cheech and the gang."

Rico looked over at the table. "Who are these young bucks?" Rico said. "They don't look like family members."

Cheech gave a nod, and they all stood up at once.

"Rottweilers, where's your mind at?" Cheech said. At once, they all displayed their brand and recited the motto:

"Why we choose peace over war? Why we value life over death? RIP Brother Rod."

Barry hugged Donna by the shoulder and walked her over to the young men.

"These are your brothers now," Barry said.

As they each took in what Barry had just said, Jermaine walked over and interrupted the moment. At first, he didn't see Rico, so Rico grabbed from behind and whispered in his ear.

"Where's your mind at?" Rico said.

"Rico?" Jermaine said.

Rico broke the hug and when Jermaine turned around he gave him a real hug.

"Rico! You made it," Jermaine said.

"I told you I would," Rico said.

"You told me you would do your best," Jermaine said.

"Do you see who I brought with me?" Rico said.

Jermaine looked over and saw Donna with an arm around her shoulder. For a moment, he thought it was Earl back from the dead. He told himself it couldn't be, and then he caught a glimpse of Barry from the side.

"What? How?" he sputtered.

Jermaine couldn't believe his eyes.

"I haven't seen Barry since...since I joined the gang five years ago," he said. "I hardly recognize him."

Jermaine walked over. He didn't even know if Barry would remember him. Barry left and never turned back. Barry saw him as soon as he got close.

"My brother Jay!" he said. "I see you are leading up a group of men."

"This is a manifest of everything you and Tony taught me," Jermaine said.

"Brother, I got out a few months after you came in," Barry said. "I had a different call on my life." Barry flashed the cross around his neck.

"Pastor?" Jermaine asked.

"Chaplain," Barry said. "Prison ministry. Giving the Word to former gang members like me. Tony gets all the credit for raising you up right."

Barry gave Jermaine a hug. It was like a big brother hugging a little brother.

Jermaine nodded to Donna. He asked, "You know my mentor?"

"I met Donna ten years ago at a gathering not unlike this one when I was these guy's age," Barry said, nodding to the new gang members.

Jermaine did the math and realized that he was referring to Brother Rod's funeral. Donna seemed okay with the reference. She was settled in with the younger members now. Sethi, who had been giving his condolences to the family, walked over to join Donna and the gang members in the circle.

"Yo! Who's this?" Rico asked.

Feeling right at home, Sethi rolled up his sleeve to show his fresh scar from his week-old brand.

"You guys let this old man join the gang!" Rico said. "We are definitely losing our street cred now."

###

CHAPTER FOURTEEN

Projects were due the following week, and Bruce hadn't seen Jermaine since Earl's passing. Although he was sympathetic to Jermaine's pain, he also had to collect the students' work three weeks before the semester ended, in order to get grades in on time.

He didn't like to show preferential treatment. In fact, he regarded it as unethical, but he saw Jermaine's potential and knew that this would not only count against him for his class, but it would also have a direct impact on his work-experience units since the two were interconnected. He decided that he would usurp the process by asking Bianca about Jermaine's whereabouts. He saw Bianca walk into class. As she did, he saw that the door was being held open by someone else's hand. As Bruce moved in and approached Bianca to ask her to call Jermaine, he recognized the voice holding the door and saw that Jermaine was right behind her. Bruce turned to go back to the front of the class before he was seen, but it was too late.

"Professor Wright! Did you miss me?" Jermaine asked.

Caught in his escape, Bruce answered curtly. "I was a little worried about you," he said. "You really need to let your instructors know if you are going to need some time away."

"My mom called the dean's office," Jermaine said. "You should be getting a funeral bulletin and all that."

"You know as well as I do that I can only excuse the death of a family member," Bruce said. "You are going to take some lumps."

"Earl was family!" Jermaine replied. "Let me make up some classes."

"It's too late for that," Bruce said. "Your projects are due next week."

"Well, let me help you grade them," Jermaine said. "I know all the metrics. I even reviewed last semester's projects and followed your format. I know your system backwards and forwards. Dare I say better than you do?"

Jermaine was thinking on his feet. He knew professors hated grading and this was his bribe to get out of a dropped grade. Bruce would spend nights and weekends going through eighteen different projects. Just the research alone was enough to drive a person crazy.

"It's not a bad idea," Bruce said. "First, you need to show me the progress on your project, but not right now. Let everyone get in their groups, and I will look at your project in a minute."

"You're going to be pleased," Jermaine said.

"I hope so," Bruce replied. "Remember this is an economics class. I need hard data."

"Professor Wright! You are talking to Jermaine here," he said. "I'm back! I had a rough week, but something really special came out of it."

Jermaine had already reviewed the project with both Donna and Sethi and had been adding their edits throughout. Bruce was curious if either were economists. Jermaine told Bruce that Donna was a business economics graduate from Kent State and a former S & E broker on Wall Street. Bruce was impressed.

"Well, I will have to invite him in as a guest speaker then," he said.

"Her!" Jermaine corrected.

Bruce responded, as he wrote information on the white board with his back to the class. "Excuse me!"

"Invite her in!" Jermaine said. "My mentor is female. From right in my hood. We are taking the hood back. One dime at a time."

Bruce didn't quite know how to respond to this, so he didn't. Instead, he got the class going and began to review projects, starting with the ones that were already turned in for review. Jermaine didn't have the opportunity to have his project reviewed by Bruce and get feedback. He took some time to look over Bianca's review and had to base his edits off of the feedback she had received. Bruce was a stickler for sustainable growth over time. Jermaine knew that. He needed to get back in touch with Lance to demonstrate how his project fit with Quarimoc's model. He hadn't spoken to Lance, or for that matter, Pamela in over a week's time. That would be his mission for the week ahead.

###

Pablo ran a check on the interns' latest numbers and posted them on the break room wall. Jermaine had not gained the ground Pablo expected but was still holding steady. He walked down the hall to report the numbers to Shirley, and Lance happened to be in her office. Pablo seemed to have walked into a tense conversation as Shirley and Lance immediately fell silent.

"What's new y'all?" Pablo said. "I hope I'm not interrupting."

"Not at all!" Lance said. "In fact, I'm glad you're here."

Shirley had a blank stare on her face, and Pablo didn't know whether he should stay or leave.

"So, it turned out IT found some activity on Shirley's computer confirming that she not only knew about the P.I. keeping tabs on Jermaine, but even after Jonathan confirmed that Jermaine was clean, this lady asked him to keep going on the witch hunt," Lance said. Speaking firmly, he pointed towards Shirley.

Pablo was stunned. He had always accused Shirley of being involved, but this put it squarely in her lap. He didn't know where to begin.

"So, he would be alive today if he didn't keep going out to dig up dirt," Pablo asked.

"We don't know why someone wanted him dead," Shirley said.

"Do the police know?" Pablo asked.

"Well, this is where it gets interesting," Lance said. "Shirley is saying that someone hacked into her computer and sent the emails, but I have an eye witness that can verify it was her."

"Yeah, who?" Pablo asked.

Lance wouldn't give Pamela up. He hoped to make this as painless as possible and have Shirley confess to her crimes.

"I don't believe in ratting people out either, but a young man is dead and if you don't admit to your part in it I have to call in the big guns to investigate," Lance said.

Shirley was concerned with not only herself, but also the reputation of the company. It would eventually all come out in the wash, so Lance thought it best if Shirley took her medicine now.

"This was all you, and you pulled Jonathan into it and look at what happened to him," he said.

"You don't have any proof of that," Shirley said.

"Well, hold your horses," Pablo intervened. "He actually might."

Pablo rushed to his office and grabbed his tablet. He came back into Shirley's office.

"I got a very cryptic email on my tablet just before things went south with Jonathan," Pablo said. "I didn't open it, fearing it was a virus. I had IT take a look at it, and they confirmed my fear. They said that the virus was launched from inside the company firewall, so somebody inside the company was responsible for it. Two days later Jonathan blows his brains out. IT found the same exact virus trolling on his computer except for the fact that he opened it."

"Well, how does that prove that I had anything to do with anything?" Shirley asked.

The virus was launched from Shirley's computer with the subject line,

They know it was you.

The IP address couldn't be duplicated. The virus that was on Shirley's computer was the same one that crashed Jonathan's computer.

"I don't remember sending that email," Shirley said. "Besides that, the subject line could have meant anything."

"Yeah! And within a matter of minutes a man blows his brains out." Lance said. "Do you have any remorse?"

Shirley stood up and shut the door to give the men a lesson in business.

"I have been at this business a lot longer than you have," she began. "In fact, longer than both of you put together. I have done some things that I am not always proud of, but I didn't sleep my way to the top or cut anyone down to climb up. I have only done what was asked of me."

"So, the board of directors put you up to this?" Lance asked.

She refused to say. She told them that sometimes she received orders, and she followed them and sometimes people got hurt, but most of the time there was no harm.

"I helped my last company become a top-50 industry," Shirley said. "When they needed a fall guy for insider trading guess who was asked to take the bullet? It came with a great payout and a nice referral to Quarimoc, but I had to leave a pension on the table. Quarimoc knew what they had in me, what the rest of you were unable to provide. Loyalty."

"I'm disgusted," Lance said. "I can't tell who I am more disgusted with, you or the board."

"You know where the door is," Shirley asserted. "Just remember, it only swings out."

Lance swung the door out and left. Pablo stood stunned. He had helped build this business from the ground up and had always operated above the board. Maybe that was the reason he never saw the big promotion or the hefty bonus. He always thought it was his moderate sales numbers, but now he came to realize that there was another game being played. The one meant to keep certain people spinning in place and the one where the rat got the cheese.

"You know," Pablo began. "I was never asked to the table."

"What?" Shirley said.

"You talk about loyalty," Pablo said. "I have been here since the beginning. No one ever asked me to get my hands dirty."

"Oh, you were asked," Shirley said. "You didn't take the invite to the golf course or to late night drinks or a trip to the Caymans. You were above that. You didn't read the signs, or vote with the majority, or respond to the wink or nod. It was all there to do or not. It's always there. It took me a long time to catch on. A colleague pulled me aside and schooled me in the ways. The deals that happen away from the boardroom. You just have to pay attention. I can teach you if you like."

Pablo thought long and hard. He had been with the company seventeen years now. He was almost fifty. Too old for Club Fed. He would have loved to have off-shore accounts, but he had been doing things the right way for far too long now. He would have had to have started earlier. It was a tough decision. He honestly wanted to think about it, but he knew his answer, that day, the next day and a week from then.

"No, I'll pass," he said.

"And so, you can never again say that you haven't been asked," Shirley said.

"True! I am too old for prison, and if you don't mind me saying, it looks like that's where they are preparing a cell for you soon," Pablo said.

"You wouldn't!" Shirley said.

"I already did," Pablo said. He revealed a recording device and played back a portion of their conversation before he walked out of Shirley's office saying, "I guess somebody had to be the rat since you or Lance refused to."

###

Bianca's project had been approved with edits. On top of that, her company decided to move her from a paid intern onto their salesforce. She was scheduled to graduate in just a couple of weeks and needed to get her business in order to be sure she didn't miss any looming deadlines. Her parents were coming from out of state with her younger sister to watch her walk in commencement.

Bianca had become proficient in buying products, such as steel and glass, from overseas in large quantities, breaking them down and then selling them to smaller companies at a rate below what the companies were paying domestically. Of course, her company had to underwrite the purchases, and she assumed a risk every time, not knowing how fast the product would move or if her purchases would ever arrive. She was doing dealings with people she hadn't met before and shopping with blind trust. She hoped that once she was on the company's payroll, she would be able to expense a trip over to China to see the country's factories and meet her sellers. Until then, she had to believe. It had all worked to date, but it was safe being an intern. Now, not only would her salary depend on her success, but also her college tuition, along with her room and board would depend on her success. She met with Bruce in his office to discuss his revisions.

"Are you ready to see me?" Bianca asked.

"Yes, have a seat!" he said. "I want to discuss the volatility of your economic scheme."

"Volatility?" she said. "Are you saying I am susceptible?"

"Not necessarily susceptible!" he said. "I have seen this strategy work before, but it's not fool-proof. You have to take a lot of things into consideration and hope that everything works in your favor. I try to look at this over the long-term. Let's say you have a banner year with over five-hundred-thousand dollars in sales, but then you take a nosedive the following year to only two-hundred-thousand dollars in sales. Can you sustain that?"

"Aren't all companies volatile in some aspect?" Bianca asked.

"Of course, but you are working with off-shore companies," Bruce said. "There is no Federal Reserve or bailout to protect your company's losses. What happens in the time of war, or even conflict, or if our government decides to close borders, or the off-shore company simply decides that it doesn't like our country's leadership?"

Bruce told Bianca that just about eight years before there was a major virus that shut down flights coming out of mainland China and how the strong companies were able to survive the hit, but small and mid-size companies folded or went into the red. Bruce shared about how there were a couple of companies savvy enough to scramble and find alternative means of income during those lean months, but it was risky.

"So, only the big boys get to play. Is that what I'm hearing?" Bianca replied. "Well, I like the risk. High risk, high reward. I still want to learn how to be flexible, if and when trouble comes. What do you suggest?"

"I'm glad you asked," Bruce said. "At the start of class, there was a debate about why products are so cheap to produce overseas. You remember?"

Bianca rolled her eyes. She said, "I remember."

"I believe you can navigate to find cheap products here in the states as well," Bruce said.

"What do you mean? Prison contracts?" she asked.

"Well, that's just trading slave labor or more slave labor," Bruce said.

Bruce referred to a partnership between the poor and underserved communities and the people who wanted to teach these skills. He knew there were many companies based in the lower forty-eight that could benefit from the business that Bianca would offer them for about the same cost, factoring in the cost of shipping.

"These are rural companies in low-tax and land-cost zones trying to bolster the local economy," he said.

"It sounds like a return to slavery," Bianca said.

"Believe it not, most of these companies are Black-owned," he said. "It's something to think about."

Bianca took the feedback and promised to do her own research and get back to him.

###

Denise had just put the girls to bed and had crawled into bed herself after an exhausting day of home care. It was go time, and Jermaine had commandeered the living room as his work lab to complete his project. He had dry-erase white boards, butcher-block paper with markers, textbooks and research papers strewn about and his laptop at his side. The next forty-eight hours were critical, but Jermaine was thinking beyond the class right now. He was even thinking beyond his internship and coin-op. He was thinking locally, statewide and even nationally. He wanted to figure out how he could make his impact felt and develop life-changing work. Something that was easily reproducible and that helped communities grow from within. What started as a mole hill had become a mountain, and Jermaine wanted to climb that mountain and yell from the top of it.

He began by mapping out his starting line with his initial mission:

To make coin-operation easy and accessible for those patrons who chose not to use credit or debit.

He then wrote down his community mission:

Inspiring more business ownership from people from within his neighborhood.

He looked at the problem:

Patrons are forced to prepay by loading money on a traceable card. Good money is being discarded in bowls, drawers, piggy banks, on desks, shelves and the like.

The map followed a continuum all the way from "how to put discarded resources to use" to "how to put discarded people and their talents and skill-sets to use." He looked at his research methods that discussed people as driving forces in social and economic structures. The research also addressed risk factors, as well as, protective factors, and provided a litany of questions that Jermaine would have to answer.

He needed to pool his resources. He called up Donna. She was on her way out to a late meet up with a friend, but wanted to make time for her protégé. She told Jermaine she could stop by for a brief minute and suggested that he catch Sethi before he headed home. Jermaine did just that.

While Sethi was closing up his shop, Donna and Jermaine hammered through the more technical side of things. She understood business economics and brought in concepts Jermaine had yet to learn. Much of the upper-level subject matter that many of the interns, against whom Jermaine was competing, already knew. His learning curve was steep.

Just as Donna was about to leave, Sethi knocked on the door. Donna began catching him up on what they had already discussed. They immediately jumped into problem-solving mode. Before they realized it, the night had slipped away. Donna called her friend to apologize and asked for a raincheck. An hour poured into two hours and then into four. Jermaine put a pot of coffee on and poured everyone a cup. They were so close. Too close to stop now.

"Mentors," Jermaine said. "That's what you both are to me. It's a key ingredient."

"Stay focused on the model," Donna scolded. "Economic solutions, remember."

"He's right!" Sethi said. "We have to look at people as our key investments. We nurture them and put them in the right place and allow them to flourish."

"People as an underutilized commodity," Jermaine said. "In fact, as the most essential resource to the success or failure of a company."

"Okay!" Donna said. "Let's follow that logic through. Who are the people investing in these resources and what is our end product?"

"If the problem is squandered assets, the solution has to be putting those assets to work," Jermaine said.

"Are we talking coins or people?" Sethi asked.

"Both," Jermaine answered.

He felt it was important to have the community members take their money and the talents they already had and connect them with the right people, such as investors, to take that raw talent and mold it into something that could be useful right there in their neighborhood.

"It's been done before," Donna said. "It's actually the impetus for the community college. The idea was to learn a trade or skill that can be put to use in a career right away."

"Okay, so we think about that on steroids," Jermaine said. "I want everyone to think as an owner, not only a worker."

"We have to add in a finance and entrepreneur component," Donna said.

"We also have to start young," Sethi said. "Junior high."

"We have this population over at the community center," Donna said.

"That's it!" Jermaine cut in. "That's our lab. Already, you have there an in. Now we need real work experience for them."

"The business owners," Sethi said. "Each business owner commits to helping a young person in the arena that applies. In exchange, that young person helps the owner around their business."

"It sounds like a lot to ask," Donna said. "We need to add in some additional incentives."

"Like a tax break?" Sethi asked.

"Even better!" Donna said. "Like increased sales. Whoever signs up becomes a valued industry, and we incentivize them with customer loyalty for their investment back into the community."

"We create our own village," Jermaine said. "I like it!"

"Okay!" Donna said. "Now it's time to make it all make sense."

They dispersed, and as Sethi and Donna opened the door to leave, they were greeted by the rising sun.

###

Cheech, Charlene and Veronika went through the security check at the courthouse where Patrice was being charged. Thomas and Phyllis were there along with Tanja and her older sister, Amber. Patrice was at a table with her lawyer. The same lawyer from the arrest the previous year for the murder of the P.I. A case that dragged on forever. There was never a murder weapon found and the evidence against Patrice was suspect at best. Besides, with the community uproar it had been deemed better to let her go free and trust that justice would prevail with her on the outside. What happened instead was Patrice's release led to another murder. Cheech and the homies were all liable for the killing of the young man. Cheech gave a signal, the homies hid the weapon, Patrice was just the trigger person. They were all taking a big risk by coming to the courthouse to hear this case. Patrice did eventually land behind bars. It was unfortunate that it took the life of another young Black man to get her there, but they were able to track her down.

The ankle monitor put her in the car at the time of the murder, despite Cheech or the homies not giving a testimony and risking being accomplices for the murder themselves. Patrice could have easily implicated them at any point in the process, but she didn't. She was where she wanted to be. As weird as it sounded, she did better inside than out. She liked the structure. She had alliances inside that had her back. She also had once left a lover back inside the prison walls. In a few months, she would ask for a transfer and try to be moved closer to her. If her lover was still there in a few months.

Cheech, Charlene and Veronika sat on the prosecutor's side, just behind Earl's family. They had chosen their alliance. Patrice's lawyer noticed this right away and whispered a suggestion in her ear which Patrice waved off. The prosecutor wanted to get Patrice for Murder One, which was pre-meditated murder. To win his case, the prosecutor would have to prove that the homies were all in on the murder. That Cheech picked up Earl to have him killed and that he sat Patrice behind Earl on purpose for the murder to happen.

Thomas and Phyllis's gut told them that was that was not how it went down. That Patrice acted out of impulse. They hadn't asked the girls, but this was what they knew to be true. The defense attorney entered a plea of "not guilty." Again, there was no murder weapon, no witnesses, and no prints. Only the ankle monitor that placed Patrice in the car. Something had to give.

Patrice was marched back to her cell to await a trial by jury. Cheech and the homies congregated in the hallway of the courthouse. Tanja walked by and pulled Cheech out of the cluster to talk.

"Did you and your homies have anything to do with this?" Tanja asked. As if the prosecutors had been feeding her with thoughts.

Cheech was caught off-guard. "I swear to God, no!" Cheech said. "Earl was my boy. Not for all the coin in the world. You know that."

"How do you know the homies didn't set him up?" she said.

"They didn't even know I was going by to get Earl," he said. "I didn't know either. I just got the whip that morning. That mess set off without warning."

Tanja reminded him, "You know the prosecutor for the state is trying to push Murder One."

"I know!" Cheech said. "I was in there. He's not going to get anywhere with that. His best bet is manslaughter, but without someone to testify or without a murder-weapon that connects to Patrice that will be hard."

"Your girls aren't saying a word, huh?" Tanja asked. "What if they get subpoenaed?"

Tanja told Cheech about the voicemail from Veronika apologizing right after it all happened. Cheech didn't know why she would call Tanja and what she would be apologizing for, but Veronika never called Tonja. The voicemail was left on Jermaine's phone. Tanja wasn't about to reveal that detail.

"I am sure I can get it and have it entered into evidence though," Tanja said.

"What do you want?" Cheech asked.

"I want one of you to testify," she said. "Before the subpoena is drawn up."

"V and I have dirt on our hands," he said. "The defense would have a field day with us."

Tanja motioned towards Charlene.

"What about Ms. Goody Two Shoes?" she said. "I heard she works and even has a year of college. No dirt there."

"Charlene ain't no snitch," he replied.

"It's either snitch or become somebody's bitch," she said.

Tanja knew Charlene was not about that life. She was just a tagalong. Tanja told Cheech to sell it to her but to wait until Veronika was not around. She thought she would bite.

"She respects you," Tanja said.

Cheech was dumbfounded. Tanja was playing hard ball. Perhaps she was doing this all for her brother. Perhaps she was still mad about Cheech keeping Earl at his place after he OD'd. Maybe she was just trying to protect them all. Charlene might not be about that life, but she was loyal. Now he was about to see who she was more loyal to. Him or Patrice?

###

While on a work trip, Pamela received a call from Shirley. Pamela was busy with a client and didn't answer the first or second time, but the call kept coming in to the point that she eventually had to interrupt the client meeting. The client was a little put off.

For the amount of money that she earned at Quarimoc, Shirley wanted Pamela's attention. Pamela stepped out into the hallway of the high-rise office building which was not the usual coin-op setting.

"Hello Shirley!" Pamela said. "Is everything alright? I'm with a client."

Shirley spoke in a calm but direct voice. "I am going to need you to open your laptop and clear your email and internet history."

Pamela didn't know what was going on and was panicking despite her calm, hushed, yet harsh tone. "Are you crazy?" Pamela said. "What is going on?"

"I will explain later, but for now I need you to do as I say," Shirley confirmed her demand and then hung up.

Pamela didn't know what to do. She had clients demanding her attention on the other side of the glass doors, while her colleague/mentor was asking her to purge files. In an instant, she picked up the phone and called Lance who picked up right away.

"What's going on?" Pamela asked.

"Quarimoc is under investigation," Lance stated. "The feds are here and have demanded that we turn everything over to them. They won't say what it's about, but they have warrants. Shirley has been shredding files with her assistant all morning. I bet it has to do with that email you saw. Do you know who it was from?"

"No! But I took a picture of it," Pamela said.

"Are you kidding me?" Lance replied.

"Well, Shirley was trying to pull that whole racist bit on me, so I thought I would hold onto it in case I needed a little leverage," Pamela replied.

"Do you still have it?" he asked.

"It's on my phone!" she said.

"Have you shown it to anyone?" he asked.

"Of course not," she said. "It's just for safekeeping."

"Good! Very good!" Lance said. "The way things are going, you will need a card up your sleeve."

"Why do you say that?" Pamela asked.

"The top brass is covering for Shirley, and they are looking for someone to pin this on," Lance said. "My money is that it will be on one of us, and the good money is on you."

"That's why she wants me to erase all my files!" Pamela said.

"What?" Lance asked.

"Yeah, she called me less than five minutes ago and told me to wipe my computer clean," Pamela stated. "She is trying to pin this whole thing on me and make me look like I am hiding something."

"Good! Let her think that," Lance said. "Clear out your computer and empty your cache, but before you, do download everything onto a hard drive. This way she will think she has you."

"Why are you helping me?" Pamela asked. "I know you don't like me."

"You have some redeemable qualities," he said. "Besides you didn't have anyone killed."

"Yet!" Pamela said. "I didn't have anyone killed yet."

"Touché," Lance said. "I will remember that. And watch my back."

###

The Rottweilers were mounted up in front of the laundromat and waiting for closing time so they could go over their business plans. Jermaine walked up.

"Are you teaching tonight?" Craig asked.

"Not tonight," Jermaine said.

"What's up? You here to listen in?" Alexander asked.

"Nope!" Jermaine stated.

"What's up then? You just stopping by?" Rudy asked.

"What with the twenty-one questions?" Jermaine said. "If you must know. I am here to present."

There was a gasp from gang members. They were waiting for the day Jermaine was finished with his project. He wasn't quite done yet, but he needed customer feedback. This made a few of them think he was only going to be presenting to Sethi, so Jermaine explained that they were all his customers and how the project had moved from coin-op to neighborhood development.

"Gentrification is already here Jay!" Stevie said. "You're late for that train."

"Funny! I am not talking about gentrification. I am talking about a different type of neighborhood development. One that doesn't force the poor and working-class out, but one that provides them the tools to own and start businesses within their own neighborhoods. Businesses that they can pass down to their kids and grandkids."

"I can dig it," Cyrus said. "Sethi is just starting to show us how ownership works."

A few last-minute stragglers left the laundromat with clothes partially dried that they would have to hang when they got home. It was their fault that they waited to do their laundry so late. As they left, Sethi switched the sign to closed and turned off the lights in the front. He held the door so the gang members could squeeze in, and they rushed to get to their favorite seats at a table in the back of the shop where they were barely visible by passersby. Jay went into the office and pulled out some of his materials that he had stored in there. He had practiced this presentation for Donna and Sethi over and over and now he wanted to see if the teens would get it.

There was a knock at the closed and locked door. At first, Sethi pretended to wave them off. He then acknowledged that it was Donna. She brought Charlene and Veronika with her. She also brought some snacks for the group. Sethi put on a pot of hot water for tea. Jermaine was set to begin. He opened up his presentation really, really broadly.

"Create in your mind the image of a perfect world," he said. He discussed the air and water quality, fruit and vegetation, animals and people living in harmony. A real utopia. "Now within that world what does our neighborhood look like?"

The homies and gang rattled off the obvious things, such as clean streets, no poverty, good schools, everyone getting along and taking care of each other. Jermaine then asked what would it take to create that perfect world?

"A miracle!" Veronika yelled out to the laughter of the rest of the attendees.

"Well, what I hope to begin is the start of that miracle," Jermaine said. "What I have discovered is that in the places that look the most like what you described, most of the wealth is self-generated. The store owners aren't big corporations or outside industry, but honest hard-working people from right down the street. The fire fighters, teachers and police are their neighbors. Their kids know each other. No one takes ninety percent of their income and spends it outside of their community. The neighborhood self-replenishes itself."

Jermaine then related this metamorphosis of the community to his project. "What I have come to understand is that every business is a microcosm of the community it serves. It either breathes life into the community, or it takes the community's resources and invests those resources somewhere else. I want to explain how coin-op can take resources that are commonly discarded and make them into something useful. Secondly, I want to show how we can take our discarded people-power in our communities and through education and mentorship rebuild our neighborhoods into our perfect world."

Jermaine went on to explain his concept and then fielded questions filling in any gaps. He was able to get a lot of key information that would prove helpful in going before his class in a few days.

###

At her apartment, Bianca put the final changes on her project. She contacted several Black manufacturers in the Deep South and added their price point to her presentation. Although the costs were higher initially, after she factored in time of delivery and shipping she could pretty much break even. Of course, it would mean pushing more products which meant upping her sales or getting more clients. She also liked that she could visit these new plants. As much as she had the desire to go to China, India, Thailand and South Korea, she knew that she did not have the money or the time to make that trip more than once a year. Besides, the weather in the Philippines was brutally hot, and she was not trying to sweat out her perm.

Her housemates, as usual, were hidden away in their rooms, but Bianca needed to bounce ideas off of someone. Jermaine had already seen her first draft. She had called him anyway, and he didn't answer. She decided to disturb her housemates. Her immediate thought was of Sheri. Sheri had been presenting and creating presentations since her first year of graduate school. She would be defending her proposal in the fall, so she had a keen eye for what these professors were looking for. Bianca knocked lightly and then a little louder. Not getting any response, she decided to crack the door and peek in. She found Sheri with her headphones on and her computer screen combing through nefarious websites. Sheri could not hear her, so Bianca stayed in the doorway a while to see what she was doing. She realized that Sheri was hacking into secure sites by bypassing their firewall. In all their time together, Bianca thought Sheri was an innocent, quiet housemate who kept to herself. It turned out she was involved in criminal activity behind the walls of the dark net. Though captivated, Bianca had seen enough. She didn't want to know so much she could get subpoenaed when everything came to light. She shut the door and took a breath. She then knocked on Dawn's door. Dawn came to the door and opened it a crack.

"Hey, sorry to disturb you," Bianca said. "I was hoping I could run some ideas by you."

Dawn was obviously disturbed. She asked for a minute while she put her things away. She attempted to close the door behind her, but it stayed open just wide enough for Bianca to see lamps peeking over a mini-nursery. Again, Bianca tried not to notice, but she was confident that Dawn was growing and storing substances in her room. She walked back to the living room and decided to wait there for Dawn to arrive. Just as Dawn got to the living room, there was a knock on the door.

"Are you expecting someone?" Dawn asked.

"No! I'm in for the night," Bianca said. "I don't know who that could be."

Bianca went over to open the door, and Jermaine was standing in the doorway.

"What are you doing here?" she said.

"Good to see you too!" Jermaine replied. He saw Dawn in the hallway. "Good evening!"

Dawn replied in a similar fashion.

"So, what are you doing here?" Bianca replied.

"I was out cruising with my boy, Cheech and I asked if we could stop by for a second to say 'hi,'" Jermaine said.

"Where is your boy?" Bianca asked.

"Down by the elevator!" Jermaine said. "I wanted to make sure you were up for receiving company."

"Tell him to come in," Bianca said.

Dawn was a little frustrated. She asked, "Can I get back to what I was doing?"

As Jermaine waved Cheech in, Cheech realized that he knew Dawn who hadn't made it back to her room yet.

"Hey what's up?" Cheech said. Bypassing any greeting to Bianca. "When did you move over this way?"

Dawn was stunned to see Cheech. They were smoke out buddies in high school and hung pretty tight throughout Dawn's first year of college. They had lost touch over the last couple of years, but picked up right where they had left off.

"I've been over here since last summer," Dawn said. "This is my housemate, Bianca."

"I have heard about Bianca," Cheech said. As he greeted Bianca his focus stayed on Dawn. Cheech asked, "You still doing your thing?"

"You know it!" Dawn said.

"Can I take a peek?" Cheech asked.

Bianca and Jermaine were dumbfounded. They had been hanging out since the start of the semester, and each of them were just now finding out that they had mutual connections.

Dawn waved Cheech back to the lab, and the two of them disappeared.

"That was different," Bianca said. "Did you know they knew each other?"

"I typically steer clear of Cheech's smoking circle, but now I do remember hearing her name associated with some good weed."

"Wow! It seems like I am always the last to know," Bianca said.

Jermaine saw Bianca's project open on her laptop.

"How's it coming?" he asked.

"I'm just about there. I have incorporated Professor Wright's most recent suggestions. You might be interested. It has to do with successful Black manufacturers who can produce my products at a fraction of the cost."

"I am interested," he said. "Anything to get you out of that slave-labor market."

Bianca cut her eyes and then hit Jermaine. She opened up her project and showed him all the information, price indexes, revenue and cost, as well as performance over time.

"Wow! You really made some changes," he said. "This is deep. Are you planning a visit?"

"It's funny you should say that. I was just thinking we should plan a trip. Seeing as that would help both of our presentations."

###

The homies helped Donna out around the arcade with various projects. She had put a bug in their ear about classes at the CC, something neither one of them wanted to hear, but Donna was persistent. She shared different economic scenarios and probabilities with them on occasion to see if anything caught their interest, but most of it fell on deaf ears. They both liked hearing Jermaine's presentation the other night, so Donna referenced it in relation to the arcade when she could. Even though they looked up to and admired Donna as Black women themselves, they had a hard time seeing themselves as business owners. All they knew were the streets. They hustled to get by, slept where they could and lived day-by-day. With no promise of tomorrow, they found no reason to plan for it. Patrice was not the first of their homies to get locked up. Just the latest. They had seen homies get killed, get pregnant, get sent away, and a handful get away, never to be heard from again. High school graduation was the big deciding point for most of them. The summer after graduation many parents hit their kids with ultimatums.

Work or go to school, or you can't live here.

Some of them had family in the South that were willing to take them in. Others moved in with their boyfriends. Some held down some minimum-wage jobs before they got laid off for stealing, showing up late or not showing up at all. Then, once in a while, when all the stars were aligned, one person would beat the odds and escape the ghetto trap. Breaking the cycle of poverty was a rare occasion. When someone did it, people wanted to analyze how it was done. Most marveled in amazement and put that person on a pedestal. Others pointed to the individual and assumed:

If so and so can do it so can everyone else.

Still others despised the person, believing that they lost their way and became "White," as if that was the only race that defined success. When someone like Donna came back into the community and gave back, it was called a "miracle." It was not often someone "escaped" a community they had been taught to despise, attended historically white colleges whose students and professors diminished the Black experience by calling it "ghetto," broke out of poverty into the upper-middle class, and then came back. Maybe if they were really rich, they would donate a park or a playground like many athletes did, but most didn't come back. Once they were gone, they were gone.

Dawn used to hang out with the homies when she was in high school. She never really lived around the way. Her parents were doctors, so they lived in the hills. No one really knew how Dawn found her way down the hill to McKinley High School. Maybe it was her grades, or she just wanted to be around more Black folks. Either way, the homies took a liking to her because she had the best weed. Home grown, so they didn't have to buy it. Of course, this gave Dawn the upper hand. They usually had to do what she wanted to do or go where she wanted to go. Places that were commonly out of the homies price range. It was some time after high school that this began to wear thin on Patrice, and she and Dawn would get into it. Dawn eventually took her weed and moved on. She was already enrolled in the university. Something her parents insisted on. She had a natural knack for horticulture and with the right letters from the right people, Dawn was able to move to the other side of the tracks. It was not as though she really lived in the hood anyway. She just spent her waking and baking hours there. She went total introvert, cut back on the weed, moved out of her parents' home and for the most part got her life straight. Of course, she still grew pot in her bedroom, but it was mostly to sell. Why throw away a gift? In a few years, it would be legal in every state in the contiguous U.S.

Donna was also inspired by Jermaine's presentation. She should have been. She helped create it. She would have loved to use the money that she had put aside to start more than one business, but she would have needed to hire dedicated on-site managers. People that she would be able to groom herself. Folks committed to the people of the community and who would do right by them. It would have been somebody like Charlene or Veronika, but they didn't see themselves as owners. Society had beaten that belief out of them already. Donna, if not anything else, was persistent. She wasn't giving up on them. They would be her lab for as long as they kept coming back. She trusted that in a few years they would have a change of heart and be ready to launch.

###

The investigation into Quarimoc had hurt the company's public image, and investors started to bail. Still others were looking at it as a blip in the market that the company would turn around and were buying while the stock was low. The company's executive board was nowhere to be found and were only answering questions through their high-priced lawyers. Shirley, Pablo, Lance and Pamela were still on the ground trying to salvage what was left. For the most part, the scandal didn't affect their clients, but they knew that could turn on a dime. Despite the information Pablo provided to the feds, Shirley's computer still came back clean, as did Pamela's. Everything was now linked to a random virus that was on Jonathan's computer. The same virus was found days later on Lance's computer. It was not enough to corroborate a murder investigation. With Shirley now calling the shots in the office, everyone was walking on eggshells. She remained pleasant in public, but that didn't help the morale. She called for a meeting to get everyone around the table.

"These have been a difficult past few weeks," Shirley said. "But we will get through it. Quarimoc has had tough times in the past. It's nothing new."

"The staff is worried about their jobs," Pamela said. "They have families to feed. Many are looking elsewhere."

"This is where we need to step up and assure them that everything is going to be fine," Shirley said. "This investigation is going to wrap up soon, and things will be back to normal."

"We can hope!" Pablo said. "I am a company man. I have my entire pension and 401k wrapped up in this company, not to mention my stock options that are circling in the toilet as we speak."

"We all want the company to do well, but if there's a mouse in the batter, we have to fish it out." Lance stated the case pointedly while looking at Shirley.

"I am well aware that there are some hard feelings for me around this table," Shirley said. "Right now, I am all you have. If I go down, we all go down. Understood."

"Is that a threat?" Pablo asked.

"It is what it is!" Shirley reiterated. "Despite wiretaps, bugs, recordings and spies. I have come up squeaky clean. The evidence bears itself out. If it doesn't fit, you must acquit."

Lance and Pablo were emotionally distraught and tried to get up to leave, but Shirley immediately stopped them in a power play.

"I didn't excuse you," she said. "Take your seats."

Lance and Pablo sat back down.

"Now, I do have a way to speed this thing along, but I need you all on board," Shirley said.

"What are you proposing?" Lance asked.

"Well, the feds want somebody," Shirley said. "Not for the charge of murder. That wouldn't hold up in court, but for the charge of conspiracy. It's not illegal to have someone followed, as it turns out. It's only illegal to put that person in harm's way. So, we need a fall guy. Not for jail time, but for probation."

Pablo raised his hand.

"I'll do it," he said. "What are we talking about? At least a quarter mil for the fall."

"It can't be you. You are already working with the feds. That would implicate them and taint their entire investigation," Shirley said. "I'm thinking Pamela."

Everyone looked Pamela's way.

"You are young, single and can move anywhere you like," Shirley said. "Six months' probation and half-a-million for your inconvenience."

"Why me?" Pamela asked.

Pamela had the most to gain from Jermaine being implicated. She was next in line to pick up Jonathan's sales area, and she also had anti-Black sentiment that led her to worry about hiring Jermaine for the internship. It was an easy sell. Shirley told her that she could make a few phone calls and land Pamela anywhere she wanted to be in the country.

"Ocean or mountains for double your salary," she said. "What do you think?"

Lance shot a wink across the table to Pamela.

“Can I have some time to think about it?” Pamela said.

“Sure!” Shirley said. “But don’t take too long. The board will need to make a decision quickly. Let’s say Friday.”

Shirley looked around the room self-assured.

“I am sure the rest of us won’t miss the racist undertones in your absence,” Shirley asserted.

“That’s for certain!” Lance said.

Pamela shot him a look, and Pablo caught on that something might be in the works.

###

CHAPTER FIFTEEN

Sethi was dressed up as if he was heading to the bank to ask for a major loan. He straightened his tie and drove over to the high school. That's where he met up with Craig, Cyrus and Stevie who all jumped in the car. Each of them wore a collared dress shirt and a tie. They rolled up to the Green Lot on Jermaine's college campus. Donna was with Charlene and Veronika, and they were already parked and waiting for Sethi and the rest of the gang to arrive. Cheech was there with Matthias, Alexander, Tim and Rudy in a separate car. They jumped out of the cars in their Sunday best, each dressed better than the next. They found their way to Bruce's lecture seminar, and each got seated before the presentations were about to begin. Jermaine did not know that they were coming, so they snuck in while he was setting up. With his friends entering through the back of the lecture hall, he didn't see them until it was time to present. When he finally saw them, he was overwhelmed. He knew that high school didn't let out until almost three p.m., and the newbies would have needed to have had an excused absence to leave school grounds. He also realized that Donna and Sethi closed up their places of business for the coming hours and were losing customers so they could be there. On top of all that, they were dressed to the nines, arrived early, and were representing their community in force on a campus that didn't regularly welcome their side of town very often.

He took a moment to let it all sink in. He couldn't delay. There were still two more presentations after his, and Bruce was a stickler for starting on time. Just as he started, Jermaine saw one more familiar face sneak in silently and take a seat. Jermaine continued with his presentation, stating most of the things that the gang and homies had already heard at their private session. As soon as he got to what they believed was the crescendo, discussing how the success of business comes from owners from within their own neighborhoods, he threw them a curveball that no one saw coming. Not even Bianca.

"As I began to research how a strong economic market is fueled by leadership from within the community, I began to think. These businesses all have to get their product from outside that community and how great it would be if there were a symbiotic relationship between manufacturer and local business owners," Jermaine said. "So, I reached out to several manufacturers regarding this idea with a proposal. Simply stated:

"If we can ensure that the money generated from these communities stays in the communities and that we only purchase from Black-owned and Black-run companies would you be willing to provide us these companies products at cost?

"I figured it didn't hurt to ask. One after the other, without hesitation, each company, to the last, said they would. They even said they would contact their competitors and ally companies to do the same."

There was a rousing round of applause from the audience, as they were amazed and astounded. A project that began with just trying to figure out ways to avoid giving out personal information which could be tracked from a card for coin-operated machines, had developed to a project about reduced slave labor in third-world markets and a project that also boosted local ownership, supported Black corporations, and did it all at a fair market price. It went beyond anyone's wildest dreams. As the applause died down, there was someone who remained on his feet in the back of the room. The same person who snuck in after the presentation started. Jermaine dropped his remote clicker and made his way up the sloping staircase to greet the uninvited guest. Everyone turned around to see where Jermaine could be heading. Cheech stood to his feet. He was in disbelief. Jermaine reached his supporter.

"It's good to see you, Tony," he said.

He gave him a big hug. Cheech ran up next while trying not to cause a big distraction.

"It's good to see you brothers too," Tony said. "But Jay, you have a presentation to finish. Where's your mind at?"

Jermaine nodded in approval and went back to the front of the lecture hall.

"Any questions?" Jermaine asked.

While Bruce and Jermaine's classmates shot question after question regarding the project, Sethi, Donna and the gang were asking Charlene and Veronika about Tony. They found out that he had just been released from prison over the weekend and was staying across the state line at a family member's house until his probation officer cleared his paperwork. They learned from the homies that Jermaine was only filling in as gang leader while Tony was away for the last year and half and that the hug was more than just a hug, but a changing of the guard.

Tony was back. The new Rottweilers now had their third leader since coming into the gang. They had heard about Tony, but didn't know anything about him. Donna didn't know Tony. He must have come in after she left for college. Even after her brother was killed. She would have remembered him from the funeral.

The questions died down and Jermaine took a seat as the next presenters came up. As was proper, he gave his full attention to his classmates but was still distracted by Tony being out. The person that took over when Greg left and raised him to be a man. He knew that Tony was proud of him. Tony always knew that Jermaine's gifts went beyond the gang. What he saw in Tony's response was a genuine big brother moment of "you surpassed my expectations." Tony would never have spoken those words. His toughness wouldn't allow him to, but Jay knew. Tony always had in mind the gang's best interest. To turn boys into men.

The bell rang, and Jermaine congratulated his classmates. He then ran to the back of the class and embraced Tony again. Tony was cold. Even rigid. Prison had had its intended effect. It would take him some time to get used to being out again. Jermaine walked him out of the classroom and into the quad. The Rottweilers all lined up and greeted Tony one-by-one. Cheech and Tony spent some time reminiscing about Earl's life and sudden death. Sethi and Donna greeted him as well, and told him how well he did in instilling great values into Jermaine. They each went back to their cars, leaving Tony and Jermaine in the Quad to catch up and talk. They spoke until the sun went down and then even more on the bus ride home. Tony walked Jermaine to the steps of his house from the bus stop, as he had many times during his teenage years. Their age difference was only five years, but in the past, their years together were all adult years for Tony and childhood years for Jermaine. There was a higher level of respect and awe that couldn't quite be put into words that Jermaine had for Tony. They stayed on his steps and talked for a few more hours until they both realized they had to cut short their conversation that could have gone on forever.

"Where are you staying tonight?" Jermaine asked.

"I don't know," Tony said. "I will find somewhere to land."

Jermaine knew this probably meant he would be sleeping on the street somewhere.

"Listen! I know it's not the best set up, but I know that Cheech and the homies have a spot they maintain on the low," Jermaine said. "Let me give you my sleeping bag and pillow for tonight and ask Cheech to get you set-up over there."

Jermaine called Cheech, and he scooped up Tony. Jermaine couldn't sleep. He was still all amped up from the day. He used the awake time to get on his tablet and research accommodations for Tony. He knew he barely had a place to stay himself, but he would gladly give him his own bed if he could. He had told Tony about the murder of the P.I. and he knew that Tony could use some time alone with Cheech, so they could have a man-to-man. Jermaine would let Cheech slide for his indiscretions with a simple tongue lashing, and Tony wouldn't put up with that shit now that he was back in charge.

###

After charter school, Roxie and Renee attended their after-school program, and they were surprised to see Jermaine's friend, Donna, from the arcade there. She was handing out flyers to parents and teachers entitled, "Young Entrepreneurs." They had both heard the term before from their brother, Jermaine. He had told them about the importance of ownership, but they were confused as to why Donna was at their after-school program. The program director, Ms. Graham, gathered the kids into the gymnasium and asked for their attention.

Ms. Graham stated loudly, "This is Ms. Donna!"

The kids all replied in unison, "Hi, Ms. Donna!"

"Can we all give Ms. Donna our attention as she explains about a new program she wants you all to know about?" Ms. Graham said.

The kids all sat down and looked toward the front of the gymnasium. Donna recognized Renee and Roxie and gave them a little wink.

"I see I have some friends here," Donna said. "I have to give credit to Renee and Roxie's brother, Jermaine. He is the one who inspired the idea for a mentorship program. I am calling it

'Young Entrepreneurs.'"

A kid from the front row raised his hand.

"Let me guess," Donna said. "What is an entrepreneur?"

"No! It reminds me of Young Frankenstein," the kid said.

The comment got a laugh from the rest of the kids. Ms. Graham quickly settled them down.

"That's true," Donna said. "And I guess you can say I am trying to create little monsters out of you."

Donna's comment rendered an even bigger laugh, and that time Ms. Graham joined in the ruckus.

"Hopefully, it's good monsters," Donna continued. "The kind that go on to do good in their community and the world."

The group settled down again.

"Well, to answer my own question. What is an entrepreneur?" Donna said. "I would explain it as someone who starts their own business."

"Like a candy store?" a young girl asked.

"Yes!" Donna said. "Perfect example! A candy store is something that you can open in any community. There is never too much candy."

Ms. Graham shot an exasperated look toward Donna, and Donna took the cue.

"Well! Only after you eat your vegetables and get permission from your parents or teachers," Donna said. “But let’s say you wanted to open a candy store here on the corner. What would you do first?”

“You have to rent the space,” Renee said. “And then buy the candy and things to put the candy in.”

“You have read my notes,” Donna said.

Renee laughed.

“No! Brother taught me that,” Renee said.

“Yes! All that is true,” Donna said. “All that is called overhead, along with equipment, utilities, taxes, and a few other things. What else is important if you want to open a candy store?”

The room went quiet.

“Well, if you don’t have the money stashed under your pillow, you might want to get a loan from the bank,” Donna told them. “Even if you don’t need a loan, it’s important to have a plan. How many of you plan for your school day before you go to bed?”

About half the room raised their hand.

"Who lays out their clothes? Donna asked.

Some of the kids raised their hands.

"Who packs lunch the night before?" she continued.

More kids raised their hands.

"Who showers the night before, so they don't have to in the morning?" Donna asked.

Most of the room raised their hand.

"Well, all that is planning," Donna said. "I want to teach you how to plan to start your own business, by thinking about what you need to do way, way before you do it."

The group giggled.

"What I want you ladies and gentlemen to do today is get into groups and get creative. Think about if you were going to start any business you wanted to, what would it be?"

The students turned towards their friends and came up with many off-the-wall ideas. Donna walked around to listen to them. As the time went on, some ideas got really far reaching, still others got more concrete. She heard ideas about fun zones for kids and ideas for cars that can fly. She didn't discourage any idea. Any idea was a good idea. As the groups broke up, they reported out. Donna gave them the assignment of coming back the next day with how they were going to make their idea into a reality. She handed out a prompt and directed the students back over to Ms. Graham.

###

As Donna walked back into the arcade, Veronika was handing out tokens to patrons, and Charlene was behind the counter issuing prizes. The arcade was running smoothly and had not skipped a beat. It was the homies first management lesson, and they passed with flying colors. Cheech walked in moments behind Donna.

"Hi Ms. Donna!" he said.

"What's going on today Julius?" she replied.

"You know! On my grind per the usual," Cheech said.

Donna had no idea what that meant since she had never seen him work a day in his life.

"I am trying to get my boy Tony acclimated again," Cheech said. "Is there anything you can do to help?"

Donna didn't know Tony, but knew that he was a good leader of men and she could use the help.

"Sure! Tell him to come by and see me tonight," Donna said. "I'll see what I can do for him."

"Can I have a word with one of the homies while I'm here?" Cheech asked.

Donna laughed.

"I'm not paying them," Donna said. "They can go and come as they please."

Cheech nodded and then walked over to the counter to talk.

"Hey what's up V?" Cheech said.

Veronika was a little reticent as Cheech approached.

"Hey, I asked Donna if I could grab your ear about something for a minute," Cheech said. "It seems like we haven't had five minutes to talk since P's hearing."

"Why? What's up?" Veronika asked.

Cheech nodded towards the front door.

"Can we step outside for a minute?" he said. "It's so damn loud in here."

Veronika gave Charlene a quick glance and then led Cheech out the front door and onto the street. Once they got out there, Veronika kept her eyes connected with Charlene who was still working the counter. Cheech had his back to the door.

"What you need?" Veronika said pointedly.

"What's with the attitude?" Cheech asked.

"I don't trust you," Veronika said.

"Where is this coming from?" he asked. "We have been homies for years. Have I ever done you dirty?"

Veronika thought about it, and Cheech was right. She didn't have any reason to not trust him based on their history together, but something about the conversation with Tanja and his attitude towards her afterwards had her on edge.

"So, I need you to convince your girl C to testify against Patrice in this upcoming court case," Cheech said.

"No way!" Veronika said. "We are not snitching on the homie."

"Tanja is being relentless on the matter, and the only way to get something that sticks is to have an eyewitness."

"How come you don't do it?" she said.

"You and I both have cases and would be thrown out as witnesses. C is the only one that can take the stand. Otherwise, the prosecution is going to subpoena her."

"This is some bullshit!" Veronika said.

"I know!" Cheech said. "I didn't even want to get you involved, but you're the homie and I had to get your side. If the prosecution gets murder one as the charge, we are all going to jail. You know as well as I do that we had nothing to do with it."

Charlene looked up and saw that Veronika was upset at Cheech. She tried to get eye contact again to see if she was alright. Veronika saw her, and they locked eyes. Charlene knew it was serious.

"I will talk to her," Veronika said.

"When can I expect to hear back from you?" Cheech asked.

"Once we figure this whole thing out," she said.

"Alright! I will be back here tonight with my boy, Tony." Cheech said. "Maybe I will see you then."

Cheech walked off. Veronika wanted to light a cigarette but hesitated. She thought about her call to Jermaine. That was the only way Tanja could have known that it was Patrice. Jermaine had let Tanja listen to the voice message. That was why no one was blaming Cheech. For God sakes, he had been the driver. As far as Earl's family knew, Cheech had set things up. Maybe out of jealousy. Possibly an old spat. It could have even been over some chick. Tanja and her family knew something that they were holding over their heads and was now threatening to have them hit with a subpoena. Veronika had to discover a way out of the corner they were being painted into. Even if it meant Patrice went free.

###

After landing at airport, Jermaine and Bianca stopped at a bookstore to pick up a few items. It was a week before graduation, yet they both took the time to go to a place they had never been to before. The Deep South. They exited the airport to sweltering heat. Once they got into their rental car, they travelled two-lane highways through former slave plantations to get to their destination. Many of the fields were empty, just rocks, weeds and dirt. As they neared their location, they began to see smoke stacks and industrial plants. There were a few more cars, but Bianca and Jermaine had no idea where the people were coming from to work out here in the middle of nowhere. They felt uneasy but were steadfast about their mission. People honked or waved as they saw them pulling up. A sense of familiarity took over. Although there was immense poverty in the area, the factory workers smiled as if excited for the task ahead. Bianca pulled up at an office, and Jermaine pulled some items out of the backseat. They walked in and were greeted warmly by a company foreman who directed them to the office of the plant manager. The manager had been anticipating their arrival. They didn't get many visitors this far out, especially people from outside of the area. Jermaine had spoken to Mr. Randall on the phone. He owned one of the largest material plants in this area. Although he was wealthy, you couldn't tell from his demeanor. There was no three-piece suit, expensive watch or high-priced shoes. He dressed and behaved as if he had just come from the work floor himself. Randall greeted them both warmly with a gentile southern charm.

"Welcome to the plant!" Randall said. "We are happy to have you here."

Bianca and Jermaine exchanged the greeting and shook Randall's hand.

"So, it sounds like you two are interested in doing some business with us to help in your community," Randall continued.

"Yes, Sir!" Jermaine said. "We both attend the local community college and are studying economics."

"Is that so?" Randall said. "I don't have much schooling, but I have found my way around the business arena. I saved a few pennies, bought some land and started a small factory some years back. It only took some dedicated employees to make it grow. Since then, my wife and I have bought out three more dying factories in this area and have not looked back since."

"Wow!" Bianca said. "That's a success story if I ever heard one."

"That's because I simplified it," Randall said. "We tend to do that in the South. I figured no young person wants to hear about the sleepless nights, not making rent, foreclosures, and all the other toil. The end result is what matters."

"I suppose you're right," Jermaine said.

"What can I help you with?" Randall said.

Bianca explained how she was working with a company and getting materials from overseas in markets like China and the Philippines. She explained how she was interested in seeing if she could get that same product from Randall's company and reduce her turnaround time.

"You have to understand we are a small outfit," Randall said. "We don't rush things here. We work hard and put out a good product, but if you are looking for large quantities, I don't know if we are your company."

"Well, I buy large quantities from China because that is the cheapest way to ship, but if I could work out a regular weekly shipment domestically, I wouldn't need as much. How often do you run trucks out from here?"

"Every Monday, Wednesday and Friday at eleven a.m.," Randall said. "We have over three- hundred employees, and some of the best equipment money can buy. I would love to offer you a tour while you're here."

"Well, if you can get me even two shipments a week that would be enough for us to stay on tab with a barge that only comes in once a month," Bianca said. "It also helps our storehouses manage inventory better."

Jermaine interjected himself into the conversation to remind Randall about his conversation with him as concerned helping local and community business owners through "at cost" pricing.

"Did I say that?" Randall kidded. "Mr. Beasley, right? I ran the numbers, and what I don't have in my factories, I can get from partner industries. We do a lot of bartering down here. I have a vending guy, a cash register guy, a young lady who has fabric and jewelry."

If his factory didn't have a product and there was a need for it, the factory sent people to get trained on how to make it. "I got fifteen engineers in Kansas City right now learning how to make new machinery," Randall said. "Those fifteen will come back and teach one hundred folks everything they've learned."

Bianca and Jermaine were impressed and grateful. Randall led them on a tour of the facilities. They got to see where the product designs were made, the technology and engineering side, as well as the assembly lines, production and post production. Jermaine saw all of the employees and immediately red flags went up.

"How are you able to keep your prices so low?" he asked.

"The sixty-four-thousand-dollar question?" Randall said.

Jermaine did not get the reference but went along anyway.

"I build only on unincorporated land. The plant is neither in the city, town or state. We are in Nowhere, USA. No zip code, post office, police station or restaurant."

"What's the population?" Bianca asked.

"Zero!" No one would live out here if you paid them. We all bus in from the train depot. Get here at sunrise and leave at quitting time. Motors shut down, and we are home with our loved ones for dinner."

"Unincorporated, huh?" Jermaine exclaimed.

"Yes sir!" Randall said. "These folks haven't paid one red cent in taxes since they started here. I pay them a fair wage, but I don't break the bank. They make out better than their neighbors."

Bianca and Jermaine had asked enough questions, and since they had decided to drive, they thought they needed to get to a place with running water and electricity before sundown. The closest hotel was about two hours away. As they left, they thanked Mr. Randall, as well as the foreman. They said goodbye to everyone else they saw as they walked in. It had been a long flight and a long day. They were ready for sleep and a quick turnaround the next day in order to make final preparations for their college graduation.

###

As the college semester wound down, high school was winding down too which would mean a lot of free time on the young Rottweiler hands. Parents believed that idle hands were the devil's workshop, so many were making plans to keep their boys busy. It was a horribly kept secret that the boys were in a gang even though gang membership was not uncommon for a lot of teenage boys in their neighborhood who were coming of age. Especially those who didn't have a solid role model in their home. They saw friends in gangs and wanted to be around those friends. The difference was the type of gang you joined. Was it the science club? The band? Or was it something more nefarious like drugs and violence? In that case idle hands were the devil's workshop. Parents knew that their kids could go either way. Sure, they would monitor who they were hanging out with, but in working-class communities a parent could only do this so much. You are lucky to get two waking hours with your child between an eight-hour work day, a seven-hour school day, dinner, homework, chores and sleep. It was a miracle to sit down for a meal together. Parents had to trust that they instilled enough values in their kids, so they could choose right from wrong, and could know the line and not to cross it.

The Rottweilers were a different brand and always had been. If a teenager was looking for trouble, they were not necessarily it. They were more of a group of tough guys who supported each other. A tough-guy support group. They could put the smack down if someone rolled up on them at school or on the block, but they rarely had to flex. Now they were learning the principles of business. As nerdy as it sounded, this was what they were motivated by. To become not only mentally tough but financially tough. The knowledge could have come through drug dealing and stick-ups, which was not sustainable, or through a legal hustle, which, if done properly, could become something that made them a living. Like Earl, they abhorred the idea of working for somebody else to make them rich for forty years of their lives and trusting that a pension or retirement plan would be waiting for them when they turned sixty-three. They saw entrepreneurs like Sethi, who wasn't rich, but was able to do good in the community and make his own decisions. They saw Donna who had worked the grind for many years and then decided to try something on her own. College was an option. They could use that time to gain some basic knowledge of how the outside world worked and to build their network, but they knew the real skill set was going to come from being in places that taught them everyday business. How to navigate with vendors, build customers, and learn the trends.

The summer would give them an opportunity to work, not just for a wage but also with a chance to learn. So, this was the time for them to became strategic. They met in front of the store, after homework and food at home. Stevie was going into his senior year and that meant decisions.

"Yo, what are you trying to do this summer?" Alexander asked him.

"I don't know, Bro!" Stevie said. "Once I age out of the system, I may have to find a program or college to get into."

"You leaving us?" Matthias asked. "We just got to know you. You should get a place around here. That way we can all smoke there."

"I don't have a choice," Stevie said. "I know the college has financial aid for foster youth. I gotta do what I gotta do. I don't know anything about paying bills."

"That's why we need to keep learning, Bro!" Alexander said. "So, we don't have to fall into the rat race."

"What does that mean?" Cyrus asked.

Alexander talked about how college wasn't designed to teach you to work for yourself but to be an employee and to work for someone else. Stevie saw this playing out in the community. He had witnessed the current system of the poor being so broke when they come out of college that they were happy to have anything. Stevie's plan was to navigate the system and have a purpose going in.

"I'm not for living hand-to-mouth like my folks, Dude," Rudy said.

"But what are our options?" Craig asked. "We don't have enough money to start our own business, and we don't want to end up like most of these dudes on the corner. We are better than that."

"We need to find a way to get that book education and not fall into the trap of becoming a drone," Alexander said.

"That professor at the CC..." Stevie said. "He sounded like he was definitely about that. Jermaine killed that presentation about community ownership. He might be able to get that prof to start something for us at the high school."

"Donna is doing something, but it's for the younger kids," Craig said. "My little cousin told me she came by the community center."

"See, if we can get somebody to do that for us at the high school that will be dope," Rudy said.

Cyrus remembered meeting Tony for the first time at the college and wondered if anyone had seen him. Matthias has seen him here and there. He knew he was crashing on the floor of the trap house, and that Donna was working on getting him a job at the community center sweeping up. Cyrus was thinking they could pull him into whatever they come up with for the summer. He knew that Tony picked up some skills in prison that could possibly turn a profit.

"Let's meet up with him now and see if he is down," Stevie said. "Sethi can help us get some rental space. It would be like a little pop-up shop."

"See, that way you can stay here next summer while you take classes," Matthias said to Stevie.

"We'll see," Stevie said. "A lot will have to go right."

###

The courthouse was packed and a charge of murder had been reduced to manslaughter. The prosecution opened with a statement that Patrice acted as a lone attacker of a weakened and feeble Earl Waiters, as the driver and passengers looked on helplessly. The change in the charges shocked half the courtroom. Tanja and the rest of Earl's family knew differently. Murder would have been difficult to prove. A motive, intent, and a murder weapon would all have been necessary to establish. Besides, the prosecution had an ace card that they were holding close to their vest. The defense presented its case. There were even more lawyers than the prosecution had anticipated. Patrice was dressed in a very professional business suit, and her hair was immaculate. She was almost unrecognizable. She was still reeling from being attacked herself, yet her wounds were undetectable.

The defense's plea was simple and straightforward: there were no witnesses to establish what had really taken place, and Earl had died of natural causes. It was a delayed reaction from his overdose, and the driver and passengers had looked on unable to get him assistance in time. Cheech was sitting with Brian, Dookie and Jermaine, and all were in shock. Cheech didn't know if Charlene would be called or not. Veronika hadn't spoken to him since he made the request. Today was the moment of truth. If she testified, it would be a scarlet letter in the community. If she didn't, she would be subpoenaed and would be forced to lie under oath. Damned if you do, damned if you don't.

The defense called its first witness. A doctor who'd had Earl in her care. She was asked about the long-term effects of an overdose of this magnitude and the possibility of a relapse. The doctor answered factually regarding her lack of experience with the level of amphetamine and its effects over time. She did, however, speak about cases where a lack of oxygen to the brain after a coma brought about asphyxia. She was careful to explain that Earl received the best care possible and was monitored closely before being released.

The prosecution cross-examined the doctor with the purpose of debunking the asphyxia claim as the cause of death. The lawyer pointedly asked about the likelihood of this type of incident and how many cases she had seen that concerned lack of oxygen to the brain leading to death weeks later. The doctor answered that it was a low occurrence, but from journals and research, she understood that scenario was a possibility.

The prosecution called her first witness. It was not Charlene, as Cheech had hoped for. Besides Veronika and himself, she was the only plausible witness to the crime. Instead it was Tanja, Earl's sister. She took the stand, and the prosecution asked her how she came to know about her brother's untimely death. Tanja expressed that she received a panicked call from Julius "Cheech" Barnes to come to the emergency room. He told her that something had happened to Earl.

"Did Mr. Barnes tell you what happened to your brother?" the prosecutor asked.

"When I arrived with my family, Cheech was catatonic," Tanja began. "I saw car keys in his hand and a car parked illegally out front, and I put two and two together that it was his. I tried to ask him what happened, as my parents rushed to the desk, but I got nothing.

"So, Mr. Barnes was of no help?" the prosecutor asked.

"None whatsoever," Tanja replied."

"So, what makes you believe Ms. Denton is responsible for your brother's death?" the prosecutor asked.

"As I rushed out the door, I left my phone at my house, so I took Cheech's phone to call my older sister and let her know we were at the hospital," Tanja explained. "As I took his phone and was about to dial, I saw that he called Jermaine last. I didn't pay it any attention until Jermaine arrived at the ER much later that night."

"Did Jermaine tell you what Cheech said took place in the car?" the prosecutor asked.

"He told me Cheech left a message to come to the ER," Tanja said. "I told him I didn't believe him and to let me hear it, so he gave me his phone to listen to the message."

"What did the message say?" the prosecutor asked.

"Exactly what he said, but there were several messages, and as Jermaine went to go check on

Cheech, I took the liberty to listen to the rest of the messages."

"Without his permission," the prosecutor asked.

"He didn't tell me I couldn't," Tanja replied.

"What did you find out?" the prosecutor asked.

"Well, there was a message from me after I just found out the news," Tanja said. "And then there is a message from Cheech's friend, Veronika."

Veronika squirmed in her seat as she remembered her phone call to Jermaine. She looked down the row to where Jermaine was sitting.

"What did it say?" the prosecutor asked.

"In a calm voice, Veronika went into precise detail as to what took place in the car," Tanja said.

"That she had nothing to do with it and that her friend Patrice had flipped."

"What else did she say?" the prosecutor asked.

"That they were casually cruising the boulevard about to take the exit for the highway, and Patrice took her bootlaces off and choked Earl to death."

"Objection!" the defense yelled. "Hearsay."

"Sustained," the judge stated.

The prosecutor finished with Tanja, and then it was the defense attorney's turn. He was relentless and accused Tanja of fabricating the entire story, and in light of there being no witnesses and no proof, he asked that her statement be struck from the record.

With this, the judge asked if the prosecution could provide proof of the voicemail. Jermaine's phone was immediately entered into evidence. The defense and prosecution listened to the voicemail in the judge's chambers while the court was in recess. The defense lobbied to have the admission thrown out, but the judge denied his request.

After recess, the jury was allowed to hear the voicemail. The defense immediately stated that the voicemail was fabricated in the weeks leading up to the trial. Veronika was called as a witness, but to Cheech's surprise, she was called on by the defense and not the prosecution.

"Please state your name for the court," the defense attorney asked.

"Veronika Caruso," Veronika answered.

"Can you tell us what happened on the day in question?" the defense asked.

"I retain my Fifth Amendment rights as the response may serve to self-incriminate me," Veronika answered.

"Fair enough!" the defense stated. "Can you tell us if that is your voice on the message the jury just heard?"

"I retain my Fifth Amendment rights as the response may serve to self-incriminate me," Veronika answered.

"Do you plan on asserting your Fifth Amendment rights with every question I ask?" the defense asked.

"I retain my Fifth Amendment rights as the response may self-incriminate me," Veronika answered.

The defense excused Veronika, and the prosecution didn't bother to call on her. Instead, the defense attorney asked the jury during her closing statement to make the determination as to whether the voice they heard on the stand and the voice from the voice message were one and the same and whether the witness's statement proved a crime of manslaughter.

###

On the block, Sethi was waiting for an equipment repair vendor to arrive when two detectives came into the laundromat and asked about Jermaine.

"He works with me!" Sethi responded defensively. "What is this about?"

"Do you know about his gang-affiliations?" Detective Lawrence asked.

"We started a group for young men who wanted to learn business and investing," Sethi snapped.

"Do you have a warrant?"

"Relax!" Detective Lawrence said. "Mr. Beasley is not a person of interest. We are investigating Quarimoc Industries, and we have reason to believe he was being targeted."

"I know Quarimoc. I do business with Quarimoc," Sethi said. "I told detectives months ago that they were responsible for that young man being shot and killed last year."

"Well, maybe you can help us," Detective Lawrence said. "We have evidence of an email that Pamela Springfield sent to Jonathan Stone about having Mr. Beasley followed. It mentions you."

Sethi was taken aback. He questioned how he was mentioned.

The email read:

Jermaine is working closely with the owner of the laundromat and can be found there when he is not at school.

"Sure! He was here a lot around that time," Sethi stated.

"We assume that he was being followed," Detective Lawrence said. "Do you have any videotape from around the time of the shooting?"

"Yes, but that was so long ago, it would be on a hard drive stored away," Sethi said.

"Do you mind if we take a look at it?" Detective Lawrence said. "Just that time period leading up to the shooting."

"It may take you some time," Sethi said.

"We have all the time we need," Detective Lawrence replied.

###

The computer records confiscated by the feds investigating Quarimoc lead to Pamela as the culprit who initiated the tail on Jermaine. The information was pushed through from an unknown source. Agents came to confiscate her computer and read her Miranda rights while escorting her out of the building in handcuffs.

Pamela had received half of her buyout early which had been placed securely into an off-shore account. The second half was to be received once Pamela was identified as a suspect and arrested. It was a waiting game.

Lance worked with a private social media company after hours to create a post that was scheduled to go viral minutes after the arrest. As the evening waned, Pamela was placed into a holding cell in the women's ward. Lance was still in the office, and Pablo was curious why he was still there and who was in there with him. He burst into Lance's office uninvited.

"Man, Pamela just got arrested, and all you can do is play games on your computer?" Pablo said.

"Go home, Man!" Lance said. "You knew it was coming."

"Were you in on this the whole time?" Pablo asked "You must be getting a cut too. I know you hated Pamela but to force her out of the company is something I could not see you stooping to."

While Pamela was in her cell, a lawyer came to visit her.

"Did the second half clear?" Pamela asked her lawyer.

The lawyer pulled out her phone and showed a cool one-million dollars in Pamela's off-shore account. Pamela smiled.

"Perfect!" she said. "Call Lance and tell him it's 'go time!'"

Her lawyer left the holding area and called Lance. Pablo was still laying into Lance when he got the call.

"Pablo, my friend! I want you to do the honors," Lance said.

The social media team cleared a path for Pablo to come around to the computer. As he looked at the screen, he saw a screenshot of an email from Shirley to Jonathan that was about to go viral. Pablo paused.

"Are you sure you want me to do this?" he asked.

"Oh yeah!" Lance said. "I've never been so sure about anything in my life."

"Well, here goes nothing!" Pablo exclaimed, He hit 'post.'"

###

Tony secured a job maintaining the grounds at the community center. Donna hooked it up. He also got to see and learn from the youth leaders there. Donna saw his capacity to lead, but she believed he could learn a lot from those who had been leading in a formal capacity. He was saving his pennies from the job, so he could eventually rent a room and would soon be in his own apartment. Jermaine arrived at the center after just picking up his graduation garb.

“Rottweiler, where’s your mind at?” Jermaine said.

Tony looked up from his task. He was still new on the job and wanted to make a good impression.

“Man, you can’t be rolling up on me in my place of business,” he said.

“I know! I just picked up my graduation gear and wanted to stop by and get you an invitation,” Jermaine said. “You're coming, right?”

“I wouldn’t miss it for the world,” Tony said. “The whole gang will be there.”

“What do you think of your newbies?” Jermaine asked.

“Those boys are legit,” Tony said. “You did good.”

“That was all Earl,” Jermaine said. “When the streets were hot, I had to step down and Earl brought in a whole crew while I was laying low.”

"I heard," Tony said.

The new guys told Tony how Jermaine took the time to show them what it meant to be a real Rottweiler. How important it was to know the history. Tony came in right after Brother Rod was killed, and principles were drilled into him. He knew that over time history was sometimes forgotten, and he saw how organizations can lose their way. Cheech had been teetering on a fence between good and evil, but knew he had crossed a line. He knew the values, but the streets spoke loudest in his ear oftentimes. Jermaine knew that there were competing messages and how important it was to stay the path or consequently lose your way.

"You kept it fresh," Tony said.

"How come you never told me about Brother Rod?" Jermaine asked.

"Like I said, we lose our way and history fades," Tony said. "The "r" became a symbol and eventually people assumed it meant Rottweilers. I didn't bother to correct them. I'm glad you brought it back."

"Again, that wasn't me," Jermaine confessed. "When Donna found out I was in the gang, she flipped on me. She told me about her brother who was killed in gang violence. She then told me the real meaning of the "r" brand. I found it in the materials and learned the rest. Life hasn't been the same since."

"You didn't tell me Donna was Rod's brother," Tony asked. "That's a trip! Now she's working with us? You know she got me the gig here, right?"

"She still struggles, but she's down for the cause," Jermaine said. "We are on this mission of promoting businesses by us and for us."

"I see that," Tony said.

The young Rottweilers came to Tony with the idea of starting a pop-up business that summer, a business that would provide a variety of services to the community. Something like a repair shop/handy-man kind of outfit that would range from shoe repair to electronics. A place for the gang members to display their skills and talents.

"I picked up a few trades on the inside," Tony said.

"Any ideas on how you are going to get space?" Jermaine asked.

"Sethi and Donna are going to help us out with that," Tony said. "Possibly there's a spot to use on evenings and weekends. We'll see."

"I'm in class all summer," Jermaine said. "Still on my grind. But let me know what I can do to help."

"Each one, teach one," Tony said.

"Yes sir!" Jermaine responded.

###

The gavel had fallen. The case was closed. Patrice was found guilty of one count of manslaughter, and she was sentenced to five to fifteen years. She didn't even blink as her sentence was being read. Her lawyer promised her that he would have the charges reduced. The voice message served to be the damning evidence with eight out of twelve jurors believing it was the same voice on the stand and that the time and date were not doctored. No snitching needed to take place and reputations remained intact. Charlene and Veronika were safe on the streets and looked forward to a new life, still in the streets, but not a part of the streets.

Brian and Dookie were not identified for their crimes. Even though Charlene and Veronika expected the brothers were the culprits, they were keeping to the code of the street and letting life go on. Cheech was happy Charlene didn't get called to the stand. He knew that, like him, the weed made her paranoid, and she probably would have probably lost her cool. Cheech wasn't down with the entrepreneur life style and refused to go straight, but he was happy that he didn't get tied into the murder of the P.I. who was trailing Jay. For the time being, he was safe, but he knew he would someday have to pay the piper. Tony turned out to be that piper, and he came down hard, removing Cheech from the gang before his twenty-first birthday. Cheech spent a while growing weed with Dawn, but eventually he succumbed to the streets and lived out his days without purpose other than waking up and starting all over.

Tony was putting his skills of carpentry and woodworking to use, making decorative art out of driftwood to put on display at farmer's markets when he wasn't at the community center. He was still leading the gang, but the gang had transformed into a network. As new members came in, they were not only taught the history of the gang, but what it meant to contribute through business ownership. Sethi and Donna were the boots on the ground for the effort. They created internships and modules for the members to learn from up to and through college. They had been inspirational in helping the members of the community to see themselves as business owners, and then teaching them the tricks of the trade. Both of their businesses were still using Quarimoc products, but after the post Lance put out went viral, the company had to be sold to its competitors who still used the Quarimoc brand.

Cyrus was removed from the gang, after it was revealed that Quarimoc was not involved in the scheme to poison the gang leader. He eventually admitted that it was Fuego's boys from the Eastside who had lured him into the crime.

Pamela was released from prison, as the email implicated Shirley and several members of the board of directors who were subsequently indicted on conspiracy charges. Pamela collected all of her money from the buyout, and since it was all off the books, she didn't have to pay one dime back. She held up her end of the bargain, took the fall, walked out in cuffs and was released before midnight. All in a day's work. She used the money to start a small coin-op outfit and was able to woo over half of her clients from Quarimoc to sign on with her. Lance and Pablo were traced back to the viral post that sent the company under, but quickly signed on with Quarimoc's competitor company and moved right back into their old offices within a month's time without losing any of their stock options. They booked a trip back to the Midwest to attend Jermaine's graduation and brought along the reward for their top-selling intern of the semester. It was two tickets on an all-expenses paid cruise through the Caribbean Islands. Jermaine invited Bianca to come along and told her that he had been considering her offer to move in together.

"So, what would that look like?" Jermaine asked.

"You would be my man and I would be your girl," Bianca said.

"We are still in college," he said. "Still young and dumb."

"I have a job now," she said. "I also get commission off of my sales. We will be fine."

"Are you gonna be okay with me staying in the hood after college?" he asked. "It's kind of the mission of my business."

"I have been thinking about that," she said.

"Yeah! What have you been thinking?" he asked.

"I've been thinking that I want to move into your neighborhood now," Bianca said.

"What? And give up that fancy apartment on the Eastside?" Jermaine said. "I can't let you do that."

"I already did it," she said. "The deposit was due last week."

"What are you going to do now?" he asked.

"Well, I have been working out a loan from my parents, and I found a house down the street from your mom that I made an offer on," she said.

Bianca showed Jermaine a picture on her phone. He recognized the house. It was where Ted used to live before his dad got transferred to a branch in Texas.

"Well, it's been on the market for the past four months, and the price has dropped to within our price range," Bianca said.

"Our price range?" Jermaine asked.

"Yes!" she said. "I want you to not only think like a business owner but also like a homeowner. What do you say?"

"I ain't got no money," he said.

Bianca had done her research. She knew that a top-selling intern not only got a fancy vacation but also got a placement in the company after completing college. Jermaine had heard otherwise. He knew from the water cooler that Quarimoc didn't like to hire from within, but with the buyout, the board had changed, and they were operating under a new philosophy.

"I spoke to Lance at the graduation and he would love to have you as a part of the company," Bianca said.

"And college?" Jermaine asked.

"Professor Wright said if you ace your two summer courses he could get you into the university right here next year," she said. "That way you get to work for Quarimoc and build clientele in your community while you complete your college applications. I have it all mapped out. Just follow my lead."

"But we are still so young!" Jermaine exclaimed.

"Yeah, we're young!" Bianca said. "But, we're ready"

Jermaine pondered this long and hard, as he stood on the bow of the vessel and watched the dolphins play in the crystal white waters.

"We are young, but we're ready?" Jermaine said. "That we are."

The ship swayed with every passing wave, and docked somewhere in the warm waters of Caribbean Sea. Bianca and Jermaine reclined on a chaise on the pool deck, sipped their icy drinks and watched the clouds drift by with their future set and now fast ahead of them.

THE END

Made in the USA
Middletown, DE
03 April 2023